Dead Re

Ronie Kendig surpasses all debut expectations. This story is well-researched, fast-paced, and centered around memorable characters. From exotic locales to romantic tensions, *Dead Reckoning* gives us everything we hope for in a modern thriller.
—Eric Wilson, *New York Times* bestselling author of *Fireproof* and *Valley of Bones*

All I can say is wow! What a fabulous story! *Dead Reckoning* is an adrenaline-laden ride that left me breathless and flipping pages fast enough to rip them.
Ronie Kendig is an author to watch!
—Colleen Coble, bestselling author of *The Lightkeeper's Daughter* and the Rock Harbor series

Dead Reckoning moves at the pace of an action-adventure movie. Ronie Kendig writes with painstaking attention to technical details of the setting, plot, and characters, while heart-stopping suspense ensues on every page.
—Deborah M. Piccurelli, author of *In the Midst of Deceit*

Dead Reckoning

Ronie Kendig

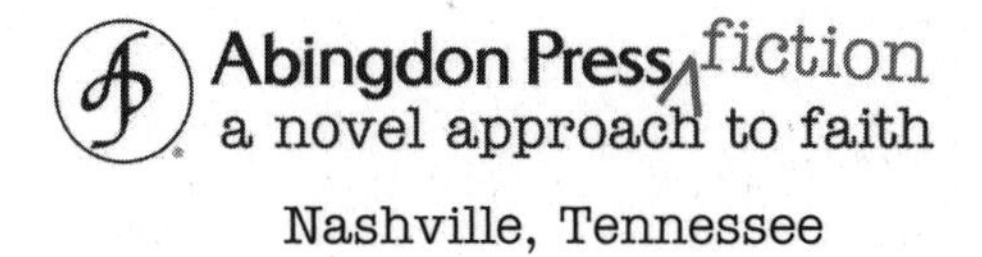

Nashville, Tennessee

Dead Reckoning

ISBN-13: 978-1-4267-0058-3

Published by Abingdon Press, P.O. Box 801, Nashville, TN 37202
www.abingdonpress.com

Cover design by Anderson Design Group, Nashville, TN

Library of Congress Cataloging-in-Publication Data

Kendig, Ronie.
Dead reckoning / Ronie Kendig.
p. cm.
ISBN 978-1-4267-0058-3 (pbk. : alk. paper)
1. Marine archaeologists—Fiction. I. Title.
PS3611.E5344D43 2010
813'.6—dc22

2009046208

Printed in the United States of America

2 3 4 5 6 7 8 9 10 / 15 14 13 12 11 10

Whatever souls are made of,
his and mine are the same.
–Emily Bronte

Brian,
I dared to dream
because of you.
For all your strength and love
my biggest Thank You!
All my love . . . .
Always,
Ronie

Acknowledgments

To my awesome Lord and Savior, Jesus. Without you, I am nothing. You gave me strength I did not have, words I did not know, and blessings I did not deserve. Forever grateful.

My precious children—Ciara—thank you for babysitting and all those sweets you baked to get me through late-nights. Keighley—thanks for your help with cleaning and whatever else needed to be done. Ryan and Reagan—thank you for being the funniest, cutest twin boys ever. I love you all so very much!

To my AWESOME agent Steve Laube—Agent-man, We did it! Thank you for believing in me and my writing, and for pulling (not pushing!) me from many ledges.

Madame Editor Barbara Scott—Wow! There's a gazillion thanks owed to you for letting this book see the "ink of print." You took a risk on this new, unpubbed author, and I'm so very thankful and grateful! You RAWK!

My "twin" Neen Miller—You are so amazing and beautiful. XOXOXOXO

Dearest friend Robin Miller—I'm so very grateful for and touched by your friendship.

Shiny Sara Mills—Thank you for talking me down with your laughter and insanity! Just remember—you rush a miracle man, you get rotten miracles.

"Big Brother" John Olson—Your humility and talent are an example for all. I am still humbled you became my advocate and cheered me on. Thanks for the brainstorming help and for reminding me not to take myself—or life—so seriously.

Lynn Dean—To Starbucks and decompressing!

Becky Yauger—I love our Thursday Nights.

Kristin Billerbeck—You were the first in ACFW to cheer me on—thank you. You watered my thirsty writer soul.

THANK YOU to friends: Camy Tang, Shannon and Troy McNear, Beth Goddard, Mindy Obenhaus, Dooley Crit Group, Cheryl Wyatt, Ane Mulligan, Pamela James, Al Speegle, Frank Ball, Steve Miller, and Tamera Alexander (for your France input!).

ACFW—So many writers with such big, willing hearts who guided me, encouraged me, challenged me, and loved me. What an absolutely amazing organization! THANK YOU!

1

Mumbai Harbor, India

SHAFTS OF YELLOW LIGHT PIERCED THE BLUE-GREEN WATERS, SILHOUETTING the dive rig that hovered on the surface of the Arabian Sea. Shiloh Blake stopped and watched a wrasse scuttle past, its tiny fins working hard to ferry the brightly striped fish to safety.

Clad in her wet suit, Shiloh squinted through her goggles and tucked the underwater camera into her leg pocket. She gripped the small stone artifact and propelled herself toward the surface. Ten meters and she would reveal her historic discovery to long-time rival Mikhail Drovosky.

Shiloh smiled. The guy would go ballistic. Score one for the girls. Between her and her new dive partner, Edie Valliant, they had surged ahead in finds. Not that this was a competition. Not technically. But everyone with the University of California–San Diego dig team knew it was make or break time.

Shiloh broke the surface. Warm sun bathed her face as she slid off her mask and tugged out her air regulator before hauling herself onto the iron dive flat. She squeezed the saltwater from her hair, the auburn glints catching in the sunlight.

"What did you find?" Khalid Khan knelt next to her.

With a smirk, she peeked at her best friend. Her own excitement was mirrored in his dark eyes. Then she noticed Edie's absence.

"Where'd she go this time? And Dr. Kuntz?"

"She wasn't feeling well."

"More like she had another date." Irritation seeped through her pores like the hot sun, boiling her to frustration. She couldn't believe her dive partner kept cutting digs to flirt with locals.

Khalid reached over to remove her dive tanks.

With a hand held up, she shifted away. "No, I'm going back down."

Footsteps thudded on the deck. "It's my turn." Mikhail's glower fanned her competitive streak.

"Sorry." Shiloh grinned. "Not for another ten minutes. You're not going to stop me from qualifying for the Pacific Rim Challenge." She nearly sighed, thinking about racking up enough dive hours for the deep-sea assignment—her dream.

On his haunches, Khalid swiveled toward her, cutting off her view of Mikhail. "What'd you find?" he whispered. Damp from his last dive, Khalid's jet black hair hung into his face. "Please tell me you aren't playing games."

From a pouch hanging at her waist, she produced the lamp. "This for starters."

He took the piece and traced the contours. "Soapstone." His gaze darted back to hers. "You mapped it on the grid, right? And photographed it?"

Any first-year grad student would know to take a picture to verify its location and record it on the mapped grid of the site. "Of course." She patted the camera in the pouch.

Not so many years ago a sunken city had been found in the area. Would she find another? Her heart thumped at the prospect. Tools. She would need better tools to safely remove the vase waiting at the bottom of the sea. Shiloh stood and hurried to the chest to remove an air pipe to suction the silt and sediment away and then grabbed an airlift bag. As she plotted how to excavate the piece, she tucked the tools into holsters strapped around her legs and waist.

"I'm coming down there whether you're done or not." Mikhail bumped his shoulder against hers and pursed his lips. "If you find it in my time, I get to log it."

Eyebrow quirked, she swept around him to the stern and sat on the ledge.

"I mean it, Blake!" Mikhail's face reddened.

She slipped the regulator back in her mouth, nearly smiling. With a thumbs-up to Khalid, she nudged herself into the water. Glee rippled through her. The look of incredulity on Mikhail's mug buoyed her spirits. Finding the lamp had been exhilarating, but one-upmanship had its own thrill. Besides, how many divers had worked this dig in the last year? Like them, she had found a piece of history. Divers and researchers had scoured this area and other sites along the coast of India.

Dr. Kuntz would have insisted on diving with Shiloh if not for ferrying Edie around Mumbai. Irritation at her new dive partner swelled. Why they had ever agreed to take on that useless woman, she'd never know. How could partying compare with the discovery of the past?

Although silt and sand shrouded the lip of the vase, Shiloh spotted its outline easily where she had marked the place with a flag. She lifted the red vinyl square from the sandy floor and worked quickly, refusing to relinquish this relic to the overblown ego of Mikhail Drovosky. He'd beaten her out of top honors for her bachelor's degree, relegating her to magna cum laude, lessening her scholarship. Enough was enough.

Why hadn't anyone else found this vase? As she brushed away the sediment, confusion drifted through her like the cool waters. A spot in the clay smeared. Her heart rapid fired. Had she ruined the relic? Yet something . . . Shiloh stilled, staring in disbelief. What on earth?

She rubbed the piece. Metal gleamed beneath the clay. The lip and handle floated away. This wasn't ancient pottery. She turned it over in her hand. What was it? It almost reminded her of a thermos. The cylinder was about eighteen inches long, and its weight surprised her. Why was it buried here like treasure? Just as she freed the object, her white watch face flashed, snapping her attention to the competition. Time was up.

Joy ebbed like the tide. Whatever this thing was, she wouldn't leave it down here for Mikhail. She held open the bag and tried to ease in the metal tube. The piece teetered on the edge, nearly falling out, so she slipped it under her arm and started toward the surface. Light again directed her to the rig. Suddenly, thrashing ripples fractured the luminescent water, stirring particulates beneath the wake of a powerful motor.

A speedboat? Why were they so close to the dive area? Didn't they see the warning beacon, the one that announced divers below? What kind of idiot would put someone's life in danger for a thrill ride?

A torrent of waves rattled her, threatening her grip on the vase. What . . . ? A half-dozen bicolor parrotfish shot past. Shiloh paused, watching their incredible color—like a psychedelic underwater show.

Thwat. Thwat.

A sound vibrated against her chest. She searched for the source but found nothing.

She continued upward, and then someone dropped into the water. Could Mikhail not wait? Sticking to the schedule ensured everyone's safety. He wasn't supposed to enter the water until she climbed out. He was in such a hurry to win that he would risk injury to her and anyone who got in his way. She'd throttle him. Only, it wasn't Mikhail.

Khalid!

A plume of red swirled around his dark form like some freakish science experiment. Blood? Was he bleeding? Her heart skipped a beat—he wasn't swimming.

Shiloh launched toward him as adrenaline spiraled through her. She struggled to breathe, threatening the nitrox mixture in her tank. Why wasn't he swimming? He'd drown if he didn't paddle back up.

She pushed into his path, and he thudded against her. Hooking her arm under his, she aimed toward the surface, scissoring her legs.

A shadow loomed over the water. Another body plunged toward her, sinking deep and fast. Mikhail's open, unseeing eyes stared back at her, a shocked expression plastered on his face. Reminding her of an Egyptian plague, the water turned red.

Watery tubes pursued him. Bullets!

What's happening?

Khalid. He needed oxygen. She wrangled him toward her so she could share her air. The metal cylinder fumbled from her grasp and sunk back into the oblivion where she'd found it. Whatever the thing was, it couldn't be worth a life—especially not her best friend's. She removed her air regulator and stuffed it into his mouth.

Khalid jerked. Pain hooded his eyes. His dark brows knitted as he gazed at her. He gripped his side and grimaced. That's when she saw the source of the red plumes. He'd been shot too. Her gaze flew to the rig. What about the captain and his son?

Khalid caught her arm. With a firm shake of his head, he pointed away from the rig. Escape.

Shiloh linked her harness to his and swam from the rig. Uncertain where they could find safety if someone was determined to kill them, she barreled away from the nightmare. If she could make it to an island—she remembered seeing a small one in the east—they might be safe. Khalid tried to pump his legs, but not successfully. At least he hadn't passed out. Or died.

Her stomach seized. No way would she let Khalid Khan die. Shiloh wagged her fins faster, thrusting both of them farther from the boat. Seconds lengthened, stretching into what felt like hours. With each stroke, her limbs grew heavier, dragging her down to the ocean floor. She pushed upward, refusing to let Khalid die.

Suddenly, she was drawn backward, pulled out to sea by the strong natural current hugging the Indian coast. Battling the forces of nature, she did her best to keep herself and Khalid aimed in the right direction. Her chest burned from oxygen deprivation.

The mouthpiece appeared before her. Surprised at Khalid's attentiveness, she stuffed the piece in her mouth and inhaled deeply, savoring the strength it gave her. Another twenty meters, and the water collided with mangroves. Shiloh struggled around the roots to a small, shallow inlet. On her knees, she tore out the regulator, dragging Khalid as she clawed her way to safety. He attempted to crawl, but collapsed. She yanked off her goggles and released their d-rings.

Khalid coughed, gagged, and vomited sea water.

Warm sand mired Shiloh's trembling limbs as she lay there, panting and gasping. The swim had been harder and much longer than she'd expected. They both could have drowned.

She squeezed her eyes shut. Thoughts of what was lost . . . Mikhail! Was he truly dead? Who would attack grad students on a dig? Why?

Shiloh pressed her hand to her forehead, tiny grains of sand digging into her flesh. She rubbed her temples and tried to make sense of the chaos.

"What happened back there, Khalid?" She flipped onto her back, the sun blazing against her pounding skull. "Who was it? Did you see?"

Silence.

Shifting, she rolled her head to peek at him. He wasn't moving. On all fours, Shiloh scrambled and shook him.

"Khalid!" His grey wetsuit glistened red from the blood that poured from his side. She clamped a hand over his wound, the warmth sickening. "Khalid, talk to me."

He groaned.

"No!" Fire flashed through her. "You aren't chickening out. Not now." Again she shook him, but this time he didn't respond. "Please!"

Shiloh examined his chest. Not breathing. With two fingers pressed to his neck, she tried to feel past the hammering of her own heart to detect his pulse. Nothing! She started compressions and breaths, counting between each to keep a steady rhythm. His blood stained her hands. While she pumped his chest, she took a cursory glance around the thick vegetation. It was so thick, she'd never know if someone stood five meters off.

They needed help—now! She activated the emergency beacon on her watch as she again searched—hoped—for help. Her heart caught when she spotted a "mechanical giraffe" staggering in the shifting fog. *Jawahar Dweep*.

"Butcher Island," she mumbled, as she tried to revive her friend. The spot only offered isolation and oil. No help. They were alone.

"At least we're safe," she said. But would Khalid die? "Don't you dare!"

She pounded his chest. More blood dribbled from the wound that seemed too close to his lungs.

A rasp grated the air. His ribs rose.

"Khalid?"

He moaned.

Tears stung her eyes as she slumped next to him. "Khalid, stay with me. I've activated the beacon."

His blue lips trembled against his chalky skin. "C-cold."

She'd always admired his dark olive complexion, but the pallor coating his rugged face worried her. Would she ever see his dark eyes ignite when she made some snide, inappropriate remark? Who would help her through her episodes? She'd told only him about her rare disorder.

"We should move you closer to the rocks to stay warm until help arrives." Shiloh once again hooked her arms under his and drew him to the side. Blood stained the sandy beach.

A wave rolled in, then out. Red streaks reached toward the warm waters. She nestled him against a large boulder and lay close to keep him warm.

"Stay with me, Khalid. No naps. This is the ultimate test, got it?" She looked to where the ocean kissed the horizon. Mumbai sparkled in the distance. So close, yet so far away it might as well be a million miles. She could only hope they would be found in time.

"You just wanted to kiss me," Khalid mumbled.

Shiloh jerked toward him, frowning. "What?"

"CPR. I didn't need it . . ." He coughed. "You just wanted to kiss me."

With her hand pressed to his forehead, she smiled. "Ah. Just as I expected—delirious with fever."

A half-cocked grin split his lips.

She tried to swallow. He had been her rock for the last four years. Despite the tight-knit relationship between their parents, Khalid and Shiloh had forged their own friendship in the fires of college life. They'd been inseparable since he came to America to study.

How long would it take Search and Rescue to locate her signal? What if the SAR team didn't make it in time? If this were American waters, it would only be a matter of minutes, but in the Arabian Sea . . .

Shiloh's head dropped to her chest. She had to believe everything would be fine. They'd be found, a doctor would tend Khalid's wounds, he'd recover, and then they'd be off to the Pacific Rim Challenge. She had worked so hard for it. They both had. For the last two years, they had prodded each other toward their common goal. Their requisite dive hours were nearly complete. No, nobody would die, especially not Khalid.

Mikhail died. She clenched her eyes shut and blotted out the image of her rival slipping through the water, sinking lower and lower.

Biting her lip, she groped for something to refocus her attention. Naming the scientific classification for the sun star. *Animalia. Echinodermata. Asteroidea. Spinulosida. Solasteridae. Solaster dawsoni.*

"Miss . . . Amer . . . ca . . ." Khalid's words, though broken, speared her heart.

She scooted closer. "I'm here. Be still, Khalid. They're coming."

"Marry me."

"You dork." She let out a shaky laugh as a shudder tore through her, threatening to unleash tears. Lips pulled taut, she forced herself to remain calm and look at him. "Rest."

His fingers twitched. She lifted his hand and cradled it in hers.

A gurgling noise bubbled up his throat. "I love . . ."

"No, shh." He couldn't love her. Not her.

"Shil . . ."

When he didn't finish, she knitted her brow. His eyes closed, and his mouth remained open.

"Khalid?"

His arm went slack.

"Khalid!" Tears blurred her vision, making it impossible to see if he was breathing.

A horn blared in the distance. She whipped around and spotted the massive white Indian Coast Guard rig racing toward them with its lights swirling.

Reece Jaxon straightened and watched the woman without watching. Seeing without being seen. She batted her auburn hair, thick and tangled with ocean water, away from her face. Hiding in plain sight on the rescue boat, he tracked her movement with ease. She hadn't noticed him yet, even though he was less than a dozen feet away.

Wrapped in a grey thermal blanket Shiloh Blake stared at the injured Pakistani on the medical stretcher as the boat churned across the water toward Mumbai. She hadn't left the man's side since the rescue.

Another man in his early fifties hooked an arm around her shoulders and drew her close. Dr. Kuntz, according to the file, was fifty-three. Married. Three grown children. An unfaithful wife and a divorce later he'd partnered with a local Indian museum to arrange underwater excavations with U.C. San Diego. Something about the man didn't sit right with Reece.

"Noor Hospital," Dr. Kuntz insisted to the Coast Guard captain.

An hour earlier Kuntz had stormed into the Coast Guard station and interrupted Reece's conversation with the officer. Surprised at the man's intrusion, Reece feigned disinterest, although Kuntz's story corroborated what Reece had relayed to the authorities after witnessing the attack. Then the emergency transponder signal erupted.

Reece noticed Shiloh stiffen under the professor's protective touch. Kuntz spoke soothingly to her, reassuring her that Noor Hospital would give Khalid the best care. Bent to shield his face, Reece tightened the laces on his boots while memorizing everything that took place in the boat's small cabin. Now, if he had judged her character right, in about twenty seconds she'd pull away from Kuntz.

Shiloh moved out of the man's reach.

Bingo.

"I need something to drink." She came toward Reece and stepped through the hatch. "They said they had coffee up front."

Dr. Kuntz laughed, his arms outstretched. "But you don't drink coffee."

"It's chilly," she called without looking back.

Chilly. Interesting. It was a mild sixty-five degrees on the Arabian Sea, and she was chilly.

Shiloh Blake strode straight toward him with her head held high. Calm. Relaxed. Confident.

Come on, look at me, Reece silently dared her.

Blue-grey eyes collided with his. He scratched his beard, wishing he had more than two weeks' growth, but it was enough to conceal his identity. With an acknowledging nod, he stayed in position. Now if she would only hold his gaze.

Oh, what he wouldn't give to smile his pleasure as she stared at him. She only tore her eyes from his when it became impractical not to. Reece guessed she would never show any weakness.

Atta, girl.

Although he'd already skimmed the preliminary data on the American students, Shiloh's impressive character made him want to know more. She had a higher confidence level than most of the people he had monitored in the region. What gave her that unshakable demeanor? Reece determined to get a DNA sample and run her through the system. Was she working undercover?

As the ship bumped Victoria dock, he leaped off and lassoed the pylons. Heavy thuds sounded against the weathered planks as the emergency crew transferred the young woman and her Pakistani friend to a waiting ambulance. Dr. Kuntz doted on her once again, but with no room in the narrow mobile unit, the professor was relegated to a rickshaw.

Shiloh huddled on a small bench in the ambulance, her glassy gaze locked on her friend as the emergency personnel worked on him. Just as the doors swung closed, she glanced toward Reece. A load of steel partially blocked his line of sight. Yet, despite the stenciling on the rear window, he saw her tilt her chin just enough to look for him over the emblem. The ambulance bumped over the sandy path, and then settled on PD Mello Road. Sirens wailed. Lights whirled.

Reece strolled down the boardwalk toward the beach, retrieving the cell from his pocket. He hit autodial. Having to report one American dead was bad enough. But having to tell Ryan Nielsen that another sat neck deep in an ocean of chaos—

"Report."

"There's a problem." What was Shiloh Blake doing at a nuclear arms dead drop?

2

Mumbai, India

"Something happened." Ali Abdul shifted on his feet, his gaze locked on the half window that afforded a view of the breezeway between the main office and consulate.

"*Kaay?*"

"A girl found the package." He tucked his chin and spoke into the phone.

Silence devoured the connection.

Movement in the narrow corridor caught his attention. He leaned to the side and eyed the hall. Only a janitor. He'd be okay. For now.

"*Kon?*"

Who? How was he supposed to know who she was? "American—she's American. That's all we know."

"You realize what was in there?" Mumbling grated on his ear. "Contact Tiger. Find out who she is."

Voices bounced off the low ceilings outside. Ali hunched into the phone. "We already have two men in play."

"Good. My team will retrieve the device. We don't need this mess. Hunt her down. Make sure it's clean."

Sweat beaded Ali's brow. "*Mai nahii samajta hu,*" he murmured.

"What don't you understand? If she is alive, you are dead."

Sirens pierced Shiloh's eardrums as the ambulance jounced over the rough road toward the hospital. Bleeping medical equipment seeped into her awareness. An emergency medical technician quickly worked on Khalid and rambled in Marathi, the local language.

Shiloh averted her eyes. Khalid had always been a modest, gentle man. Somehow, it seemed wrong to watch as they laid his chest bare. Maybe she should have let Dr. Kuntz ride in the ambulance with him. But her professor had argued, said she needed to be checked, and then he had hopped into a rickshaw. She could only hope Dr. Kuntz arrived at the hospital alive. Whoever wreaked this havoc on the team could come back to finish what they'd started.

Determination ignited. She wouldn't take this without a fight.

The attendant sitting next to her lifted Shiloh's elbow and slipped a pressure cuff around her upper arm.

The clink of metals wrapped around her mind like a vise. *Please don't die, Khalid. God*... No. She wouldn't go there. God was only a fanciful delusion for weak minds. Khalid had faith, but it was . . . different, somehow.

"What is your name?" the tech asked her in English.

Shiloh gazed at him. "Shiloh Blake."

He grinned. Just like Khalid, this tech had lovely dark skin and eyes. "American, yes?"

She wrestled to maintain her composure. Whoever had attacked the rig—the crew in this vehicle could be in league with them. Finally, she nodded and resisted the compulsion to blurt out her living arrangement as a student in cooperation with the College of Advanced Maritime Studies and Research. What he didn't ask, she wouldn't volunteer.

Life took on a sinister hue, coloring her world in daunting shades of red.

She focused on Khalid and his battle for life.

Something niggled at the edge of her mind, but Shiloh braced herself as the ambulance wobbled and sped around a corner. One of the two working on Khalid shouted at the driver, who snapped back. She pretended not to understand the bets they waged on Khalid's life—that he wouldn't make it to Noor Hospital alive. That he was better off as fish bait than being attended at the hospital.

"Your papers?"

She studied the tech, suspicious. "Why do you need my papers?"

"Why you not give me papers?"

The ambulance jolted to a stop. Doors flung open.

Shiloh seized the opportunity to evade more questions and hopped out of the Noor mobile unit. Clearing the way for the gurney carrying Khalid, she trained her eyes on his body and her ears on the chatter as the staff assessed his condition. *Little chance of survival. Great blood loss.* They didn't help her frayed nerves.

Maybe she should tell someone about the attack. But who? The police? What if they were in on whatever had happened? She couldn't allow herself to trust anyone. Shiloh scanned the parking lot for Dr. Kuntz. A rickshaw would take forever. Brutal reality slapped her in the face. She was alone. Again.

A nurse motioned Shiloh toward the double-door entrance. As they entered, the tail of the gurney whizzed out of sight around a corner.

A group of doctors huddled and cast disconcerted looks her way. Only then did her attire register. Shamefully aware of her inappropriate wetsuit, Shiloh's cheeks warmed. Thank goodness this wasn't Saudi Arabia. She'd be arrested just for wearing it. Here in Mumbai, the melting pot of India, conservatism had its place, but she wouldn't be in trouble with the authorities. Still, she noticed the disapproving glares of men and women alike. Catching the nurse's arm, she tugged her aside. In her best Marathi, she pleaded for a pair of hospital scrubs to change into.

"Wait here." With a smile, the nurse hurried off.

Perfect opportunity to call Dr. Kuntz. A phone sat cradled on the wall. Shiloh rushed toward it, lifted the handle, and dialed his cell number. When his voice mail picked up, she groaned. Where was he? She tried Edie. Again, no luck.

The nurse reappeared with the scrubs and a pair of lightweight shoes, then ushered Shiloh to a restroom. Grateful to shed the neoprene hugging her body, Shiloh changed quickly. If she could fit in rather than stick out like an orca in a tank of dolphins, all the better. Less attention equaled more safety. The fact that someone had murdered Mikhail—and nearly killed Khalid too—warned her that their attackers didn't want survivors.

She stared at the wetsuit. Ditch it? The thing cost too much. From a nearby shelf, she grabbed a towel and wrapped it up. Back in the hall, she stopped by the nurse's station and inquired about Khalid. The nurse shrugged and said it was impossible to know anything this soon.

Shiloh clenched her fist, glanced down the long, sterile hall where they'd whisked Khalid, and headed toward the waiting room. Settled into a vinyl-cushioned sofa, she let out a deep breath. She bent forward and cupped her head in her hands.

Marry me. A half-smile drifted across her lips as Khalid's words flooded back to her. Insane. Clearly the injury near his lungs affected his brain or he would have never made such a ridiculous request. They'd always been close, but not like *that*.

And yet he'd been her lifeline for the last four years, ever since he had witnessed her first seizure.

Had he really meant it? In a strange, twisted way, every gesture and wink from him held new implications. Nervous jellies swam through her stomach.

He *did* mean it.

No. He was delirious . . . dying . . . hovering between Paradise and the horrible reality of life on earth.

"You are Miss Blake?"

Shiloh glanced up, dread spilling across her shoulders. Two police officers stood before her. Dressed in their heavily starched tan shirts with the red- and blue-striped ascots and dark slacks, they waited. The younger man shifted his hat under his arm. How did they know who she was? Had the EMT steered these men her way?

"We like speak with you. We have questions." He spoke with clear but broken English.

The atmosphere in the room shifted. A mother hugged her daughter closer. Men scooted so their backs were to the officers. Others hid their faces behind magazines.

This wasn't the time to let her anxiety show. "So do I."

The older man spoke, a partial bow revealing his thinning hairline. "I am Officer Kodiyeri, and my lieutenant, Ramesh Srivastava." They pulled plastic chairs close to her and sat. "You have your visa?"

Something about the way he asked told Shiloh he already knew the answer. Despite her misgivings, she smiled. "No, I was diving when we were attacked." With her hand on the towel, she slid back the top to reveal the thick, black suit. "There's no way to carry my papers when I'm in the water."

The men exchanged looks. Kodiyeri scowled at her. "The law states you must present your visa to authorities when asked."

Tingling up her spine warned her to be careful. "Within twenty-four hours of such a demand," Shiloh added. These men . . . something wasn't right.

"That is yours?" Srivastava pointed his black pen toward the neoprene.

"My suit. As I said, I was diving when the others were attacked."

"Can you show it to us?"

Shiloh unbound the suit and laid it out on the chair next to her. She crossed her arms and studied the two men. What was up with them wanting to see that?

"And that's all you have with you? No visa? No . . ."

Irritation clawed at her. "Nothing." Why were they questioning her like this? Were they going to blame her? "Look, I can bring you my visa first thing in the morning."

The heavier-set and sweating Kodiyeri grunted. "We aren't overly concerned."

Not concerned about her visa? Interesting.

"Can you tell us anything about the incident?"

"No, I'm afraid I can't."

Kodiyeri's eyebrows rose. "But you were there."

"Fifty meters underwater."

"You didn't see anyone or what took place?"

"No." And that very point grated against her. Without a lead, how could she track down the killers?

Kodiyeri sneered. His arm raised in question, a yellow cord of rank pulling taut as he did. "You saw nothing—at all?"

"That's what I said."

"What about the body our divers found, or what happened to—" he glanced at a notepad, "—Mr. Khan?"

"Mr. Khan was shot."

"And you save him?"

"No, actually, I hope that's what the doctors are doing right now." *Stay cool, Shiloh.* This was routine—and better than being hauled down to headquarters, where she could easily disappear if they wanted her to. Or the Minister of Tourism would rake her over the coals for bringing trouble to his quiet state. They wouldn't take kindly to such an incident. She certainly didn't. "I dragged Khalid to the cove."

"How did you signal for help?"

"Emergency transponder."

What was with these questions? And why were the pants of the younger officer two inches too short? The hair on the back of her neck prickled. She swallowed.

It was time to turn on the charm and get away from these two. She crossed her arms. "So, Raman." She forced a smile and shifted toward the younger officer. "Your men have done such a great job. I mean, I'm impressed they've already recovered a body and learned so much about our dig. I take it you've examined our dive rig by now? And you didn't find my visa?"

He glanced to the side. "No, we found no visas."

"Ramesh," said the older officer.

Feigning innocence, Shiloh said, "Excuse me?"

Kodiyeri's eyes darkened. "His name is Ramesh, not Raman."

"Right." *Then why didn't he correct me?* "If you'll excuse me—" Shiloh stood, smoothed her long tunic, and retrieved the wetsuit—"I need to see if there's any news on my friend."

If she thought the ride to the hospital foreboding, this interview with the police sent chills down her spine. *Relax, girl. Your imagination is getting the better of you.*

She walked away, and they didn't stop her. As she padded down the narrow hall, she kept her ears attuned to the room she'd just left. Drawing in a deep breath, she neared the swinging doors.

She was stranded. Without her visa. Without money. Even with a Consulate here—it was the weekend. And she was more than forty minutes away by car—a car she didn't have. Which meant at least two hours on foot. Besides, she couldn't trust anyone here. Whatever had happened on the water, someone wanted it kept quiet. Deadly quiet.

Behind her, she heard rhythmic clopping. Two sets of feet. One a bit heavier than the other. She hurried toward the emergency room corridor.

The pursuers quickened their pace.

Shiloh slipped through a door and burst right. A team of doctors stood nearby. She darted toward them. "Excuse me? Is there any news on the shooting patient?"

A female, her gaze roaming over Shiloh, broke away from the group. "You are relative?" With an easy smile, the woman wrapped an arm around Shiloh and led her to the side, out of sight of the two pursuers.

Shiloh tucked her hair behind her ear. "A friend. I came in with him."

"Ah." The woman's smile flattened. "He in surgery. That all I can say."

In surgery meant still alive. "*Dhanyavaad.*" With her thanks, Shiloh moved back.

Light shattered the dull illumination as the back doors swung open. The ambulatory team entered, and with them, Dr. Kuntz.

At the sight of the professor the tension drained from Shiloh's body. Her muscles ached.

His thick brow drew together. "You look dreadful. Are you okay?"

"I'm fine." She directed his attention down the narrow hall. "They won't tell me anything about Khalid except that he's in surgery."

"Well, we shall see about that." Dr. Kuntz pulled his shoulders straight and stomped toward the doctors.

In the glass of the surgical theater doors, Shiloh caught the reflections of the two police officers standing behind her. Then she focused her thoughts on the long hall just beyond the surgery doors where several bays appeared to jut off. Somewhere down that stretch of glaring white sterility Khalid clung to life. He had to live. Had to.

Mikhail had been murdered. The somber thought tightened her chest. Would he have lived if she had tried to save him too? Had she played favorites in saving one and not the other? No—Mikhail was dead when he hit the water.

And what of Edie? How convenient the Brit had left only minutes before the attack. Coincidence? Shiloh gave herself a mental shake. Of course it was. The petite, five-foot-two girl didn't have a mean cell in her body. Her claws only came out when she spotted a good-looking guy and tried to sink those sharp hooks into him.

Dr. Kuntz returned with a long sigh. "He's touch-and-go, but he is fighting." His gentle tone did nothing to ease the brutal words. "I'll call his family."

"No." Shiloh caught his arm. "I'll call. He was my friend—I know his parents."

"Are you sure?" Even when she nodded, Dr. Kuntz hesitated, but then deferred and handed her his cell. "Very well. Once you're done, I can take you back to the hotel, and you can rest. You saved his life, you know."

"He isn't out of the water yet." She wanted to slap herself for the insensitive, unintentional pun. "I'm going to step outside to make the call."

Again, clicking shoes followed her down the hall. She stopped just outside the door and hoped her close proximity to help would keep them at bay. It did. Humidity blanketed her as she scrolled through Dr. Kuntz's contacts to locate the number for Khalid's family.

Her heart sank. How could she tell his parents that he might not make it? They had readily welcomed her and treated her as one of their own. Even his mother had embraced Shiloh with her very large heart. Of course, the vast difference in their beliefs remained a wedge in the family. His parents refused to talk about his newfound Christian faith.

The connection went through. A woman answered.

"Nisa? This is Shiloh . . ."

"Ah, beautiful Shiloh. How is it with you? You are well?"

"Yes—no." She swallowed the conch-sized lump in her throat. "I have bad news. There was an . . . attack." In the minutes it took to explain the situation and comfort Khalid's mother, Shiloh struggled with her own raw emotions. After promising to remain by his side for as long as she could, Shiloh clicked off.

A dull ache pulsed at the center of her forehead. Kneading the spot with two fingers, Shiloh closed her eyes. Was this really happening? Although her life had never been quite in sync, it seemed wildly insane at the moment. What would happen to Khalid?

She heaved a sigh and opened her eyes—and sucked in a harsh breath.

A man in tan pants and tunic half-bowed before her. "You are American woman from boat? Yes?"

Shiloh stiffened. How could he possibly know that?

"A man, he ask me give this you. You lost it." He held out his hand.

The lamp. The one she'd retrieved from the site just before the attack—the one she'd passed to Khalid—sat in the man's palm.

She stared at the artifact, unable to move.

"It is yours, yes?" His hand bounced closer.

She blinked as she lifted the piece. "Yes. Dhanyavaad." The man shuffled away even as she offered her thanks. Her gaze skated around the parking lot, searching for whoever had sent him. Who could have retrieved the artifact from the rig . . . from Khalid? Only someone involved in the murders.

A sickening weight pressed against her stomach. They knew where she was. They knew she was an American.

Yet here she stood out in the open with nothing to protect her. The realization sent her sailing back into the air-conditioned hall. She quickly spotted Dr. Kuntz talking with the two officers.

Stuffing the small lamp into the pocket of her scrub tunic, she walked toward the professor. She could only pray Dr. Kuntz hadn't given them her entire life's story. He was too trusting. Far too trusting. Urgency leapt within her to get the professor away from these men. Steadying her heart, she straightened her shoulders.

". . . at the Mumbai Palace." Dr. Kuntz shook Kodiyeri's hand.

She could strangle the professor for telling these imposters what hotel the team was using. Dr. Kuntz's thick, dark brow furrowed against the white wisps of hair that hung over his forehead. "Shiloh, is everything okay?"

"Fine." She cast her gaze to the police. "If you're through . . ."

Kodiyeri nodded. "For now."

Without another word, Shiloh stepped away with Dr. Kuntz but kept her eyes on the men hovering in the background like a bad storm.

"How did Khalid's parents take the news?"

"Not well." She handed over the phone. It took a concerted effort to concentrate on relaying the phone call to Dr. Kuntz. Between the imposters in the corner and the lamp in her pocket, she felt dizzy. "Khalid's father is going to come. His mother is shaken up. They don't have—"

The weight of a large man knocked Shiloh off step as he swept past them. Head down, he mumbled, "*Kshama keejeeae.*"

Despite his excusing himself to pass by, she glared after him. He had half the hall and—

Familiarity dashed through her. Her mind spun. Those broad shoulders. She strained to see if he had a scraggly—*beard*!

"Shiloh?" Dr Kuntz caught her arm as he looked after the stranger. "What's wrong?"

The man, at least from the back, looked like the one from the Coast Guard boat. But it couldn't be.

"Nothing." Pulling her eyes back to her professor, she fixed a smile on her face. "I'm good, just a bit tired." Again she searched for the big guy. Was it really him? Was she being followed?

Get out. Get out now. She bit back the warning that seared her mind. *Be calm, be reasonable.* Her father had taught her those life-saving skills. At least she could be grateful for that despite her deep-seated resentment of him. Then again, those skills had her standing here making spook and ghoul out of every person who crossed her path.

Concern wrinkled Dr. Kuntz's face. "I think I should take you back to the hotel."

"N-no." The hotel, where their names could be accessed by anyone searching the hotel registry, was the last place she'd go. Shiloh calmed her voice. "I'm going to stay here with Khalid. Hopefully, they'll let me see him once he's out of surgery." The opportunity to get the professor to safety presented itself. Shiloh patted his arm. "Why don't you go to the embassy? Tell them about the attack and work out arrangements to fly Mikhail's body back to the States. See if you can find Edie."

"Oh yes. I wonder where she is now." Dr. Kuntz wiped his brow with a handkerchief. "I can't believe Mikhail's dead. That wasn't—what infidel would do such a thing? Incomprehensible!"

"I know. There's probably a lot of legal red tape to work through." Shiloh urged him toward the exit. "You could get a head start. Maybe even arrange for the team to head home early." Did he hear the quiver in her voice?

She breathed easier once he was gone. At least with him heading away from here, he was out of danger. Hopefully. But then . . . her pulse raced in protest. Once again, she'd be alone. What if the two police officers made their move now?

Olive suits rounded the corner, looking in the other direction.

Shiloh dove into a darkened room. *Click.* The handle caught just as harried voices dashed past her in the hall.

"Where is she? The woman?"

"*Maaf kijiye,*" a man mumbled his apology. "I didn't see."

She gripped her temples. None of this made sense. Why were they targeting her? Surely those men were only posing as officers. Or they'd have known their own names and worn clothes that actually fit.

Safety, like the ebbing tide, seemed out of reach. The embassy was too far away. Her only ride had just left. If she ventured onto the streets of Mumbai, she'd be noticed right away with her fair skin and auburn hair. Obviously, a foreigner. No money. Dressed in hospital scrubs.

"Did you find her?" the Marathi words grew frantic.

The noisy rumble of a gurney and medical staff rushing through the corridor drowned out the voices. Shiloh craned her neck to the side and peered through the small, square window. The hall looked empty. But looks were often deceptive, especially since she could only see a few feet in either direction.

Tick. Tick. Tick. The noise drew her attention to a wall clock. She'd wait ten minutes and try to slip out unnoticed. Until then she needed a better hiding spot.

Lockers lined both walls and split the room in two. Chairs huddled around a table in the far corner. A white lab jacket hung on a hook by the door. To her right, a bed lay cordoned off by a ceiling curtain. Shiloh hurried to a locker. She chose number 24—her age—and opened it, stuffing the dive suit inside. After spotting a paper clip, she picked a lock on one door and used it to secure "her" locker.

"Check every room. We must find her."

Shiloh spun and searched for an exit. Her gaze fastened on the window at the far side of the room. She ran back to the door and peered through the portal. Her pulse spiked as a man and woman strode toward the seemingly thin barrier. She turned and darted to the windows. Hands on the sill, she paused. What if she was overreacting?

Your mind registers an inconsistency, an incongruence. Go with it, Shi. Always go with it. Had her father's espionage tactics made her paranoid?

No, she wasn't overreacting. Two of her friends had been shot. One dead. The other—

Her heart skidded into her ribs. She had told Khalid's father she'd wait here until his arrival. But if she stayed, she might end up as dead as Mikhail. Could she leave Khalid here, alone? What if the killers came back to finish him off?

And what would you do, genius?

Shiloh reached for the latch.

Forgive me, Khalid.

"We've got complications," Reece said into his secure phone as he sat in his Jeep.

"You always do."

He ground his teeth. "A group of college kids got messed up in the drop site. Americans. Three dead. A student and two locals—the boat captain and his son. One student injured and in the hospital."

"What part of *clandestine* don't you get, Jaxon?"

"Do you want this information or not?" Reece growled. His eyes darted to the hospital at the far end of the parking lot. "There are three stragglers: Professor Daniel Kuntz, Edie Valliant, and Shiloh Blake. I think the others are in shock, but this Blake girl, she—"

A gasp burst over the line. "What did you say?"

Reece stilled.

"What was that name?" Nielsen prompted. "Reece? Are you there?"

Since when did *Nielsen* get excited?

"Reece?"

"Go ahead."

"Give me those names again."

What was going on? He'd submitted the data on the American college students last week. Nothing flagged. "Daniel Kuntz, Edie Valliant, and Shiloh Blake."

A curse hissed into his ear. The director's voice muffled, and then Reece heard a loud bang like a door being slammed. "Okay, listen . . ."

The ensuing static grated on Reece's unsettled nerves.

"This Blake girl, you've got to stay with her. I mean it."

Staring through the windshield, Reece squinted up at the hospital. Shiloh had snagged his attention from the start. If any of the dive team knew anything about the dead drop, it would be her. She was smart . . . alert . . . fearless.

Was she the contact he'd been trying to nail for the last six months? Is that why Nielsen wanted her tagged? That was insane. No young, attractive American woman like her would betray her own country and risk her life for a nuclear compromise. She didn't have the earmarks.

"Can you get a biometric to confirm her identity?"

Glancing at his multi-purpose watch, Reece transmitted the data. "On its way."

"Okay, um . . . listen." That was the second time Nielsen had used the word "listen." But again, only quiet pervaded the line.

Reece hitched an eyebrow. "I'm baking out here. If you have something to say, spit it out."

"I can't. Not yet. Just don't let her out of your sight. Consider her your new target and don't show your hand. Got it?"

"Whoa, wait. No way." Reece straightened. "I've got bigger fish to fry, remember? A dead drop that could unseat international peace relations between a half-dozen countries. Several suspicious money transactions. Evidence that someone is transporting missile material and technology out of here. I'm not about to spend my time tracking some preppie around Mumbai."

"You will if you want to keep your job."

Reece clenched his eyes and bit back a retort to tell his supervisor where exactly he could stick this job.

"I want to know anyone she comes into contact with. Locals, good guys, bad guys. Everyone. Got it?"

How had his day gone from intriguing to fire-and-brimstone torture? "Fine. Start with the two men posing as Maharashtra police and tailing her. Also, a floater who delivered an artifact to the target."

Another curse stabbed the line. "Intervene only if necessary. If anything happens to this girl—if she's who I think she is and she gets hurt? You can kiss your sorry job good-bye. We don't need another disaster like the Taj. *Capiche*?"

Reece hung up and threw the phone onto the passenger seat, staring at the device as if it had somehow infected Nielsen with stupidity. Why did he have to bring up the Taj?

He snatched the scanner and waited for Shiloh's signal to register. If he guessed right . . . He glanced up at Noor Hospital, ignoring the traffic that buzzed along Mohammed Ali Road.

With his thermal imaging binoculars, he scanned the building. There! Alone in a room, her signatures raised and red.

The colorful silhouette showed her at a window, but casting a glance over her shoulder, staring at a door. On the other side, three signatures. Two males and a female.

"Follow your instincts, girl." Whoever she was, she had better gut-level reactions than most trainees he'd drilled. Better than Chloe.

When he'd bumped into Blake to plant the microchip, he had managed to lift the small lamp from her pocket. He turned the piece over in his hand. They were getting bold. No, downright brazen. To eliminate her team on open waters in the middle of the day screamed their arrogance. Then to deliver this artifact . . .

Her image turned back to the door.

"No. Get out of there." His muscles constricted under tension for the first time in years. He lowered the binoculars and slumped against his seat. He couldn't have read her wrong. She's a smart girl—why would she go back? Maybe he should take the initiative.

Intervene only if necessary.

"Life in danger" definitely qualified. He reached for the door handle.

3

SHILOH'S FEET HIT THE SOFT GREEN GRASS. SHE SPRINTED TOWARD A line of Neem trees that acted as sentries guarding the hospital from the street. When she slipped between two of them to catch her breath, the pinnate leaves tickled her cheek. She shrugged the branches aside and scanned the area. No movement in the sparsely populated parking lot except a man folding himself into his car. Pale blue scrubs probably served as a homing beacon against the dark bark. She'd need to remedy that.

Am I losing it? Playing spy girl in the middle of India. Hiding in the hospital. Climbing out a window. Leaving Khalid.

"I'll be back," she whispered and stepped from beneath the teasing foliage.

"*Rukho*!"

The shout to stop made her plow through the parking lot. *Never look back*, her father had always said. *Run until you can't run, then run some more.*

Rocks dug through the thin material of the hospital shoes. Pain shot into her foot. Heedless of the sensation, she wove around cars and headed for the street. Get lost, find a way to scrounge some money, then . . .

Then what? Shiloh blanched. She had no clue what to do, where to go, who to talk to. Could she hoof it to the American Consulate? Impossible—a two-hour trip by car, which she didn't have.

Sirens screamed behind her. They were closer than she thought. She pushed harder.

Cars zipped past. Honking and shouting assailed her. The piercing noises propelled her down busy streets. If she could reach Yusef Meherali Road, she could lose the tail, possibly even herself, in the insanity of the markets. She was too far to make it to Crawford Market, but the smaller ones would work. The thought spurred her on.

Whirling blue and white lights spun around her, bouncing off the low muddy-brown buildings and smearing across taller structures. She darted down Nagdevi Street, spotted Yusef Meherali, and flanked right. She ran past buildings, rickshaws, and people—the very people who'd helped Shiloh fall in love with Mumbai . . . with India.

But today, danger pulsed through the air. Once beyond Sheikh Menon Street, she'd head southwest. Somehow she had to make it to Chowpatty Beach and the sparkling waters of Back Bay. She had to. Khalid was counting on her.

A blur of red silk emerged from a shop, right into her path. Shiloh dodged the woman. Then, a small child appeared. She spun around him.

A quick glance over her shoulder proved her fears. Less than two blocks back, the familiar Jeeps with their spinning lights stabbed their way through the thick crowds. She shot left and cut through traffic. It was like trying to do a breaststroke through the mangroves that lined much of the Indian coast.

Shiloh checked on her pursuers. A grin tugged at her lips. Stuck. Jammed in gridlock traffic, they couldn't get through. She had to switch clothes and identities. Seizing the chance, she hurried beyond the Santa Maria church and into a clothing shop. Although the religious structure across the street bore a crucifix, the sanctuary catered to every religion—a haven for all.

Voices nudged her farther into the shop. She feigned interest in the *saris* and *cholis*. Her fingers caressed the silk. The lightness of the material made her wish she could buy something. Satin, crepe, blues, purples—oh, the greens! She lifted the *faal* of one and traced its intricately delicate pattern between her fingers, attention trained on the door. Men moved into view.

She slid her hand over a rack of less ornate garments. Once again she admired a teal one and let the crepe fabric drape across her arm while she assessed the threat.

A short, round woman shuffled toward her. "You like try?" A *bindi* of pink crystals ending in a teardrop focused attention on her chocolate eyes.

Telling this woman she didn't have money would alert her to Shiloh's predicament. An American wandering the streets without money? "*Kai kimmat*?" Asking the price should stay the woman's suspicions. When the seller revealed the cost, Shiloh shook her head. "Sorry."

"Trade?" The woman pointed a bejeweled and henna-tattooed hand toward Shiloh's hemp bracelet that sported a pearl embedded between two shells.

Her heart caught. Khalid had made it for her on their first dig in the Caribbean. Opening her mouth to decline, she stopped as sirens pervaded the busy street. A man shouted, "She came this way."

Shiloh had to change clothes. Now. She gritted her teeth and agreed to the exchange.

The woman lifted the teal sari and choli from the rack and held out her palm.

Stomach knotted, Shiloh slid off the bracelet. "I'll come back with money," she promised herself and the woman, who took the bracelet and shoved the clothing toward her.

Had she done the right thing? The exchange hardly seemed fair, and now she was without the only gift that tied her to Khalid. *What have I done*?

Shiloh snatched a pair of sandals, too, then rushed behind a curtain and changed. A breeze danced around her bare midsection, making her feel half-naked. Even in America where fashion applauded peeking midriffs, she'd always worn conservative baby doll T-shirts.

"You there! Have you seen a girl, an American?" The thick Marathi words spilled through the warm structure.

A sliver of space between the two tapestries gave Shiloh a clear view. Outside, the two imposters chasing her stood talking with an elderly man.

Sari wrapped around her head and mouth, she slipped out. The woman bustled toward her.

"*Bindi*." She gripped Shiloh's shoulder and stuck a jewel to her forehead, then appraised her. "*Aap khubsoorat hain*!"

Beautiful? Since when? Heat crept into her cheeks.

"Dhanyavaad," Shiloh mumbled her thanks. She hurried to the side of the shop where a narrow opening afforded her a clear escape. A knot of bodies swarmed the church entrance.

Behind her the woman's shrill voice rang out, soon followed by irate Hindi as she ordered the police out of her shop, declaring they were cursing her profits.

Shiloh fled down the tight passage and up a flight of red-painted stairs and entered an open door. Darkness consumed her. She stepped to the side and waited for her vision to adjust. To the far left, candles swayed under a gentle breeze. An aged woman in an orange sari knelt before an altar and poured oil over an idol.

Shouts came from the alley. "This way. A man saw her."

Tugging up the sari, Shiloh strode to the altar and knelt. Perhaps the police wouldn't take notice of two women kneeling before the round-bellied Buddha. She lifted a candle and lit the wick, offering prayers not to the stone god, but to the Christian God. He'd always helped her parents. *If you're there, God, I could use some help*. Would He listen or even care?

The sanctuary darkened. They were here! Her pulse quickened. She ducked her head and pressed her palms together. God had never answered before. Why would He now?

The woman next to her chanted. Shiloh moved her lips and hoped it looked convincing.

Air stirred nearby.

The soft rustle of fabric snapped open her eyes. The woman stood. So did Shiloh. As the bent woman attempted to shuffle around, Shiloh hooked her arm through the fragile arm. Though surprised by the help, the woman murmured her thanks. In this culture, helping one another was almost a duty, not an inconvenience as in the States.

They neared the front doors, and Shiloh dared a glance back. The men stood at the side exit, scanning the alley as they spoke into walkie-talkies. She drew a breath. Just maybe she'd be okay. With a nod to the woman, she wished her well and sped away.

The attack had happened only a few hours earlier, but it wore on her like a lifetime. She spotted a fifty *paise* lying on the sun-baked ground and surreptitiously picked it up. A few more coins, and she could ride the bus to the beach. Easy. Perhaps too easy.

She scoured the ground as she walked, sure nobody would notice her down-turned gaze. Women here were still lower life-forms.

Someone's watching. Of course someone was watching. Jaw set, she kept moving. Her fair skin drew attention no matter how hard she tried to fit in.

Shiloh paused. Her gaze tracked over the reflected images on a dirty shop window. A woman, hunched slightly from the crying child secured to her back with a stretch of fabric, pushed Shiloh aside. His screams punctuated the thick hum in the clogged street. Laughter trailed a small girl as she wove through the tangle of bodies. Amid the chaos, the delectable aroma of curry teased Shiloh's hunger. Just as fast, incense stung her eyes and nose.

She lifted her chin for a clean, clear breath. Instead, rank sweat and a smell she could not identify assaulted her. A car honked, and she flinched at the sudden noise. Her senses buzzed. Yet . . . this was normal. This was India.

She adjusted her choli and continued down MJ Market Lane.

Cross the street. Heeding her instinct, she pivoted and peered around the edge of the sari to check for traffic. Maybe anonymity had found her after all.

"I need a trace."

"Why?"

Sweat dribbled down Reece's temple as he looked out the passenger window. "I've lost her."

"You what?" Ryan's voice bordered on outrage. "I don't have to tell you—"

"When was the last time you were in the Mumbai markets? An elephant could get lost in here!" He craned his neck forward, assimilating every detail of the busy street.

"Do I have to remind you that your job is at stake?"

"How about you get your boys on that tracer?" His white-knuckled grip did not help the ache in his shoulders. "And get the link to my satcom so I have immediate feedback. We don't have time for runaround. If they've captured her . . ."

"Already on it."

Steering around a corner, he let the car idle as a stream of pedestrians crossed the hot pavement. His gaze struck every person as he searched for the blue scrubs Shiloh wore. How hard could it be to spot her?

"Okay, we've got her signal. She's on . . . uh . . . looks like Market Lane."

"*I'm* on Market Lane, Nielsen!" His temples throbbed as he finally got a break in traffic and pressed the gas pedal. He cruised past one shop. Nothing. Another.

"She's right there."

"Where?"

A blur of green flashed into his path. Reece nailed his brakes and hammered the horn at the sari-clad woman he'd nearly creamed. Heart racing, he hissed his frustration.

"Reece, your signals are overlapping."

He pounded his horn again as he searched the busy street, the shops, the vendors. "I'm telling you, she's not here." There. A woman in blue. He grunted. The woman wore a sari, not scrubs.

At every juncture where he'd expected her to fail, Shiloh Blake had surpassed his expectations. And now, she went in one door and out another without him ever noticing.

Again he honked and demanded the woman in green clear the road. She flashed her palms at him, a scowl etched into her face as if saying to hold his horses. He leaned out the window and shouted for her to move—and froze. No way. He narrowed his eyes. Hers widened.

"I'll be the son of a monkey," he murmured.

She hustled into a throng of people on the sidewalk opposite him.

Reece tossed the phone on the passenger seat and glued his eyes to the road ahead. Hands planted on the steering wheel, he peeked in the rearview mirror as his mark tucked her head and rushed onto the sidewalk. She quickly disappeared into a shop.

Whipping down the next street, he knew he'd have to dump the Jeep and follow her on foot. She'd spotted him. As he jogged back up the street he stuffed his arms through a *kurta*. The thin tunic would buy him some time in tracking her. He donned a pair of sunglasses. Hands in his pockets, he rounded the corner and didn't slow.

Then he located her. She hugged the door of a shop and watched the corner, feigning interest in a black bag with crystal beads.

A couple of yards east, Reece stopped and purchased a plain black cup of thick coffee. Sipping it, he crossed to Shiloh's side of the street and slowly made his way toward her. Amazement mingled with frustration as he took in the sight of her. A choli left her tanned, trim waist bare. The brightly colored sari accented her auburn hair and blue-grey eyes. He'd never forget those wide orbs staring at him when he'd nearly run her over.

Incredible. She didn't have any resources, yet she'd managed to change clothes, exit unnoticed, and almost lose him. Brilliant.

Who was this woman?

Shiloh licked her dry lips. It was him—the man from the Indian Coast Guard boat, the one with the brown beard who'd bumped into her at the hospital. At first she thought paranoia had tied her mind in knots, but now she had no doubt he was following her.

Who was Mr. Brownbeard, and who were the other men? Were they working together? Separately? The second seemed unfathomable. What could be big enough that two different forces would pursue her? Maybe they thought she saw Mikhail's murder.

More than ever she wished Khalid was here. With his help, she could talk through this. Alone, her mind couldn't stitch together the threads of information.

Shiloh shrugged off the thoughts. She needed time to figure it out, but first, she had to ditch her tail. She surveyed the busy marketplace. A mother and daughter shopped a few feet away, admiring the bindi and bangles laid out across a scarved table. Arms crossed, an Indian man chatted with another who sat in his car, his elbow sticking out the open window. Her real focus, however, lay on the opposite corner of the street. Ten minutes and the man still hadn't appeared.

Perhaps she was finally safe. Nearing the sidewalk, she stepped into the last rays of sunlight twinkling past the small huts. She reveled in the warmth and breathed in deeply of the scent of curried chicken. Now to make it to the beach. She was certain she could find food there. Her stomach rumbled.

"Okay, let's get this over with." Just as her toes touched the curb to cross the street and head south, she glanced right.

Brownbeard. Though Shiloh wanted to snap away her gaze, she steeled her response. Definitely him, but now he wore a white kurta and black-tinted sunglasses. She'd recognize those broad shoulders anywhere, especially in a sea of shorter Indian men.

She veered away from him and had taken only a dozen paces when uniformed men leapt out of the throng. Hostile eyes met hers—Kodiyeri and his minion.

Her heart jack-hammered. Trapped between Brownbeard and fake police.

The edges of her field of vision washed grey.

Oh no. Not now. Please not now! Khalid wasn't here to help. To steady herself, she reached for an electrical pole and looked for a place to hide. She spotted a gap between two shops. But it was too late. She couldn't move.

4

SOMETHING'S WRONG.

Reece considered the approaching agents and Shiloh. Why wasn't she moving? Reece tossed down the coffee and started toward them. This he didn't expect—Shiloh to freeze up. From what he'd seen, she was tougher. Smarter.

He pressed the autodial on his phone. "I'm going to need you to keep a tracer on me."

"Jaxon . . . what are you up to?"

"Just keep a live feed. Something's wrong with Blake."

"Reece, stop. Wait."

He kept walking. She still stood with her arms locked, facing the opposition. Auburn hair billowed over her shoulders blown by a gentle breeze that swept a light, spicy scent toward him.

"Reece, what's happening? Answer me or—"

"*Namaskar*," he said to the two agents and blocked their path to Blake. "*Tu kasa ahes*?"

The heavyset man scowled, his unibrow diving deep into the bridge of his nose. "Get out of my way!" he growled in Marathi.

Reece knew his linguistic skills concealed his nationality. "I think I may have seen the woman you're looking for."

The dingbat duo froze. "What did you say?" Malice painted a wicked mural across the older man's face. "How did you know we were looking for anyone?"

"I was in a shop earlier when you asked for her," Reece said. "I saw her around the corner—that way." He pointed across the street.

"Stay here. We will handle this." The fat agent stomped past him.

Reece shifted and rammed his shoulder into the agent's. When the man swung a fist toward him, he stepped back and apologized. "*Maaf kijiye.* I didn't mean anything." He could play the pretender—at least until Shiloh found her exit.

"She's gone." The younger man spun, searching the crowds. "The girl is gone!"

Reece smiled inwardly. Shiloh had taken the opportunity and split.

"*Chup raho.*" After ordering the underling to shut up, the bigger man turned his sneering eyes on Reece. "I ought to drag you down to the station and show you how *badmash* like you are handled." He threw a punch, and Reece let it connect.

Bent and feigning pain, Reece offered false humility with his apology.

The man shoved him.

Reece gave a half-bow and stumbled down the street, still clutching his ribs and watching as the two stormed in the wrong direction. The way she'd stood there, feet pinned to the cement, wasn't like her. What happened?

"Ryan?"

"Good save, Jaxon. Your satcom should be working. You won't need us now."

In the safety of his vehicle, he lifted his watch and flipped to the tracer readout. Her signal blipped, showing her nearing Bhuleshwar and Kalbadevi Roads. Reece clicked off the tracer. *Why would she go back?*

Oh, no. He knew exactly what she was doing. And why.

Smacking the steering wheel, he started the engine. Stupid. He'd love to wring her neck. Never had a target so mangled his mind and options. After the stunt she pulled on Market Lane, and now this, her naïveté might prevent him from keeping her alive.

Long repressed memories surfaced. Darkness. Clanking. A scream followed closely by a thump. And he'd lost Chloe Staite.

Reece shook his head and rubbed his eyes. Let the dead remain buried.

He sped down Kalbadevi Road, keeping his eyes peeled. What had gotten into her? In the last fifteen minutes, she'd made two serious mistakes. Freezing up in front of those two and heading back to her apartment. She had to know better!

His phone chirruped. At the intersection, he held the brake and retrieved the phone. "Go ahead."

"We've got an agent in place inside Mumbai Mansion. Just hold."

An agent in place? "Who?" He'd been the only agent working this area. "What's going on? Why didn't you tell me about this before?"

"He's been there since the attack. Just sit tight."

"Sit tight?" He spun the steering wheel and pulled onto Bhuleshwar Road, this time coming from the east. The attack. He meant the one that had hit the Taj Mahal Palace and Tower . . . and killed Chloe.

Parked along the curb, he glanced up at the multi-storied building where the UCSD students had taken up residence. He glanced at the Laxmi Narayan Temple across the street. Would that the gods there actually did any good—at least for Shiloh right now.

"Okay, he's got her in sight. Looks like she's going in."

"Ryan," Reece worked to keep his voice calm. "If she goes in, she'll walk into a trap."

"I know."

Reece stilled. Were they not listening? "She's dead if she goes in there."

"I know, I know. We're working on it."

A dog with its tail tucked scampered across the road, skittering out of the way when a horn squawked at it. Reece lifted his thermal binoculars and peered through the lenses toward the building. A dozen or more signatures lit up the screen. He tossed them aside. There would be no way to find Shiloh in that crowd, not at this time of day with everyone gathering for dinner in the main lobby and café.

Several men in suits jogged up the street from the south. In a city of white kurtas and khaki pants, this had the look of high-powered trouble.

Reece reached for his Beretta. He popped the magazine out and cleared it. Double-checking the players, he returned the clip, chambered a round, and released the safety. An AK-47 rested under the arm of one man; another carried what looked like a carbine. A lot of firepower for dinner.

From under the seat, Reece ripped free his Glock and did a press check. He opened his door and climbed out. Something far more sinister was going down. He'd pound the answers out of Langley when this was over.

"Reece, what are you doing?" Ryan's voice wavered. "Your signal's moving—you're moving."

"She's my target."

"Reece, stay out of this."

"Too late."

Scuttling across the lobby, Shiloh hugged the walls as she made her way to the stairwell. The people clustered near the front desk seemed harmless enough, but the two men near the east exit served as a warning not to stop.

Sweat tickled her back as she took the stairs two at a time. When she rounded a corner and looked up, she propelled herself faster. Her floor. She exhaled and then slowed, listening. Scraping on the steps above pushed her back against the wall. Side-stepping, she covered the last few stairs and reached the landing for the third floor.

"*Ye*! Come here! Down one more," a voice shouted.

Footsteps pounded overhead. Her gaze shot to the door. She jerked it open. Although she might be confronted in the hall, she had no choice. Getting trapped in a stairwell meant death—no way out. As soon as her foot hit the threadbare carpet, she paused and checked both ways. Clear. She sprinted to the right.

Behind her, the door squeaked open.

Shiloh darted into a closet marked Supplies. Palm against the wood, she eased the door shut. She swiped at the sweat on her forehead and upper lip with the back of her hand. Her shirt stuck to her back. Angry voices drew nearer. She tucked herself behind a tall stack of paper towel boxes in the corner.

"*Tu kaay kela aahe*?"

What did you do? Shiloh's heart skipped a beat. That sounded like Dr. Kuntz.

"Tracking down your problem," came another voice.

"I have no problem, you infidel." Definitely her professor—he loved that word! "If you had left her alone, she would be in our hands by now. Mess this up, Burak, and it's over."

"Do not threaten me, old man."

Shiloh squeezed her eyes. What was going on? What were they after? What did they think she knew? She couldn't believe Dr. Kuntz was a part of this.

"Meet me at the office in two hours. She should return by then. She'll think it's safe," Dr. Kuntz said.

"What if she doesn't?"

Dr. Kuntz's sarcastic laugh penetrated the walls of her hiding place. "Come now, *mera dost.* She thinks of me like a father."

Shiloh frowned. *Not quite.*

So, he called the leader his friend. Exactly what kind of friends had the professor made since arriving here?

"You'd better be right. If she knows anything, you know what we'll have to do."

"She made an unfortunate discovery," Dr. Kuntz said. "Do not worry. I have things under control."

With the men standing just outside the supply closet, Shiloh feared she might be discovered.

"You are careless. Perhaps you have forgotten how much we paid you or the importance of what we are doing."

"I don't care about your ancient beliefs. And yes, you paid me well, but the rest is due."

The man prattled, his words seeming to alter from Marathi to another language, using words outside the conversational use Shiloh had mastered. She struggled to understand and keep up. Despite the dropped words, his sharp tone could not be missed. The argument escalated.

Then Dr. Kuntz pleaded in fear. "Burak, there's no need. Please!"

"You've cost me too much."

BANG!

Shiloh jerked at the gunblast. She drew back and balanced her stance, ready to fight.

"Drop the gun!" A commanding voice broke through the chaos.

Another shot. Another. Dozens. Plaster exploded around her. Puffs of white, chalky gypsum crumbled and burst into the air. Gritty dust clouded the closet. Cordite stung her nostrils. She swallowed a cough, but the powdery substance burned her throat. Searing heat trailed across her arm. She clamped a hand over the spot and bit her lip to keep from moaning at the pain of the bullet graze.

"He's getting away," the same commanding voice shouted. "Stop him!"

Shoes thudded, growing more distant with each stomp, until finally, there was silence. Shiloh assessed her arm. Minor. She'd worry about it later. For several minutes she listened and then eased herself from behind the boxes. She hesitated. Was someone still out there?

Broken gypsum crunched underfoot as she inched toward the door.

Through a gaping hole left by several bullets she saw a blur of black. A suit jacket. Someone was there. Rooted to the floor, she held her breath, and then released it slowly. She swallowed hard and waited. Soon footsteps echoed in the hall.

"Maharashtra police!"

Running.

Doors slammed.

Quiet.

Shiloh seized the moment and eased open the door. In the hallway, she glanced to the left, the direction the steps had faded into. She had to retrieve her visa and passport and grab some money. With a quick look to the right, she started to her room—and tripped. Her hands thrust out to break her fall; her fingers grazed something sticky. Hair fell into her face. The sari slid from her shoulder and hung limp around her waist.

On the floor . . . a man dressed in a black suit . . . bleeding.

"Dr. Kuntz!" Anger and panic warred within her at the sight of her old friend. His head was propped at an odd angle, chin touching his chest, as he sat against the wall. She felt for a pulse and found a faint one. "What did you do?" she whispered, grieving. Why had he betrayed her?

Blood flowed from his mouth, down his jaw, and onto the once-pristine white shirt. "Sor . . . ry."

"Shh." She touched his shoulder, trying to assess his injuries.

"Here," he choked out. His hand flopped against the floor. "Take it."

She gulped. With a shake of her head, she looked down. An object, covered in blood and unidentifiable, lay in his palm. It was round and hard, like a coin.

Thundering footsteps in the stairwell drew her attention. She'd never make it to her room now. In the far distance thrummed the call to prayer for the Muslim community. The melodic chanting from a nearby mosque lent itself to the eerie sensation consuming her.

"Rrrun . . ." Dr. Kuntz's word slurred. A guttural hiss issued from him, and he sagged.

Strength rushed out of her like the tide. She wanted to save him, but she knew he was gone. Just like Mikhail. She had to move . . . now.

Pushing herself toward the tall, narrow window at the end of the hall, she vowed to discover how deeply Dr. Kuntz was involved in the attack. What had been worth the lives of two friends and possibly a third?

She shoved back the glass pane and climbed onto the ledge, toeing it shut just as shouts vaulted through the tight corridor. Heat from the sun-warmed wood and plaster radiated through the choli and her waist as she stood on the beam, fingernails digging into the siding.

The window swung open.

Shiloh froze and watched the pane.

A shiny black head peered down the fire escape, then up and to the left. If he looked her way—

Her foot shot out, nailing him in the face as he turned. He flew back against the sill with a sickening crack. She hopped onto the fire escape, scaled the outer rails, dropped to the silky grass, and landed in a roll.

With his Beretta cradled to the side between both hands, Reece grinned, mesmerized as Shiloh sped across the street and hopped onto a bus without missing a beat. He didn't know how she'd managed to escape from the death squad unscathed, or where she'd been hiding, but when he saw her sailing through the air, his heart caught. She had outsmarted a deadly enemy.

Using his advantage, Reece assessed the scene. The authorities would be here soon, so he had to work fast. First he snapped photos of the dead professor. Then he took photos of the hall and window where Shiloh had made her stealthy escape. Quietly he picked a lock and let himself into Shiloh's room. He scanned the furniture and bed. Undisturbed.

Voices in the hall pushed him against the wall.

Mumbled words carried through the thin plaster as a man affirmed Reece's suspicions. The dead drop and the dead men in the hall were connected. One of the radicals was identified as Burak al Nabiri.

Reece eased himself out the window, lowered himself down one floor, and made a quick escape through the room. The UCSD dive team had two members left, possibly three if Khan was still alive. With the way al Nabiri's people were picking off the Americans, they'd be oh-for-four in no time flat. That wouldn't do.

Reece had his assignment, and he would make sure at least one member made it home breathing. He pitched her backpack in the rear of his Jeep and climbed behind the wheel. Using the secure-link patch to locate her, he let out a sigh. Moving south. He pulled onto the crowded street.

At his shack he ditched the Jeep. He kicked off his shoes and tossed her backpack on the unmade *charpoy*. After a quick shower and shave, he shoved the bed aside and knelt in the corner. As he pried a loose brick from the wall, he let his mind drift through the events of the last twenty-four hours. The attack on the water was unexpected, but nothing he couldn't handle. Khan still lay in Noor Hospital hooked up to machines. According to Human Intelligence that guy was a vital part of her life. And HUMINT was generally reliable. Was Khan a romantic interest? Maybe he provided a balance for the angry, driven Blake. Because that's surely what she was. No average woman had so much fire and a willingness to snap a man's neck with her foot. He readily recruited types like her.

But she was out of reach. The hands-off policy was a mystery, which he intended to solve, but first he needed to get the heat off her.

Reece lifted his phone and dialed the hospital. "*Namaskar*, I'm calling from *The London Times*. We've received word that an American university dive team came under attack. Reports are that two have been killed."

"Oh, no," the woman on the other end answered. "Only one."

"Is that so?" Reece pressed her as he retrieved a box from the hidden compartment. "Does that mean the other two are under your care there?"

"I'm sorry, sir. I can't release that information."

Once he opened the safe, he withdrew a wad of *rupees* and other foreign bills. "Right. You only want to protect your patients. Just last summer, I was down there in Juhu Beach—beautiful place. My friend took a bad spill in an accident. The doctors were atrocious."

"Oh, our doctors are completely competent."

On his knees again, he dragged out a bag from the dusty compartment. "You know, now that you mention it, there was this one doctor, sort of balding, with thick glasses."

He described in detail the man Reece had seen when he'd bumped Shiloh.

"Dr. Biswas?"

"I think you're right. Very good doctor." He lodged that name in his memory bank as he stuffed clothes into the duffel. "Dhanyavaad," Reece thanked her. He ended the call and immediately dialed information, asking for the surgery desk, switching his tone again.

"Noor Hospital."

"Calling from St. George," Reece said in Marathi. "I need to speak with Dr. Biswas."

"One moment, please."

He packed a few extra supplies in Shiloh's bag and donned his leather jacket.

"This is Dr. Biswas."

"Doctor, we've received a patient here, apparently washed up onshore—from the same accident your shooting patient came from."

"Is that so?"

"Yes, a woman." Reece could only hope those after Shiloh would intercept the information and end up in his wild-goose chase. "How is your patient? These Americans are so intolerant."

"Mr. Khan is still in ICU. We believe he's out of danger but are keeping him under watchful eyes."

"Of course, of course. Have you had any contact with a representative? We haven't been able to reach anyone. It's been so hard to track them down."

"As a matter of fact, their sponsor was here moments ago."

Only if the dead still walked. Dr. Kuntz should be at the morgue by now. The doctor just confirmed what Reece feared. The threat was growing. He clenched his teeth, but kept his reply relaxed. "If he returns, will you tell him he's needed here?"

"Of course. How is your patient?"

"It doesn't look good."

"Too bad."

"Indeed." After thanking Biswas, Reece closed his cell phone and stalked out the door armed with two bags.

In the alley he peeled back a false tin wall lining his hut and squeezed into the three-foot space. He ran his hand along the fiberglass body of the bike, still warm from the heat of the now-gone sun. His baby, the one indulgence he'd allowed himself for the mangled streets of Maharashtra and playing on the beach. Ducati Monster. Danger never looked so good.

Packs secured, Reece slipped on the red and white helmet. Using his knees, he eased the Ducati out of hiding. He revved the engine, allowing the rumble to vibrate through his chest. After another rev, he released the brake, pressed his chest to the spine, and roared into the night.

Whether or not Shiloh Blake was ready, the time had come.

5

A CANOPY OF STARS TWINKLED OVER THE EBONY SEA AS REECE LEANED against his bike.

"Her name is Shiloh Blake," Nielsen said.

"Tell me something I don't know." He stood up and lifted her pack from the tank.

"Listen to me. She's Shiloh *Blake* as in Jude *Blake* as in former Director of Affairs in Europe, the agency's Middle Eastern expert? Bangladesh? Sound familiar?"

Reece caught his breath. "Want to explain why you yanked me out of the mission when you knew this?"

"You don't understand. There is a special directive regarding Blake's daughter—"

"Give me a break, Nielsen. Every top-level director has extreme protection guaranteed for their family."

"Yes, but this . . . look, there's history here you can't know about. That comes from so high up the chain you'd never believe it. Her father negotiated with the agency to maintain the highest level of protection. A few years ago, she walked away from it."

"And right into my territory." She'd come to India as part of her college studies, but Reece suddenly knew she'd really come to hide. He understood. Despite his faith in God, he still had wounds that were better buried. Hidden. Forgotten. He turned back to his bike.

"As for getting yanked, it's complicated. We'd gotten HUMINT that al Nabiri had crossed India's border. I tried to get a few things lined up but the situation worsened."

"You could say that." If the girl was Blake's daughter, that explained a lot, especially if the bad guys knew about it. Could she lead them to those responsible? "Couple al Nabiri's presence with the Muslim grassroots movement—this thing could be ticking right under our noses."

"Exactly."

"So, I get her on the first boat home."

"No."

Reece waited.

"An asset has relayed information that it may be detrimental to put her or Khan on any type of traceable transport. Then we have the beauty of a dilemma here—someone suggested to my superiors that she may have seen those responsible for the attacks. She might be able to identify them. So, not only do we need to assure her safety, but we have to convince her to trust us."

"You want me to—"

"Protect an asset of the United States."

She wouldn't cry. Not here. Not now. Not ever. She'd done enough of that as a little girl. It never helped.

Rolling and lapping, the tide continued its endless reaching as if unable to find the object of its search. Just like her. The melancholy thoughts dug at Shiloh's heart, wearing down her resistance to the tears begging to be unleashed. Legs drawn to her chest, she leaned against the Mumbai beach retaining wall. Uneven rocks dug into her back, but the lingering warmth made it worth the discomfort. A cool breeze teased her with the scent of curry from the café fifty meters away. With the sun setting, laughing families gathered on the beach to enjoy the last rays of light. Their happiness haunted her. Why would anyone laugh on a day like this?

She shivered and tossed the long end of the sari around her shoulders, hoping to block the chilly air. Across the rippling waters, the sun melted into the Arabian Sea. Orange spilled over the strangely grey waters. Gone was the vibrant blue-green she'd savored earlier this morning. How ironic that the sea she'd adored at the waking of the day became the one that assaulted her by close of it.

Holding her wrist, she bit her lower lip. Without Khalid's bracelet, her arm felt naked, empty. Like her soul. She pressed her head into the heel of her hand. Although she'd lost the precious gift, she had gained her safety. He'd understand. She was sure of it.

Marry me.

She clenched her eyes shut. Why did she have to remember those words? Hadn't she buried them on Butcher Island? If—no, *when*—he got better, he'd regret it.

Images of blood, like a bad leak from a radiator, swam in her mind. First Mikhail. Then Dr. Kuntz. What if Khalid died too?

Where was Edie? Was she one of their victims as well?

A low growl rumbled through Shiloh's stomach, reminding her of the last meal she'd had—dinner last night. Without her pack, she didn't have any rupees to buy from the vendors who littered the beach. Though she had scrounged the beach for food, families had stared, so she slipped off to a quiet corner to wait for dark and anonymity to scavenge. She had found a half-eaten apple about an hour ago, but it hadn't gone far in sating her hunger.

Hunger. She sighed. That was the least of her worries.

She'd always had strong instincts that kept her edgy . . . competitive . . . at the top of the academic food chain. In fact, she often ended up being the butt of jokes. Some at UCSD had given her character nicknames. There was a reason they were graphic novel superheroes—they weren't real.

Today reality smacked hard, and those graphic novels sprang to life. At the hospital the inconsistencies about those two men screamed, *imposters!* She'd followed her gut instinct then, and they'd pursued her through the city.

Her mind snapped to Brownbeard. With those muscles and his uncanny ability to appear out of nowhere, he could've easily overtaken her, but he hadn't. As a matter of fact, now that she thought about it, he seemed more intent on following her. The thought forced her to scan the beach for him, and she felt relieved when she didn't spot his large frame. Was he expecting her to lead him to something? Perhaps the same thing as the other two?

From her pocket, she slid out the object that Dr. Kuntz had given her just before he died. She sighed. What was it? A coin? An electronic device? She'd considered washing it, but what if it had some kind of sensitive circuitry? Water could destroy it. Then again, the blood probably had done that. Still, she didn't want to risk damaging the piece any further. Somehow, it was a part of what happened today.

Wait a minute. Where was the lamp, the piece she lifted from the sea bottom this morning? She searched her other pocket. Empty. Had she left it in the scrubs with the choli vendor? She cocked her head to the side and realized when she removed the tunic, the lamp hadn't been there. Had she lost it while running between the hospital and the shop?

Dusk settled quickly on the beach. Shadows skittered here and there like spirits in a ceremonial dance. Shiloh shook her head. Soon the last of the families would be gone, and she could attempt to clean up in the rank bathroom and maybe even lap water from the faucet. Disgusting, but her burning lips demanded hydration.

But then what? There had to be something she could do, someone she could contact. Yet, as she ran through a mental checklist, she came up blank.

"Oh, Khalid," she whispered, rocking herself in the sand. "What happened? I wish you were here." A knot welled in her throat. Eyes on the stars glinting against the black, she whispered, "Please don't die. I need you."

Drained, she stared at the swollen waves that tumbled onto the sandy beach. A pulsing headache throbbed through her skull and pulled at the back of her corneas.

Less than a dozen feet away, masked in the dusky light, a father shouted to his children squishing the remnants of a sandcastle. Still laughing from their play, they picked up their things. The deep-throated sound of a nearby motorcycle coated the air as the family strolled out of sight, heading for the parking lot behind her.

One down, one to go. Shiloh closed her eyes, waiting to hear the purr of their vehicle. Almost in sync with the starting engine, the other family that had lingered on this sandy stretch of beach headed for the parking lot.

Sand crunched and rocks popped against the undercarriage of their car as they drove away. Finally, she was alone. Dusting off her legs and backside, she plodded toward the bathroom. She weaved a little, her coordination partially thrown off in the fight for her life, but also caused by stiffness left over from her seizure at the marketplace.

Swarms of thick, foul odors assaulted her as she stepped into the bathroom and switched on the one dangling lightbulb. Though she tried not to take in the smell, she couldn't avoid it. She coughed and rushed into the first stall. After relieving herself she stood before the badly scratched and dulled mirror, water trickling over her hands. A smile threatened her dour mood at the sight of the pink and white bindi adorning the middle of her forehead and settling between her eyes. Absently, she traced a finger over the crystal pieces, surprised at the way they felt. Cold. Lifeless. Why did everything remind her of death?

She tossed off the thoughts and washed her hands. After noticing the rusty hue of the water, she opted against sipping it. She would need to find another source of hydration. She could sleep tucked between the retaining wall and rocky beach. Hopefully, the police wouldn't notice her.

Warm sand squished between her toes and welcomed her into the quiet air and chilly breezes. Once again, she pulled the sari around her shoulders, quickly surveyed the beach, and started back to her hiding place.

With her options limited, she had to find a way to get information on Khalid's condition. Since certain fake cops scouted the hospital and the hostel, she'd have to sneak in through the back tomorrow. If she needed to stay with Khalid until his father arrived in a couple of days, she would find a way. Somehow, she would.

A dolphin lurched out of the water less than twenty meters from shore, arched, and then dove back in. Shiloh walked to the edge of the rippling liquid and slipped off her shoes, letting the cool seawater tease the tips of her toes. She drew in a deep breath and slowly let it out.

God . . . The prayer lodged in her throat. Would He care about Khalid, about this insanity gripping her life? Surely He would. Khalid was a Christian. Granted, a new Christian, but he believed in Christ, the Messiah.

Yeshua. She could hear him speaking the name he preferred to the Anglicized "Jesus," saying it gave him peace. And she had to admit that peace rose in her even now. She ached for the soft whisper of Khalid's voice. To hear him lecture her about her relationship with God—or lack thereof. Guilt hung around her heart. She had always rebuffed Khalid. He couldn't understand. Her life had been marred by cruel and unusual punishment—punishment for her parents' mistakes. She wasn't the average American college girl, even though that's what she'd longed for with all that was Shiloh Blake.

She pivoted and started back to the rocky outcropping. As she neared, her heart skipped a beat. Then another.

My pack! The bag sat on the ledge with a bottle of water.

Stopping cold, she attuned her senses to the surroundings. Shadows flickered across the sandy terrain. Shiloh pushed forward cautiously. Suddenly, the lapping ocean sounded deafening, drowning out everything but itself. Nothing seemed out of place . . . except for the unexplained appearance of her backpack.

Her mind worked the labyrinth of details. One family had left. A motorcycle went by. Another family left. Even in the bathroom, she'd not heard anything or anyone approach.

She scanned the beach as she closed the last few feet between her and the pack. Was it really hers? Black and tan with a starfish keychain her mother had given her hanging from the zipper tab. Definitely hers. From her hotel.

Somebody had brought the pack and water. Somebody aware not only of her location and needs but of her identity. Her stomach plummeted.

There! To her immediate right. Metal or glass glinted.

As she stood in front of her pack, she let her hands wrap around the strap and then hoisted it up, testing the weight. The nylon bottom bulged outward. Hopefully, it would be enough if she needed it as a weapon. She shifted one foot back to brace herself against an attack.

"Planning to use that on me?" Amusement radiated through a man's tone.

Shiloh shrank from the deep voice. *No, don't pull away.*

It took several seconds for her eyes to adjust, to spot him. In shock, she saw that he sat right in front of her on the rocks. Dressed head-to-toe in black, he had been camouflaged directly under her nose. Shoulders broad, neck thick . . . the guy was nobody to mess with. Brownbeard.

Would he toy with her first, then torture, rape, and kill her? Leave her body for the sand spiders and vultures?

"Who are you?" She lifted the pack and held it close. It weighed at least twenty pounds. Had he packed all of her belongings?

"Sit down. Let's talk."

The undulating sea sparkled under the caress of the moon, forming a silhouette of her figure. Nice. He'd never paid attention before. He wished he hadn't now.

"I don't think so." She drew herself straight, moving the bag away from him.

Her defensive posture didn't worry Reece. He'd have been disappointed if she wasn't ready to fight. "You're alone. Your sponsor and a colleague are dead—murdered."

"So you speak Marathi and listen to police scanners. Should I be impressed?"

"As of an hour ago, Khalid was still alive." He tossed the bait and waited.

Gradually, her shoulders lowered as she set the bag back on the rock. "What do you want?"

"To talk."

"Alone, in the dark, on a deserted beach?" Sarcasm coated her words, but he heard the uncertainty there too.

"I had to be sure of a few things." He nudged the bottled water toward her with his booted foot. "It's spring water. Untampered."

"Says you."

The corners of his lips quirked, but he stopped the smile. "You're dehydrated and weak."

"Says you."

"You're wasting time, Shiloh."

She drew in a quick breath.

Reece scooted to the edge of the rock and rested his elbows on his knees. "A lot happened today." He looked to the sea. "I imagine you want some answers."

"And you have them?"

"Some." Tempted to stand, he opted to give her the appearance of control and remained seated. He lifted the water, took a sip, and handed it to her. "If you want to live to see your boyfriend, you might want to start with this."

She snatched it from his hand, glaring down her straight nose at him. "You know a lot about me. I'm at a disadvantage."

Nice try. He wouldn't let her drag information out of him.

The wind kicked up, tossing long strands of hair off her shoulders. She lifted her jaw as she pushed her gaze to the street. "How do you know who I am?"

"That's not important. That you have a powerful terrorist organization after you is. As you witnessed today, they aren't afraid to kill."

With a sidelong glance, she twisted the lid off the water. "That was you on the Indian Coast Guard boat. The hospital. Then on Market Lane."

He shrugged his acknowledgement and held out the small artifact he'd lifted from her pocket in the sterile environment.

She took the piece without a word and stuffed it into her pack. Cool as a cucumber. All the same, he had seen the wariness and surprise in her eyes moments ago. He had taken her by surprise. Now with the lamp, he had her undivided attention. An ounce of disappointment clung to him at how easily she'd been ensnared by his advantage. Then again, she wasn't trained to hide what piqued her curiosity. But it wouldn't take much to make her a top-notch agent.

Reece controlled his thoughts. That wasn't why he had intentionally crossed their paths. Her safety was.

"You shaved," she said.

"You changed clothes."

"I thought it was fitting."

"And smart."

This time she turned her head. "My father taught me not to talk to strangers." She dumped the water out in front of him, tugged up the pack, and started toward the street.

"He taught you more than that."

She flinched but kept walking.

Reece shoved to his feet. "Where are you going, Shiloh? Too many people are scouring the city for you."

"They won't find me."

"I found you."

She stopped, her head tilted back as she stared at the sky. "I suppose you put a tracking device on me or something." Slowly, she turned toward him, her face bathed in the pale blue of moon glow. The eerie hue made her appear vulnerable.

He shoved a hand into his jacket pocket and withdrew a phone. With a flick of his wrist, he tossed it to her. "When you're ready to talk, use that."

Defiance hardened her face. "Do you really think I'd want anything to do with you? It's not like you've helped . . ." Her words faded. Her eyes dropped.

No, keep your head up. Always keep your head up. Reece bit his tongue. He couldn't guide her, although her skills outshone most he'd trained. "I've put a *lakh* of *rupees* in your pack. Find a hotel and food for the night, then call me."

Shiloh studied the phone. Finally, she glanced back at him. "What makes you think I will?"

"A guy can hope."

She bounced the phone in her hand.

By the look on her face, the questions screaming through her mind begged to be released. Who was he? Why was he helping her? Why had he intervened earlier? Could she trust him? Without those answers, she didn't have control. And it would eat at her until morning. He bent and lifted his helmet then strutted down the beach away from Shiloh.

Noon. At the latest.

If she can wait that long to call, I'll give her my bike.

6

A BOMB? SHILOH STARED AT THE PHONE SITTING ON THE CHARPOY. HAD he rigged the thing to blow when she used it? No, if that man wanted to kill her, he'd make sure they were face-to-face. Still, better safe than sorry. She slowly slid off the back cover and removed the battery. Everything looked normal. As normal, she supposed, as the circuitry of a cell phone could look.

What did she know about defusing a bomb? Had there really been one, she probably would've been splattered on the walls by now. Brownbeard had helped her with the . . .

Shiloh gripped her stomach. *You have a terrorist organization after you*, he had said. What on earth did terrorists want with her? With the archeological dig? The cylinder flashed into her mind. She frowned. What was that thing? Is that what they were after?

Battery replaced, she dialed the number of the American consulate. She'd memorized it before she ever stepped on the jetliner. The lights on the pad blinked and then flicked off.

She frowned. The thing had completely powered down. Shiloh turned it on, pressed the buttons, and waited as the keypad once again glowed blue. With a huff, she punched in the numbers again. It died again.

Mashing the keys, she powered it back on. This time she scrolled to the programmed numbers and groaned. Only one number was in the registry. The name simply read: Me.

Shiloh tossed the phone onto the charpoy and slumped against the thin mattress. With the toe of one shoe, she pried off the other and rubbed her feet on the dusty, frayed rug. A lone light hung from the middle of the ceiling, casting odd shadows along the walls. She grabbed her pack by the bottom, upended it, and stared at the contents splayed across the thin blanket.

Jeans, T-shirts, tanks, boots . . . Heat fanned her cheeks. Underwear. Bras.

Indignation welled within her. How dare he? The thought of *anyone* going through her unmentionables nauseated her, but to think of that oversized . . . She lifted the sock stuffed with money. It had paid for the room.

A *lakh* of *rupees*—two thousand American dollars. Did he realize how far she could get on that?

She sighed. Yes, he knew exactly how far—a hotel room, food, supplies, and a visit to the hospital. She couldn't—wouldn't—leave while Khalid lay injured. Did the big guy realize that? Somehow he knew she had a special connection to Khalid.

Who was the brute? What did he want?

To talk.

"Not in this lifetime." A quick glance at the clock sent her scurrying. If she wanted to see Khalid, she needed to get moving. She shoved her clothes and belongings into the backpack and carted it to the small bathroom. With fewer guards and staff on duty, darkness also would aid her in sneaking into the hospital unnoticed.

She turned on the shower, and a tiny stream of warm water trickled out. Her muscles ached for a hot, pelting spray, one that kneaded the kinks and knots from her shoulders and neck.

At least she could wash her hair and slip into clean clothes. After she snuck in to see Khalid, she might manage to come back here for a couple hours of sleep.

Her mind drifted back to the man with the brown beard. She guessed since he shaved, she'd have to find a new name for him. Brutus. If she encountered him again, it would be one lifetime too soon.

Yet she could feel herself crumbling, piece-by-piece. Life had spun out of control. Fear tracked her through the desert of isolation like a starving lion. Her shoulders sagged. She felt vulnerable, and she didn't like it. Shivering, she clenched her fists.

Enough. Get dressed. Find Khalid.

Shrugging into her black T-shirt, she rehearsed what she remembered of the hospital. Double front doors with Noor labels. Yellow-hued vinyl, highly polished. Slick. Forty feet to the information desk. Surgery to the right. Waiting area immediately to the left of the entrance. Side exit. She'd have to use that. No doubt Kodiyeri would be watching for her. Was there a back entrance? She had to find a way in that wouldn't arouse attention or suspicion.

Shirt tucked into her jeans, she bent to retrieve her boots. Silently, she thanked Brutus—she couldn't live without her Columbias. They supported her ankles, which were throbbing from all the trotting around town avoiding terrorists. The word still sat bitter on her tongue. Brutus had to be wrong. He wanted to frighten her, knock her off balance. She gritted her teeth as she secured her hair in a French twist.

Well, she had a lakh of rupees. In the morning, when life in the city rose to a boisterous level, she'd venture to Market Lane, buy back her bracelet, then head to Crawford Market and stock up.

Keeping to the shadows and with her pack slung over her shoulder, Shiloh wound her way through town to the hospital. Alert for her pursuers, she pulled into hiding places when cars whizzed by and tucked her chin when strangers appeared on the sidewalks. Scattered and lonely cars sat in the parking lot as she cased the medical facility. Bright lights illuminated the emergency and front entrances. Her hand trailed over the wall as she crouched along the perimeter of the building. Finally, she spied a steel door at the back and watched for a few moments. No foot traffic. Confident the coast was clear, she hustled to the entrance.

Suddenly, the door swung out and hit the wall with a bang. Shiloh pressed herself against the cement siding. Adrenaline exploded through every vein.

"*Apna khayal rakhna*," a voice inside shouted, apparently from across a large distance, for someone to "take care." A man stepped into the night, waved, and carelessly slammed the door behind him. He never looked back.

Shiloh lunged and caught the handle. Inside, she huddled next to a thrumming refrigerator as she eased the door shut, assessing her situation. To the right, movement. She peeked over the sheen of a steel table. One . . . no, two men working a machine of some sort. Silence filled the left side of the room. Light from a doorway spilled across the waxed-to-a-slick-shine floors.

Lowering herself to peer under the steel center island, she spied her escape route—a semi-darkened hall. She kept her eyes on the men as she inched around the island. A cart shielded her from the workers as she calculated the speed and maneuverability she would need to make the hallway without being seen. With a deep breath, she burst across the open area, bringing herself to her full height just as her foot touched light.

"Oh!" A woman in scrubs gasped when Shiloh surprised her.

"*Mujhey bhookh lagi hai.*" Shiloh pressed her hand to her stomach, forcing a hungry look into her face. Would they believe she was visiting someone and looking for a cafeteria?

The woman considered her for a moment.

She still hadn't eaten, so the confirmation of a growling stomach didn't surprise her.

The woman's knotted brows eased. "I will show you." The nurse motioned for her to follow as she pivoted and headed in the opposite direction toward the cafeteria. "Down the hall, then right."

"Dhanyavaad." With a nod and thanks, Shiloh breathed easier with each step that took her away from the woman.

At the end of the hall she spotted a directory hanging on the wall. According to the map, two flights up there was a station directly above her. She pushed through the door and took the stairs two at a time, reaching the third floor in less than thirty seconds.

Slowing her breathing, she stepped into the hall and paused to let her eyes adjust. Squeaky shoes approached from the left.

"*Kya mein aapki madad kar sakti?*" The nurse in blue scrubs stopped, her expectant expression echoing her offer of help.

"I know it's late," Shiloh whispered, hoping her Marathi didn't sound too distinct. "I'm looking for a patient. He had surgery. He's my . . . *mera dost.*"

The woman raised her eyebrows at the endearment, then smiled. "Come, we'll look." The nurse walked to the desk and plopped into a chair. "What is his name?"

Shiloh glanced around the area, hoping she hadn't drawn attention. "Khalid Khan."

When the nurse started shuffling papers, Shiloh's fingers itched to prance over the computer keyboard. Why didn't she just look it up on the desktop?

Finally, the nurse typed Khalid's name. "Ah, here we are. He's"—she traced a finger over the screen—"second floor, room twenty-five."

"Dhanyavaad." Spinning on the balls of her feet, Shiloh stifled her glee. If she found his name in the registry, that meant he was here. Alive!

Isn't that what Brutus had said? She shrugged.

Jogging down five steps, then around the landing, then down five more, Shiloh hoped Khalid would be alert. What if he was in a coma? The thought stalled her heart. She'd have to leave him and find a way to the American embassy on the western coastline.

Through the darkened hall and around a corner, Shiloh found the room. She slipped in, straining against the low-wattage lamp near the bed that threw light across Khalid's face. His chest lay bare, a wide bandage around his abdomen. The stark white medical tape contrasted sharply with his olive skin.

Feeling as if the world had just righted itself, Shiloh dropped her pack at the foot of the bed and heaved a sigh. "Oh, Khalid," she whispered as she moved to his side.

For a moment she let her eyes track over his body. An IV taped to his hand pumped vital fluid and medicine into him. His hair drooped into his eyes. Without thinking, she swept the silky black strands from his face. When she withdrew her hand, she stilled. Dark eyes held hers.

"Hello," she said, emotion thickening her words.

"You're late." His voice sounded dry, tired.

A smile stole into her face. "I'm always late, remember?" Why did she suddenly want to cry?

The left side of his mouth tugged upward, and his eyes slowly closed. Had he fallen asleep?

"Khalid?"

His hand moved toward her and grasped hers tightly.

She wanted to tell him everything. How the two men had tracked her all over the city. Then Brutus. Dr. Kuntz. Instead, she stood there, staring at his handsome face, disbelieving the last twenty-four hours. Maybe they'd been a dream. Here with Khalid, holding his hand—when had they ever done that?—everything seemed okay, right.

"How are you feeling?"

"Weak." His head lobbed toward her, eyes slowly drifting open. "Mikhail?" When she averted her gaze, he asked, "The professor?"

Refusing to move or reveal more through her traitorous expressions, Shiloh stood rigid.

The foggy haze clinging to his face cleared. His brows knitted against sparkling eyes. "Are you safe?"

She squeezed his hand. "I'll be fine."

"Hey," he said, his voice growing hoarse. "Miss America, you're not invincible."

"No, but I'm smart."

"That's why I love you."

Lips parting to speak, Shiloh shook her head instead. She noticed a cup of ice on the stand next to his bed and lifted it. "Here, your throat sounds sore." Plucking out a piece, she worked to steady her nerves.

Khalid opened his mouth, but she could feel his eyes boring through her as she set a chunk in his mouth. "Shiloh . . ." he mumbled around the obstruction.

"Khalid, please don't." The words tumbled out so fast, she nearly tripped over them. She sighed and once again pushed a smile onto her face. "Just rest." Running her fingers through his hair, she pretended not to notice the hurt reflected in his soulful expression. "You need to gather your strength."

Silence devoured the moment. Shiloh shifted on her feet and propped herself on the edge of his bed.

"I can't pretend anymore, Shiloh."

"About what?" But she already knew. Only, she didn't want to know. Again she glanced down, watching as he rubbed his thumb over the top of her hand.

He strained to sit up.

She nudged him back. "Stop being a hero."

His grip tightened, and he tugged her closer. His IV-trapped hand swept her jaw. "I'm in love with you. A brush with death gave me a new perspective. You're afraid of love, but Shiloh, you don't have to be afraid with me. I know you say you hate God, but that's the anger over your dad. We'll work through it. You'll—"

"Khalid." She shoved to her feet. "I just need you to get well."

"You don't *need* anything. You're always telling me that."

"They—" She bit her lip.

"Who's 'they'?"

"Never mind. I . . . it's nothing."

His dark, deep eyes narrowed. "What's happened? What are you hiding?"

"Nothing." Nearly choking on the lie, she scrambled to correct it. But there was too much to explain. "I just . . . we need—"

Voices in the hall interrupted her. Hide. The bathroom. Backpack in hand, she darted to safety just as the door opened.

"Shiloh, wait. What—"

"Mr. Khan, you're awake at this hour?" a sing-song voice said. "I'll increase your drip so you can get some rest. You have lost a lot of blood."

"No, please. I'm . . . fine."

Shiloh peeked between the jamb and the door. By the time the nurse released his flow of meds, checked his vitals and left, Khalid had slipped into la-la land.

Sneaking back into the room, Shiloh returned to his side. Even though peace enveloped him, it struck her that he always looked that way. Awake. Asleep. It made no difference. Maybe that's what she liked about him—his quiet strength. Something she didn't have. He'd always made her feel like the Queen of Sheba.

"I'm sorry, Khalid. I don't deserve you, my Arabian Prince." The nickname she'd given him forced a deep ache into her soul. "Get well, *mera dost*." She bent and pressed a kiss to his cheek. "I'll be back." With one last glance, she slipped out of his room.

I know you're afraid of love. How could he say something so cruel? Anger wrapped a tight coil around her chest. Why couldn't he just leave things be? They were friends. Good friends. But, no, he had to ruin things.

Outside the hospital, her façade evaporated. Knees weak, she stumbled toward the retaining wall and leaned against it. Why did it hurt so much to hear Khalid say those words? What was the fire that burned in her chest?

If anyone knew how to truly love, it was Khalid. And he knew her backward and forward, didn't he? How could he love her?

Could she love him back? No, she *wouldn't*. Love hurt—always.

"Oh, no. Not you."

Arms splayed to each side, Reece stepped into the office. "What?"

Toby Roberts, Consular Section Chief, tossed a file toward the young woman standing between him and Reece. "Get those copied and back to me ASAP." He turned his attention to

Reece and groaned. "Every time you show up, there's trouble. I don't need trouble. Got it?"

Chuckling, Reece clicked the door shut after the admin made her escape. "Such a welcome greeting, Chief Roberts."

With a huff, Toby stomped around the desk and shuffled through a pile of papers on a conference table. "You're more pain than you're worth." He snatched a manila folder and shoved it at him. "That's everything we have."

File in hand, Reece lowered himself into a thickly padded chair and crossed an ankle over his knee. He thumbed through the pages. "Uh . . ." Flipping the folder over to ensure he hadn't dropped anything—like half the file—he nailed the man in the rumpled white button-down shirt with a glare. "You're kidding, right?"

"No, I'm not." Toby ruffled his hair and stomped back to his seat. "I have no idea what's going on down there. We're not getting answers, and we're not getting cooperation."

"There's no U.S. investigative report on the shooting. Is your team still writing it?"

"No."

Reece fanned the pages. "Then where is it?"

"There isn't one. No report. No team."

Reece sat forward. "Come again?"

"Deputy Minister Abdul won't let our people on-site. He's given us the complete runaround, claiming there is a dispute about where it happened, and that it didn't involve Americans. He even tried to say it happened in international waters or something."

"Bull."

"I've sent two teams to the beach, and they've been turned away flat." Toby wiped a hand over his sweaty lip. "They won't even let us set up guard around the survivors at the hospital. No weapons or display of force. Of course, it's a bit of a mess with the *burglary* at the Mumbai Mansion and a missing girl."

"Burglary." Tension knots pulled tight in Reece's shoulders. He'd been there. Heard the rapid fire of AK-47s. Saw the swarm of nationals.

"Yeah, I'm not buying it, either. Unfortunately, Abdul is placing the blame for the murders on—"

"Shiloh Blake."

"Exactly."

Thumping the folder against his shoe, Reece chewed the facts. A shooting on open water. Several dead in the bay. More killed in a massacre at the hotel. India not letting the U.S. investigate. "They're stalling."

Toby looked at him from the corner of his eye. "What was your first clue?"

"Your foul mood."

"Just full of charm, aren't you?" Toby stormed to the door and barked for iced tea for them both. "If I didn't like your sister so much, I would never have agreed to work with you."

"How's that going?"

"I haven't seen her in three months."

"Smart girl." Reece wouldn't tell his embassy friend that Julia had gone to South Africa on a mission trip for the summer. Let the guy sweat it out; he'd appreciate Julia's return all the more. Despite their differences, he knew Toby Roberts was a good man.

At his desk, Toby dropped into the chair and buried his face in his hands. Finally, he sat back. "I hate to say it, but you were right about this dead drop."

Chuckling, Reece flicked the file onto the table behind him. "Boy, bet that hurt."

"You have no idea." Toby eased against his chair as the admin hurried in with two tall glasses of iced tea. "Irene, hold my calls unless it's the ambassador."

"Of course, sir."

They sipped quietly for a few minutes. Reece savored both the silence and the refreshing, albeit too-sweet, drink. He'd probably have a sugar buzz by the time he left the temporary consular offices.

Something didn't fit. What was India hiding? Were they behind the dead drop? He'd heard and seen them protect their own, and what country *liked* having another country investigating a crime within their borders? It was all about control. Still, it didn't make sense for Abdul to stall, not like this. In order to snap the neck of the dragon ready to breathe nuclear fire all over this globe, Reece had to pull these threads together fast.

He glanced at his watch. 8:59 A.M. His thoughts bounced to Shiloh. Would she call? Keeping her under his thumb meant she stayed alive, and through that, he might unearth more information.

"Maybe you should chat with Perry again," Toby said.

Perry Titus. Reece didn't need to tell Toby that's where he was headed after this meeting. The fewer people who knew what he was up to, the less chance of having his cover blown or ending up dead. All the same, it wouldn't hurt to have a second brain to work through this mission. Besides, it always amazed him to hear the knowledge Perry had that most government aides and lackeys didn't.

Reece set his glass on the tray. "Set up a meeting with Abdul for me under the name of Simon James."

"Abdul? You're joshing." Toby scooped several spoonfuls of sugar into his glass and stirred.

"I never joke. I especially never *josh*." Reece slapped Toby's shoulder. "Get it set up. We've got to get in there and find out what they don't want us to know. And Toby?"

"Yeah?" He was on his feet now.

"I hope you have a lot more than three pages next time." Reece let the seriousness in his tone carry the weight.

"Someone's killing innocents to cover up a really bad gig. I'm ready to stop it. I can't do that if your people aren't on their toes."

"We're doing everything we can."

"Do more."

On the other side of Mumbai, Reece strode up the dusty path to the three-story, white plaster structure—one of three buildings on the campus. He shoved aside his irritation over the morning's events. Too much had been revealed, and yet, too little. He strode down the hall and knocked on the door.

"*Varu,*" a voice intoned from within.

Nudging the door open, Reece relaxed at the sound of his old friend's voice. "Hello, Perry."

The greying man looked up from a table where he sat with two Indian students. Surprise pinched his eyes. "Simon." He patted the backs of the two men and bade them good-bye. "What brings you here, *mera dost*?" The American-born man had spent most of his life in India, and it suited him perfectly.

Reece waited for the room to clear and then shut the door. He allowed Perry to hug him, and even laughed. "I suppose it has been too long."

"Far too long." Perry started toward the far corner, where a small desk sat piled with books, bags, and papers. "Come, I'll get my wallet and we'll go have something to eat."

"Are you sure I'm not interrupting?"

"No, no, it's good." Perry hustled toward him, tucking his wallet into a fold of his long tunic. "And friends never interrupt." He patted Reece's shoulder. "Tandoori chicken, right?" He'd never forgotten Reece's favorite.

"If we can find something this early," Reece said. He glanced at his watch. Only one hour left before he'd have to transfer ownership of his Ducati to a beautiful young woman.

"Always in Mumbai there is somewhere to eat."

They weren't more than a dozen paces from the college building, when Perry's grip tightened. "You've come not a moment too soon. Things are beyond imagination."

7

"SHE NOT HERE."

Shiloh blinked, staring at the short Hindu man before her. Grey heavily streaked the hair at his temples and peppered the rest. "When will she return?" She had to get her bracelet. Khalid couldn't know she'd bartered the precious piece yesterday.

"She not come back."

Her heart raced. "What do you mean?" When she leaned in, the sari slid down her upper arm. She tossed it over her shoulder. "I need her."

"She quit. Go back to Pradesh."

"Pra—*no!* She had my bracelet." *Oh, please.* Shiloh stepped closer, gripping the edge of the table. "Did she leave a bracelet here? A twined one with shells? It's very important to me. I told her I would come back with money." She flashed the rupees under his nose.

"No." He waved his hands in a criss-cross pattern. "No, she not leave anything." He shook his head. "Glad she gone. Lazy woman."

Swallowing hard, Shiloh glanced around, as if she could find the missing piece. "You're sure? Is it under—"

"No bracelet." He raised his chin and stomped away.

Heartsick, she shuffled out of the shop into the chaos of traffic and shoppers and headed toward Noor Hospital. Khalid would notice the missing bracelet. Notice and never understand. No, that wasn't true. He *would* understand—and that was part of the problem. Because then she'd have to explain what happened—about the men, the professor, and Edie. There still had been no word from her vivacious diving partner. Shiloh didn't want to add to Khalid's stress or create health risks for him. The whole thing seemed like a surreal nightmare.

A half hour and a load of guilt later, Shiloh sat next to Khalid, reminiscing. Their lives had intertwined in college, netting them memorable tales.

"Remember that time we visited Dome of the Rock?"

Shiloh scooted to the edge of the hospital bed and grinned. "I never felt so out of place."

"Well, it didn't help that you entered the main synagogue."

She chuckled. "A few men weren't exactly appreciative of a woman in their worship area." Head shaking, she tried to suppress the bubble of laughter. "I can't believe how archaic they can be."

Khalid's dark eyes sparkled, his smile fading as he reached toward her face. "Yet you honored their wishes, gracefully." His fingers swept her cheek. "That's what I admire about you; even if you don't agree, you respect the culture."

Hunching her shoulders, Shiloh sandwiched his hand against her face. "Let's just say I don't like attention. It was easier to slip into the women's courtyard than make a display."

"That was the first time I knew I loved you."

She flinched, but tried to hide it behind a shrug. "Just rest, goof. We need to get you out of here."

"You need to reconcile with God, Shiloh."

"Khalid, please don't do this."

"I've always let you get away with that. But it's important. My parents raised me not to marry someone who does not share the same beliefs. This is a priority—"

"My priority is getting you out of here to someplace safe."

Frustration soaked his dark features. "Where is the bracelet I made for you?"

Shiloh tensed and ducked her head.

"You still haven't told me what's going on." He shifted up in the bed and grimaced. Hand clamped over his side, he settled against the pillows.

"I just think . . ." She brushed loose hair from her face. He'd get upset if he knew everything that had happened in the last thirty hours. In his condition he didn't need any more trauma. "I don't like seeing you in a hospital bed. Besides, we need to log more hours for the Pacific Rim Challenge. It'll be nice to get back out on the water."

"I can't dive for a while. The doctor said there was damage to my lung. It needs to heal first." He held her hand, lacing his fingers with hers. "At least I'm alive. I didn't like lying on the beach, wondering if I would ever see you again. Thinking you might find someone else to watch out for you."

She sat up straight. "I don't need anyone to watch out for me."

"But I like being there for you, helping you through the seizures."

"Me too." They'd talked about it once. Somehow he knew when to be there, when to whisper soothing words and act like they were just enjoying each other's company so that nobody else figured it out. He had always protected her dignity.

The air in the room thickened. Shiloh scooted off the bed and cleared her throat. "So, did they say how long you'd have to stay? What about your father?"

"Shiloh." His tone held a gentle reprimand. "Don't run from me."

"Khalid, please."

"No."

His firm tone surprised her.

"I've always backed down to give you room. But I won't walk away from this or pretend it isn't there anymore. I love you." His dark eyes glistened with determination and intensity. "No more hiding from me . . . or God. We need to face this."

"Face what?" a voice boomed from behind.

They both jerked toward the door. Tall and impressive, Baseer Khan glared at them. His hands rested on his hips. Instinctively, Shiloh took a step from Khalid and retreated into a corner of the room. Khalid's father always made her nervous.

"Father, you made quick time."

Baseer let the door swing shut as he moved to Khalid's side. "My only son in a hospital? Would that I was here yesterday!" He gripped the bars of the bed and leaned down. "How are you?"

Khalid shifted. "Tired, but they say that's normal."

His father studied Shiloh. "And what is it you two have to face?"

Fire licked Shiloh's cheeks. *Don't look away. Be strong.* She'd always been able to face down anyone—anyone but Baseer.

"We must talk, Father." Khalid's voice wavered. "I have intentions toward Shiloh. I want your blessing to marry her."

Baseer straightened. While he wasn't the tallest man she knew, somehow his presence seemed to choke out the last molecule of oxygen from the room. His dark brow dug toward his nose, and his black eyes glowered. "What of university? And your future?"

"My future *is* Shiloh."

"Khal—" His name caught in her throat. Why did he have to do this? Why now? She winced at the pain in his face as he struggled to sit up. Shiloh rushed to his side and pushed him back. It brought her within inches of Baseer. She dared not look at him. "Rest, Khalid. There's time later."

"No," he groused. "I nearly died. Yeshua got my attention with this incident. I don't need another to know what I want and what is right for me."

"What of you, Shiloh?" Baseer asked.

Panic raced through her. "I'm not sure what you're asking."

Baseer laughed. He *laughed*. "You have always avoided speaking your mind—"

"Not really." She clutched a clump of Khalid's blanket.

"You didn't let me finish." Baseer hitched an eyebrow. "You have always avoided speaking your mind in matters of the heart."

Anger laced a tight band around her chest. Why did they have to push? She didn't want to talk about marriage. "I beg your pardon, but there are *matters* that are more pressing."

"As in?" Baseer seemed amused.

His grin irritated her, and she saw the taunting challenge in his eyes—the one that said women knew little and should speak less. "Men chased me through the city last night."

Khalid lunged upward, and then he dropped back against the mattress, his face contorted in pain. He groaned.

"I'll get the nurse." Shiloh bolted from the room—anything to free her of the suffocating conversation that pinned her between the two men. Once the staff brushed past her into Khalid's room, she waited in the quiet hallway, savoring the tranquility. If she went back in, he'd ask more questions, or put *the* question to her again. His father would interrogate her.

No, she couldn't go back in.

His father emerged a moment later. When their eyes met, he stopped and studied her.

She jutted her jaw, refusing to squirm. "How is he?"

"They've given him something to help him rest." Baseer nodded toward a chair. "Would you like to sit?"

"No, I—"

Dark eyes bored into hers. "What does your heart say about Khalid?"

She stilled. "He's my best friend."

"What of marriage?"

"It scares me."

"Good."

She gaped at him. "Good?"

"Yes." He folded his arms and leaned against the wall next to her. "That tells me you are aware of what it takes to make a marriage work. That it's not taken lightly."

Her heart sank. She'd been certain that once Khalid's father knew how she felt, he'd withhold his blessing. The way this little chat seemed to be heading, she'd be married by sunset. Khalid deserved better . . . *someone* better.

"I don't want to fail him." Her stomach twisted. "I'd never forgive myself if I let Khalid down."

"It is as it should be." Baseer nodded. "He is worried for your safety."

"I'm worried for his, for mine—and Edie. I can't find her." She squeezed back the thought that Edie could be dead.

"You said two men followed you?"

"They were here yesterday." Shiloh brushed her hair from her face. "I just had this feeling that they weren't who they said they were. Then, I saw them trailing me through the city. I wasn't sure at first, but when I started running, they ran after me."

She wouldn't mention Brutus . . . or the coin Dr. Kuntz had given her. It had significance, she was certain. She'd also keep the fact that Brutus had paid for the hotel to herself. What would Khalid think about that? What would his father say? Taking money from a strange man while Khalid made a plea for his father's blessing on a marriage she wasn't even sure she wanted. He deserved a humble wife—one who'd be willing to stay home and bear him a horde of children to bring honor to his name and family.

"I take it you lost them?" Baseer's words yanked her attention back to the present.

"No, I haven't." She looked at the clock hanging at the end of the hall. Eleven-fifteen. No wonder her stomach rumbled after skipping breakfast. "I spotted one of them out front this morning, so I came in through the back."

"You don't think you're overreacting?"

"Why don't you ask Khalid if I'm overreacting? Ask the surgeons who spent hours putting his body back together." The storm churning within her threatened to unleash. She took a steadying breath and shrugged. "Whoever these people are, they aren't playing games. I saw their weapons—fully automatic. Whatever they want, they think Khalid has it, or I do."

Baseer exhaled. "Then it would seem wise to get Khalid out of here as soon as possible." He stroked his thick, black beard. "I have friends . . ." He stared into space.

Shiloh let him formulate a plan while she figured out what to do next. The thought darted through her mind to call her father, but she squashed it as quickly as she would a roach. She didn't need his help, or want it. He'd never been there for her anyway.

Half an hour later, she managed to escape the hospital with an agreement to return by sunset to help smuggle Khalid to safety. She'd spend the afternoon gathering supplies and food and then meet Khalid and his father with a rental car. That was the only way to get Khalid across town to the nearest hotel and then to the airport. Somehow, Baseer had vowed, he'd get them home to Pakistan.

The plan wasn't foolproof, but it would have to do. In addition to the unease in her gut about Baseer, she wouldn't leave Khalid until he returned home safely. She wished her intentions were sparked by her love for him. Were they?

Maybe Khalid was right. Was she hiding? Running from love? He was such a brilliant man . . . caring . . .

She gripped her temples. *Stop it. Just stop it.* Love was not the issue right now. Staying alive and getting back to the U.S. was priority number one. Pack slung over her shoulder, she steered herself through the chaos of Mumbai's busy streets. Curry and other spices mingled with the thick humidity. A white and brown dog chased a rickshaw, barking as it bounced over the uneven road. Laughter trailed a crowd of youngsters disappearing around the corner.

She shuddered. Crowds. She hated them. What she wouldn't do for the pleasure of cool open water. Her eyes shifted to the west, where she knew the bay glimmered under the morning sun. She squinted up at the sky. It was close to noon—perfect dive time for the next two hours. Oh, to dive beneath the surface, to be enveloped in the silent serenity of the depths. She sighed.

There. Her heart sped as she caught a flash of black. Was it Brutus? She ducked behind an orange cart and picked up an orange as she peered across the open street to the other side. Yes. He sat with an older man at a sidewalk café.

So, mystery man, what are you doing on this side of town? Maybe she could turn the tables on him. If she could get the advantage . . .

"*Kyaa aap ko yeh accha lagta hai*?" The vendor shook his hand at her, waiting for the payment.

Mumbling an apology, Shiloh paid the vendor and moved away from the cart, shooting a quick glance back to Brutus. She didn't think he had seen her.

It was still early enough that she didn't have to rush to retrieve Khalid and Baseer for several hours, but she needed to buy supplies. That would only take a couple of hours. So she had a bit of time to spin the scenario into her favor and follow Brutus.

Down the street a block, she bought some *pazham pori* and a soda. Then she tucked herself into a table that afforded a partial view of her mystery man and his friend. As she took the first bite of fried plantain, she remembered where the money had come from to buy the snack. She almost tossed it to the nearby dogs. But she was hungry. And tired. She deserved this treat if for no other reason than to spend the money of a man who had tried to control her.

What was his game? He had tracked her all over Mumbai. Although she didn't witness the bloodbath at the hotel, she recognized his voice during the shooting spree—the one yelling for the killer to stop. She tilted her head and stared down the sixty or seventy yards to the thick-chested man. The way he leaned on the table, he looked like a relaxed panther. Yet she suspected the eyes behind those black sunglasses were alert to any danger in his environment. Was this just a casual chat, or was the meeting related to the attack?

Who are you? He knew too much about her not to be government-connected. Embassy? She almost laughed. No way. He was entirely too rough around the edges. He could collapse any peace negotiations just by walking into an embassy. No, this guy didn't waste time on small talk. All those years with her father helped her know—this guy looked and acted like CIA.

Shiloh stuck her thumbnail between her teeth. Why hadn't he stopped her? He'd even given her money. Did that mean he wanted to buy her loyalty? Or her trust? Both?

Slouched in the chair, Shiloh crossed her legs, and cringed as she sipped her warm soda. She'd kill for a tall glass of ice.

Reaching for her food, she heard the *scritch* of claws nearby and glanced down. The little white and brown dog sat giving her the puppy-dog pout. Shiloh tore off a piece of plantain and dropped it for the canine.

Movement across the street forced her to abandon the feeding. The table was empty. Her heart tripped. Where was . . . ? There. Brutus had left the café and was a half-block closer to her.

Shiloh scowled. What did he know that she didn't? He had answers. Was it something that could keep her alive? Her muscles twitched to follow him. Counting to ten, she tried to steady her nerves and remain invisible to him. If this man was who she thought, then she was about to step into a clandestine world: spying on a spy.

Casually, she rose and forced herself to follow him. What was Brutus doing near the Christian college and government offices? He moved at a brisk pace, and after several blocks, her breath labored.

Then he rounded a corner. She hurried, afraid of losing him. She needed answers, and she was sure she could find out what he was up to if she could keep tabs on the brute. Hugging the building, Shiloh peeked around the corner and spotted him at a vendor. He popped the money toward the seller, tossed a mango in the air and caught it, and then struck out again.

Shiloh stayed with him. Where was he going? He acted like a tourist. Didn't he have someone important to interrogate or kill?

Around one building and then another. Down the street, and up a different one. She stuck close. Cramps shot pain up her calves. Perspiration plastered her T-shirt to her skin. Why couldn't he just get on with whatever dirty deed he was up to? To avoid being spotted, she crossed the street with a knot of pedestrians, keeping Brutus in sight. A group in front of her stopped and trapped her in the middle of their steamy body heat. Feeling the suffocation of the crowd, she pushed out—and froze.

Where'd he go?

Shiloh shoved forward to the curb. She scanned the crevices between shops. Was he hiding? She darted to the other side, straining on her tiptoes and craning her neck. A few staggering heartbeats later, he emerged from a shop with a bag tucked under his arm. Too close. Shiloh hung back and waited for him to get ahead a bit more.

Suddenly, he spun and came straight at her. Shiloh ducked her head, and with a pounding heart, she rushed into a store. The thick tobacco smoke and stale scent of a convenience shop strangled her. She hustled down one aisle and up another, weaving farther into the shop and out of sight. From behind a rack of books, she peeked out the word-painted window. He stalked past, chomping into a mango.

What are you doing, you big oaf?

A man at the front of the aisle cut off her view. Hands at his side, he frowned at her. Shiloh apologized and hurried back outside, anxious not to lose the big guy. A sea of bodies swarmed around her.

Not again. Where was he? She probed the throng of white and tan tunics and pants and spun around. Not behind her. She jogged forward. He couldn't have disappeared that fast. She expected him to leap out at her from a stoop just ahead, but instead she only found the barrenness of a boarded-up shop. A frustrated groan worked its way up her throat despite her best attempts to squash it. She'd trailed him for twenty minutes—only to lose him.

Fine. Enough games. Time to find out who he was and how he knew so much about her. Once more she scanned the crowds for his face before plunging her hand into her backpack. Game over. She withdrew the phone he had given her and flipped it open. Irritation ripped at her as she pressed the TALK button and started the trek back toward Jail Street.

"Miss Blake."

Her heart skipped a beat when his deep voice boomed through the phone.

8

FURY NEVER LOOKED SO BEAUTIFUL.

"Don't you know it's not nice to follow people?" Reece chuckled when the line went dead. He slid the phone back into his pocket and leaned against the door, watching as Shiloh stomped toward Princess Street.

Once she blended into the crowd, he stepped from the stoop and headed back to his bike. Did she seriously think he didn't know she was tailing him? He'd wanted to laugh when he switched directions, sending her spiraling into a convenience store. She had a few things to learn, but he had to hand it to her, she had guts.

Disappointment stuck to him the way the Indian heat glued his jacket to his back. He knew she'd call. Man, he almost felt let down to have her pegged so accurately. He liked a little surprise every now and then. Or maybe it was that he had hoped she would prove him wrong—show herself smarter than most. He'd expected a lot more from Jude Blake's daughter. With a quick glance at his watch, he . . . stopped.

No. He tapped the crystal of his watch as he stalked to his motorcycle. It wasn't possible.

He slumped against the hull of his Ducati Monster, staring down the busy, jumbled chaos of the street. Maybe he was wrong. He double-checked the time. Maybe the watch was wrong. He tugged out his phone and scrolled the incoming calls.

Jaw out, he grunted. One-fifteen. Who would have guessed she'd hold out this long? Reece stared at the fiberglass body under him. His off-the-cuff bet with himself taunted him. *I'll give her my bike.*

He palmed the black fairing of his bike. *Get a grip.* She didn't even know about his private wager. No worries. The bike was still his.

When was the last time someone had outwitted him? The thought agitated, yet excited him. He admired the fact that she'd thought she could play his game. One thing was certain—he wouldn't underestimate her again. After spotting her at that café—her ivory complexion a stark contrast against a tapestry of olive—he'd let her play cat and mouse with him.

His phone buzzed again. Was she that easy to play? One corner of his mouth curled, but his good mood fled at the ID. "Go ahead."

"The meeting is set."

He straddled the Monster and stuffed the key in the ignition. "When?"

"One hour."

"One—" Reece stopped short. "Toby, that doesn't give me time to prep your guy."

"I know. I'm sorry. Abdul didn't give me a choice. He's leaving the country tomorrow on a business trip." Toby huffed. "I'm sending a car to your shack right now."

Phone in his pocket, Reece tore through the city toward his house. Without time to rehearse their stories, there were so many things that could go wrong with this meeting. He wouldn't have a chance to make sure the embassy grunt stuck to a script. One wrong word and the guy could put everyone's lives at risk. He revved the engine and eased back on the seat.

By the time the shiny black car slid to a stop along the curb, Reece had showered and changed into a slick Italian suit. He folded himself into the back passenger seat and shut the door. Attuned to the darkness, he resisted the urge to smile. "Couldn't get one of your lackeys?"

Toby shifted. "Don't give me any of your mouth. I knew you didn't have time to prepare someone, so I came."

"About time you got into the field." Reece grinned and unbuttoned his jacket. He hated the way the heat turned the silk blend into a sauna suit. "I met with a friend. He has it on good authority that our Hindu deputy minister isn't exactly loyal to his country."

Toby shifted from the window. "What do you mean?"

"We need to buy some time. We're just asking questions, performing a routine investigation into the deaths of the American college student and his professor." Reece tugged at the noose around his neck.

"You'd better quit messing with your tie, or they'll think you aren't an embassy official."

With a quirked eyebrow, Reece glanced at the man next to him. "But I am."

"Yeah, whatever."

Minutes later, they pulled up to the security checkpoint outside the walled, barbed-wired, sniper-protected government building. A team of guards allowed the car to enter but halted them just inside the compound. After the gate closed, the car was escorted to the *porte cochere*.

"Think they have enough snipers?" Toby asked.

"Keep it cool." Reece stepped from the car and rebuttoned his jacket.

Two columns of armed soldiers protected the entrance to the building. Although Reece hung back to give the appearance that Toby was in charge, he memorized every detail. The mirrors behind the reception counter were new. Cameras? Security? As Toby gave the woman his card and waited for her to notify Abdul of their arrival, Reece eased away, studying the long corridor to the left.

Footsteps echoed from the other direction—two people in a hurry. Rubbing his jaw, Reece turned and drifted toward the paintings on the wall to get a look at the men, who hustled down the hall and disappeared around a corner.

"Ah, Mr. Roberts."

Reece swung his attention to the minister as Toby and Abdul shook hands.

"Thank you for meeting with us so quickly," Toby said. "This is my associate, Mr. Simon James."

Reece nodded toward the much shorter Hindu. "Minister."

"Mr. James." Abdul gave a half bow. "If you'll come this way, we can talk in private."

Inside the office, Deputy Minister Abdul eased the door shut and pointed toward the chairs in front of a large desk. "Please, have a seat. Would you like a glass of water?"

"No, thank you." Toby settled into a chair and looked a bit uncomfortable. "What we want will not take a lot of time, Minister."

"Ah, right to business, is it? You Americans should relax."

Lowering himself into the leather chair, Reece surreptitiously examined the office. A security camera lurked in the corner. The potted plant probably contained a hidden microphone. Or maybe it was in the desk lamp.

"I'm afraid a lot of time has already been wasted, Ali." Toby swept his sandy-blonde hair from his forehead.

Seated behind his desk, Minister Abdul folded his hands over a pristine surface.

No clutter. No paperwork. Interesting for a man too busy to meet with American embassy officials. Where were the itinerary and files for his upcoming business trip?

"Yes, most unfortunate misunderstandings." Abdul's smile seemed plastered on with determination. That is, until he looked at Reece, who gauged the minister with an unwavering stare.

Abdul pressed his glasses up the bridge of his nose; his lips pulled downward.

"Misunderstanding or not, we are here to secure your official approval for our investigators to inspect the crime scene and interview the witnesses." Toby opened his briefcase and handed Abdul a piece of paper. "This is a persons-of-interest list."

"Ah, yes, I see." Abdul set the paper to the side, folded his hands, and returned his attention to Toby. "When I return, I will personally escort you to the diving boat and bring these people here for you to interview."

Toby leaned forward. "When you return?"

Abdul shifted. "Yes."

"And when will that be?"

Reece heard the edge creeping into Toby's voice. He prayed the guy could keep his cool.

"Two weeks."

"I'm sorry." Toby half laughed. "That simply won't do."

"That is the best I can offer." Abdul dabbed his forehead with the back of his hand.

The overhead fan circled lazily, stirring the thick air.

"Ali, you do understand this is going to bring the anvil down on your head? My superiors are already displeased with your stalling tactics."

"No stalling." Ali shook his head. "President Chiranjivi and I leave in the morning. He thinks he can convince the French to help us. But no, we are not stalling. We have official business out of the country."

Toby's brow knitted. "If you aren't stalling, why can't we see the boat right now? Let's get this out of the way."

Ali scooted back his chair, swiping a hand over his mouth. "The boat has been stored and is not easy to access. We must bring it from dry dock so you can examine it. Not easy to do. And you have one student at Noor Hospital and another at St. George Hospital. We must interview them first to be sure they are not responsible for the crimes. Murders have happened at the hotel."

Reece's heart stalled. St. George. He signaled Toby his readiness to leave.

Toby launched to his feet. "Minister, we have always had a kind and friendly association. Unfortunately, I must file a grievance with the U.N. and with our governments. This is unacceptable. Lives are at stake, and the murderers have no doubt escaped by now."

With great care, Reece drew himself straight. He didn't want to give away his hand and reveal that he knew without a doubt—whether directly or indirectly—that Ali Abdul was connected to the murders.

Shiloh tensed and braced herself to prevent banging her head on the car's roof. Baseer's import seemed to aim for the endless potholes as he steered through the tangled streets. It had to be painful for Khalid. The thought pulled her attention to him. His head rested against the back of the seat. Were his eyes even open? Sneaking out of the hospital had been much easier than she would have imagined. She had simply wheeled a fully dressed Khalid through a side entrance to Baseer in the waiting car.

Each hole jarred her. But no more than the phone call to Brutus. When had she given herself away while following him? Her face flushed with anger at the memory of how he'd answered the phone. She gritted her teeth and chafed at the chaos of foot traffic swarming their car.

Don't you know it's not nice to follow people? His words stoked her frustration. It wasn't that he'd known she was on the other end of the line—but the way he seemed to enjoy it. It hit her—he knew. He had expected her call. How was he always one step ahead of her? Yet, she felt the spark of a smile crowding out the storm in her life. He had a sense of humor . . . and a nice voice.

But would she ever get ahead of him? She'd have to if she didn't want the spy learning all her secrets. He and two other men were acutely interested in *something* she knew, or what they thought she knew. The coin in her possession was somehow a clue to this insanity.

The slowing car yanked to the right into an open courtyard cradled by a u-shaped hotel. Brick arched over the entrance to the cobblestone terrace. Littered with tables and fruit and vegetable vendors, the courtyard unfolded a warm welcome to the Taj Mahal Palace and Tower.

An uneasy tremor rippled through her. How could Baseer afford rooms in a high-end hotel?

Standing at the curb, Shiloh watched people flow in and out of the expensive hotel. Bellhops unloaded and hustled bags into the lobby. Blue-white waters rippled in slotted views beyond a wrought-iron gate. The hotel itself was nicer than most. Small squares below each window gave the promise of air-conditioning. Wasn't this the site of the 2008 terrorist attack?

Why had Baseer chosen this place out of all the hotels in Mumbai? Sweeping aside her questions, she opened Khalid's door.

"I will take care of that." Baseer rushed to her side as the trunk popped open. "I will help Khalid and then check in. You wait."

In other words, he didn't want Shiloh touching Khalid in a public building, nor carrying any of his belongings. While his archaic social customs grated on her, Shiloh knew they needed to appear as normal as possible. The less attention, the better. She'd yield . . . this time.

Baseer hooked his arms under Khalid's and drew his son out of the car. Although Khalid didn't grimace, his flat lips and flaring nostrils told her the pain he suffered. After his father had propped him against the small rental, Khalid hobbled around and faced the hotel, his palms pressed against the car behind him.

"When you are ready." Baseer reached into the car and withdrew a briefcase. Then he patted his son on the shoulder, met Shiloh's gaze, and headed into the hotel.

Shiloh took a step closer when Khalid didn't move.

"I'll be okay," he mumbled, watching his father's receding back.

"In about six months."

One side of his lips quirked upward. He flipped his hair from his face. "How many paces between here and the nearest chair?"

With a step back, Shiloh mentally measured the distance. "About fifty."

With squared shoulders and fists balled, he took the first of the fifty steps toward the hotel. Shiloh swallowed. She dared not say anything. His pace was slow and pain-filled. She heard him suck in a breath every six steps or so. Her heart twisted, and she wished she could just wrap her arm around his waist and ease his burden.

"I have an idea." Shiloh darted past him, grabbed a luggage dolly, and wheeled it back to him. "Grab the pole."

Agony morphed to relief as he held the brass pole. No more than a dozen feet lay between them and the front door.

Ten minutes after Baseer had checked in, they rode the elevator up to the fourth floor.

"Get on." Shiloh pointed to the dolly supporting Khalid. His eyes widened. "Get on and pretend you're just goofing around. Your father can push you."

His father scowled. "I will do—"

"Look at him, Mr. Khan. He either rests or keels over," Shiloh pleaded with the two men.

"There is only one more hall," Khalid mumbled as he slumped against the mirrored glass elevator. "Once I get to the room, I can rest."

"Khalid! Pride isn't worth the strain it's putting on you."

"It is not pride; it's honor."

Shiloh bit back her groan. This wasn't a battle she could win. Why it had to be a battle in the first place, she didn't know. Khalid would follow his father's wishes. He always had. Which made her wonder about his decision to turn from the Muslim faith and become a Christian. She knew it had rent his relationship with his father, but nobody spoke of it. It made her wonder how Khalid would ever get Baseer's blessing to marry her since the man seemed to resent her.

Shiloh stared at the shiny numbers on the black door as Baseer slid a key card through the reader on room 313. Was it an unlucky number? He pushed open the door and held it as Khalid stumbled into the suite. A table and chairs, small bar, and sofa welcomed them.

"Your room is there," Baseer nodded his head and handed her a card. "You can access it from the hall or from here, and you may lock both doors. Tomorrow, I will go into the city and arrange our travel plans." He seemed to hesitate, his mysterious eyes monitoring his son as Khalid eased onto the sofa with a groan. Baseer pivoted toward her. "While I am gone, I'd prefer if you stayed here in the hotel. You . . . stand out."

Clearing her throat, she looked at Baseer. "When will we leave for Pakistan?"

The man's eyes darkened. "If Allah wills, in less than two days."

She relaxed her face as she met Khalid's eyes. "Good night. Rest well."

"Good night."

Shiloh let herself into her room and flipped on the wall switch. Light flooded the room, and she nudged the door shut behind her. She locked the deadbolt and slid on the chain lock. Two red, tufted chairs sat before the gold brocade curtains. She dropped her pack in a chair on her way to the window. Drawing the thin material aside, she unlocked the glass door and stepped out on the tiny balcony. She leaned against the ledge. Sun-warmed plaster bathed her palms. Fewer people populated the tables and vendors below. A woman bent over her cart, stretching a tarp over her produce.

Knocking drew her around. She paused as another rap thudded on the adjoining door. Khalid! She unlocked it and yanked it open with a smile.

She froze. "Baseer." A half-smile. "Did I forget something?"

Thick brows shadowed his dark eyes. His mouth turned downward, drawing his bearded face into a scowl. "Khalid is asleep. We should talk."

He dragged a chair to the door and sat.

I guess this isn't an invitation. She copied him and settled into a crimson chair. "Okay. Is something wrong?"

"I want to know what happened in the harbor."

"I told Nisa." Shiloh folded her hands to hide her agitation. "We were diving—the last leg of our assignment."

"Right." Baseer scratched his beard. "Why was Khalid shot?"

She blinked. “I have no idea.”

“Why weren’t you shot or killed?”

Although she tried to swallow, her tongue felt thicker than fried plantains. “I was underwater when it happened.”

He nodded.

“If I had been on the boat, I probably would’ve been shot.”

“You have no idea what these men wanted?”

Confusion draped her. “What men?”

His eyes widened.

“The men at the hospital?”

“Yes, yes. Them.”

“I told you and Khalid, I don’t know what they wanted. It’s my guess they want me dead because they think I saw or know something.” She laced her fingers and squeezed.

“Then you don’t know these men?”

Shiloh straightened. “Know them? How would I know them?”

“I am not sure. I would just like to understand what happened.”

“As would I, but—” A thought hit her. Her cheek under her left eye twitched. “You . . . you can’t possibly think I had anything to do with it, do you?”

“One wonders.”

Her mouth fell open. She stared, disbelieving. Finally, she hung her head and rose to her feet. If he thought her capable of the attack, then . . . “Do you intend to leave me behind?”

He sat for a minute without answering. By the look in his eyes, she could tell that very thought had crossed his mind. The affront stunned her.

“I see.” She knew Baseer had never liked her—or maybe it was more that he hadn’t ever been friendly to anyone—but to have him accuse her of the attack, of nearly killing Khalid, clawed at her soul.

"I am sorry." Baseer looked down. "It is a path I must consider in the protection of my son." His dark eyes came back to hers. "He intends to make you his bride, but I am not convinced you are willing or right for him. That makes one wonder if you would—"

She held her mouth tight against the trembling. "I may not be the most affectionate person, but I would never, ever hurt Khalid. It is insulting that you can equate that with murder."

On his feet, he moved toward her.

Shiloh took a step back, bracing herself for an assault.

But he stopped short, his gaze darting to the bed. Was he remembering that propriety demanded he not be in an unmarried woman's bedroom? He averted his eyes and stepped back into his suite, pulling the door closed. "Good night."

When the door clicked shut, Shiloh slapped the bolt into place. She whirled around, her chest pounding. How could he accuse her of murder . . . of intentionally harming Khalid? She stomped to her pack and jerked it onto the bed, where she plopped onto the stiff mattress. As she dug through her bag, she tried to think coherently. Her anger, frustration, and the weight of the last several days seemed to have smothered her ability to think clearly.

Is that what Brutus thought too? That she was responsible for the murders? Is that why he'd given her the phone and tracked her through the marketplace? She pulled the secure phone from her backpack. Running her thumb over the spine, she ached at the thought that she had been judged so quickly, especially by Brutus.

No, there was something about him . . . something different in his eyes . . . something more positive than condemnation or accusation.

Belief. He believed in her.

It was a crazy thought. Khalid believed in her, too, yet it was different. But how? Either you did or you didn't. Right?

Or maybe it was acceptance. No, that couldn't be it. Khalid knew her darkest secrets and still he had proposed. Foolish guy!

So what was it with Brutus that seemed to tear down her carefully constructed barriers?

Who cared! She tossed the phone back into her bag. Returning to the balcony, she wrapped her arms around her waist and rested her forearms on the ledge. A thick, salty breeze tousled her hair, and the fine strands tickled her almost-bare arms. The scent of the sea begged her to immerse herself in its blue-green waters. When would she be able to dive again?

With a heavy sigh, she looked at the sky. Something in the twinkling black blanket above reminded her of the night Brutus had bequeathed her the rupees and a thousand-pound box of questions. If she ever saw him again, she'd make sure to drag some answers out of him.

Maybe she could ask him if he knew anything about Baseer Khan—like did he have connections to the men who tried to kill her?

9

"So, what was that all about?" Toby shut the door to his flat.

Reece shed the jacket and hung it over the back of a living room chair. "At least you had the good sense not to talk in front of the driver."

"Hey, I'm an embassy official, not a moron." Toby sauntered into the kitchen where he ripped off his tie and yanked open the fridge. "How 'bout a Coke? A real one—it's even cold."

"I'll pass." Reece lowered himself onto the brown leather sofa and rested his elbows on his knees. "Abdul's involved in whatever's going on."

Toby popped the top to a glass-bottled soda and took a long draught. "Well, I could've figured that out."

"Yeah, after I brought the guy down."

Laughing, Toby kicked off his shoes and untucked his shirt. He looked like a slob as he plopped into his recliner. A tuxedo cat leapt to the back of the chair and arched into Toby's neck with a long meow. He scratched the black and white fur as the feline purred. "So, what was your clue? What tipped you off?"

Reece slumped against the sofa, the leather letting out a mournful hiss. "Several days ago, I attempted to divert attention from the female student." Reece prayed Toby didn't mention Shiloh's name. A strong possibility existed that his flat had been bugged. "She had tails and a close encounter of the ugly kind, so I set a trap."

"Smart."

"After what I saw on the street, I knew I had to get some heat off her."

"Which takes heat off you." Toby swirled the dark liquid in the bottle. "So, how does any of this connect to Abdul?"

"I called Noor posing as a doctor from St. George, told them I had a female student who, unfortunately, didn't look like she was going to make it."

"Ahh." Toby set his drink down and lowered the cat to his lap. "So, when our good friend, the minister, mentioned the hospital—"

"Like I said when we went in there, I just had to get him talking. I knew he'd slip up. He might look smart, but there's a reason Chiranjivi won the election."

"Yeah, and good thing you never mentioned that. I hear the two still aren't talking."

Reece processed the tidbit. It had been a heated race. Abdul tried to play on Muslim sympathies, but India had long battled to preserve their Hindu legacy. "Abdul's divulgence helped me know where to concentrate my efforts. If we didn't look interested in the attack, they'd know that we have the girl in our court."

"We do?" Toby's eyebrows hitched.

A shrug. "It's only a matter of time."

"So you know where she is?"

His friend seemed a bit too interested. Reece couldn't believe she still had the cell phone. He'd expected her to toss it after the last incident. She'd been really ticked. But he wasn't going to force her to his side. Eventually, she'd have no choice. He only prayed she'd wise up before someone else got hurt.

Surely, she would. After all, she'd tried to turn the tables on him. Spunky.

"You do realize it's against the moral codes to spy on her like *that*."

Reece scowled. "What?"

"That smile on your face didn't look like it came from allowed practice."

"You're out of your mind."

Toby nudged Mitty off his lap. "I might not be a spy with all the smoke and mirrors, but I know when a guy has a thing for a girl."

"The 'thing' I have for this young woman is protecting her and getting her out of the country safely."

"What about the guy who was shot?"

Quirking an eyebrow, Reece rubbed his hands together. "They're together, with his father."

"You don't sound happy." Wood floors creaked as Toby moved to the mail drop.

"It's hard to be happy when an asset is in the hands of a suspected terrorist." Reece pushed off the couch and made his way to the kitchen where he lifted a glass from the cabinet and poured water into it.

Toby returned with a stack of letters. "Haven't checked my mail in several days. It'll take the whole weekend to go through these." He tossed them onto the counter. "So you think the son is a terrorist?"

"Father. Reportedly connected to some Pakistani radicals. My theory is Sajjadi."

Toby's eyes widened. "Osman Sajjadi? Aren't you swinging that bat a bit high?"

"You trace the paths. The Pakistanis are notorious for covering their tracks, but more than once I've seen the road lead to Sajjadi. Then al Nabiri, his right-hand man, was gunned down at the Mumbai Mansion."

Grabbing a pen and paper, Toby came around the counter. "I need the father's name and location."

Unwilling to hand over the information just yet, Reece dumped the water down his throat and set the glass on the Formica. "Give me two days to cement this—at least."

Challenge crossed Toby's expression. Lips taut, eyes slightly narrowed, he stared at Reece. "Our relations with the Indian government have improved since the NPT, but we still walk a fine line. Unless you have absolute proof about Sajjadi, or you can bring me your data about this girl, I can't entertain your theories. I need names."

The safety and life of an American college student depended on his withholding that information. Toby knew better than to ask for details. With or without the non-proliferation treaty, relations were tenuous. Of course, if Toby had the data Reece had gathered, there might be quite a bit more tension. But Reece wasn't ready for things to heat up.

Toby eyed him for a minute and then banged a fist on the counter. "You know something." He grunted. "I can't believe nobody informed us about this," he muttered, apparently realizing Reece wouldn't give an inch. "I expected a little more respect from you."

"This has nothing to do with our relationship. You know that." Obviously the guy had a few things to learn about cooperative intelligence and the fact that it wasn't always quite so . . . cooperative.

Rapping on the front door drew them both around. Toby huffed and stalked to the foyer.

Check the peephole. Reece shifted backward, edging to a point so that once the door opened, he'd still be concealed in case an unfriendly burst through. He tugged his weapon free and held it, ready.

Toby peeked into the tiny hole, and gasped. "What the devil!" He jerked open the door. "What're you doing here?"

"That's the welcome I get after three weeks?"

At the sound of the woman's voice, Reece relaxed, sliding his weapon back into the holster on his belt.

Toby hugged her and nudged the door closed at the same time. "I didn't . . . I . . ."

They released, and she stepped into the living area, her eyes alighting on Reece. "Well, isn't this a surprise?" Long gauzy material clung to her lanky form as she sashayed across the room. Her dark brown hair hung in lazy ringlets past her shoulders, adding to her gypsy look. "So, little brother, what're you doing here with a lowly embassy servant?" She tiptoed and planted a kiss on Reece's cheek.

"Keeping the guy out of trouble." Amazing how Julia's presence eased his tension, yet cranked it up at the same time. Though she was three years older, he'd always felt the need to protect her—from herself. "How was Mozambique?"

She glared at him. "Bloody."

"Hey, don't get mad at me. It was your choice to join the Peace Corpse."

"It's *corps*, little pimple." Despite the venom in her words, he saw the grin urging her lips apart.

"Same difference."

Ignoring him, she whirled on Toby. "Let me guess, you haven't checked your mail since last Saturday?"

The poor guy blanched, his eyes darting to the pile of envelopes.

"You were supposed to pick me up at the train station an hour ago."

Although Reece loved seeing Toby squirm under Julia's snarkiness, he should get going before Toby remembered their discussion prior to the wild one's entrance. "I'll leave so you two can decide if you still have a 'thing' for each other."

Too late. Revenge lurked in Toby's eyes. "Does Julia know about her?"

Reece clamped his jaw tight.

As she spun toward Reece, Julia's dark brows shot upward, her mouth gaping. "There's a *her*?" Hope flickered through her expression. "After all this time, some woman has fanned the wet kindling of love in my little brother's heart?"

Fists clenched, Reece speared the putz with his fiercest glare. "No," he said through ground teeth, driving his attention back to his petite sister. "There are things I can't discuss, and you should know better than to believe Toby would have the scoop on anything in my life."

"Gee, hum." Toby rubbed his jaw. "That's why you sat on my sofa grinning like a banshee, lost during our conversation about this woman."

"Banshees don't grin, they scream." Julia studied Toby for a minute, then turned her olive face back to Reece.

"I'm out of here." He grabbed his suit jacket and stuffed his arms into the sleeves before looking back at his sister. "You in the city for a while?"

Her bracelets jangled as she crossed her arms over her chest. "A few days."

Shrugging to smooth the kinked fabric of his shirt, he nodded. "I'll call you." As he stepped into the stairwell, he felt a light touch on his sleeve but kept moving.

"Reece?" Julia followed him down the single flight to the front steps. "Who is she?"

Despite the soft lilt in her voice, he grew frustrated. "She's a case, okay?" Sunlight bathed him, chasing the chill he felt in Toby's flat.

"Please talk to me."

Halfway down the concrete steps, he paused and pivoted to her. "Look, Toby doesn't know when to keep his mouth shut."

"Is she that special that my speck of a boyfriend can get you angry?"

Scratching the back of his head, Reece groaned. "Good-bye, Julia. We'll do dinner."

Her laughter trailed him into the thick crowds. Soon the din of the busy city teased the tension creeping into his shoulders. Regardless of the gnat of an embassy official and his gypsy sister, he knew how things stood. Shiloh Blake was nothing more than an asset of the United States, his assignment. A really beautiful one.

"You're beautiful, you know that?"

Sand caked her sandaled feet, warm and comforting as she sat on the beach with Khalid. Shiloh bent and brushed the tiny grains off her legs. "You're delirious with fever." He'd never been this forthright during their friendship. Would they ever get back to San Diego and finish their studies? She squinted at the glimmering water. What about the Pacific Rim Challenge? It all seemed lost.

Baseer's aggressive behavior last night stirred a concoction of dread and depression in her gut. He might be her father-in-law. The man came from a totally different culture where women were little more than a means to an end. She'd always known that, but something in his eyes last night twisted the noose tighter.

"What happened last night?"

"What?" His question startled her.

Khalid reached over and tucked a strand of hair behind her ear. "I heard my father talking to you. What did he say? You've been so quiet."

Leaning against her legs, Shiloh drew circles in the sand with her finger. How could she tell him what his father had accused her of? Would Khalid believe her?

"Why do you do this? I want to marry you. Will you ever be honest with me?"

She snapped up her head. "When have I ever lied to you?"

As he bent forward, his hair fell into his dark eyes. "You speak in half-truths, giving only what you think I want to hear. Afraid to anger or upset me."

Heat fanned her neck and cheeks. "You just underwent hours of surgery. Of course, I'm going to do what I can to protect you."

Outrage flared in his eyes. "It is *I* who should be protecting you!"

Shiloh gathered the tattered edges of her nerves and pulled them in tightly. "I'm not going to argue or fight with you. Not in your condition. Not here." She pushed to her feet and brushed off her backside and legs. "I'll get us something to drink. What would you like?"

"Stop coddling me, Shiloh. I'm a grown man." The frustration and defeat on his face convicted her. He dragged himself upright, a sheen of sweat bathing his forehead. "In my world, respect is everything. Respect and love." His eyes searched hers.

"Respect is earned—and you have that completely, Khalid. You know that. How could you ever doubt that?" Love. He wanted her to say she loved him, as well as respected him. Shiloh clenched her hands tightly at her sides to control the tremors. A rift opened between them.

"You can't even say it." His downcast expression chipped away at her courage.

But still she couldn't say what he wanted to hear. She took a shuddering breath. "I'll get you an orange soda." Self-hatred followed her up the steps to the parking lot, digging into her like the tiny grains of sand between her toes.

Across the street, she spotted a shop. A rickshaw squeaked past, tailed closely by several ultra-compact cars. Waiting at the curb, she glanced back at Khalid. Would the chasm ever close?

She doubted it. Her aversion to his faith hadn't fazed him. He had promised to help her through her anger issues, which only made her angry. But her stubbornness and independence would destroy their relationship.

A man walked with several women toward a shop. Something flagged her attention—his shirt! It bore the same symbol as the coin Dr. Kuntz had given her. Shiloh raced after them, dodging pedestrians to get to them.

"Excuse me!" She held up her hand and stretched on her tiptoes.

The man looked back but didn't see her and kept going.

She pushed through the sea of bodies, and finally, she reached out and touched his shoulder. "Excuse me," she apologized and shifted into her broken Marathi. "Your shirt. I've seen that symbol before. Could you tell me what it means?"

The man's chest puffed, but the way he shot a nervous look around the busy square and to his friends told her he didn't want attention drawn to it. "Allah's Sword of Justice. We are a peaceful organization."

Shiloh nodded. She'd never heard of them. She thanked him and stepped away. A flash of white-blonde hair caught her eye. *Edie?* She rushed forward, straight into the path of another rickshaw. With a yelp, she lurched back, her heart ramming against her chest.

Where did she—there! Long blonde hair, short frame, walking east. "Edie!" The chaos of the street muffled her cry. Shiloh checked both ways for traffic, and then launched herself after her friend. Weaving through the swarms of Hindu people moving en masse toward the beach, Shiloh continued to call Edie. Maybe it wasn't Edie. After all, why would she be farther east, when the airport and quickest passage out would be north?

However, if Edie was still here, she was in danger. "Edie Valliant!" Shiloh shouted when her friend neared a shop.

The woman paused, glanced Shiloh's way, and then disappeared into the building.

How could she miss me? "Edie, wait!"

Two men emerged from the building. Kodiyeri.

Shiloh skidded to a halt, nearly losing her balance. Her pulse catapulted. What was he doing here? She ducked and spun, her feet quickly carrying her back toward the beach. She risked a glance back.

Kodiyeri's black eyes bored into her. He lunged after her. So did several uniformed men. Sirens sprang to life. Two police cars pulled from the side of the road and raced after her.

Dear God, help me! Shiloh sprinted down the street as realization flashed like lightning through her mind—she couldn't lead them to Khalid. She needed to lead them away from him. Maybe fate was separating their paths.

Shiloh weaved her way through the crowd, thumbing through them like a catalog—past a woman, a man, a teen. An elderly man grunted as she nudged him aside.

"Sorry," she mumbled. *Where are you going, Shiloh?* Panting, she banked right at the next intersection. Heavy footfalls thudded behind her.

"Stop! I'll shoot."

His words propelled her forward. She tore around a car, zipped across the street, and hurdled over a dog. Glass shattered. She pushed herself. Harder.

After rounding the next corner, she looked back to check on her pursuers—and barreled into a solid mass. Hands grabbed her . . . restrained her.

"Let go!" She writhed and kicked out against the man in the white tunic.

"Shiloh."

The deep bass voice rattled her. She gazed up into dark eyes.

"Baseer," she breathed. Old alarms blared inside. With a yank she tried to pry herself from his grip and glanced over her shoulder. "Let me go." Would he hold her for them? Was that it?

"Keep still."

Why else would he restrain her? She whimpered, "Please."

He shook her. "Shiloh. Be still."

Maybe he was the enemy. She didn't know. But he'd protect his son. "Let me go," she pleaded. "If they find Khalid—"

He shoved her toward a car. "Get in."

She seized the moment and burst from him. Only, the alley dead-ended.

Shiloh spun. Across the street Kodiyeri and his men scanned the area.

No options. No outs. Her lungs burned. Her limbs shook.

"Shiloh, come." Baseer held open the door. "We'll get Khalid and return to the hotel."

Was there really no other way? Although she feared Baseer, she feared Khalid's stinging disappointment more. It would be worse than a rejection.

Licking her lips, she met his father's mysterious eyes. "I don't trust you."

"It's me or them," Baseer said, nodding behind him.

Hesitation held her in place for several long seconds. Finally, she dove into the car. Seconds later, they peeled out around the corner. Shots erupted. Glass crackled. Covering her head, she bent double to shield herself. Seconds felt like hours until they no longer heard shots or screams.

"I believe we are safe."

Shiloh straightened and glanced back. Crowds had scattered across the open area, their faces revealing shock . . . the same shock Shiloh felt. Turning to Baseer, she brushed glass from her lap and shoulders. "We'll never be safe as long as we're in Mumbai."

"We have train passage for tomorrow night." Baseer's gaze remained on the road, his expression hard.

After one more glance back, she dabbed the sweat from her forehead. "Am I included in that 'we,' or is that you and Khalid?"

An angry flame shot through Baseer's face. "He plans to make you his wife."

"Why would you give your blessing? I must be the only one who's not blind. It's no secret you don't approve of me. I don't even share Khalid's faith." Shiloh gripped her hands to hide the trembling.

Baseer's knuckles whitened against the steering wheel. "It is not *you* that I do not approve of, but your country. My son will be persecuted. As an American you will never be accepted. The children, perhaps."

"Then why did you ever shelter my father so many years ago?"

Baseer darted a look her way, then back to the road. He pointed out the windshield. "He's waiting."

Khalid leaned against a stone wall, cradling his side. Shiloh bailed into the backseat as he rushed toward them, his eyes hardening. "What happened?" The car shifted beneath his weight as he settled into the front seat. He glared at her. "How did you end up with my father?"

"They seem to be one step ahead," Baseer growled.

Did Khalid notice how his father evaded that question? Would he call his father on it?

"We'll return to Karachi, and that will make your mother very happy." He nodded to his son. "Your mother needs good news, eh?"

Khalid gave a silent nod, his gaze still on Shiloh.

She blinked and tore her eyes from his. Her heart broke like the glass on the floorboard. Once he knew everything, he would release her from their engagement. Why didn't he just do it now? The longer he pretended nothing was wrong, the more people would get hurt. Especially if his father was aligned with the very men who pursued her. More and more, she suspected he was. What was Baseer Khan hiding?

10

"You are sure?"

Headphones on, Reece toggled the volume control and visually confirmed the conversation was being recorded. He'd planted the bug in Abdul's office telephone two days ago. With the short lifespan, it wouldn't work much longer.

"Yes," Abdul said.

"If you can make this happen, you will be greatly rewarded. Here and in Paradise."

Reece didn't recognize the other voice.

"*I'nsh Allah.*"

"You understand—he must be at the summit or this will not work."

"Baseer just left. He assured me it would be so."

"Good. Two weeks, my friend."

The connection cancelled.

Reece blinked. That was it? He leaned on the small desk in the hotel room and scratched the stubble on his jaw. What did it mean? Rumors abounded that something big would happen at the Summit of the Agreed—a convention of trouble led by Syria, Iran, Pakistan, and Russia. Would India send a representative? Surely they wouldn't violate their pact with the U.S. and France.

Of course, Chiranjivi didn't exactly adore the French Prime Minister. Still, the Hindu leader seemed to have better sense than to let personal vendettas cloud what was best for his country.

Time ticked toward an international nuclear nightmare. Reece had tolerated Abdul and Baseer for the information they could provide, but learning Baseer had visited Abdul today had increased the stakes. No more hiding. No more nice guy.

Reece needed to keep a laser sight on Shiloh Blake now. The players had just proved his worst suspicions. Baseer Khan had an alliance with Ali Abdul and was one tiny step away from Osman Sajjadi. The connection almost felt tangible.

He flipped open his ringing phone. "Jaxon."

"Hello, my friend."

Synapses half lulled by listening to the conversation awoke. "Professor. What can I do for you?" He pulled himself out of the chair and removed the recording. "Need another good meal?" He stored the small device in the floor safe.

"I have something you will want to see."

"On my way." Reece didn't need the location. They'd only met at one place—the sidewalk café. Within minutes he sat across from the semi-balding man and activated the jamming device on his watch. "You've found something?"

"Have your people check the Kashmir Mountains."

"There's been unrest there for years."

"Yes, but nuclear?"

Reece quirked an eyebrow. "What do you have?"

"A friend visiting the Shangri-La Resort said they spotted a caravan of trucks ambling up out of India through the mountains like a pack of mules. Said he was certain there was a missile in one of the covered trucks."

Swallowing, Reece considered the man before him—a man who knew better than to send Reece on rabbit trails. "I'll check it out."

Perry smiled. "Good."

They carried on a casual conversation as Perry devoured another plate of Tandoori chicken and Reece drank a warm soda. If anyone was watching, they looked like old friends sharing a meal. Finally, they said their good-byes and Reece strode away. He opened his secure phone and hit an autodial button. "Toby, I need a satellite shot."

"Where and when?"

"Last twenty-four hours. Kashmir Mountains."

"Uh . . . what're we looking for?"

"Nukes."

"On it."

"Good. Flash me the images." Reece hung up and stepped onto the curb outside his shack and shifted to full alert. The door sat ajar. Cradling his Glock between his hands, he inched sideways toward the entrance.

Crash! Rrrrrip!

With his toe, he nudged the door open farther and peered into the small room. A man sliced into the charpoy with a knife. Another guy stood at the side table, flipping through magazines and mail.

In one fluid move, Reece swung inside and aimed his weapon. The man at the table reached for a weapon. Reece fired before the silver gun came out of its holster. He spun and sighted the second. Something large and black hurled through the air. He fired off two rounds before the thing broadsided his face. Reece stumbled. His vision blurred.

Whatever hit him crashed at his feet. He blinked through the psychedelic spots. Shuffled back. Shaking his head, he tried to clear the shock from his system and assessed the room.

Two men lay on the floor. He looked down, surprised to find the brick-sized safe he'd hidden in the floor. How they found it, he didn't know. He lifted the fireproof box. Still locked. He'd made it just in time. A grin prickled his lip with pain. With the heel of his hand, he tested the area, and winced at the sticky swollen spot.

He kicked the door shut and made quick work of stuffing his belongings into a pack. Reece sneaked into the hidden compartment where his black beauty waited. Within minutes, he headed north on his Ducati toward the resort where Baseer Khan had holed up with Shiloh and his son.

Tension stiffened his spine as he wove through the darkened city toward Shiloh Blake. He hoped she was still alive. His helmet-com activated, and Nielsen's face appeared on a heads-up display embedded in his visor.

"Got my images?" Reece asked.

"Already relayed."

He opened the throttle, nice and steady, easing into the intersection. "Go ahead."

"We don't have all the data, but it appears Baseer Khan might be an agent provocateur."

Heat spread through his shoulders. Provocateur meant Baseer could be working with the Americans or the Brits, trying to force Abdul to do something that would prove his guilt.

Nothing Reece had seen pointed to that. To collusion, yes. Not entrapment.

"Do you have proof?"

"Hey, we untangled these feeds, and that's the consensus. We've intercepted data that indicates he's working with someone. He seems to be in the right place at the right time. How he's aware, we can't figure out yet. He hides his trail well."

"Dig deeper." Reece slowed and guided his bike around a knot of pedestrians. "And fast. Someone just ransacked my shack."

A curse hissed through his helmet. "You're compromised?"

"No." He eased the bike to stop at a light. "I have my bona fides. Run the voice analysis and confirm. But the damage they did tells me they didn't know what they were looking for." Which meant they didn't know who he was—and that was good. Very good. "I'll transmit an intercepted communiqué between Abdul and who I believe to be Sajjadi."

"Sajjadi? Are you kidding me? We've just about got a noose around Abdul and India's neck on this thing. Now you want to implicate Pakistan? You've always had a grudge—"

"Just run the analysis. Let that prove me wrong." He stretched his jaw, certain he'd have a bruise by morning, if he didn't already.

If what Nielsen suggested was true, he'd have to watch Baseer Khan a little closer.

Cities and their crowds frazzled her nerves. Leaning against the splintered windowsill, Shiloh crossed her arms over her chest. Honking. Beeping. Voices. Droning cars and industrialization. Creaking rickshaws. If only she could find the solitude familiar to her on the water. Serenity and pleasure soaking into her as the warm rays reflected off the blue-green expanse. She closed her eyes, transporting her mind into the invigorating salty spray. Sea enveloping her as she submerged.

Shiloh smiled. Fish wiggled past in her fantasy.

Red.

A floating body.

She snapped open her eyes. Swallowing hard, she gripped her throat. Would that garish image forever burn in the back of her mind? Death had now replaced the tranquility of the one thing she loved most—diving. Fulfilling her dive hours for the Pacific Rim Challenge had crawled out of reach.

"Are you okay?" Khalid's whispered words made her stiffen.

Casting a glance at him, she nodded. "Fine."

His beautiful smile swam out to her as he drew closer. "You look pretty shaken." Behind her, he gripped her shoulders and pressed a kiss to the back of her head.

"Just tired." Was he going to pretend that nothing had happened between them?

Khalid rubbed her arms. "When will you trust me?" His breath skittered across the back of her neck.

"I do trust you."

"But you hold back. You never say how you feel."

She clamped a hand over his, hoping the gesture conveyed what she could not muster in her heart: conviction. "I tell you more than I tell anyone. You're my best friend, Khalid."

He eased onto the sill in front of her. Hands resting on her hips, he looked up and smiled. "Then marry me, Shiloh."

She furrowed her brow. "How can you ask me that? You know me—better than anyone else. You know what I'm like, how I feel about God, how I . . ." Shiloh choked down the volley of emotions. Chewing the inside of her lip, she traced the thick clouds with her eyes.

Khalid rose, blocking her visual escape, and nudged her chin so their gazes locked. "I've fallen in love with you, everything about you. And I know that as smart as you are, some day you will release your anger against God." He peeked down at her. "Today would be good."

Shiloh shook her head. Always prodding. Always pushing. "You deserve someone like Ruth."

He scowled. "Ruth? Who is Ruth?"

"You know—Ruth, from the Bible. Humble. Pious. Thoughtful. Left all she knew to take care of her mother-in-law. Gathered scraps from the fields so they could eat." She pressed a hand to her chest, fending off the panic and tears. "I'm not like that. I'm not wife material, Khalid."

"Hey," he whispered, drawing her closer. "Easy on yourself, Miss America. I'm not looking for a servant to glean my fields," he said with a laugh, the humor lost. "You're all I want. Just as you are. I'd give my last breath for you."

Shiloh gritted her teeth and willed herself not to move, not to break his hold. Why couldn't she just accept his proposal? Khalid Khan was the best thing that had ever happened to her. If life could bring anyone to love her, if she could find happiness, it would be with Khalid. He believed in her. Wanted the best for her. But . . .

"You've always been so good to me," she murmured as she searched his face, the dark brows that drew attention to his penetrating eyes so dark against his smooth olive skin. Beyond his looks, Khalid had everything a woman could possibly want in a husband. Wealth. Kindness. Gentleness. Faith. Yes, even faith, despite her dislike of it. Studies across the globe showed those with faith lived longer, fuller lives. If she ever married, she'd want reassurances that it was forever.

"So is this your way of saying no?" He shifted back. The light in his eyes faded. "I see."

An aching regret constricted her lungs. How could she refuse? He'd nearly died in her arms, and even on the verge of Paradise, he'd reached out to her.

"I shouldn't have pushed you." He walked away with his head hanging low. "I thought . . . it seemed like we had something special and deep."

"We do." Could she be any more cruel? This was her fault.

Over his shoulder, he looked at her. "How can you say that and yet refuse me?"

"I'm not—" Her voice cracked and she gulped. "It's not . . . Oh, Khalid. I don't know what to say. I don't know how or what I feel. It's all jumbled. The one thing I do know is that I don't want to be apart from you." The words startled her into silence.

Khalid studied her. Finally, he returned to her side. "Then do me this honor, Shiloh. My parents have given their blessing—a miracle in itself!" His always chilly hands tracked down her arms, fingers lacing with hers. He lifted her right hand to his lips. "I tried to call your father to ask—"

She sucked in a breath. "You *what*?" Arctic wind blasted through her chest.

"It's okay, Miss America." Khalid cupped her face. "I only wanted his blessing, but he wasn't there. In my culture it's very important to have the blessing of both fathers. I know you aren't speaking to yours, but I wanted to give him the opportunity."

"Do not *ever* do that again. I don't want that man in any part of my life."

"Your father would not be in our marriage. Just you and me and God."

She tensed, but he tugged her closer. Always pushing.

"Say yes, Shiloh. Say yes, and make me the happiest man on the Earth."

Her life would be empty without him. Wasn't that love? "Okay." *What are you doing?* Chin lifted, she nodded. "Yes." She could do this.

A smile the size of the sun beamed back at her. He bent and kissed her.

At first, she stiffened—how odd to kiss him! But he was tender and gentle. A reminder that this would only be the beginning of intimacy she would eventually share with him. His arms snaked around her and squeezed as he hugged her.

"Then it is settled?" Baseer appeared from the other room. "You are agreed?"

Khalid swung toward his father, arms still wrapped tightly around Shiloh. "She said yes!" He then swiveled her and held her shoulders, as if presenting her to his father. "Your new daughter."

Baseer stared hard at her.

She smiled but knew it didn't reach her eyes.

With a cockeyed nod, he pursed his lips. "If you love my son, then that is all the blessing needed."

If you love my son . . . If.

"Your mother will be angry she was not here," Baseer said to his son. He took Shiloh's hand and held it up. "Where is the ring?"

"I forgot!" Khalid laughed as he dug through his pant pocket. He produced a ruby ring and slid it onto her finger. "My grandmother's."

"Khalid, I can't." The ring sparkled back at her. Several small diamonds encircled the crimson stone. Why did it have to look like a droplet of blood? She shivered.

"You are family now." Baseer's smile carried more than congratulations—a threat seemed to lurk behind those words. "It is yours." He shook Khalid's hand and drew him into a manly hug. "You are my only son. It is up to you and Shiloh to produce sons to continue the name."

Shiloh inhaled sharply. Children?

The two men hugged again and then dove into an animated conversation about telling his mother and sister. Within seconds, they dialed Pakistan. The phone bounced from Khalid to Baseer to Shiloh, who stumbled through Nisa's nearly screamed congratulations. Finally, she handed the phone back to Khalid.

Glancing out the window, Shiloh felt a gentle throb encircle her skull. A seizure. She tensed. Not now. Tightness captured her muscles, holding them hostage.

Almost instantly, Khalid stood in front of her. "It's okay. It'll be over soon, Miss America." He massaged her arms, then her hands. "Just relax and let it pass."

Fury shot through her. Why did she have to suffer this debilitating disorder? Hot tears streaked down her cheeks. *Tears?* When was the last time she cried? She could kill her father for what he'd caused . . .

"Hey," Khalid whispered, wiping the drops away. "Shiloh, take it easy. You're getting too worked up."

Finally, she exhaled and slumped into his arms. "I hate it." She groaned. "They're getting worse, Khalid. They're getting worse."

"No." Khalid crouched so they were eye-to-eye. "You're stressed. That's going to increase the seizures. The neurologist told you stress will do that, remember?"

Half-nodding, half-shaking her head, she wanted to be . . . normal.

With his arm around her shoulders, Khalid led her toward her bedroom. "I think you should rest, and I'll do the same. Our wonderful news has left me feeling a bit winded."

She allowed him to direct her to the bed, then dropped onto the mattress. "Are you sure this is what you want for a wife? A cripple?"

Khalid sat next to her, his hand on hers. "You're not a cripple. And without a doubt, you're what I want, Shiloh. Every day that God has ordered for me, I want to spend it with you, with our family."

Heart scalded, she could not bring herself to tell him the truth. She'd never told anyone.

He kissed her temple. "Get some sleep. I need to rest. See you in a couple of hours."

Shiloh couldn't meet his gaze. Would she need to tell him before they married? Would he cast her aside then? He'd vowed his love for her, but where was the line? At what point would he walk away? She pressed her palm to her stomach. He deserved a woman who could bear him a son or daughter.

Bereft, she eased herself against the mattress and bunched the blanket close. Getting engaged should be the happiest day of a girl's life. She batted the rogue tears and closed her eyes.

Nightmares invaded her sleep, taunting her with ghostly forms of Mikhail. She awoke with a start. Sticky and damp, she pushed herself from the bed. After a quick shower and a clean change of clothes, she wandered to the window that overlooked the courtyard.

Brilliant rays embraced her, permeating her with warmth and issuing an invitation to savor the new day. If only she could. She looked at the ring—the *engagement* ring.

What have I done?

A movement in the courtyard distracted her. She scanned the bricked area. What had caught her attention? A dark blur—there. By the alley. Seated at a table for four. Brutus.

Fuming, she sneered at him. Just then he lifted a glass and toasted her with a smile.

That no-good, low-down . . . He'd followed her! Adrenaline flooded her veins. He leaned back in the chair and sipped his drink as if this were just another day at the beach.

She'd love to kick the chair out from under the lug. Knock him flat on his back. Bring him down a few notches. How could he be so impudent? She needed to put an end to this right now. Her opportunity to drill him full of questions had presented itself.

Shiloh shot out the door and down the stairs. By the time she reached the ground floor, she wanted to pound some pain into the thug, but she had to play this cool. The heavy ring on her finger reminded her that she wasn't her own anymore. If anyone saw her with the brazen idiot, her chastity could be called into question. While she didn't give a shark's fin about that, she did care about how it would affect—and hurt—Khalid.

Stifling her rage, she crossed the open area and strode straight to the food vendor. Let Brutus sweat it out. She'd make him come to her this time. With each step, she felt his gaze boring into the back of her skull. At the vendor, she bought a platter of curried chicken and a bottle of water.

Seated at a table for two, she felt a haunting presence. She peeked up at the fourth floor of the hotel. Khalid. She waved, drawing a large smile from her betrothed. How could she confront Brutus in broad daylight with Khalid looking over her shoulder? Shiloh concentrated on not choking on the spicy curry, but it only agitated the acid boiling in her gut. Food finished and water mostly gone, she eyed the window. Closed. Curtain drawn.

Okay, enough.

On her feet, she strode straight for Brutus.

11

CONFIDENCE OOZED FROM HER BLUE-GREY ORBS. INDIGNATION TOO. Maybe outrage. Amusement trickled through him as Shiloh sat down across from Reece. If Shiloh Blake hadn't been so enigmatically clever and perceptive, he might have chalked her up as a spoiled brat. But there was a method and decisiveness behind every move she made. Intriguing.

"I'm sorry." Reece leaned forward and motioned toward the rickety wooden seat she occupied, toying with her. "That seat's taken."

"Yes, actually, it is."

Undaunted. How admirable. He pressed his spine into the spindles of his chair and lifted his soda from the table. It had taken two bottles of water, a lime soda, and a cola to drag the siren from her pen. "Is there something I can do for you?"

"Leave me alone."

"Excuse me, but aren't you the one interrupting my fine afternoon?" Arms held wide, he looked up at the sky. "Here I am, enjoying a drink under the glorious Mumbai sun, and you barge in." Reece clicked his tongue. Then with a serious look, he paused. "You aren't following me, are you?"

Eyes narrowed into slivers, she scooted to the edge of her seat. "What do you want with me? Just go back to your hole and climb in!"

He widened his eyes and opened his mouth to speak.

"Don't!"

He almost grinned.

"Look, I know everything you're doing. I knew you were down here. I knew you were watching me." She swiped at a loose curl the wind had tossed into her face. "Your actions and methods scream the obvious—you're a spy."

He laughed.

"Just stay away from me and my—Khalid. We aren't hurting anyone, we didn't do anything wrong, and we aren't in any danger, so back off!"

His humor vanished. Elbow resting on the tiled table, he set down the bottle with a clink. "That's where you're wrong. Dead wrong."

She scowled, hesitant for the first time. "You'd like me to think that, wouldn't you?"

Leaning to the side, he hunched closer. "Shiloh, you've got instincts, good instincts. So, you tell me. Would I be here, consuming a disgustingly warm drink just to lie to you?" He tipped the bottle and guzzled more. "Besides, I thought you knew what was going on."

She glowered at him, but he saw her uncertainty too. That was more like it. Quick study.

"Who am I in danger from now? I've escaped three incidents, so I'm not exactly worried. It's getting a bit old, actually."

"Just take a short walk with me. I'll show you."

"You must think I'm an idiot."

"Quite the contrary." He nudged his head toward the alley. "Take the walk."

"Why, so you can kill me and then dump my body somewhere?"

"Do I look like the type?"

"A killer?" She arched her eyebrows. "I wouldn't know. I didn't get a chance to introduce myself to whoever murdered my friends."

Reece considered her as he finished his soda and chucked the bottle in a nearby trashcan. "If I wanted to kill—"

She held up a palm to him. "Don't feed me some lame cliché."

"It's about as cliché as you marrying Khalid." Touché.

Her lips snapped into a hard line. Though he kept his eyes on her tightly controlled expression, he caught her turning the gold and ruby addition to her finger. Good. Get her thinking. And mad.

From his pocket, he withdrew a small plastic bag. Rubbing it between his fingers, he debated handing it over. Was it ethical? He chided himself, remembering the way she froze up on Jail Street and nearly got herself killed. What if she locked up in the water? Or driving? He tossed the bag on the table.

She glanced at it.

"A drug not yet available to the public. It'll stop the seizures. It's designed to combat your frontal lobe paralysis."

No matter how good she was, Shiloh couldn't hide her surprise this time. It rippled over her face, and her lips parted ever so slightly. She blinked. Her nostrils flared. For a second he wasn't sure, but he thought her chin quivered. Then lightning-bolt fast, her encased, tight control clicked back into place. She hadn't thrown the pill back at him. That he could work with.

Reece knew how to play her game. "Get up, walk down the alley behind you, and turn right. I'll meet you at the end of the street in five minutes." He stood and strolled away. Don't give them time to refuse. Don't give them time to think. Thinking killed instinct. Just like all the thinking she'd probably done convincing herself it was a good idea to marry Khalid Khan.

Nielsen had insisted Reece hand over the potential cure that her father had secured. Even sent a special courier with the tablet. But Reece was smart enough not to mention that little detail. If he had, she'd probably stomp the tablet to dust. He'd done his job and delivered the medication, but it niggled his conscience like an aneurysm. Bartering for her cooperation with a way to potentially cure her . . .

God, help me. Although he wasn't sure what, Reece knew something was different about this mission. Of course, here was his deep-seated suspicion that the powers behind the dead-drop site had to be bigger than what Langley suggested.

As Reece slipped through the hotel, he lifted a baseball cap from his back pocket. He slid it on and tugged it down to shield his face. He'd take a diversionary path to the coordinates. Couldn't afford to have the lackeys who were tailing Blake figure out his identity. Of course, she wasn't the most discreet person he'd ever met. Her little stunt in the courtyard could have cost both of them their lives. However, his internal radar told him they weren't compromised—yet.

He waited in the door well of a shop. His mind played over the recording taken from the hotel suite she shared with the Khan men. She'd agreed to marry the guy. How did that happen? Would he ever figure her out? He shrugged. Why did it bug him so much?

It didn't matter. Shiloh would be on the first plane back to the States as soon as he could solve this little riddle. He would have sent her back sooner, but she seemed to be a magnet for trouble—the trouble he'd been trying to extinguish for the last five months.

With a glance at his watch, he tucked himself into the shadows. It had been five minutes. He wasn't worried. Shiloh

Blake was tough; she'd try to assume control by arriving later than he'd instructed. Two minutes more. She probably needed that long to figure out if she should trust him and take the pill.

How could he win the confidence of a woman who didn't trust anyone? He could relate. Better to keep the invisible walls erected than to get a little too close and end up dead. Like Chloe. Roughing both hands over his face only heightened his frustration. *Keep thoughts on positives. Thoughts on positives.* If he chanted the mantra enough, maybe he'd flush the images of that disaster from his brain.

Exactly two minutes and twenty-eight seconds later Shiloh stood on the corner of the street, checking out a rack of scarves. If he'd played his cards right . . . Yep. A dozen paces behind her. Across the street . . . two men followed her. But who controlled these puppets? Who called the shots?

Shiloh remained where he'd told her to meet him. Reece strolled up beside her. Facing the opposite direction gave him a view of the other two thugs.

He leaned against a pole. "Take your time, but sight the two guys by the papaya vendor."

Shiloh ran her fingers through those long, auburn tresses and played it cool as she searched the street. "Tan shirt and pants."

"They've been following you since you left the hospital."

"I've seen them." Unruffled and borderline arrogant.

"Behind you, two dozen paces, an older woman and a young man." Reece bent and tied his shoelaces. "I believe she cleaned your room this morning." He heard Shiloh's sharp intake of breath. "Keep it easy. Cross the street."

Without a moment's hesitation, she obeyed.

Good. She trusts me. He trudged in the other direction, stopping at a vendor and smelling the mangoes. Lifting one fruit and then smelling another, he caught her staring at him from a half-block away. Purposefully, he stepped around a man and his son, pausing next to them. Would she notice? The two had stalked her for days.

Her chin dropped as she shifted back toward the hotel. Yep, she recognized them. She had yet to let him down. Then again, why was she walking so fast?

Reece pressed a rupee into the vendor's hand as he bit into a mango. Having her out here involved a tactic he'd never reveal to her—luring out the *real* bad guys. The people following her now were only henchmen; they weren't the firepower. If he got her into the open, then perhaps he could force the real threat to show their hand.

Bingo! With a careful flick of his wristwatch, he snapped photos of the two men emerging from a shop. Men in dark suits. Men with poorly concealed M16s.

Reece eased himself out of sight, sprinted down a side alley and through one intersection, narrowly avoiding a rickshaw. He banked left, heading straight for the hotel. Another intersection. He slowed. Around the corner, he spotted Shiloh approaching.

Their gazes collided.

"Are you trying to scare me?" she said.

The men were far enough away. "You said you weren't in danger. I thought you should see what you're up against and why I'm not leaving until I know you're safely out of this country."

"That's not happening. Not without my fiancé. If morons like you would just leave me alone, we'd be fine."

Reece trained his attention on the two men coming fast from the southeast. One reached for his weapon. "I think I know a couple of guys who wouldn't agree with you."

Shiloh hesitantly glanced over her shoulder, then yanked back to him. "Who are they?"

"Bad guys." He grabbed her arm and tugged her aside. "Step into the alley."

"Maharashtra police! Stop!"

"Run!"

Brutus's words propelled Shiloh down the packed street. She whipped through families and mothers with children perched on their backs. Around cars and carts. Over dogs. In her periphery, big guy kept even with her. His hand reached toward her, and instinctively, she grasped it. He jerked her right, through an alley. Faster.

Thunderous steps. Her heart matched the noise. A metallic taste—the bitter aftertaste of the pill—filled her mouth. She pressed on. Behind them, shouts.

Brutus darted down another narrow street. Skidding on the dirt road, Shiloh nearly missed the turn. Her fingers dusted the ground, and her knee scraped concrete. She used the building to launch herself after him and quickly caught up. Almost as soon as she did, he broke off in another direction.

Wood erupted around her. She ducked and yelped. Shooting! Sirens wailed.

"Here," Brutus said, once again snatching her hand and pulling her into darkness.

Flattened with her back against stucco, she steadied her breathing. He stood next to her with his back pinned against the wall too. She tried to peek past him but couldn't see around his broad chest. Head tilted up, she gulped air. The big guy pressed a warm palm against her stomach. Gently, but firmly, he urged her farther into the dank recesses.

Running footsteps approached.

A beam of light struck his navy shirt. He tried to lean away. If they didn't move, they'd be caught.

Her fingers slid along the wall, searching for an escape. The texture changed. She craned her neck left. A door! With care, she twisted the knob, hoping it would open. Creaking.

She checked Brutus. He watched the street.

Despite the noisy riot of the city, silence pervaded the street. Her skin crawled. Turning. *Click*. Her fingertips pushed back the door until she eased out of the stoop. He didn't seem to notice but scooted closer to her as if searching for a hiding place. Shiloh gripped his arm and tugged him into the dark space.

Brutus spun, apparently searching for his bearings. Their hands brushed. Nudging the door closed, she focused on the imprint her two-second recon afforded. Light evaporated less than a foot from him. Blackness. A lone streak of sunlight sliced into the abandoned shop. He lurched toward the opening, watching through the tiny slot between the door and jamb.

"Who are they?"

"Quiet."

The beam fractured. Someone was coming!

He reached for her, made contact, and shoved her into the blackness of the corner. His arms wrapped around her as he tucked them both into the tight space. Dust tickled her nose, and plaster dug into her shoulder blades. The gentle creaking of boards seemed as loud as foghorns. Taut arms pushed against hers. A fresh, crisp scent filled her senses like a cool night on the beach.

He pulled up the hoodie on his sweatshirt and ducked his head. Hot breath swept her cheek and neck. Face-to-face, he let out a barely audible "shh" and nudged her head down.

Seconds later light erupted but never reached the far corner that concealed them. She gripped his arms. What if they were discovered? Would their pursuers kill them?

Sweat trickled down her spine. Shouldn't it be weird—creepy, even—being this close to a man she barely knew? Though the darkness hampered her sight, Shiloh peeked at him. His profile seemed exaggerated with the light from the door. Head ducked, he watched as two men rushed in, shouting.

Shiloh stiffened.

The men mumbled something.

Brutus didn't move, still monitoring their pursuers.

A salty bead dribbled down her face, over her neck, tickling and itching at the same time. She ground her teeth, demanding her body not twitch or freeze. Wouldn't that be great? A seizure. During the paralysis, it would be fine, but coming out, she nearly always collapsed.

Gentle rubbing—his thumb along her forearm—awakened her to the fact Brutus was trying to calm her. How could he think with such dual purpose—preserving their lives and calming her? Maybe he figured she'd give them away. She considered him. Is that what this was about? His strong, angular jaw stood out against the dark material. A straight, slightly hooked nose added to his intensity.

His gaze hit hers. Her heart raced. Though she couldn't see the color of his eyes, she remembered the way they sparkled like Mumbai Harbor. His nearness made her feel safe instead of suffocated.

Outside noises invaded her thoughts: blaring horns, metal scraping metal, yelling voices. Shiloh flinched.

"They're gone," Brutus whispered. He moved and squinted through the crack in the door.

Shiloh shuddered and exhaled deeply. She suddenly felt cold from the absence of his body heat.

"You okay?"

"Fine." She fought the nausea swirling in her stomach and wrapped her hands around herself as Brutus considered her for a moment.

"Sit tight."

"You're not leaving me here alone." Shiloh hurried with him as he slipped out, remaining in the shadows.

Past him and beyond the curb, a crowd gathered around the mangled wreck of two cars. A small child raced through the onlookers as two men shouted and shook fists at each other. Barking amplified in the narrow street. Smells of rotten food and sewage filtered into her senses.

She scooted behind Brutus. He reached back and clamped a hand on her, catching her waist. "Come here." He pushed her back inside the store.

"Look, Brutus, I'm not a slab of beef." Wriggling free, Shiloh worked to steady her voice and pounding heart.

Pausing, he scowled. "What did you call me?"

Heat licked at her cheeks. "Shouldn't we be running for our lives?"

"We'll take a few minutes, put more space between us and them." His hands slid around her neck. Heebie-jeebies skated down her body as he secured her hair and tucked it into the band of her choli.

She jerked back. "What're you doing?"

He caught her arm and held her firmly. "It'll help if we can alter our appearances." His fingers swept the sides of her face as he smoothed the strands away.

This was too bizarre. Shiloh forced herself to nod, to let him know she heard him over the drumming of her heart. "Where did you get the pill?"

"Don't worry about that."

"I will worry. How does it stop the seizures?"

He checked over his shoulder. "Dunno. They said it'll reestablish the neural connections or something. Taken long enough, you'll be seizure free."

"Impossible."

He winked. "Go out, around the corner to the right, through the fence, down the alley and past the church. Your hotel is on the right."

"We're splitting up?"

"Not unless I'm dead."

"That's not exactly reassuring."

Chuckling, he arched his hands over his head, gripped the back of his shirt, and removed the hoodie, revealing a thin, green T-shirt. "Put this on. Your choli and sari make you an easy mark. We need to throw them off." Scrunching up the hoodie, he slipped it over her head and tugged it into place.

Whoa. Okay. Too much touching. Shiloh stepped from his grasp, glaring as she positioned the shirt.

Was he grinning at her? "I'll escort you to the courtyard. It's up to you to get to your room. If you see them, don't stop."

"Exactly *who* is 'them'?" Threading her arms into the heavy material, she tried to think past the cologne tingling her nostrils.

"Why don't you tell me?"

She arched her eyebrows. "Me? You're the spy."

"You have instincts or you wouldn't have figured out what I am. So, pop quiz: Who are the men after you?"

This little test tightened the rope of agitation and frustration inside her. If he knew, why didn't he just cut to the chase? She shrugged to adjust the hoodie, peeking up at him. It wasn't any use. If she didn't spill her thoughts, he'd never open up with his. Somehow, she also didn't want to be shown an idiot in front of this man. The thought alone drew her chin up an inch.

"They aren't Maharashtra state police."

"Brilliant."

He was mocking her. She gritted her teeth. "Whatever this is about, they—and you—think I have or know something." She glanced at him, hoping he'd confirm that.

"I'm the good guy, remember?"

"Well, you're good. Whether or not you're on my side remains to be seen."

"I'm helping you now, aren't I?"

Lips quirked, Shiloh tried to stop the smile. "I don't know, are you?"

He raked a hand over his short military crop. "All right. Back to the men. Think. What put them on your trail?"

Did she frustrate him? Or was he avoiding that question? Shiloh refocused her thoughts on his interrogation. A competitiveness rose from within her to figure this out. "The dive site—when I was out there a week ago."

"Go on."

She huffed. What could it have been? "That cylinder . . ."

Reece gripped her arms. "Hold up. What cylinder?"

12

WILD BLUE EYES STARED UP AT HIM. FROZEN IN HIS GRIP, SHILOH PARTED her lips.

He shook her. "What cylinder?"

"I—" She swallowed. Scowling, she jerked out of his hold.

"Just tell me what you found."

Defiance flared on her face. "On the bay, I located what I thought was an artifact. I thought I'd finally got one up on Mikhail Drovosky." Her vibrant eyes clouded. "It was a tube of some sort. At the time, I was irked, wondering who'd compromised the site, who'd been there before me." She sighed. "But now? Now I know everyone's after that thing. I mean, that's what this is all about, right?"

"What did you do with it?"

She flipped her hair out from beneath the hoodie that draped her torso and hips. "I had to leave it when the shooting started."

Reece mentally paced up and down the news. What was in it? Who'd planted the cylinder? He'd watched that site for weeks. He hadn't seen anything. Divers swam to the drop. Still, nobody had come within a mile of there until the—

The college team. A perfect cover. Was it the professor? Khalid Khan? The stunning woman before him?

Head tilted, she looked at him. "What?"

Reece let his mask of indifference slip back into place. "Nothing." He reached for her arm, but she swung away. "We should get you back to the hotel. Wouldn't want your fiancé to worry."

"Wait. I—" She closed her mouth. Finally, she jutted her jaw as if summoning her courage. "Since you're a spy—"

"Operative."

"Whatever. Can you check up on people?"

He paused, surprised by her question. "What do you mean?"

Her eyes seemed to probe his, and then she bunched her shoulders. "Nothing. I shouldn't have brought it up."

Double-speak. A line that meant I'll tell if you ask again. He wouldn't.

Seconds stretched between them as she shifted away a few paces and cradled her body with her arms. She pivoted and dropped her arms to her side. "Can you check out Khalid's father?"

Reece kept his expression impassive.

"See if he is . . . if he has . . ." She huffed. "To see if he's on the up and up? Can you do that?"

"And why would I?" Something akin to pride trickled through his veins. The girl blew him away. How did she nail Baseer Khan? Toby Roberts, experienced consular grunt, didn't even see it coming.

She scratched her temple and wrinkled her nose. "I know, it's crazy. I shouldn't have brought it up."

"Tell me what you saw."

"It wasn't so much what I saw as what I felt."

"Go on."

Uncertainty tiptoed across her face as she shifted on her feet. "He seemed a bit aggressive the other night. Then, earlier today, I bumped into him on the street near the government offices." Kneading a muscle in her shoulder, she looked as distraught about the information as if she'd caught the guy red-handed in something illegal. "What would he be doing over there when the train station is on the other side of town? He knows people have been killed and someone probably wants me dead."

"No probably about it. I'll look into Mr. Khan." He checked his watch. "Time to head back. Once inside the hotel, trash my shirt and hoof it to your room. Lock the door and don't come out for anyone you don't know."

She nodded. "Who exactly am I hiding from?"

He started for the door. "Bad guys."

"Bad guys?" She rolled her eyes. "I'm not a child. Tell me who we're dealing with."

"Do names matter when the guy in front of you is holding an AK-47?" He cleared the stoop and stepped out.

She was right with him, staying at his elbow. "I guess I lied in the courtyard."

He reached behind her, caught the hood, and tucked her hair back under the material. Sweat slid down her face. "How so?" He slipped the hood up.

"I said I wasn't in danger." She tugged at the strings hanging down the front of the navy sweatshirt. "Pretty stupid when they've murdered my friends and seem to know where I am."

"Don't worry. I won't let anything happen to you." He swept a few stray strands of hair from her face.

Her eyes fluttered.

What was that? Reece shrugged off her reaction. "Let's go."

Getting her to the Taj Mahal proved much easier than he'd expected. Hopefully, they'd delayed long enough to throw off their tail, but he wouldn't count on that.

Reece waited until Shiloh appeared on the balcony and gave him the all clear before he sped away from the hotel. At his place, he powered up his laptop, hit the secure site, burrowed into a nested site, and scanned the taps he'd planted. The satellite images waited. He opened them, zoomed in, and hung his head.

Perry's friend had been right. India had sent nukes into Kashmir—the perfect location to launch a strike against Pakistan and avoid the blame. He prayed that wasn't the plan. Prayed they weren't that stupid.

He closed it out and scanned his inbox. Another email provided the tap results on the fax line. He read the document, a standard business letter to an unspecified recipient. At least, that's the way Abdul wanted it to look. Reece knew enough about the way networks worked. One glance told him it referred to a meeting. He forwarded the information to analysts, who would decipher the code words and figure out the when and where.

Tonight, while the ministry offices were closed, he'd sneak in and surf the files in Abdul's office. Baseer, his son, and Shiloh would board the train at one a.m. Reece exited the nested sites and grabbed the phone to call his sister. With the way things were heating up, he'd better catch a few moments with her before this case took him to Pakistan. After changing into a fresh tunic, he headed out the door to meet up with Julia.

Strong spices overpowered him as he strode into the restaurant and spotted his sister in a booth.

"A quick dinner?" Julia burrowed into her seat and crossed her arms. "Since when do I get crammed between events? And you're late."

"I can leave now."

She clicked her tongue. "You've lost your sense of humor. I ordered for us."

Soon the hostess set three platters of food between them. The curried spices rose in a spiral of steam, tingling his nose. Without a moment's hesitation, Reece piled some rice onto his plate, followed closely by a mound of the yellow chicken and sauce.

A vegetarian, Julia served herself a portion of the curried vegetables, nibbled on the food, and then set down her fork.

Mouth full, Reece glanced at her. "What?"

"I'm going to marry Toby."

Reece tried not to choke. He swallowed and hurriedly drank some water. "He proposed?"

"We talked about it after you left the other night." She sighed. "We haven't agreed on my job, but we're both willing to compromise."

"Whoa." Reece eased back, wiping his mouth with a linen napkin. "When did you get so domestic?"

Something twinkled in her eyes. A light he didn't recognize.

"I love him. Despite his quirky, almost nerdy mannerisms, he's the only person I feel comfortable and complete with. He's not demanding or forceful."

Reece grunted. "I don't need to know this, not about Roberts." He rested a hand on his leg and leaned to the side. "As long as you're happy—you are happy, right?"

She smiled. "Yeah, I am."

He nodded. "Thought so."

"Don't sound so depressed." She tossed her napkin at him.

Laughing, he pressed his spine against the chair. "I just didn't expect you to ever get married—and definitely not to someone like Toby. We made a pact, remember?"

With a loud half-groan, half-laugh, she shoved her hands into her dark hair. "I was twelve. You were nine."

"So?"

Giggling, she reached across the table and tapped his head. "Yep, still as hard and thick as ever."

Reece dug into his food and tried to ignore her knowing look, but he anticipated her next topic of conversation. Toby had planted ample fodder in her mind. She probably had it all planned out—him madly in love, married, and expecting a baby. With Shiloh, of course. Finally, he let his fork clatter against the plate and folded his arms on the table. "Go on. Get it out of your system before you explode."

"Tell me about her."

He grunted. "Jules . . ." Tossing his napkin down, he exhaled again, stifling a grin. "She's tangled up in a mess. I was already involved, but things came to light that made her the asset. I have to admit, she's tough. Smart too. She pegged something even Toby hadn't figured out."

"Really?"

"Yeah. If I were still training, I'd recruit her in a heartbeat." Was she buying his story?

Julia sat back and chewed her lower lip. "Wow, she got your attention, didn't she? What does she look like?"

"Stunning. Reddish-brown hair. Out by the bay, it looked almost golden, like a goddess on a Grecian urn."

She smacked his arm—hard. "You're playing me."

He burst out laughing. Fist over his mouth, he tried to stop, but he couldn't.

"Reece Jaxon, you are pure evil."

He wiped tears from the corners of his eyes. "You asked for that one."

"You can be a jerk, but at least Toby showed me her picture."

His smile vanished. "He *what*?" He drew back, pulling up his shoulders.

"Oh, don't get all protective."

"He compromised her safety. I'm barely keeping the sharks off her tail." Shaking his head, he balled his fist. "I could kill that puke."

"Hey!" Julia's brow furrowed over pouting red lips. "That *puke* is going to be your brother-in-law."

"Yeah, don't remind me. What a stupid—he knows better. Those files are confidential. She's been through too much already."

"I thought you said she was tough."

He shook a finger at her. "Don't even go there."

"Why would Toby say you had a thing for her? She's very pretty."

He nudged his plate aside. "What do you want from me, Julia? To say I've fallen madly in love with the girl and we're running off to Paris together?"

"No." She smiled that sweet, big-sister smile that had more syrup than Saturday morning waffles. "Just to know that you won't die the way our father did."

The little food in his stomach soured. "I'm *not* our father."

"I hope not." She crossed her arms and leaned on the table. "Have you let go of what mom did? Or is that still eating at you too?"

Reece tapped the table and raised his hands in surrender with a snort. "What is this? Suddenly you're a shrink?"

Julia's dark brows wrinkled. "Will she be in danger?"

"She already is."

"You like playing the hero, don't you? I think that's your way of trying to prove you're not like dad."

"I need to get going." Scooting his chair back, he waved over the hostess for the bill.

"Not so different from Dad after all, are you?"

Despite the soft tone of her words, they pummeled him all the same. "What is that supposed to mean?"

"He ran when Mom's scandal broke. Left us, left her. When things got tough, he walked."

He hunched his shoulders. "What exactly am I running from? Besides an overly romantic big sister." When the petite Hindu woman arrived, he handed her enough rupees to pay for the meal and stood. "I'll tell Shiloh you'd prefer I bed her than protect her to make sure she makes it back to the States alive."

"Shiloh, huh?"

Reece froze. Had he really said her name? In public?

"I like her already."

Reece stomped off, grateful a trip to Pakistan would put distance between him and his nosy sister . . . and her fiancé.

Dampness pervaded Shiloh's senses as she sat back against the hotel room headboard. Rain threatened the ending of a day that had started out with sunshine and peace. Drawing the comforter up to her shoulder, she glanced at the hoodie on the bed next to her. She had looked for a place to trash it, but all the bins in the lobby were too small. Even in here she didn't have a place to hide it. Khalid and his father were down in the restaurant eating. Feigning illness, she had stayed in the room, her mind buzzing from the encounter with Brutus.

She walked her fingers across the silky spread to the cotton sweatshirt and tugged it closer. Soaked in the scent of him, she inhaled. The shirt gave her a strange comfort, one she hadn't felt since she was a child . . . before her mother's death.

Her mind whipped back to the present. The little adventure with Brutus slammed home the danger that surrounded her. She'd thought herself alert, cognizant of what was happening around her. But he'd pointed out more than twice the number of goons she'd sighted. How foolish to think leaving the other hotel and taking up residence under assumed names would be enough! Had she put Khalid and his father in jeopardy?

Why was Brutus helping her? Did he think she had answers to this puzzle? But he hadn't interrogated her. That'd be the prudent route. Drill her full of questions until she sunk in a sea of guilt. Only, what guilt did she bear? That stupid dive trip wasn't her fault. He sure seemed interested in the cylinder, though. Silently, she entertained the idea of finding her way to the bay, diving, and figuring out what was in that thing. Was it even there still?

Who were the men from the street? The ones with the big weapons?

A scent, clean and crisp, sailed over her. Brutus. He'd held her so close in that abandoned shop, sheltered in his arms. Though his grip was tight, it hadn't been rough. She'd found it oddly reassuring—his strength and those muscles . . .

Shiloh blinked. *What am I doing?* She stared at her engagement ring, but it blurred in the background. She drew the navy sweatshirt close; the odor of sweat, not pungent but clearly there, and something like Old Spice mingled together. Heat seared her abdomen as she remembered his blazing eyes.

Rolling onto her back, she groaned, remembering how she'd shuddered at his touch. As they had stood by the door, a tinge of light haloed around him, accenting his jaw, the intensity in his eyes, and the way his T-shirt stretched across his bulky, well-toned chest.

At the sound of loud rapping, her pulse catapulted. She scooted upright and visually inspected the locks she'd snapped into place hours earlier.

"Shiloh?" Khalid's voice jabbed her with guilt. She slid the sweatshirt under the pillow and drew the comforter over it. More rapping. "Shiloh, let me in."

Material peeked out from under the pillow. "Just a minute." Heart pounding, she grabbed the hooded sweatshirt and stuffed it in her pack. "I'm not decent. What is it?"

"Open the door a bit—I've brought you something."

What was so urgent? With the chain still in place, she eased back the lightweight door. A black mound of cloth slipped through the small crack.

"Wear this. Bring your things. It's time to go."

Unfolding the garment, she resisted the urge to groan. The *burqa* would cover everything but her eyes. They'd be in Pakistan by morning. Already, she felt the shackle of ultra-conservatism tightening around her neck.

I can't do this. No way could she wear a burqa and live in that country. Married to Khalid, she'd be expected to remain at home and bear his children, which she couldn't do. Even if she had a choice, she *wouldn't*.

Upending her pack, she buried Brutus's sweatshirt at the bottom. It was stupid to keep it, but it seemed like a good-luck charm or something. On top she planted her clothes, money, and toiletries. Her heart filled with dread as the reality of what she was about to do smacked into her. It was almost midnight.

Where was Brutus? At this hour, would he be awake? Would he know where they were going? Her stomach seized. What if he didn't? Why did she feel safer with a man whose name she didn't even know than with the man she was pledged to marry?

She glared at the pack that contained the forbidden sweatshirt. "I love Khalid Khan, and I'm marrying him."

"Well, that's good to know."

She whirled, heat singeing her cheeks. "Khalid. What . . . ? How did you get in here?"

He pointed toward the door joining their rooms. "The chain slid off when I nudged it." Chuckling, he came to her and slipped his hands around her waist. He bent to kiss her.

"Khalid!" His father's voice seemed to rattle the windows. "Inappropriate! You should not be in her bedroom."

With a snort, Khalid pecked her on the lips and broke away. "Of course, Father."

Although fully clothed and buried in the burqa, Shiloh felt naked and exposed in front of the two men.

Thud, thud, thud!

Baseer and Khalid exchanged alarmed glances, and fear wedged into the recesses of Shiloh's heart. Both men started toward the other room. Khalid tossed her a backward glance. "Stay here. Don't come out." With that, he pulled the door closed.

Why was everyone telling her what to do? She was perfectly capable of taking care of herself. Defiance hardened her resolve. Who could be knocking on the door at nearly midnight? The question hung in her mind like a dark cloud and lured her to the adjoining door. Ear pressed against the wood, she held her breath and listened.

There is no time to waste.

Our men are in place. Reassurance coated Baseer's words.

Their men? What must Khalid think of his father's mysterious connections?

You are sure it's safe?—Khalid's voice.

If the authorities find you or her there is no telling what will happen.

Shiloh stared at her pack. Was it too much to hope Brutus would trail them and keep her safe? How crazy that she found so much security in a stranger. The idea of going to the station, boarding, and traveling to Pakistan under Baseer's protection carved a river of fear through her.

Rushing to her bag, she prayed she had time. She flipped open the phone Brutus had given her. Her heart plummeted. The battery! Not even a whole bar left. What did she expect? An endless lifespan? Tempted to call him, she stared at it long and hard. Finally, she pressed the TALK button. Then cancelled it.

What if her fears were unfounded?

Trust yourself.

Chewing her lip, she let Brutus's words seep into her brain. She opened her pack, withdrew a pair of jeans, slipped them on under the gauzy material, and tucked the phone into the pocket.

Her door swung open. Khalid entered, his face grim. "It's time."

13

QUIET BLANKETED THE DARKENED HALLS OF THE MINISTRY BUILDING. With the use of his cell phone, Reece jammed the signals controlling the motion-sensitive cameras. At this hour, his worst foe inside should be the night-cleaning crew and the tired security guard at the main desk. Outside would be a different story. Stealthily, Reece glided down the slick floors toward the stairs. He easily bypassed one checkpoint after another, marveling that India had kept its secrets this long.

At his eleven o'clock, a shadow stretched into view. Whistling pierced the empty corridor. Reece ducked into the public restroom and waited, his back plastered to the wall. Steps grew louder. The whistling stopped. He inwardly cursed his choice of hiding places. The guard was coming straight to him!

Shoes scuffed. The door cranked open. The guard entered, his wide girth filling the tight, cramped bathroom as he moved toward the bank of urinals.

Reece slid around the open door as it swung shut.

"Hello?" The guard's hesitant question propelled Reece toward the stairs. As his foot hit the first landing, he heard the door to the bathroom creak open and another muttered hello. On the second floor, Reece disabled the cameras and darted for the deputy minister's door.

In the office he planted four discs, two on opposite walls from each other. Once activated, the discs would reflect the coded image—a wall-to-ceiling duplicate of the minister's office from last night. A gentle hum pervaded the artificially cooled air, massaging it with a special form of trick photography. The façade would allow him to scour the desk, files, notes, computers, trash . . . anything that might prove a connection between Baseer Khan and Osman Sajjadi, but more importantly, the source of the dead drop. And if he was really fortunate, the reason for the two-week deadline.

Time trickled through his fingers. Tension bunched his neck muscles, and a bead of sweat rolled down his temple. He swiped at it and kept searching. He didn't have much time before the train shuttled Shiloh out of his hands. Maybe following Baseer Khan to his hometown outside Karachi was the best thing to do. Let the guy lead him to the connection.

If only.

Reece had chased enough dead ends regarding Sajjadi to last several lifetimes. This situation, involving the possible dissolution of the nuclear proliferation pact between India and France and India and the U.S., demanded an aggressive approach. Too many links in the latest developments pointed to the mastermind—the brute force, the efficiency, the extensiveness, and worst of all, the dead ends.

Kneeling behind the desk, he felt along the mahogany panels, pressing gently. There had to be a concealed compartment somewhere in this office. His fingers slid over the floorboards, checking for depressions or pressure-sensitive spots. Nothing.

He hunched, one arm propped on his knee, and looked around the room. Where would Abdul hide—

Reece grinned as he noticed an almost imperceptible change in the pattern of the trim around the top of the desk. He cocked his head and inched closer. Fingers against the wood, he pushed. *Click!* The half-inch trim popped out. A blue folder peeked up at him. He set it on the desk and flipped it open. A coded document, too encrypted to be decipherable at a glance, lay on top. He used his watch and captured a snapshot of the page. He'd work through it later. Next he found several sheets of paper with three columns of numbers and letters. Nonsensical, random arrangements. Hundreds of them. He took a shot of that image too.

A small stack of photos in the far, back corner snagged his attention. Reece thumbed through them. A woman. Child. Two children. A family—

Abdul had a family hidden somewhere? Interests to protect. Interests nobody knew about. That could be useful. He snapped a copy.

What else lay in the secret shelf of a ministry official? Like glacial formations, the pieces slid and collided against Reece's imagination. A key. No identifying marks. An account slip from a bank in Switzerland. Last, a hand-scrawled note.

The timing must be perfect. Anything less will bring this down on everyone's heads. I entrust this matter into your hands, my friend. –BK

While the field warbled and protected his location and signal, Reece sent the images spiraling through the air as a minute particulate straight to Langley and his private laptop on a secured, access-only signal.

Staples held a stack of diagrams together. Reece fanned the pages. A half-dozen schematics of a boat. Details filled close to ten more. What was this about?

Voices in the hall. His adrenaline spiked.

In the exact order he'd removed them, he replaced the pieces, then shut the secret compartment. He planted a bug underneath the desk, snatched the devices, which deactivated the interference screen, and rushed into the adjoining room. A small desk straddled the space between the connecting door and the exit. Darkness embraced him as he peered through the scrollwork on the frosted glass.

Abdul strode in, a woman trailing him. "Does the Prime Minister know?"

"No, sir." The receptionist scurried behind him. "You told me to bring this information to you first."

"Good." Ali grunted. "You can leave."

Had he left something out of place? Reece watched the deputy minister move around his office, loosening his tie as he placed the phone to his ear.

"It's in place." Abdul glanced at his watch. His head snapped up, eyes wide. "Do you realize what will happen?"

Craning his neck to see through the clear space, Reece prayed he wasn't signing his death certificate by sticking around. Something told him this was worth seeing.

"Call me when it's done." Abdul clicked the phone shut and dropped into his chair, head in his hands.

Seizing the moment, Reece rushed to the exit and carefully turned the knob. Checking right and left, he stepped out just as voices skated into his awareness. He yanked back and pulled the door to, peering through a slit of space.

Several men stalked toward him. As they drew closer, the grouping separated. One stood at the juncture between the stair and the hall, another stopped a dozen feet away, and yet another rushed to the opposite end. The tactical positioning sent Reece's instincts buzzing. This had the smell of a protective insertion.

As if to confirm his silent assessment, one thug called, "Clear."

Anticipation mounted as Reece waited for the mystery guest who felt the need to secure a government building that had been shut down for the night.

An entourage clogged the narrow hall: three in front, three behind. The huddle warned him they were protecting someone important, someone who didn't want to be bothered or seen. Their approach pushed Reece into the shadows, his eye still focused on the slight opening. Who had come to Abdul? Would this be the break he needed? The proof?

Dark suits swam by the door.

A tall man, partially balding with a dour expression to match, sauntered past as he mumbled to the team. Light skimmed his face. Kodiyeri, the man who had followed Shiloh.

A chair squeaked and thunked, apparently as Abdul shot to his feet. "Why are you here?"

The disbelief and fear in Abdul's question stopped Reece cold. The way Abdul had spoken sounded more like an underling speaking to a superior. Didn't Kodiyeri work for Abdul? Despite the warnings blaring through his thick skull to make a hasty exit before he got caught, Reece hesitated. This could be colossal. But colossal could mean dead.

Yet without big proof, the case was dead.

The hulking man shifted toward the minister, a scowl etched into his dark brows. "We have unfinished business."

Kodiyeri's words drew Reece back to the scrollwork glass.

"You could ruin me!" Panic laced the minister's words.

"You are already ruined, old man." Kodiyeri took a seat, two guards flanking him, making it almost impossible to see his face.

A dark, sinister tension weighted the room. What Reece believed to be fact—that Kodiyeri worked for Abdul—had just been upended. If Kodiyeri wasn't Abdul's hireling, then who did he answer to?

The familiar knock of opportunity rang in his ears. Nielsen hadn't believed Sajjadi, a Muslim radical based out of Pakistan, would be aligned with a conservative Hindu government official like Abdul. Could Kodiyeri be the missing link?

If Reece could snap a picture and record a bit of this conversation, perhaps he could get the proof he needed. Angling the camera watch toward the glass, he aligned the lens with a clear spot in the frosted pane. He clamped his teeth. From this angle, he got nothing but the backside of a heavily armed mercenary.

"Why do you come here? It is a delicate position. If the Americans learn—"

"The Americans are being dealt with."

Abdul gasped. "What do you mean?"

"You had your orders. You failed. Now, you're out of time."

Kodiyeri *was* the link, Reece's fast-track to pinning this mess on Sajjadi. He had to snap an image of them together.

"We are being watched, and you come here, spouting off about some horrible thing you have done." Abdul paced and pivoted back to the all-too-relaxed power player, who lit a cigarette. "Have you killed them all?"

"Do not worry, my friend," Kodiyeri said. "You will not be implicated."

Reece ducked and swung to the other side of the door. Get the shot and get out.

At his desk, Abdul lifted a file and slid a piece of paper toward the man. "This girl—she is trouble. Too many contacts, I think."

Reece snapped the photo just as the words hit him. Abdul was talking about Shiloh. He froze. He should have left when his instincts ordered him out. Was he too late? Had they already gone after her—or worse? Completed the mission?

"She is not long for this world." Sick laughter slithered around Reece's mind and stomach like a viper. Kodiyeri waved a dismissive hand at the deputy prime minister. "Such a pity, don't you think? So pretty."

Go! Now! Heart thumping, Reece darted a glance at the door.

"Wait!" Ali's breathless admonishment drove Reece out. Had he been discovered?

Chaos erupted on the entire second floor.

Armed with the element of surprise and his Glock, Reece burst out of his hiding place and shot the nearest guard. As the guy dropped hard, Reece had already taken aim and fired two rounds at the blue suit by the stairs. In a fluid motion, he spun. Zigzagged down the hall and eliminated the last guard who protected his exit.

He flung himself at the fire escape door. Clanging open, the door rebounded, but Reece rolled around it.

Ping! Ping!

Sailing over the steps, he ducked and hoped the bullets didn't ricochet straight into the back of his skull. Seconds thundered in his head.

Rounding a corner, he ignored the sweat that dribbled down his back. He headed for the side exit and punched the door, nearly breaking it from its hinges.

"There! There!" Shouts erupted throughout the open area.

Several guards jogged from the building and dropped to their knees. Gunfire punctuated the night. Reece broke into a sprint, aiming for the side wall. Floodlights swirled toward him.

He dove behind a car. After a pause, he craned his neck to see through a window. At least a dozen heavily armed men raced into the open. He checked the rooftop, dust and dirt partially clouding his view. Yet through that haze, he saw them. Snipers.

God, I could use a little Elijah action here—just transport me straight to Shiloh.

Glock in hand, he sized up the safest route. A mere twenty feet lay between him and the wall. But those were twenty heart-pounding, bullet-piercing steps. Fairly certain he could make it without taking one through the head, Reece worried about scaling the wall. Eight feet tall and made of white, cracked plaster. Could he get enough traction on its smooth surface to climb over it?

Ping! Ping! Crack!

Reece pulled himself into a crouch. Shuffling toward the middle of the car, he prepped himself to cross the distance. Prepped himself to die. He used his shoulder to wipe the sweat from his neck. This wasn't the place to die. Shiloh needed him, and with what he heard in Abdul's office, he didn't have time to mess around.

"Okay, God . . ." he mumbled and glanced to his right, his gaze tracking over the lit-like-day compound, searching for hostiles. And saw the power box. He grinned. "Thank you." Peering down the muzzle, he lined up the crosshairs of his Glock and fired.

Sparks flew. Hissing, popping. *CRACK!* Darkness reigned.

Reece launched himself toward the plaster wall. Dirt burst up at him, as if reaching for his ankles to yank him down. The acrid smell of cordite enveloped him. Hurling himself at the wall, he prayed his landing wouldn't hurt much. Plaster stabbed into his hands as he clawed up the barrier. Exploding paint chips peppered his face. Hooking an arm over the top, he grunted at the vibrating cement beneath his hands.

With a heave, he flipped, but not before fire tore down his left calf. He concentrated on landing with both feet, despite the wound needling his leg. Darts of pain shot up his calves on impact. He sprinted between two buildings. Through the maze of streets, he pushed himself toward his bike. His pants pulled against the wound, sticky from coagulating blood.

Sirens screamed. Light swirled as police cars cruised the streets, flashlights knifing the slivers of darkness separating the buildings. Reece gritted his teeth and hiked his bloodied leg over his Ducati. Helmeted, he jabbed the key into the ignition and cranked the engine. He eased the throttle and roared into the night.

"Open com." Cool wind bathed him as he pressed his gut to the fiberglass spine and tore across town. "Nielsen, I've relayed a series of images."

"Just got 'em."

"I have my Sajjadi proof."

"I'll decide that. But, apparently, we have you to thank for a gun battle in the middle of an Indian ministry compound."

"It hasn't even begun."

"What do you mean?"

Reece nailed a corner, practically laying out the bike. His gut twisted, not from his maneuvers, but from the threat still echoing in his mind. "I'm on my way to the transit station. Call in support. Get the GBs on alert."

"Whoa! Slow down. What's going on?"

"Just do it!"

"Not till you tell me—"

"There's a hit ordered on Khan and Shiloh."

14

I THINK YOU SHOULD TAKE THE RING BACK." SHILOH TWISTED THE GOLD and ruby jewelry around her finger as she sat on the bench, a cool draft rustling the black burqa.

Silence choked their conversation as a family of three strolled past, dragging their luggage. Small and rosy-cheeked, the little girl with deep, green eyes stared back at Shiloh. It reminded her of the photograph from one of those national magazines that captivated the heart of the West. Brandishing a small stuffed animal, the girl smiled.

Shiloh ached. No more putting off the truth. She had to come clean. "Khal—"

"The train will be here soon." His father joined them. "A short delay outside Calicut." He leaned against the nearby wall.

"Let's walk." Khalid stood and held out his hand for her.

They walked in silence to the end of the platform, where a metal rail protected passengers from stepping into the street. There, she lowered her backpack to the ground.

Khalid reached over and clasped a hand over hers. "Just because we argue does not mean it's over." His smile touched that inner place in her heart that so few even knew existed. "We are different people from different cultures. We will not always agree." Gentleness in his tone coaxed a smile from her. "But I will not love you any less."

She glanced at his hands. He didn't know. "Those are easy words when you think the future is bright and promising."

Movement drew her gaze. Baseer had walked closer, watching them. It felt as though sand filled her mouth.

With a warm palm against her back, Khalid smiled. "Do not fear this time, Shiloh. I know we are in danger. But I believe God has us firmly in His grasp."

"Okay, see?" Raw burning seared her throat and heart. "Right there—I can't believe that. The whole God-thing doesn't work for me. Never has."

"You are hurt. But I can help you through that. My mother—"

"I can't have children." The blurted words rang in her ears.

His eyes grew round and then narrowed. "Can't? Or don't want to?"

Indignation rose in her chest. "Experts made that diagnosis, not me."

His ragged breath sounded loud in the thick air. "You . . . you never told me."

"There wasn't a need. I never intended to marry." She steadied her quivering lip. "I can never give you what you deserve and want so badly. The one thing in your culture that gives a woman merit."

His absolute resolve cracked, just a glimmer, but enough for her to know the revelation had the effect she feared. The vehemence in his sparkling eyes dimmed. At the edge of the platform, he stared out across the tracks to the small lights twinkling in the distance.

She'd known he'd reject her for this, that he would change his mind. Isn't this what she had imagined for so long? So why did it hurt so much?

Shiloh closed the physical distance, yet knew the emotional distance between them had spread wide. "Here." She tugged off the ring, lifted his hand, and tucked the piece into his palm and closed it. "I understand. I really do."

He edged closer, his expression strangely serene. "No, I don't think you do." Khalid gripped her wrist and pulled it to his chest. He slid the ring back on. "I asked you to marry me." His smile was thin. "If this is as God has ordained, it is my honor."

"You can't mean that," she said. Suddenly, her rationale for not marrying him crumbled, leaving her exposed. No more fooling him—or herself. "Khalid, it's not just that."

He nodded. "I know." Sorrow dragged down his tranquil features. "I thought if you'd just give me the chance to show you how much I love you, how deep my feelings are for you . . ." He hung his head. "This whole time, I've used every possible explanation and reason to convince myself that you loved me too." Bent over the railing, he folded his hands. "I'd never force you to do something you don't want to do." He rubbed a hand over his face, the *scritch* of his stubbled jaw echoing in the silent night. His gaze rose to the night sky. Hazy clouds streaked around a dull moon. "Oh, God, why did you fill me with such love for a creature too wild to accept it?"

"Wild?" Shiloh quivered.

A scream pierced the night. She spun.

The little girl lay on the ground a few feet away. A dark puddle spread out like a halo around her head. Wailing, her mother slumped and drew the limp body of her child into her arms.

"Help me! Help! My daughter—" Her words morphed into another scream.

Shiloh's heart skipped a beat. This seemed so familiar. Feeling distant yet trapped, she watched the man clasp his wife's shoulders and try to drag away the sobbing woman.

"What's happening?" Shiloh whispered.

Dark stains suddenly appeared across the man's tunic and pants. He crumpled like a blanket.

Whizzing and popping drowned the night sounds. Light twinkled against the barrenness of the black sky.

A hard yank snapped her out of shock.

"Run." Khalid grabbed her pack and thrust her from the railing.

Pushing herself, Shiloh raced toward the building. Wood exploded, splintering and flying like tiny daggers. She shielded her face as she lunged around the corner and took cover. Khalid landed next to her, his back pressed against her shoulder.

With deep, gulping breaths, she tried to make sense of the chaos. "What's happening?"

"I don't know." Khalid peeked around the corner, but jerked back. "I can't see anyone."

Shiloh's mind caught up with the adrenaline surge. "Kodiyeri."

"What?" Khalid looked over his shoulder at her. "What did you say?"

"The man who's been chasing me—his name is Kodiyeri." Could he really have found her? How? They'd hidden. Brutus's little revelatory trip seeped into her mind. He'd shown her the brutal reality of her situation. Why did she think they could escape? And where was Brutus? He'd always been on her tail. What of his promise to watch her back?

The rumbling of a vehicle neared. Shiloh slowly turned toward the sound. Only then did it hit her. Despite having taken cover from the direction of the gunfire, she now stood with nothing but warm, sticky air and darkness between her and the open road. "They're coming this way!"

"The office." Khalid grabbed her hand and pulled her around the corner.

Thwat, thwat, thwat, thwat!

Shiloh ducked. Hunched over, she and Khalid snaked along the wall toward the depot door.

Shattering glass resounded in her ears and showered onto her head.

He stumbled but kept going. "Just a few . . . more . . ." A limp marked his gait.

Something marred the concrete under her feet. Shiloh squinted at it—blood! Her eyes shot to Khalid. "Are you hurt?"

An ominous howl rent the air.

Khalid answered with a loud, reverberating grunt as he whirled and threw himself at her. "Down!"

Boom!

Heat flashed over them. Wood, metal, and rocks showered the station. A squawking noise devoured her hearing. She looked around with narrowed eyes, trying to decipher the sound. Khalid's lips moved, but she couldn't hear him; the explosion had deafened her.

"Khalid!" His father's voice, normally deep and resonating, sounded like a distant, underwater call.

A muzzle flash lit the dark, narrow alley.

Khalid struggled to his feet. Blood streaked his face and dripped down his chin. No time to nurse wounds. If they didn't get to shelter, they'd both end up in Paradise. Well, at least Khalid would.

"Hurry!" Baseer leaned out of the office, a weapon in his hand, and fired several rounds.

Behind her, Shiloh heard two thuds that sent her spiraling toward him. A sudden shove against her shoulder made her stumble—straight into Baseer.

Then, the oddest of sensations. Her body lifted into the air. Baseer's wide eyes struck fear into her core. As if in slow motion, she saw him hunch his shoulders and cringe, all the while propelling her to the side—into the building—with both hands.

Another whistle, but longer—higher-pitched.

Boooooom!

Her spiraling body rocketed through the air. Silence gripped her in terror. Her torso twisted. Arms crossed in front of her face, she braced for impact as she sped toward the concrete.

Someone hit the fast-forward button. Without warning her legs experienced a supernatural thrust. Head over heels, she hurled toward the far wall. No control. She tumbled. Blurred images. Chaos.

Thud! Crack!

Her head hit first. Pain stabbed her neck and back. Her body flattened against the pebbled concrete.

For a moment, everything went black.

She blinked open her eyes, dazed. How long had she been unconscious? Light swirled and spun. Fire licked the ceiling and walls. Red-hot embers rained down. Shiloh blinked again. Burning papers drifted aimlessly toward the debris-littered floor. Black murals smeared the furniture that was still intact. Smoke and ash singed her lungs.

The hollow scraping of her own head against the cement roared in her ears as she tried to regain her orientation. Although the door should have been to her right, she peered down the length of her body into a gaping hole in the wall. No door. No office. Half the building lay in ruins.

Khalid. Her heart lurched. Where was he? He'd been right behind her. And his father.

Shiloh peeled herself off the floor. Pain ripped through her back and shoulders. Wincing and moaning, she finally sat up. She clenched her stinging eyes tightly and called, "Khalid?" Her trembling fingers struggled to support her as she pushed to her knees.

On all fours, she took a ragged breath. Her head swam. Loud whirring and tweeting filled her ears. Excruciating. She cried out, clamped her hands over her ears, and collapsed into a huddle to protect herself from the noise. But it came from within. She shook her head hard.

Slowly, the shrieking dimmed. Gunfire devoured the seconds between the hiss and crackle of the flames. Disbelief choked her as she took in the scorched structure. Whoever did this wanted them dead. Drained of all strength, she didn't have time to wimp out.

She struggled to one knee and froze in shock.

"No," she whispered. The word sucked oxygen from her lungs. "Khalid!"

Unmoving, he lay on his stomach, facing away. The back of his shirt was charred. Smoke and ash clung in snaking vines around him.

As rocks dug into her burning palms and legs, she scrabbled over the debris. "Khalid!" At his side, she rolled him into her lap. Shiloh flinched.

His dark, beautiful eyes stared back empty.

She shook him. "Khalid! Khalid!" Again, she rattled his shoulders.

A blink. For a fraction of a second, he seemed drawn back from the edge of death, his gaze locked on hers.

"Thank . . ." A half-grin. He coughed. "Miss . . . —mer . . ."

"Shh, it'll be okay," she whispered. "I'll get us out of here." Searching the darkness beyond the missing wall, she wondered if she could. "There has to be a way. Just don't—"

She paused and looked at his now blank expression. Eyes empty. Smile gone.

"No." She gripped his shirt. "Khalid, don't!" Drawing her legs out from under him, she eased him down. "Please, please don't . . ." Unable to say the words her mind railed against,

Shiloh stared at his beautiful, ash-smeared face. He didn't move. "Please." Tears blurred her vision. "Khalid." She pressed her ear to his chest. Nothing. She pounded his chest. Turning her arm, she opened her fist. Horrified to find blood, she looked at his shirt—covered in blood.

Coagulated blood. How long had she lain there unconscious?

Shiloh bent and held him close, his face still warm against hers. "Oh, please, God! Where are You? Please don't let him die."

Tears streaming, she let out a gut-birthed sob—one that freed her ears in a painful way. The stark pain was of little consequence. "Don't die, Khalid!" She ground her teeth, forcing the words out. "Don't leave me here alone. I need you. I love you!" She buried her face in his shoulder, crying. "I love you."

"He's gone."

Glock in hand, Reece hunched next to the smoke- and ash-covered woman. After that double aerial she'd pulled, he didn't expect to see her alive, let alone moving.

Eyes wild, she whirled and lost her balance. Sooty auburn strands clung to her tear-stained face. Rivulets of tears streamed down her dirty face and tore at his heart.

"We need to go."

She shook her head, recognition slow in coming. "Brutus." Her gaze slid back to her friend. "No, I . . . I have to help him."

"You can't help him."

Defiance flashed in her eyes.

News like this wasn't easily delivered, so he softened his voice. "He's dead." Reece held out his hand and prodded her. "Come on."

"I can't leave him." Trembling, she looked down at her fallen friend. "Not like this."

He clasped her shoulders. "Shiloh, there are men trying to kill you. If you don't leave—"

"Then let them." Her lips pressed into a taut line.

Nostrils flared, he holstered his weapon and tore off the flak jacket. "We don't have time for this." He swung it around her and lifted her arms. She struggled against him, but he threaded one arm into the jacket. "If I have to drag you out of here, I will."

A right cross connected with his jaw. He stumbled backward, but caught himself. In position, he reached for her other arm and caught her fist midair. With his fingers wrapped tightly around hers, he reminded himself she was still in shock, still reacting, still irrational. He used his grip to thread that arm through the vest.

The wound in her right shoulder didn't seem to faze her. Again, the shock.

"I'm not—"

Gunfire drowned her words. Shouldering her pack, Reece drew his weapon. Holding it to the side, he scanned the void beyond them. The void that once held restrooms and a waiting area. Settling debris caked the air.

Shuffling. He raised his weapon, right arm straight but slightly bent as he settled back with the same foot.

"What're you doing?" Her whispered words reminded him of his mission: her. He had to protect her.

"Get behind me."

The scraping of feet came faster.

Reece side-stepped until he stood in front of Shiloh. "Move to the wall." He tried to direct her to safety, but she wouldn't budge.

"How do I know you didn't do all this?"

The accusation snapped his head around. "What?!"

Her red eyes widened as they focused on something in the corner. "Baseer!"

He turned and stared down the sights of his Glock into the clouded eyes of Baseer Khan. The weapon in the man's hand put Reece on full alert. "Drop it, Khan."

Standing within a dozen paces, Baseer stopped, his dark eyes lowering to his son. "They vowed to kill him if I did not help." Grief seemed to battle within him—but with what?

The rest of the family. A wife and daughter. Stomach clenched, Reece inched toward Shiloh, his gaze still on Khan. "Put the gun *down*." He shifted, his grip relaxed but firm. "Now."

Shiloh rushed around Reece toward the man.

Baseer shook his head and bounced his shoulders at the same time. "Look what they do to those who do not obey." His gun aimed straight at Shiloh.

"Don't!" Reece ground out.

With a gasp, she pulled back. "Baseer."

Mournful and grief-etched, his dark orbs met Reece's. Something in them seemed to send a message . . .

Shock flooded Reece. "No." He drew himself straight. "This isn't the answer."

"It is the only way." He squinted at Shiloh. His weapon dipped as he applied subtle pressure to the trigger.

Reece fired first.

Boom!

Baseer stumbled, the bullet penetrating his shoulder. Just enough to thwart the man's aim.

Shiloh's cry clawed at Reece. He couldn't let Khalid's father fire a shot at that close range.

Bent on his course Baseer staggered and aimed again.

God, help me! He's making me kill him.

Boom! The weapon's recoil rattled through Reece's arm.

A sob-like sound burst from Shiloh. "Stop it!" She thrust a hand toward Reece while she held another at the man trying to snuff out her life. "Please, Baseer, come with us."

"Khan! Drop it," Reece roared, his pulse throbbing in his neck and temples. "I'll end this. So help me, you know I will."

"No!" Shiloh shot him a glance. "Baseer, just put the gun down. Please!"

A crooked smile faltered on the embattled man's lips, a stream of blood oozing out as he looked at Shiloh. "He loved you so very much." His knee buckled. Although he swayed, he remained upright. "Nisa wanted you in the family even though you had no faith in God. I argued with her. But she loved you as a daughter." The smile dropped into a frown. "They will rape and murder her. You know this, yes? Then my daughter—poor Aatifa. I can't . . . can't let that happen." His finger coiled around the trigger, his hand shaking. Eyes glassy, he aimed at Shiloh again.

Boom!

Baseer spun. Fell. The weapon skidded to the side.

Shiloh rushed to him. "Baseer! Why? You could've come—taken Nisa to America. You could've hidden."

Reece stood over them. The mentality—the fear that destroyed the lives of normal, decent men—angered him.

"Here . . ." Baseer gasped and stuffed something into Shiloh's hand. "Gerard Mo . . . Mor . . ." Trembling, bloodied hands encompassed hers. "Take to him. Tell Nis . . . love . . . er." He slumped with his last wheezing breath.

Shiloh sniffled as she bent over Khalid's father.

Shouts outside.

Reece grabbed her shoulders and yanked her back. "We're outta time." With a firm but gentle grip on her arm, he led her to his bike just inside the building. The blown-out wall had given him the perfect entrance and exit.

Tires squalled nearby. Sirens blared.

Carefully, he fitted a helmet on her and secured the chin strap. With a tap on the top, he pronounced it good to go.

"We'll be on the road all night. Will you be okay?"

Liquid blue-grey eyes drifted to his. A somber nod. He pointed to the graze on her shoulder. "If that bothers you, let me know. Tug on my jacket." He hunched so they were eye-to-eye. "Got it?"

Another nod.

He flipped down her face shield, mounted the Monster, and shifted back to her. She stood, stared at the bike, and slowly hiked up the absurd burqa, revealing a pair of jeans. Surprise lit through him. Why had she worn jeans? Somehow, she knew something would happen tonight.

Proud that she had obeyed her instincts, he held out his hand. Shiloh placed hers in his and swung her leg over the back. He bent and lifted her foot and set it on the footrest. He repeated the move with her other foot. As he stabbed the key in the engine, he felt the subtle pressure of her grip against his leather jacket. Reece tugged her hands around his waist and patted her arm.

"Hold on—tight."

He revved the engine, released the clutch, and the bike screamed forward. Rubber tires clawed for traction. He felt her tense. Her fingers dug into his jacket. Then she moved closer. No lady-like distance between them.

They burst out of the building. Sparks flew off the fairing—bullets missing their target. With a bounce, the Monster screeched and jerked forward, propelling them down the darkened street. He accelerated and up-shifted, ready to embrace the night.

Lights shattered the darkness. Ahead, several cars appeared on the road.

Left foot downshifting, he tucked his head and glared. *Lord, we need an—*

The alley! Urging the bike to the far right, he spotted the turn and fired down through the gears to second. Barely slowing in time, he felt her muscles constrict. A glance at the speedometer—60 mph—warned him this corner would be terrifying. Hoping to give her a silent message to trust him and go with his movement, he pressed his elbow against her arm.

Then he banked left, leaning hard into the turn. Down . . . down . . . Shiloh countered his momentum, trying to stay upright instead of following his lead.

He pulled harder, arching his side toward the road and once again accelerated. Kiss of death? *Come on, come on,* he prodded her mentally.

Her weight eased into his. Aha! There, she'd figured it out. The scathing warmth of the cement sneered up at him. A fraction more and his knee would sizzle. Just a little farther. They nailed the corner.

Nice and steady, he tugged his body straight, and she came right into position, pressed to his spine, stopping the bike's curve trajectory. At the next street, he repeated the maneuver, thrilling over the way Shiloh had adjusted and flowed with it as they roared toward the interstate. The wind whipped against them, and he hammered through the gears. The arms encircling him bound tighter and tighter. It wasn't until he flicked the bike into fifth and smoothed out at one-twenty that she started to relax. By the time they'd reach the Green Beret camp, her legs would feel like jelly.

But he wondered if the Shiloh Blake he'd met on Mumbai Beach two weeks ago still existed. Tonight's ordeal ranked up there on the catastrophe scale that left people with major issues.

God, protect her mind and heart. Help me get her to safety.

He concentrated on the winding road to avoid the potholes that felt like landmines. Whatever Baseer Khan had given her, Reece would have to convince her to hand it over. That could be the answer, the key to this whole disaster. Beside his wife and children, the man had a secret worth dying for.

Reece could only hope nobody else knew about it.

15

Northern India

PRE-DAWN COLORED THE WORLD IN A GREY HAZE. A SLIGHT BREEZE swirled cool mist around the street. Trees stood guard along the winding path to wherever they were going. At this point, she really didn't care where, just as long as they kept going. And going.

At a trash bin, Shiloh tossed the burqa. Her gaze darted to Brutus, who haggled with a street vendor. His frame seemed enlarged next to the short woman tending the stand. Never would she forget the image burned into her mind of him killing Baseer. Shot after thundering shot. With a quick shake of her head, she tried to push the image far from her mind. But her thoughts danced with it in some sick serenade. Khalid in her arms . . . his last breath.

Why did God do that? Why did He take Khalid? He was such a good man.

He's gone. She blinked fast and dropped her gaze to the UCSD T-shirt she wore. Why didn't God protect him? Isn't that the way it should work? Khalid lived his life for God. Shouldn't the Almighty return the favor and let him live?

Brutus approached, armed with two bottled waters and protein bars pulled from his pack. "It's not much, but it'll get us through till we make camp." He handed her one of each. "How're you?"

What a question. How did he think she'd be after watching her best friend and his father killed? Her shoulder ached, and her head pounded like a distant echo of his firing weapon. Ignoring him, she twisted off the water bottle cap. After a couple of sips she closed it and set it in her bag.

The early morning hues shrouded his face in shadows. "We're not leaving until you down that bottle."

Shiloh studied him. His almost flat brows seemed to sit in a perpetual line. His lips were tight, his jaw set. Did it even bother him that he'd shot a man to death?

"We've been on the road since midnight." He glanced at his watch. "It's nearly four. You haven't had anything to eat or drink since last night."

"So?"

"So you need to guard against dehydration." Without waiting for her reply, he retrieved her water and handed it to her. "The water and at least one protein bar."

"Or what?" She heard the hollow jeer in her own words. It didn't matter if she ate or drank. Nothing mattered. Everything seemed senseless.

Straightening to his full height, he stepped closer and slid the protein bar into her hand.

Heat shot through her chest. In a tantrum, she threw it across the dusty street. Without a word, he offered another.

Eyes searching his, she felt the hammering in her chest. "You killed him in cold blood. You just shot him where he stood."

Brutus didn't flinch. His gaze held hers, constant and steady.

"Not once." Her voice rose, and she shoved him. "Not twice. *Four times!*"

Despite her shove, he didn't budge.

"How can you stand there"—another shove—"and not say anything?" Right jab to his gut. "You shot him."

His hands rose slightly in a defensive move. "Shil—"

With all she had, she slammed her fist toward his stomach, but he caught her strike.

And he let her go just as quickly. "I'm not going to fight you." Hands held up, he took a step back.

Her fury fed off his words. Her palm stung when it connected with his face, slapping him again and again.

In one fluid move, he wrapped her in a tight hold. Blood roared through her ears. Unable to reach his face, she writhed in his grasp and pounded his sides.

"I hate you!" She hit him again. "I hate you! You killed his father." Tears poured down her face. "You made me leave him." *I loved him.* "Like a dog in the street."

Her vigor renewed, she pummeled his sides. Occasionally, he grunted from a blow, but remained steadfast in holding her tight and close. It felt like she beat him forever . . . until she could hardly hold herself upright.

Finally, she slumped her forehead against his chest, fingers coiling around his supple leather jacket, and she sobbed.

Spent, Shiloh eventually shuddered and drew in a ragged breath. She remained in his arms, wishing that the enclosure was some portal to a different life, a life without raw pain and shattered dreams.

Sudden awareness of what she had done embarrassed her. *You must look like a complete idiot.*

Brutus released her.

Humiliated, she couldn't bear to look at him. He moved out of view. Seconds hung like doom. Had he left? Would he leave her like Baseer had planned to? She swiped a hand under her dripping nose. Though an ache burned her neck, she dared not look up.

Then, his feet returned—large, booted feet. He stuffed another protein bar into her hand and waited as she gobbled it all and guzzled the water.

He held out his large black helmet. "We should get going."

She couldn't figure him out. Why didn't he hate her back? How had he controlled his anger at her accusations? He hadn't struck her once as she beat on him.

"Why?" Her own words snapped her from the stupor. She hauled her eyes to his. "Why aren't you angry?"

One corner of his mouth lifted. "We have a long ride ahead." His soft words held understanding as he lifted the helmet from her and set it on her head. He crouched closer, working with the strap and securing it. "Looks good." He straightened and looked at her with his incredibly blue eyes. "Ready?"

Something stirred within her as she nodded. No condemnation? No order to grow up and act like an adult? Her father would've said that.

He straddled the motorcycle, started the engine, and then glanced back at her. "By the way, it's Reece."

"What?"

"My name. Reece Jaxon. Not Brutus. Deal?"

Heat climbed into her cheeks. That, too, frustrated her. "Deal."

Hand planted on his muscular shoulder for balance, Shiloh swung her right leg over the back of the bike. She plastered her body against his. It wasn't romantic . . . just necessary. As *Reece* had proven last night, if she didn't sit close and tight, she'd end up as roadkill.

The engine revved, and the bike lurched forward. Shiloh wrapped her arms around his waist and gripped her own wrists for a tight hold.

Once the motorcycle settled into high speed, she relaxed a bit. Her thoughts tumbled over what had just happened. It was so unlike her to lose control like that. But she'd never felt so close to plummeting off a mental cliff.

Shiloh rested her head against his back so she wouldn't end up with another crick in her neck.

The whole time she'd hit and kicked out at him, he just stood there taking it. She felt so stupid, like a three-year-old child trying to beat up a high-schooler. The thought pried a smile from her unwilling lips. She sighed. He'd had no choice with Baseer. She knew that. And yet she had accused him of murder.

Reece possessed a steely quality she didn't have. How could he kill someone for the sake of his job? What he'd shouted at Baseer reverberated in her memory. She'd heard something in his words. Anger? Was he angry over what he'd been forced to do? Yes, but it was more than that. His voice revealed . . . what? Grief? Regret?

His leg bounced against hers as he downshifted. She peeked over his shoulder and spotted a road jutting off the highway. He aimed for it. At least it wasn't a turn. She wasn't sure she could take another screamer.

Again he upshifted. Shiloh tensed her arms, hugging him tighter as the propulsion tugged her back, the wind trying to rip her off the bike. Then just as suddenly, he downshifted again. Their speed must have been cut in half. She glanced over his shoulder at the speedometer. It read sixty but it felt like they were crawling. Then she saw the turn.

Reece looked back at her, their eyes meeting despite the shield. Oh no! She scooted closer and clung to him. Just as she felt confident she could hang on, the bike laid right. At first, she tried to pull left, but remembered and let herself ease into his back and follow his lead. *Trust. Trust. Trust him.* If he wanted her dead, he would have pumped her full of lead in Mumbai.

Within seconds he rose upright, and she followed him. Another half-hour passed before he steered onto a dirt road, slowing considerably. He eased the bike to a stop. With both legs stretched out, he balanced the Ducati as the engine idled.

Confused, she glanced around, wondering why they had stopped.

"You handled that corner beautifully," he said.

"Thanks."

Reece retrieved his cell, dialed, and put it to his ear. "Five miles out." After he stuffed the phone away, he glanced at her. "The terrain is rough from here on."

In other words, painful.

The engine sprang to life, numbing her legs with the vibration. During the next ten minutes as they bounced their brains senseless, including six terrifying seconds when they went airborne after taking a small incline too fast, Shiloh wondered if she'd ever walk again without a limp. As the road straightened, Reece picked up speed. Would this ever end?

Dark movement blurred to her right. She glanced back, her pulse spiking at the sight of another biker burning up the road behind them.

There was no way to warn Brutus. He must have noticed, too, because he upshifted, increasing speed. He bent closer to the bike. She leaned forward to stay with him and then peeked back.

Unbelievably, their pursuer had gained on them. Whoever he was, he'd have to keep both hands on the handlebars, so he couldn't shoot. Right? The black-clad rider pulled even with them.

Reece dodged trees, downshifted, and spun the bike around, whipping Shiloh's mind into a mural of colors and chaos. They stopped. Hard. She looked for the other rider but instead saw a half-dozen men step from the woods with fully automatic weapons trained on them. Her heart skidded into her stomach.

She loosened her hold on her bike partner, but he seemed to think it was funny. Reece actually laughed!

A man ran toward them. Shiloh stiffened, recognizing the black rider. He gripped Reece's hand and pulled him close, patting his back, both men laughing.

"I creamed you!" the man practically yelled, jabbing his finger at Reece.

"Keep telling yourself that, Miller."

Awkwardly and on shaky legs, Shiloh pushed off the bike. Her knees almost buckled. The perimeter of men closed in.

Reece took his first breath that didn't feel like he needed pure oxygen. He turned to Shiloh and helped her with the helmet. Wide eyes met his, uncertainty blanketing her features.

"You okay?" He held her shoulder, waiting until she nodded.

"Were you followed?"

Reece shifted toward the voice and saw something in his friend's face that made him pause. What it was, he couldn't be sure. "Just this slow guy who thought he could beat my Ducati." He couldn't help but grin. It felt so good to be back among men he could trust.

Miller slapped Reece's chest. "Keep telling yourself that." He winked. Then snatched the helmet and tossed it to another man. "Stow the bike, Stick."

Reece shot the scrawny guy a silent thanks, then turned back to his friend. "Who's your medic?"

"Ron Hinck." Miller glanced back at Reece. "Did you take a bullet?"

"Both of us."

His buddy spun and started toward a building. "Come on."

"I'm fine." Shiloh said, her voice quiet.

"Won't hurt to check it out." Motioning for her to follow Miller, Reece noticed the way the men seemed dumbstruck, gawking at Shiloh as if she'd descended from heaven in a chariot of fire. He fell into step behind her and trailed her to the hut.

As they plodded up a worn path in the high brush, Miller pointed to the side. "We've got that hut set up for her. You'll be right next door." He dragged himself up over a boulder. "Hinck will be glad to have someone to play doctor with finally."

Half an hour later, Reece emerged from Hinck's tent. Gripping his right thigh, he hoped he could knead out the fire still shooting up his leg where the wound had been cleansed. "He's mean."

Miller nodded with a grin. "And you met him on a good day."

Reece looked at Shiloh, who sat on a log nearby, her shoulder bandaged. "How are you?"

She shrugged. "A graze."

"Come on." Miller stood. "Get some rest. You both look like you need it."

The screen door squawked as they stepped into the ten-by-twelve space.

"Gita cleaned it up." Miller stood in the middle of the cramped hut. "It's not the Mumbai Palace, but it'll keep you warm." His gaze moved to Shiloh. "Glad you made it out okay." He extended a hand. "Captain Cole Miller."

At the gleam in Miller's expression, Reece had a sudden urge to step closer to her but resisted. Shiloh's face still wore the telltale signs of fire and battle. She glanced between him and Cole.

"Yeah, I wouldn't trust him, either," Reece said. "Seriously, he's a good guy. Leader of these bunch of misfits."

"Captain?" Shiloh shook his hand then stuffed hers in the pockets of her jeans.

"Green Berets."

Shiloh wrinkled her brow. "Green Berets? What're you doing way up here?"

A sardonic grin pinched the corners of the man's eyes. "Besides clean lake water and no air pollution? Training the locals while their government looks the other way."

Miller slipped between them and strode to the door. "I'll get Gita. She can show you the showers."

Reece tossed her pack onto the bed made from leafy trees and most likely stuffed with feathers of local birds. In a GB camp, everything was local. "You'll be safe here, but it never hurts to stay on guard."

She whirled toward him. "You're leaving?" Panic streaked the edges of her eyes.

Surprised at what he heard in that simple question, Reece paused. She didn't want him to leave. She *feared* he would leave. "I'll never be more than fifty feet away. Clean up and get some rest. Then grab some grub."

"Oh." She seemed to relax. Her gaze shifted to the furnishings: the bed on one side, the chest sitting against the far wall. "Who's place is this?"

At the foot of the bed, she lifted the mosquito netting, and her fingers stroked the sheets.

"Probably one of the guys. I'm sure Gita changed the bedding," he said, hoping she heard the humor in his words.

"I'm not tired."

"Trust me, once you clean up, it'll hit you."

She turned and let out a long breath. "Maybe."

Did she have to look so vulnerable? So frail, not in a weak sort of way, but the kind that made him want to ensure she never left his sight again. "Grab fresh clothes, and I'll meet you outside."

Bathed in the early warmth of the morning, Reece lowered to a stump. Miller strode toward him with a young Hindu woman. "This is Gita, our resident cook, maid, and launderer. Not that we make her. She actually enjoys it."

Standing, Reece greeted her in Hindi, thanking her for the preparations for Shiloh. With a glance toward the hut, he wondered what was taking her so long. Just as he was about to explain her delay, she emerged with clothes tucked under one arm.

Gita smiled and half-bowed to Shiloh. "Shower?" She wrapped an arm around her and ushered her away, mumbling in broken English. Halfway across camp, Shiloh's gaze came back to him.

Impulse taunted him to sprint across the camp and escort her himself. Propriety and the dozen grunts scattered around the camp nailed his feet to the ground. He clamped his mouth shut.

"She looks shell-shocked." Miller slapped his gut as he walked past. "Let's get some grub, and you can tell me what happened."

Reece joined him in a small, covered kitchen area. A portable, generator-powered stove sat on a plank-top table. His friend moved to a bin, where he withdrew a small cup, poured something black from a thermos into it—could it be coffee?—then slid it across the table to Reece. "Have a sit and tell me about it."

With care, he eased onto the bench, hoping the bruises from Shiloh's meltdown didn't ache the way he expected them to. "Full-scale assault. RPGs, M4s, snipers—took out an entire train depot." Cradling the warm brew in his hands, he compartmentalized the action from the emotion.

"She lost her fiancé and his father, who I had to neutralize right in front of her. She didn't take that well."

"No kidding. What did the father do?"

"Aligned with whoever's after her. Tried to kill her."

Miller scooped eggs from a pan and slopped them onto a tin plate. "Most people can't take that much, but other than the dirt and grit, she looks like she's holding together okay."

"I hope she does." But he knew better. Her fight was gone. She moved robotically. Her little eruption on the road gave him hope that she might come through. Maybe that was expecting too much. With Khalid and Baseer dead, he didn't imagine she had very fond feelings toward him right now. As a matter of fact, the *I hate you. I hate you!* might be real. When she'd said it, he'd rationalized the words as remnants of her anger and pain. He wasn't sure anymore.

"Who's on her tail?"

Scooting the eggs around the plate, he grunted. "That's liquid. At first, everything pointed to the minister of defense."

Hands tucked into the pits of his arms, Miller balked, "Abdul?" He snickered. "He doesn't have the spine."

"I know, but the guy's in so deep, he can't see his way out."

"Deep? How so?"

"Sajjadi."

The casual smile on Miller's face vanished. "You got proof?"

"Enough to keep pushing." Reece scraped the plate as he finished off the eggs, grateful for the energy slowly working its way back into his limbs. He shoved the plate aside and scratched his head. "We need to lay low for a while. At least a week. Can you guys handle that?"

"No sweat. We're dug in pretty solid for now."

"Good." His gaze drifted to the place where Shiloh had disappeared into the woods with Gita. Running his tongue along his teeth, he wondered where this little mission would go from here. What else would he have to do to keep her alive?

"Who is she?"

Reece looked at his buddy. "Come again?"

"When you got off that bike and doted on her—"

"Doted?" Laughing, Reece dragged his legs out from under the table and settled back against the wood. He sipped his coffee. "She's an underwater archeologist caught up in the dead drop I was scoping."

Miller's eyes narrowed in thought. "Underwater? She's a diver?"

"Yep."

"Impressive. No wonder you're so attentive."

With a snort, Reece let his gaze probe the woods again. Should he check on her? Surely Miller's team would be on guard. He tensed, hoping the guys kept their distance and weren't playing peeping Tom.

"Stop worrying. Women take forever to get ready."

"She's not like that."

That drew up one of Miller's blond eyebrows. "Wanna explain that statement, soldier?"

"Not to you." Reece laughed and bent forward, his elbows on his knees. "She beat the tar out of me a few hours ago."

"Decompressing. Good sign."

Nodding, Reece ordered his attention to remain on the dirt caked to his boots. *I hate you. I hate you!* Her words rang as gongs against his conscience. But it only made him more determined to end this chaos, solve the case, and get her on the first jumbo jet back to the States.

"Her name's Shiloh Blake."

Miller shrugged.

"Remember Jude Blake?"

"Who doesn't?" Miller's eyes widened. "Wait. You aren't telling me—"

"His daughter."

Miller let out a low whistle. "Which probably means you have half of Langley breathing down your neck."

"More like breathing fire." Wrestling with the memory of holding her while she blew her top, Reece roughed a hand over his mouth and face. "And the killers after her always seem one step ahead of us."

"Insider?"

He squinted back toward the woods. "Possibly." A yawn sifted through him, freeing a ton of weariness and aches—and body odor. He cringed at himself.

"You look like you need some rest."

"I need a shower more."

"Well, it's free now."

Reece snapped his head toward the path, automatically rising to his feet as Shiloh walked through the camp with Gita. The sight tugged a smile out of him. With the dirt and ash washed off, her face shone under the twinkling of the morning sun peeking through the branches. Her reddish-brown hair hung darkly down her back, a loose curl draping her soft face.

Gita ushered her charge to the kitchen bench, served her a plate of food, took her dirty clothes, and then hurried away with a promise to return.

"Gita made the grub," Cole said, standing over her with a smirk. "So it's edible, unlike anything else the men cook up."

Shiloh bounced her gaze from him to Reece.

Miller thumped his arm. "Weren't you going to clean up? Here we have a beautiful woman in camp, and you look like the beggar's dog."

Oh, Reece could have punched him for that. With a smirk, he leaned toward Shiloh. "Don't trust anything this man says. He's been known to con princes out of their crowns."

"Hey," Miller said. "Prince Albert was busy in a race. What can I say?"

A small smile.

"I'll be back." Could he leave her? If he sat here reeking and hawking over her, Miller would never let him live it down. "Get some rest. I'll wake you for dinner." He touched her shoulder. If his buddy weren't here, he'd wait until she tucked in before heading down to the showers. As it was, he felt Miller's eyes boring into the back of his skull.

With his heart still sitting on the bench across from Shiloh, Reece tromped off, grabbed his rucksack, and headed down the path. What was happening? Was he going soft? In his gut, he couldn't stand the thought of her going through any more. Yet he knew this ordeal was far from over. He'd held her hours ago as she worked through the first layer of emotion elicited by the traumatic situation. And suddenly, he wished he could do it again and make this entire nightmare go away.

Under the cold, drizzling shower spray, he let his mind wander to the train station. Ending Baseer Khan's life. Palms to the wall, he hung his head. *God, forgive me.* While he knew he'd acted out of necessity, he wondered if she could ever understand. Some people couldn't. God hadn't designed every person to fill the role he worked in protecting U.S. interests. A tricky but vital game. Still, the regret ran deep over everything Shiloh had witnessed. Khan knew what he was doing. Shiloh probably wouldn't understand or forgive him.

Worse, she believed Reece a murderer.

16

RUBY RED GLEAMED ON HER FINGER, A SPARK OF EARLY MORNING SUNLIGHT catching the crimson jewel in Khalid's ring. Shiloh's stomach knotted. Should she have left it in her pack? She almost had, but *not* wearing the ring seemed like a cruel betrayal of the man who had given it to her. Yet more than two days after the attack, the painful reminder screamed at her as she sat on the grass overlooking a placid lake.

Focused on the body of water that spread out before her, she twisted the ring until the stone pressed into her palm. She unlaced her boots, set them aside, and rolled up her pant legs. Feet immersed in the cool liquid, she squinted at the sparkling lake. If only the sight of water didn't remind her of the attack on Mumbai bay and the man who had died in her arms at the train station.

It seemed like a bad dream. Holding him, screaming her declarations of love, words that rang hollow in her own ears. What kind of person withholds their words of love until after someone dies? She didn't even care about the Pacific Rim Challenge anymore. It felt empty and worthless without Khalid. Gentle water lapped at her ankles.

No, she couldn't allow herself to remember. Last night she had awakened twice from her nightmares. Reece had come both times to check on her. Just his voice calling through the screen door had soothed her tremors. Even now as he talked with Captain Miller, she could hear his voice a couple dozen feet away and felt secure for it . . . for the sternness, the resolution.

She felt bad for screaming at him yesterday. For hitting him and acting the fool. But he didn't yell back at her or tell her to grow up. He just let her beat on him.

Swallowing, she brushed a strand of hair from her face, watching as several of the men swam and played football in the lake.

Splat! Water splashed up at her. She blinked—immediately shoving aside the fear that knifed through her—and spotted a football at her feet. It hovered on the surface, spinning.

"Toss it back!"

Uncertain at first, Shiloh lifted the ball and palmed the hide. In the middle of the lake, arms flailed, trying to persuade her to send it to them. She picked a guy nicknamed Map and fired the ball at him. Like a trout swimming upstream, the largest of the group dove through the air, clipping Stick and knocking him over before intercepting the ball meant for Map.

Map gaped at her. "She's on my team!"

Back on his feet and shaking the water from his hair, Stick groaned. "Not fair!"

"Come on, Shiloh. You can take Stick's position." Map waved at her. "Bronco and I will gladly take you over him."

"Hey!" The scrawny guy swooshed water at Map.

Playing games. Laughing. All things Khalid would never do again. The thought wrapped around her, tightening. "Sorry, not up to it."

A chorus of objections and pleas pushed her from the bank. She hurried up the bank and crested the small hill. Her gaze connected with Reece's. He looked so steady and intense, as if he saw right through her actions to the pain drowning her. Heart heavy and aching, she hesitated. *How could he be so unswerving?* She felt as though she'd been knocked to the ground and would never rise. But he just stood there . . . waiting. Waiting for what?

Breaking their look, she rushed to her hut and stepped inside a mural of browns. Brown bed. Brown floors. Brown chair. Brown desk. Brown tarp ceiling. Dreary, dull brown that felt constricting and choked her. Yet it was the only place she could be alone. She slumped onto the bed and sat with her legs crisscrossed. Closed in and shut off. She'd go crazy if she had to stay here. Every man in camp had tiptoed around her last night while she ate curried chicken. She hated the pretense, the awkwardness.

The engagement ring poked her hand and conscience. Without another thought, she tugged off the ring and tucked it in the side zippered pocket of her pack. She dragged the pack to her lap and dug through the contents, searching for the small stone lamp. Where had it gone? Upending the pack, she dumped everything onto the bed and sorted through it.

Her hand grazed the navy sweatshirt. Did it still carry his smell? She lifted it and took a whiff, and smiled. Yeah, definitely.

A rapping at the door startled her.

"Come in." She tossed down the hoodie and stuffed her things back into the pack.

Boots thudded across the floorboards and a body cut off the light from outside. "Did you bring shorts?"

Her gaze shot up. Reece stood a few paces away. "Uh, yeah." The sweatshirt. *Please don't notice it.* How would she explain that she still had it after he said to toss it?

"Good. Get changed, and I'll meet you by the lake."

She faltered. "The lake? You mean, like to swim?"

Arms folded over his chest, he waited. Again with the waiting. What was with him?

"I'm sorry, I don't want to. I can't . . ." The rest of the words caught in her throat. *Not without Khalid.*

"Maybe you misunderstood." He lowered his arms, planting his hands on his hips like a drill sergeant. "I didn't ask."

"Excuse me?" It would be a lot easier to get angry and indignant if he glared or yelled or *reacted* like a human being instead of a robot without feelings. But he didn't. He just stood there like a pillar.

Then again, she wasn't the compliant type. Even Khalid knew that. Did this brute? "What if I refuse?"

For a moment his expression was blank, and then . . . a smile? Did he really smile? "I'll carry you down there and throw you in myself."

She froze. "You wouldn—" Shiloh gulped back the words. She knew without a doubt that he would. He absolutely would. And he'd enjoy it. She yanked the drawstring on her pack, her eyes catching sight of the sweatshirt. "Just leave me alone, okay?"

He clomped closer and without a word, he reached down and lifted the hoodie, *his* hoodie.

A blaze shot up her neck and into her cheeks. She could only pray the dim natural light didn't give away her humiliation. Regardless, no way would she meet his gaze. Even when he handed the shirt back, she avoided his eyes and jabbed the hoodie into her pack.

Then he reached down and lifted the coin—the one Baseer had pressed into her hand just before he died. "Is this what Khan gave you?"

She nodded.

"What did he say when he gave it to you?"

With a lazy shrug, she said, "Gerard Moore, at least, that's what it sounded like." She forced her eyes to his. "Do you recognize the name?"

"No." He handed the coin back. "You have three minutes to meet me at the lake." Some of the edge had left his voice as he walked out.

The screen door slammed behind him. He'd left no room for argument, as if she should act like an obedient puppy. Shiloh grabbed her bag by the harness, flung around, and sent it sailing out the door after him.

"Two minutes, fifty-five, Blake!"

Shiloh plopped onto the bed and dug her fingers into her scalp as she stifled the scream crawling up her throat. She would not be ordered around like some recruit. The men here might be soldiers, but she wasn't. And he wasn't in charge of her.

Cringing, she realized how much that sounded like *you're not the boss of me*. She huffed. Well, he wasn't. Accosted by the humiliation of being hurled into the lake in front of all those men, she dug through her pack and found her jean shorts and a black tank top. Shiloh changed quickly behind the curtain rigged for privacy.

When her foot hit the boards of the steps outside her hut, she glanced up and spotted Reece stalking toward her. She didn't know whether to be irritated or laugh. He looked ready to kill.

He stopped short, surprise lighting up his expression. After a once-over, he nodded, the intensity returning to his eyes. "Let's go." He had that military pivot down pat.

Feeling like an insolent child, she stalked behind him. Where was the team? Had everyone moved down to the water? She wasn't going to let him humiliate her in front of a dozen men. She slowed, her stomach weaving into knots. *Go back, Shiloh.* Her foot hit a rock and pitched her forward. If she didn't pay attention, maybe she'd wrench her leg and have a legitimate excuse to head back to her hut.

Trudging down the path, around the line of trees, she rounded the corner. Glimmering waters wreathed her with peace. She shook it off, unwilling to let anything ease her conscience. Khalid was dead. As dive partners, they'd spent so much time together in the water.

Reece stood on the bank, his feet already in the water. "Swim out to the buoy and back."

She paused several paces away. Bobbing in the distance, the buoy taunted her. "I'm not swimming."

He didn't move. "To the buoy and back."

"Maybe you misunderstood," she said, tossing his words back. "I'm not swimming."

One step closer. "I didn't ask. This isn't a request."

"Look, Brutus, you're not—" She clamped her mouth shut, realizing she'd nearly spouted off about who was the boss. "I'm not going. That's it."

"Reece."

"I know who you are. But Brutus fits better."

He quirked an eyebrow, his eyes sparkling. On the incline, he shifted—one leg behind and one in front as he squinted at her. "Shiloh, you need to get back in the water."

She held his gaze, lost for a second in how warm and inviting his eyes were. She let her attention drift to the glass-like lake. "I can't." Too many memories.

He inched closer. "You have to overcome this. The sooner, the better."

Again she looked into his eyes, feeling their warmth all the way to the pit of her stomach. Maybe he was right. She'd let the fear drown her, disabling the exhilaration she always found in the water. So, yeah, he had a point. "Maybe."

A half smile. "Good."

She let him lead her to the edge of the water. "We're alone," she mumbled, glancing around.

"Yeah, they had a training exercise, but we've only got a couple of hours." He crossed his arms, grabbed the edges of his shirt, and pulled it off. Shiloh averted her gaze, heat rushing into her cheeks. He nodded at her.

"What?"

"You first."

"Oh." Wiggling her toes, she watched the water and sand squish between them. She slowly walked in, allowing the water to seep over her ankles . . . her calves. She felt his assessment. Was she too slow for his liking? Finally, she folded her arms. "I can't do this with you watching."

Without a word, he shallow dived into the water. A huge fountain of white foam roared up from where he impacted.

This was her chance. She struggled for footing and then hurried back to the grassy knoll. She spotted Gita, standing atop the hill. Shiloh waved and smiled. The woman waved back—and then her eyes widened.

Shiloh turned. Reece barreled toward her. He bent and flopped her over his shoulder like a sack of potatoes.

"No!" she gasped, wriggling and pounding his back. "Put me down!"

He jogged into the water.

"Put me down! NO!" she screamed as her body flew through the air.

The surface loomed before her. She inhaled deeply and snapped her mouth shut just milliseconds before she went under. Cold glory enraptured her. Yet fury drove her to the lake floor. Serve him right if she drowned. Make him sweat? The idea curled around her like a water moccasin.

But he didn't come for her. Rising, she promised herself he wouldn't forget this. He'd pay. And she'd make sure he paid good. She burst from the lake and whipped her hair from her face, searching the area around her. Hands skimming the water, she turned in circles. Closer to the lake now, Gita laughed.

"Where is he?" Shiloh shouted.

The woman shrugged.

Shiloh's legs whipped out from under her. Underwater, she fishtailed, probing the depths. *There!* She swam toward Reece. He torpedoed away. Up for air, she batted the strands that drooped into her face. She kept her movements small as she circled, hoping to spot him before—

"No!"

Shiloh spun at Gita's warning, but not in time.

Lurching, Reece grabbed her shoulders and dunked her, wishing he could laugh. When her face went under, he noticed her mouth open and released her. Wading a few feet away, he watched her sputter and cough.

"I'll kill you!" she growled, pinching the bridge of her nose. "You idiot. You could've drowned me."

Good. Her mind wasn't on the fear. "You're too good of a swimmer for me to take you that easily."

Although she was good, Shiloh would need some tips on aquatic games. He saw her plotting, pretending her eyes were stinging worse than they were. Maybe in chlorinated water, she'd be in pain, but right now, she was buying time. He'd wait. Let her think her plan could work. She would launch at him—her hands going for the jugular probably. She didn't know he was a former Navy SEAL. He'd been trained for this.

Shiloh dropped below the surface.

His heart skipped a beat at the unexpected move. He saw her slithering toward the far side where the reeds clogged the water. At least they were in the mountains, or she'd be swimming in sewage.

Lowering himself so only his eyes were above water, Reece watched the ripples and bubbles, effectively monitoring her movement. Reeds swayed. Then . . . nothing.

Curiosity piqued, he eased himself under. Nothing. Where did she go? He peeked above. How had she—

A swift knock against his skull sent him spiraling into the water. He reached. Grabbed her shirt. They wrangled. She wiggled free.

He rose to the top and broke the surface, waiting.

She erupted, shouting, "Ha! Nailed you!"

"You're a fast learner." With firm strokes, he moved himself farther out in the water. "But can you do it again? Without the reeds for distraction?"

Challenge glinted in her blue-grey eyes.

Reece dove straight to the very bottom. Almost right away, he spotted her attack. He torpedoed out to the buoy, pausing halfway. Her lithe body streamed through the lake less than ten feet away. *Atta, girl.* Once within reach, the buoy would give her a moment to catch her breath. This was a walk in the park for him. Hand resting on the metal bobber, he rose and waited.

Shiloh was right behind him. She poked her head up and splashed him!

He shook his head, wiping the lake water from his face. "You're a brat."

She chuckled and held onto the contraption. Angled around, she clung to the buoy—her body bent in half with her toes nearly above the water. "So, you tired?"

"What?"

With a huge push, she shot up and dove in. Using a wicked breast stroke, she sliced through the water with great speed.

Unbelievable. He'd taken that break for her! He grinned. Then with butterfly strokes, he barreled after her, chiding himself for once again underestimating her . . . but she was injured. Had been through a traumatic experience.

He treaded water and glanced toward the shore. She wasn't more than eight feet ahead. What he wouldn't do for a prop to scuttle past her. Pumping his arms again, he prayed he could catch her, or he'd never live this down. With each rise, he measured the distance, glad to find himself gaining steadily.

Closer . . . he had to catch her. Miller would love this.

His finger grazed flesh—a foot.

Rising one last time, he found himself almost even with her. Arms wrapped around her waist, he pulled her down and then burst up. Together, they were instantly bathed in the warmth of the Indian sun. Slick rocks beneath their feet made traction difficult. Shiloh wobbled and slipped, a laugh seeping from her chest.

Reece couldn't help but grin as she panted and sloshed toward the bank. She gripped her knees and bent to catch her breath.

With a hand on her back, he chuckled. "You're a she-devil, you know that?" Inhaling deeply, he waited for his heart rate to slow. Then let his breath out.

Shiloh dragged herself upright, her head tilted back. "I haven't swum that hard in years. I thought I would drown trying to beat you." She eased herself down, sitting so only her head and shoulders remained above the water.

Something swished toward her.

What was—

Shiloh sucked in a breath. "There's something in the water." She scooted around.

"Keep still." Reece tensed, uncertain what sort of hairy creature swam this lake.

She yelped.

Like a flash the furry animal darted upward. It sprang toward Shiloh and latched onto her shoulder. With a scream, she batted it off. The thing scampered onto the bank and sat staring at them, brown eyes blinking.

Hand clamped on her neck, Shiloh spun and gaped. "A monkey? In the water?"

Reece noticed a red trail of blood sliding down her neck. "You okay?" He sloshed closer.

"Just a scratch." Shiloh winced.

"Let me see." He lifted her hand from the scratch—she faltered, but he caught her and held her in place. Sure enough, a two-inch scratch. "You're up-to-date on your shots, right?"

"Of course." She frowned and shrugged away from him. "Can't believe that thing was swimming!"

He cleared the hair from her shoulder to keep it from irritating the wound. "The scratch isn't deep, but get Hinck to put something on it. The waters here aren't polluted like the lowlands or cities, but you'll want to make sure." The stitches in her shoulder caught his attention. Gently, he fanned his thumb over them. "Your stitches held, despite that killer breaststroke."

"I had someone to beat." Blue-grey eyes skidded into his, and she froze.

His hand slid down her arm. The way she seemed to shudder under his touch sent warmth through his chest. Stalled, his heart tried to recapture a normal rhythm. Her gaze tiptoed around his. He brushed the strands of hair from the side of her face, drawing her eyes to his again. So incredible. Her skin was so soft . . . eyes so beguiling. Her lips drew him closer.

Snap out of it, Jaxon!

The mental stab jerked him back. What was he doing? He took a step away, only then realizing his arm had been around her waist.

"I see you two have met Aras."

Reece whipped his head toward the voice. Miller stood with the monkey and a look that said he'd seen everything.

"That beast nearly sliced my neck." Shiloh trudged from the lake, stomping her feet on the bank. She wrung her hair, acting as if nothing had just happened.

Reece wished he could say the same thing. His buddy wouldn't say a word about this. He'd wait for Reece to bring it up, which he wouldn't. Ever. Right now, right here, he left whatever misguided emotional rebound had taken place.

"We thought of dyeing her hair blue so she couldn't sneak up on us. Besides, Aras is a little wild. We think it would fit her personality," Miller said, walking up the hill with Shiloh.

Reece appreciated his friend giving him space. Unable to follow and wanting to recover from the insanity that had blindsided him, he dove into the water, ready to beat his mind and body into submission.

An hour later, he sat on the grass, limbs aching as he studied the sunset. What kind of jerk takes advantage of a woman less than thirty-six hours after her fiancé and his father are killed? He needed to back off. Way off. Shiloh's heart belonged to another man, and Reece had no business encroaching on that. Even if he had a suspicion she'd talked herself into that engagement, she must have some pretty deep feelings to be willing to give marriage a try. Then there was the whole matter of faith. From all appearances, she had a beef with both her heavenly Father and her earthly father.

Obviously, the magic he'd sensed between himself and the amazing Shiloh Blake had been one-sided. Her reaction to him in the water—Stockholm Syndrome. Had to be. She was vulnerable and shattered.

He vowed not to cross the line again. He had once before. Visions of Chloe swarmed his mind, stinging reminders of how he'd failed her, failed the mission, failed the agency, failed himself. He'd gotten too hung up in what he thought was love. And she died.

This time he wouldn't make that mistake. He snatched his shirt and stomped back to camp. In his hut, he grabbed clean clothes, only then noticing his secure cell light blinking. He and Nielsen had agreed on no contacts until the dust settled. It hadn't even been thirty-six hours. Flipping open the phone, he tensed.

17

HE'D ALMOST KISSED HER! HOW SHE WANTED HIS KISS.

And that was the problem. She was ashamed of herself. Khalid hadn't even been dead three days. The enigmatic thing choking her reason was how she'd never wanted Khalid's kisses. He'd kissed her twice since arriving in India. Each time made her tense.

Not with Reece. How could that be? She didn't even know the man the way a girl should before something like that.

"Shiloh? You with me?" Reece leaned in, staring from his spot next to her at the picnic table.

Only then did she notice the camp had gone mysteriously quiet.

"S-sorry." Clearing her throat, she tried to gather the remnants of conversation from her subconscious but came up blank. Did he know how unnerving his presence was? She didn't want to look at him. Didn't want to talk to him.

He straddled the bench, facing her as she cupped a bowl of stew. "I have to leave to take care of some things."

Her courage failed. She studied the murky meal with chunks. "You said you wouldn't leave me." She hated the desperation in her own voice, but it consumed her. "Fifty feet—you said you'd never be more than fifty feet from me."

"Shiloh . . ." The way he whispered her name pushed her to her feet.

He caught her hand and then slowly released it.

In the distance a storm rumbled, mirroring the one in her heart. She needed to get away from him. She started toward her hut.

Reece followed and tugged her around. Quietly, he closed the space between them. "I would never leave you here if I felt there was danger. Miller is my equal in every way."

"No," she snapped. "He's not you." Aware that the guys in the camp pretended not to listen, she fled toward her only sanctuary.

"I'll be back Friday."

She waved over her shoulder and let the door clang shut. No, Miller wasn't anything like Reece. He hadn't been there when Reece saved her. The Green Beret's interest wasn't vested in keeping her alive.

On the edge of her bed, she bent and buried her face in her hands. It felt as if God was playing Russian roulette with her life. How many bullets were left? Which one would take her life? She'd already taken one to the heart. The bullet had Reece Jaxon's name carved in it.

Never had she felt this way about Khalid. The revelation burned. How could she know Khalid all her life, not have those feelings—that suffocating thrill—but know Reece less than two weeks and long to be tucked into the safety of his arms?

But I loved Khalid! Tears trickled down her cheeks. She eased herself against the mattress, grateful for the release in her muscles as her body reclined. Through the screen door, she spotted the captain talking with Reece, who'd already rolled his bike from the shelter.

An ache squeezed her heart. *Please don't leave.*

Helmet on, Reece jabbed the key into the engine. The venomous roar punctured the quiet of the camp, drawing Shiloh to the door. *Please.*

The engine revved. So did her heart.

Hand on the screen, Shiloh struggled not to push it open. Reece wouldn't leave her, would he? He wasn't like her father.

Reece glanced in her direction. He bobbed a single goodbye, let the engine rip, and disappeared down the road, swallowed by the elements.

She pushed herself back to the bed and lay listening to rain splat against the tarp. He'd withdrawn his kiss. Why? Scattered thoughts mingled with the rain. The way he'd protected her, yet pushed her to be better and smarter.

Captain Miller knocked and entered. "Storm's coming. Pretty rough one. We'll be fine."

Why didn't that reassure her? "Thanks." What about Reece? Would he wipe out on those gut-wrenching turns he loved so much?

"He'll be okay." The captain's gentle words drew her gaze. "And he'll be back."

"So he said."

"Might want to put that blind down so your gear doesn't get wet. Matter of fact—" He clomped to the window and secured the shade. When he turned, he tripped over the hooded sweatshirt, paused as if he knew whose it was, and then set it aside. "Well, stay dry."

She eyed the hoodie. "Thanks."

He hesitated at the door and looked back at her. Shiloh stood and folded her arms. "What is it, Captain?"

"Nothing."

"You recognized the sweatshirt."

A sheepish grin tugged at his lips. "I gave it to him one night when the temperature dipped," he said. "I figured he threw it out."

"We were being chased, and he put it on me so we could slip past our pursuers." Embarrassed, Shiloh lifted it and ran the string between her fingers. "He told me to throw it away when I got to the hotel."

"But you didn't."

Shiloh laid it on the bed and shrugged.

"Look, it's none of my business—"

"No, it's not."

"Understood." He headed to the door.

"Captain, I'm sorry." She hung her head. "Please . . ." Though she might not want to hear what he had to say, she couldn't be rude. "Say what's on your mind."

Miller shifted. "Jaxon hasn't always been the brightest bulb in the pack regarding women. He got hurt real bad once. I think—" He snorted and laughed. "No, I know he likes you. I've never seen him, well, I didn't mean to snoop, but I came running when I heard you scream at the lake. I saw the two of you. Reece hasn't ever lost control. Ever."

"Lost control? Is that what you call it?"

"He stays locked in a tight box, protecting everyone—including himself. He's one of the CIA's best. He trains their operatives. Two years ago, he lost a girl in an op gone bad. I can see him trying to find his way where you're concerned, but I think it scares him."

Shiloh laughed. "Scared? Reece isn't afraid of anything."

Captain Miller's green eyes studied her. "Except you."

Pounding rain hammered the Mercedes. Ali squinted through the tinted windows as the vehicle slid around a corner and the warehouse came into view. Roiling anxiety wiggled through his gut. He swallowed. This had to be taken care of before things spun out of control. The driver slowed the car as they drew closer; his phone rang.

Ali bent forward, straining to hear what his man mumbled into the phone over the din of the storm. "What did he say?"

"We're clear."

The car pulled into a tunnel. Silence devoured the interior, a startling difference after the driving rain. In black, two guards stalked toward the vehicle and opened the door. Uzis rested against their arms.

Ali climbed out. Dust seemed to cling to the air, thickened by the rain. A former factory with an open train tunnel, the building had ceilings that soared upward a hundred feet. Walls climbed three stories. Trusses hung open and rusted. He coughed and glanced at the two thugs. "Where are they?"

"This way," the bigger of the two grumbled and led him through a doorway.

Ali found himself in a narrow hall that led to at least twenty offices. Straight ahead, the hall dumped into a smaller open area. Black film covered the windows lining both sides. Rain thumped against the glass.

In the center, ropes restrained a woman slumped over in a steel chair. Blond hair escaped the brown hood covering her face. With a wicked grin at Ali, one of her captors rammed his fist into her head. She groaned.

"Do not kill her," Ali growled.

"She is not cooperating."

Clothed only in a blouse that had been ripped to shreds, the woman had red burn marks that marred her arms and legs. Disgust swept through Ali. "You raped her?"

The man sneered. "I was told to break her."

"You fool!" Ali whipped out his cell. "No doubt you have left DNA for the Americans to collect. And what good will this do if you are found and taken into custody? Do you really believe you could survive their interrogation methods?"

The sneer lost its gleam.

Turning away, Ali waited for the call to connect.

"What do you know?" a voice asked.

"Your fools are not effective."

"Tell them to do whatever is necessary. I must know who that girl is and what she knows. She has contacts. I want names. We will make these American infidels pay."

"We are endangering our operation. The longer she is here, the more chance they have to find us."

"I do not care how long it takes. If you must move her, do so. Then kill her when you have what I need."

Ali held his breath. This entire operation worsened with every day.

"Do you understand, Abdul? Do you understand what this means to your family and to our country?"

Threats. Always the way of his contact. "Yes."

"Good. I would not hesitate to make an example of you."

"That will not be necessary."

"Then get what you need and kill her."

Sheets of rain blurred his vision. Reece squinted low against the Ducati as he roared toward Mumbai. He activated the infrared vision on his helmet's visor and increased his speed, but not nearly as much as he wanted. He'd never get there if the rain didn't let up. The mission had a short timetable, and the elements were fighting him. With every mile, his foul mood increased.

The oil-slick roads slowed him to a crawl at times. His back wheel slid to the side. The bike wobbled. Heart crashing, he accelerated in the hope of regaining control. Finally, the bike steadied out.

The call for the mission had come less than fifteen minutes after he'd nearly shattered protocol on his primary objective.

He hated the look in Shiloh's eyes as he left. He wanted to tell her why he was leaving, that it wasn't her.

Shiloh's face flashed into his memory. He revved the engine and left her image behind. Refusing to be distracted, he mentally went over the Intel relay. An internal contact had notified the American embassy of a potential hit. Without intervention, they'd lose an asset. The dangers for covert operatives never went away. He glanced at the GPS. Less than ten miles out.

Father, protect me and give me wisdom.

Lightning knifed the sky, and bright white exploded through his field of vision. The helmet immediately compensated. He silently thanked the engineer who had designed the technology. Otherwise, he'd be smeared across the pavement.

Following the rail tracks would lead him to the last known location of the asset. Unfortunately, because of the remote site, Reece doubted he'd find anyone worth interrogating. He knew exactly what he'd find out here—grunts, pawns, and a lot of brutality. Tension wound a tight coil in his gut.

With each layer of this game peeled, the complexity grew. He'd had enough. Enough circles. Enough targets.

A couple of miles out, he downshifted and aimed for the small house in the middle of a field. Behind it sat a large steel building, like a garage turned workshop. Dodging puddles, he took care in not getting stuck. His visor gave him thermal readouts. One signature. He rolled to a stop ten meters from the door and waited.

A tall, lanky man emerged from the house. "'Bout time you showed up." Heath Whitcomb, an operative he'd worked with on many missions, carried a sniper rifle.

Grinning, Reece climbed off his bike and walked it toward the house. He stowed it inside, shut the door, and jogged toward the shop. Sheltered from the rain, he still felt a chill seeping through his wet clothes. At the tailgate of a black Humvee, they strapped smart armor onto their chests and wired themselves for the operation.

"Hop in." Heath closed the rear hatch. The thick, reinforced windows thudded hard against the ten-inch hull.

As they tore out of the garage and down the jarring road, Reece checked his Glock. "What's the word?"

Heath shook his head. "Spotter just got there. Once he's set up, he'll report." His gloved hand squeezed the steering wheel.

"You have the extraction point?"

"Wired in just minutes—" Heath held up his hand and pressed it to a remote hanging around his neck. "Go ahead," he whispered into the mic.

Field after boring field of grain and fruit orchards whizzed past. Low clouds danced along the horizon, rolling and tumbling. Thunder shook the vehicle.

"He's in place," Heath said to Reece. "Seven tangos. Three outside, one in a vehicle, three inside. Target's inside and bound."

"Point of entry?"

"Best possible is the side. One door. In and out."

"Worst?"

"Front—wide opening, bottlenecked hall leading to destination."

Reece assimilated the intel. What were the chances they'd get the easy route? Would this be the last mission he worked with Heath? Or would they succeed and part ways until another hot spot erupted? He prayed it was the latter.

"Just play it smart."

"Smart gets people killed." Reece grabbed the paint crayon from his pocket and greased up, drawing long, black lines over his forehead and down his cheeks. He smeared the OD-green greasepaint over his face.

A block later, they turned into a building. Once they removed the weapons from the hold, they climbed two flights of stairs, then up a metal wall-mounted ladder to an opening in the ceiling. On the roof, they lay flat at the edge of the building next to Whitcomb's spotter.

"Two more vehicles just pulled up." The man peered through his binoculars. "They've added five more to the game."

Reece took the high-powered lenses and focused on the building across the tracks. He made out four tangos in a small room anchored between two large, open areas. In the area to the right, two stood with weapons aimed at the objective. He scanned the perimeter.

"We need to hit them hard and fast."

"No time for quiet." Heath tossed Reece the keys to the Hummer. "Pick us up at the cross-street one mile away."

Back downstairs, Reece climbed behind the wheel of the armored SUV and stuffed his M4 next to him. He positioned the vehicle so he could rocket onto the street. The revving engine made him wish this thing handled like the Ducati, but he needed the reinforced steel and glass, or nobody would come out of this alive. Tires squalling, he held the Hummer in place. Finally, he let her rip.

The SUV lunged out the open-bay door, hit a ditch, and flew over the tracks. Landing with a jolt, he steadied the M4.

An explosion inside the building turned darkness to light. Reece hoped they'd hit the location where the four had assembled. He punched the pedal and aimed for the open room. The Humvee barreled through the wall. Metal folded like an accordion. One panel spiraled ahead of him. Guards dove to the side.

He whipped the vehicle to the right of the asset, circled, and squealed to a stop on her right. With a punch, he shoved the door open, grabbing his M4.

Thud. A body fell into view from behind the SUV. Reece knew the guy probably had one sniper bullet through the skull.

Clearing the room, he felt every nerve tingle. Where was he? Where did the other one go? A whimper dragged his gaze to the bound-and-gagged woman. Her half-naked body bore witness to the hell she'd endured. Reece jerked open the passenger door.

"Tango at your seven," Heath warned.

Reece snapped to his left and fired. The second guard slumped to the floor. Smoke snaked into the area behind the body. The moorings groaned against the fire ravaging the building.

"Move it, move it! They're heading your way."

He tugged the hood off her head. Angry welts and grossly swollen eyes marred her once-beautiful face. Kneeling at her side, he monitored the environment while reassuring her. "Everything's fine now."

With his folding Emerson knife, he sliced through her bonds. Hurrying, yet taking care not to aggravate her injuries, he scooped her into his arms and shuttled her into the back of the Humvee.

"Package in custody." Just as he stuffed himself behind the wheel, Reece spotted three armed men in the doorway.

A ball of fire torpedoed toward him, felling the enemy.

Reece gunned the engine. His stomach clenched as they bolted through the flames that danced over the armor plating.

Ping! Ping-ping!

"Shooter spotted . . . neutralized," the voice in his headset said.

A mile later he flickered the lights and pulled to the edge of the road. Heath and the spotter emerged and climbed into the SUV. By the time they returned to the house, a Little Bird waited, rotors whirring.

Heath raced to the back and removed his gear, leaving Reece to take care of the former hostage. He hopped out of the SUV and opened her door.

Her head lolled toward him.

"How you doing?"

She gave a soft snort and shook her head.

"That good, eh?" Reece lifted her into his arms again and transferred her to the bird. A medic immediately slid an IV into her arm. She'd spend a few weeks at Landstuhl Air Force Base in Germany recuperating before she returned to the action. She'd survived, and that impressed him. "Take care. We need you back in the field."

Through gritted teeth, she braved a smile despite her split lips. "How's Shiloh?"

"Wondering about you."

"Take care of her."

"Will do, Edie."

18

SERENITY SOAKED INTO HER MUSCLES AS SHE GLIDED THROUGH THE QUIET lake. Rolling onto her back, she gazed up at the sky, still veiled in pre-dawn hues. Nothing imbued her with peace so completely as swimming. The tension of the water pressing against her, then relinquishing to her movements. The cooling touch of the liquid caressing her aching limbs and heart.

Turning onto her stomach, she swam out to the buoy. Holding onto the side, she remembered the way she'd nearly beaten Reece. He always challenged her, left her wanting to be better, smarter, faster.

Prettier.

She flinched. Would he have withdrawn his kiss if she'd been prettier? Is that what made him hold back? Or was it his job—dedication to the call and all that?

Self-hatred chided her for pining after a man she barely knew. Yet she felt as though she had known him forever. He definitely knew everything about her. And it hadn't taken him ten years to develop that uncanny ability to counter everything she said or did before she could speak or act. Still, while she hadn't learned to read him, she did have a good sense of what to expect from Reece. For example, if he had returned by now, he would probably be standing on the shoreline watching her.

She let herself look. *Idiot.* Of course he wasn't there. Lowering herself into the water, she stared down at the glassy surface, surprised at how much she'd hoped to see him. He said he'd be back today, but it could be midnight before she heard the purr of his Ducati.

Laughter filtered through the early morning quiet. Gita must be whipping up breakfast. With a push, Shiloh glided toward shore in a backstroke. The luminescent moon seemed transparent as the sun pushed it from its high orbit. In the six months she'd spent in India, she had come to love the country, with its ancient history and majestic views. There was something to be said for the slower pace of life. Sure, there were hot spots in the city, but she savored the tranquility that fed her soul in this country.

Out of the corner of her eye, she spotted wide brown eyes amid a furry face floating toward her. She giggled. "Hello, Aras." The monkey clambered onto Shiloh's stomach. "Looking for a free ride, huh?"

She kept her strokes even as they came to shore. Easing back, she dragged herself to where the water lapped against her legs. With Aras on her knees, Shiloh stroked the monkey's fur.

"So, what do you think? Will he come back this afternoon or tonight? I want him back *now*."

Aras's head tilted as her eyes locked on something behind Shiloh. The monkey let out an intermittent screech.

"What?" She glanced over her shoulder and jolted. "Reece." She stood as Aras scampered off. Flustered that he'd snuck up on her, and yet thrilled at seeing him again, she yanked her towel around herself.

"Monkeys are not known for cooperation during interrogations."

"Ha. Ha." She started toward the camp.

"Shiloh, let's talk."

Nerves buzzing, she didn't trust herself standing alone with him and so kept plodding up the path toward camp. "So, talk."

"We have to go back to Mumbai Harbor."

She stopped, the wind knocked out of her lungs.

"You're the only one who knows where the cylinder was, and it could contain very important clues to the case." Pebbles and dirt crunched as he joined her on the path. "We might be too late to retrieve it, but we have to try."

He wanted her to return to where Khalid had been murdered. To where he'd killed Baseer. Where Mikhail drowned. Her breath shuddered as he came into view next to her.

"I can't," she whispered.

"Listen," he said, positioning himself in front of her. "We'll leave at dusk and be back before sunrise."

She dragged her gaze to his. "You don't get it. I don't want to go anywhere but hom—" The words lodged in her throat. *I have no home.*

"Want to try that again?"

Why did he always have to know what she was thinking? Glowering, she turned and paced the path to the lake.

"With the cover of Miller's team, we'll make the dive, grab the cylinder, and be out before anyone is the wiser."

Shaking her head, she sighed. "Going back is stupid. They know who we are, what we look like." She whirled toward him. "Won't they be watching the site?"

"Yes."

Shiloh studied him. Not a single line of concern or crease of worry on his rugged face. Blue eyes betrayed nothing but confidence. Insecurity scratched at her, especially with Reece and his unwavering, undaunting, un-*everything* personality. Like a brick wall. Nothing got past him or affected him. Why couldn't she be strong too? She didn't want him thinking she was weak. But honestly . . . she wasn't sure she could pull this off.

He held out a pill.

She huffed. "Buying my cooperation?"

"Wouldn't want anything to happen in the bay."

Pill in her hand, she stared at it. Another sign of her weakness. An inability to even control her own body. "I've never had a seizure in the water." Should she ingest the miracle cure? "The neurologist thinks the combination of water pressure and how much it relaxes me prevents the tangling of the electrical signals that seize my muscles." Did he have more confidence in her if she took it? Would he believe in her then? She stuck the white tablet in her mouth and swallowed. "There. Happy?"

He closed the distance between them and tipped up her chin. "I'd never put you in jeopardy."

Cotton coated her tongue as sky-blue irises glistened back at her. "I-I thought anything could happen—that's why you're always prepared, expect the unexpected."

His eyes traced her face. "Exactly."

Stomach swimming at being so close to him, Shiloh pulled away. "You know what? You're arrogant." She stepped around him and continued up the path.

"Confident."

"Same thing." She trudged toward camp with him right behind her. *All right, Mr. Confidence.* After a glance back to gauge his proximity, she dropped to the ground. Fingers planted against the dirt, she swung her legs around to sweep his feet out from under him.

He leapt into the air and as he came down, he pinned her shoulders to the hard earth. Immediately, he snatched her wrists and held them over her head with one hand.

Shiloh gasped, stunned as a jolt of pain shot down her back and through her shoulders. Dirt and her own stupidity ground into her face. What was she thinking?

A chuckle—a deep one. "You're too easy."

Mind racing, she thought to whip her leg up and smack him in the back. But with one leg, he had both of hers secured. Teeth gritted, she chose to feign surrender. "Fine. You win."

Amusement trickled through his eyes and into his lips. "I don't think so." His grip on her hands and legs didn't lessen.

Angry—yet wanting very much to laugh—she let out a half groan. "Okay."

He didn't budge.

"Get off me, you big oaf!"

Reece chuckled again and scooted back onto his haunches.

Freed, Shiloh stomped off to her hut. She hadn't meant to wrestle with him, but he aggravated her to no end. Still . . . he might have gotten her this time, but she'd find a way to prove she could out-think him. If it took her to the end of her natural life.

"I'll be waiting, Blake."

Jaw clamped, she balled her fist.

More laughter.

Bring it on, Brutus.

She waited through breakfast, through the noon meal, each time hoping a brilliant idea would leap into her mind so she could pay him back. There had to be a way to outsmart this fox. How exactly did one go about upstaging a U.S. government-trained operative who'd probably seen more brutality than one could imagine?

Clunk!

Shiloh jumped.

Reece slid his tin plate across the picnic table and bent toward her. "Give up yet?"

No way would he bait her that easily. She'd find the perfect opportunity. Patience, her new best friend, would afford her the prime moment. Then he'd know not to underestimate her again. He'd respect her, admire her.

Miller joined them at the table. "Everything's set. We'll head out under cover of night to the river, take it down to the bay." He shoveled some curried chicken into his mouth. "I've tagged Stick and Bronco."

It felt like guppies scuttled through her stomach at the thought of the mission that would take her back to Mumbai. She stared at her food. The acrid odor clogged her throat. Fork set down, she sipped her water.

"We're ready." Reece didn't miss a beat in eating or answering.

Shiloh considered him. "*He's* ready."

His gaze jerked to hers. "You chicken?"

The accusation narrowed her eyes.

"We're ready," he repeated.

"Good enough. I'll meet you two lovebirds at the dock at twenty-two hundred."

Blue-grey twilight hugged the sky. Reddish-orange streaks tucked the sun in for the night, drawing out the moon. Four hours ago, Miller had spoken words that put the fear of God into Reece. Responsible for every life on this mission, he railed at the thought of love being a factor in this gig.

On the edge of his bunk, he sat with his fingers steepled and pressed to his forehead. He drew in a deep breath. *God* . . . He pulled his shoulders up a bit and sighed. What? Exactly what did he expect to hear God say about this? Too often man expected God to salvage the mess they made out of situations. He'd seen it time and again. People living the way they wanted, serving no one but themselves. Then when the first problem comes along, they slap God with the blame, expect Him to run SAR and drag their sorry carcasses out of the jungles of their own stupidity.

No. He wouldn't create a mess with this one. It'd happened once before and Chloe paid. Eyes closed, he clenched a fist. He'd hesitated . . . a deadly mistake with her life on the line.

Weariness dragged his shoulders back down. He hung his head and stared at his boots. This close to the goal he couldn't let anything interfere with the completion of this mission. Then he would escort her back to the States.

If she goes back, I'll never see her again.

When she'd come up out of that water with Aras, Reece couldn't believe his ears. She'd anticipated—*longed* for his return. Even now, nearly a full day later, the thought still poured lava through his mind. The way her grey-blue eyes sparkled with relief and . . . attraction—

No.

He grabbed his pack and stomped out of the hut. Get to Mumbai, get back, get her out. Three simple requisites haunted him as he strode into the thick humidity of the night. To the right, a screen clapped shut. He glanced over and spotted Shiloh heading his way.

"Diving at night isn't exactly smart." She slung a pack over her shoulder.

A smile tugged at his lips. Tenacity. That's probably the one thing he loved most about her. *Loved?* Muscles constricting, he stared at her.

"Don't worry. I'm not going to try anything when we're diving." A coy smile softened her features under the allure of the pale moon, reminding him of the night they'd first met.

The team assembled around two trucks loaded with their equipment. Reece tossed his pack into the bed and checked the oxygen tanks. Satisfied, he stored them along the inner portion next to the ice chest holding MREs—the nasty meals-ready-to-eat—a first-aid kit, and emergency radios. He shook hands with Stick and the wall-of-a-man known as Bronco, assessing the men in that brief second.

"Don't worry, chief." Stick grinned at Reece. "We got your back."

Bronco nudged the guy. "Goes without saying."

"Your priority is protecting our objective." Reece darted his eyes toward Shiloh, then back to the guys. "No matter what happens, you get her out alive and unharmed, or you'll deal with me."

Straightened, she planted her hands on her hips. "What about the 'nothing's going to happen' line you pitched me earlier?"

"Let's go, people." Miller climbed into the boat and started the prop.

Reece waited for Stick and Bronco to take their places in the boat before he moved toward Shiloh. Her words had carried a light tone, but he could see the doubt rippling through her. Closer, he tried not to appear as though he towered over her. "Trust me."

"I always have." Her soft words nearly escaped his hearing.

Before he could muster a response, she climbed into the front passenger seat next to Miller. Over the next hour, Reece studied her profile, wondering what they'd find—if they found anything. When they arrived at the river, the team quickly unloaded the supplies into the dive prop. Shiloh settled on the far, middle side. Within minutes they were en route, the monotonous drone of the motor almost lulling him to sleep. He closed his eyes, relishing the words Shiloh had spoken.

Exhaustion from the all-night excursion seeped into his bones. Reece allowed himself to drift into a light sleep, hoping to build some energy reserves for whatever they met on Mumbai Harbor.

"Yeah, he can sleep in the middle of an RPG attack." Miller's deep chuckle stirred Reece.

Without peeking, Reece slid down so the back of his head rested against the rubber craft. "I get sleep when and where I can."

Dreams skittered through his awareness, flicking out just as quickly. Heaviness bore down on him. Angelic and serene, Shiloh's face floated before him. She stood in a wide meadow amid a billowing field of waist-high flowers, wearing a coral-colored sari and choli. She laughed—a sweet sound that filled the open area. A breeze swept over her long auburn strands, rustling them. Reece waited at the edge of the plain, watching, smiling. Then, something to the left dragged his attention away. A sign. *Reece, look!* Shiloh's laugh dissipated as he looked back—she held that rat of a monkey and laughed. Again, he glanced at the sign. LANDMINES. His heart lurched. Something tugged at his hip.

Reece's hand flew out. He tightened his grip around the little pickpocket.

A whimper.

Laughter jolted him from the nightmare. He blinked several times—and found blue-grey eyes staring back at him. Only then did realization hit—Shiloh was the thief.

"Trying to disarm me?" Reece taunted as he pried her fingers from the handle of his knife.

Stick and Bronco high-fived.

Shiloh slumped back. "I had it."

"No, you *almost* had it," Reece corrected, re-securing his Emerson.

"She got farther than anyone else ever has," Miller hollered over the drone of the engine.

Her gaze skidded back to Reece's. He acknowledged the truth with a shrug. That's when he remembered the dream. His psyche had known she was there but didn't register her as a threat. He stared at her. No, he didn't ever want to think of her that way. Yet she was a threat to everything he'd carefully assembled and worked to protect. It gnawed at him to think of her at all in those terms. He'd give anything for her. And that fact unsettled everything in him.

Within twenty minutes of the drop-off point, he and Shiloh assisted each other in gearing up. He admired the fluidity and confidence with which she moved to get ready. No hesitation, no fear. This was familiar ground for her. He liked this version of Shiloh Blake. Could he get her thinking and acting like this in any situation?

Definitely.

The motor lulled to a stop, the boat rising and falling on the tidal pull of the waves.

Sitting on the edge with his back to the water, Reece waited for her. She gripped his shoulder as she lowered herself into position.

"Radio when you're ready for extraction." Miller slapped his back.

Reece nodded and shifted to her. "Once in, regroup and we'll tie off." Regulator in his mouth, he shot a sidelong glance to Shiloh and lowered his mask. She did the same. Together, they flipped backwards into the water.

Once they came to the surface, he used his carabiner and secured a tether between them. Hooked, they drifted down. Reece activated his halogen lamp several feet below water, and they began the mile-long swim east to the dead-drop. As they neared the coordinates, Miller radioed the all-clear. No unfriendlies sighted.

Shiloh gave hand signals toward the last known location of the cylinder. He didn't expect they'd find it—after all, more than a week had passed. His mind stalled on the revelation. A week, ten days? Is that all it'd been? He'd felt like he'd known Shiloh much longer. As if they'd spent years together.

She swirled toward him. His light glanced off her neoprene-clad form. She raised her hands in question. Pointing toward the surface, he paddled his feet. He slowed his ascent and let his head break the waterline slowly.

Seconds later, Shiloh's face emerged inches from his. She tore her regulator out. "It's not here. What now?"

He had to ask. "Are you sure you remember where it was?"

"Positive. I remember taking the picture of it ne—" Her eyes widened. "The camera!"

"What about it?"

"I stuffed it in a locker at the hospital."

"Noor?"

Shiloh nodded.

He knew what she was thinking. And he didn't like it. "Not safe."

"It's our only chance. If we can find it, we might be able to tell what it was, or what was in the cylinder." Treading water, she stayed close. Her fingers grazed his arms.

In dive suits, they'd be spotted instantly on the streets. "We'll head back to the prop." He rushed on before she could interrupt. "Let's bank, and get Miller to check it out."

She relented and within a half-hour, they were rumbling toward the rocky shoreline. Miller cut the engine and they used paddles to make a stealthy landing. They dragged the prop into a shady cove. Miller and Stick disappeared into the trees, aiming for Noor.

Reece pried off the dive shirt and stuffed his arms into a clean, black tank. He would offer to let Shiloh change in the trees, but he had a feeling she wouldn't take him up on that. She bent over the boat and tugged something out of her pack. When she slid it on, Reece couldn't help but grin.

"It's warm," she grumbled as she slid her hand under her hair and freed it from the hoodie.

"I know."

Shiloh shot him a glance.

He chuckled.

She walked to the edge of the shady protection and glanced up. He heard a shuddering sigh as she stood there. His gaze followed hers. Dazzling against a blanket of black, the moon shone brightly, a larger version of the stars dancing around it. He moved closer, knowing that even a few feet could be a lethal distance if someone leapt out of the shadows. Behind her, he allowed his gaze to wander to her.

Unlike in his dream where her hair billowed, her hair hung dark and wet down her back. Under the wash of moonlight, her face softened and her eyes lightened.

"How do you always know what I'm going to do?" Her soulful gaze came to his.

Did she know how beautiful she was? He broke the hypnotic tug of her eyes and strolled around her. "In my business, you learn to read people." On a nearby boulder, he planted his foot and stared out at the bay.

Shiloh followed, stepping up onto the rock, which brought her almost even with his height. "I've always thought I could judge people pretty well."

"You do."

She darted him a glance.

Lowering his leg, he stared out at the diamond-encrusted waters. When she looked at him with that remnant of hope, of wanting him to believe in her, all Reece wanted to do was pull her into his arms and kiss her soundly. *Change the topic, genius.*

"Am I predictable?" She did it for him.

"Everyone is," Reece acknowledged. "Most people fit into a certain type, so it's easy to peg what they're thinking or what they'll do. It works most of the time." It was why he had faith she'd come back to God.

She batted her hair from her face, her chin tilted so that she peered down at him. "So, what am I thinking?"

Reece couldn't stop his grin. "You're trying to figure out what you can do that I won't expect."

She grunted and slid off the rock. The lapping water bridged the silence that overtook the conversation. A moment later, Shiloh yanked around and eyed him.

"Did you figure it out?" He shouldn't taunt her, but this was too much fun.

She rolled her eyes and glanced away. Seconds later, she whipped toward him. Something flickered in her expression. Her gaze shifted.

No, *something* shifted. The change was so subtle, it almost didn't register. A nuance. It unsettled him. Familiar, yet foreign.

With the moon skimming the quiet waters, shadows danced across her face. Seconds stretched into what felt like minutes as she stood, unmoving. What was she thinking? Why couldn't he read her? A shrill alarm squealed through his mind. What muddled his instincts? *Step off, Jaxon.*

Her hands came to his shoulders as she stood on tiptoes and kissed him.

19

LOCKED IN THE INTENSITY OF HIS GAZE, SHE STARED AT HIM WITH A THUNdering heart. Her stomach flipped then flopped as she stood, unable to move away. Not wanting to.

His hands snaked around her waist. A hand slid up her back and cupped her head. Heat fanned across her chest and slithered into her cheeks as his eyes bounced between her lips and eyes. Her breath caught as he lowered his head.

Lips dusting hers . . . warm, gentle. He nudged the small of her back, tugging her deeper into his arms. For a second, he eased back. He waited, as if asking permission—or warring with what he felt and what his silly professional rules dictated. He might say they had to keep their distance, but his reaction to her screamed otherwise.

She wouldn't lose this moment. Her world suddenly felt bearable. She let her fingers trickle up his shoulders and around his neck. "Reece . . ."

He captured her mouth with his.

As Shiloh melted into his arms, his grip tightened her against him. Bathed in his passion, she sensed the security and peace she'd found only in the depths of the ocean. But a different depth engulfed her now—a magical one sprinkled with happiness.

Like an ice storm, he broke off. Pushed her away. He hissed a curse, lodging his rejection into her heart. He pivoted with his hands threaded behind his head. He mumbled and paced. Finally, he turned back to her.

And she saw it. Regret.

Rage wove through her. When her chin quivered, she clamped her jaw.

"Shiloh—"

"No!" she ground out, laboring through each breath. "Don't you dare!" A hot tear streaked down her face. She slapped it away. "Don't you dare apologize."

Why had she taken the risk? Handed her heart to a covert operative. This is what she got—this is what she'd known she'd get from day one. Her father had brought nothing but rejection and pain. Why in this dark universe did she ever think it'd be different with Reece?

He slumped onto the boulder and cradled his head in his hands.

Tears unleashed, she stomped back toward the craft. "Weak, stupid . . ." *Schoolgirl.* Isn't that how he saw her? As a silly schoolgirl with a crush? She spun back to him, ready to unleash her fury. But stopped short when she saw him barreling toward her.

He took her into his arms.

"Get off!" With a shove, she broke free.

"Shiloh, listen—" He caught her, pulling her toward him.

She writhed against his grip. "No! I won't . . . I can't . . ." Rage melted into sheer agony. Why had she trusted him? *Give your heart to a spy, you only end up betrayed.*

"You're right. I have no business apologizing."

She snapped her head up and glared at him.

"I can't apologize because I'm not sorry. But I never wanted to hurt you." Torment and confusion rushed across his terse brow. He shook his head. "You haven't even had time to grieve for Khalid. This . . . thing between us could just be a blowback from his death."

"A blowback?" Shiloh stared at him, blinking. "Is that what you . . . ?" She swallowed and averted her eyes. Her breathing deepened. Crushed. Did he really think she . . . ? She raked her hair out of her face and shoved back the tears.

Maybe he was right. A blowback. She dared to meet his gaze. *Transference.* The unconscious redirection of feelings from one person to another. She took a step back, her legs feeling like jellyfish.

His gaze dropped.

Yeah, he thought she'd transferred her feelings from Khalid—now dead—to him. Is that truly what had happened? Her mind's eye swam through the thick emotions that burned when Reece held her, kissed her, reassured her . . .

Reece roughed a hand over his jaw and huffed. "I don't know what to do about this, about you."

Sorrow clung to her as the remnants of his powerful kiss still lingered. "Why must you do anything about me? Khalid's gone." The words caught in her throat. Her eyes burned. *Please don't let Reece be right.* She needed what he'd just given her—a taste of happiness. "It's different between us—you and me."

She hated the desperation in her own voice, but Reece moved something deep in her, something never touched before. Yet it scared her. Made her wonder what sort of insanity consumed her to get mixed up with a man whose very existence depended on deceit. Why hadn't she ever felt like this with Khalid? Guilt rubbed her raw.

"Maybe we should give each other some time."

She flared her nostrils. "Why? Is this just a game—do you show every woman that kind of passion?"

The nerve she hit exploded across his face. "You know the answer to that."

Frustration gripped her. Tightened its hold. Strangled her. "Why is this wrong?" Her voice cracked.

Once again, he pulled her into his arms and cradled her. Shiloh slumped against his chest. Strong biceps made the world slip away. All the trials, all the enemies . . .

Daunting understanding seized her. She knew why it was dangerous for him to get involved with her—his guard fell, his mind succumbed to intoxication. Did she have the same effect on him that he had on her?

Without explaining her revelation, Shiloh sank into the safety of his hold and let the world slip away once more. A shudder rippled through her, coaxing a sigh as he pressed a kiss to the crown of her head. They stood under the moonlight, quiet and peaceful. Yet Shiloh worried over their future, over the possibility that she unconsciously projected. Once they left, once he was thrust back into his world of espionage, what would happen to them?

"So, what do we do?" She tilted her head back to look up at him.

A small smile. "I like to finish what I start. Since I can't, no more kisses for a while." He grinned. "A long while."

What if they backed off and never found their connection again? "In that case—" She tugged his face down once more. This time, *she* deepened the kiss.

"Hey!" someone shouted behind them.

Reece jerked, his gaze snapping down the darkened beach.

Shiloh shifted back as she searched for the source of the interruption. There, about fifty yards off, stood Bronco.

"Miller radioed," he hollered. "They've got trouble."

Running through the sand proved arduous as the gritty grains pushed against her. Still, Reece seemed to fly effortlessly over the terrain back to the boat. Shiloh wasn't far behind when he barked orders to Bronco. Orders to maintain watch over the boat . . . and Shiloh.

"I'm not staying here." She planted a foot and caught his arm.

Reece hooked a fist up and under her hand, breaking her hold. He stepped into a pair of jeans over his now-dry trunks, then donned a shirt, and slung a pack over his shoulder. The familiar shink of the weapon's slide echoed through the night. Intensity flamed into his face, every action strategic and practiced.

"Reece . . ." She let her voice trail off although she wanted to argue, to demand her rights. But something told her not to, to hold her peace. Hadn't she said she always trusted him? Then this was the time to prove it. "Come back."

He met her gaze briefly, gave a gentle nod, and jogged out of view without a word.

For several moments after he left, she stared at the foliage that had swallowed him. She didn't want to lose him the way she'd lost Khalid. Rubbing her arms, she strode toward the trees. She'd just handed him her heart, and now he had rushed off into a deadly conflict.

"Stay close to the prop."

At Bronco's warning, Shiloh stopped pacing.

Reece Jaxon had filled a hole long vacant in her life, and only now, with him off fighting the perils of the night, did it strike her how much she feared caring about someone. Isn't this why she'd hidden her heart, shielded her emotions from everyone about everything? Her father had always read her openly—much like Reece. It was because of her father she'd mastered schooling her facial features and finding ways to answer without answering.

She walked the edge of the shore where the water kissed the still-warm sand. Yes, she'd spent her entire life running from her feelings and her father. Her father would enjoy this, knowing she'd fled his watchful eye only to end up in love with a man just like him. She closed her eyes. *How can I be so stupid?*

What was she doing falling in love—period? With a spy, no less!

No. She didn't love Reece Jaxon. They barely knew each other. This was just an infatuation. Maybe she needed to let things cool off. Even he said things between them had to level out.

I like to finish what I start. His words tickled her conscience. Didn't that hold a promise of a future? Why did her heart race at the thought?

She squeezed her eyes and shook her head. Raking a hand through her hair, she heard Bronco approaching and glanced at him.

He held out a small earpiece. "Thought you'd want to keep an ear on the traffic, considering you and the chief."

"Considering what about us?"

He looked at her like she'd lost her mind but clamped his mouth tight.

Irritated with her own defensiveness, she took the device and tucked it in. Activity leapt into her ear canal. Confusing lingo ensued, but then she grabbed the edges of the stiff conversation.

"Bravo One, report." Reece's voice came through strong and commanding.

Captain Miller responded with the information. If she understood the scenario, Miller and Stick had encountered two hostiles outside the hospital and were trapped. Had they found the camera?

Rustling and static rattled her nerves over the next several minutes. Shiloh kept her eyes on the water, focused on the rhythmic lapping in the hopes of staying calm.

"Behind you!" Miller shouted.

A crack and thud.

Shiloh spun toward Bronco. "Shouldn't . . . can't we do something?"

"We wait."

Shiloh ground her teeth together.

Rapid-fire weapons hammered her ear. Shiloh stopped cold when silence shrieked through the coms. Again she shot a questioning look to Bronco, who shook his head. She listened, hoped to hear something. Anything.

Her heart lurched. What if Reece died?

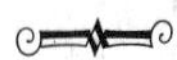

Reece hoofed it across the narrow stretch of grass between the street and the hospital. They had risked this trip for what? A trap? Irritation rose up his spine but he shoved it aside. He had to provide a distraction for the guys to get out alive. Half bent, he hurried toward the white van parked at the far edge of the lot. Back pressed to the hot metal, he peered around the front fender.

"In position, Bravo one."

"Copy."

From the pack, he withdrew the clump of Semtex. He reached up under the vehicle and set the Russian C-4 against the wheel hub. "Package in place. Ready in eight . . . seven . . ." He sprinted toward the waist-high wall.

At the first hint of detonation, he dove to the ground.

White lit the night. A thundering concussion slammed through the smoldering air. Heat skimmed the back of his legs and his spine. Once it passed, he waited out the back-draft, then pushed himself from the grass. "Bravo One, gimme a sitrep."

"Two unfriendlies down. En route to rendezvous."

With the confirmation that their diversion had worked, Reece kept his eyes alert, mind processing his surroundings. A Maharashtra State Police Jeep sped down the road with its blue, white, and red lights stirring chaos. Pedestrians gawked at the emergency vehicles descending on the private hospital.

With his face hidden from the authorities, Reece blended into the shadows of the tall trees. Crunching footsteps nearby sent him rushing behind the biggest trunk. He leaned against the bark and peered out.

A stream of light probed the dense foliage and swept left and right. More crunching as officers inched between the trees then stopped, apparently afraid to go deeper into the small forest. If they moved in farther, their flashlights would strike his chest. He glanced over his shoulder, spotted a slightly larger tree, and shot toward it.

Shouts erupted.

Bark ruptured, peppering his face and arms. He wove to the left and bent into a crouch.

Hurried and frantic words swirled through the area, choking his hope that he could make it to the boat in time.

"Over here," one hollered, their Marathi coated with urgency as they drew closer.

Dangerously close. Reece searched for an exit strategy.

Snap! Crunch.

Another five yards and they'd have a clean shot.

His heart skipped a beat. Miller and the others were most likely pushing out into the water. They'd better get Shiloh to safety. The thought of her getting captured weighted his muscles. His mind skidded into the memory of her soft, sweet kisses. *God, help me!*

"Help!" a woman's voice called.

The officers spun, stared toward the road, and jogged away from him.

"I saw a man," the woman said, her dialect a bit . . . off.

Not just a woman. Shiloh! Reece's tension ratcheted. A metallic taste shot through his mouth. He wasn't going to lose

Shiloh the way he lost Chloe. Caught between racing to safety and ensuring hers, he shifted for a better view.

With a convincing amount of emotion in her voice, Shiloh stood, shouting that someone had stolen her car. She pointed down the road and insisted they stop the man in the red import.

The authorities didn't seem to buy her story.

"My baby is in there. The man had a backpack and a gun." Those words sent the two racing away, but only after they ordered her to wait there.

Reece's pulse spiked when Shiloh didn't rush into the trees. *Come on, Shi, come on!* He whistled to signal her, momentarily forgetting Shiloh wouldn't recognize the sound. He fisted his hands as seconds ticked off. If she waited much longer . . . He took a step forward.

Just then, she burst through the shelter of trees—and barreled right into him. He caught her hand and together, they zigzagged through the pines.

"Bravo one, what's your twenty?"

"Fifty red."

As they ran, he glanced at Shiloh. Determination etched into her face, she maintained course without hesitation. Ten more feet.

Sand spurted upward. Stinging grains prickled his legs and arms.

Shiloh grunted.

The black waters beckoned.

"Fifty meters southeast, go!"

Fingertips touching, she dove into the water. Reece launched in behind her. He kept pace, knowing if she ate a bullet, she'd drown. Mentally, he prodded her to swim faster. Yet her pace tonight slaughtered her competitive swimming at the camp. The sense of foreboding had never pervaded his senses the way it did with Shiloh. She'd foolishly put herself in danger. She should've stayed put.

At the rig, the agitating motor stirred the waters as Stick and Bronco hauled him and Shiloh aboard. She flopped in like a fish, her lungs heaving. Reece slid onto his rear as he worked to steady his breathing, watching her.

Her head rolled to the side as she looked at him. A crooked grin. She licked her lips.

"Not smart," he said with a ragged breath. "Never compromise yourself or your location."

Propped on her elbows, she wrinkled her brow. "I saved your life!"

"You compromised your position and put the team at risk."

"Everyone's fine." She pushed up as a full scowl took over her delicate features. "The cops were within five feet and would've killed you if I hadn't drawn away their attention."

"And in doing so, you implicated and endangered yourself."

"Fine. I'll leave you to die next time."

"That's exactly what you should do." He watched the shock course through her, creating a tumultuous wake like the frothy waters behind the boat. "I'm trained for situations like this. You aren't. I told you to stay with Bronco." Reece turned his glare to the burly man at the back of the boat. "I'll deal with you later." Special Forces and the guy couldn't even maintain control over one untrained asset.

"She sprinted—"

"You won't deal with anyone on my account," Shiloh shouted over Bronco's objection and the motor. "I'm a grown woman. I assessed the situation and did what I thought was best."

Why did he feel so enraged? "You were wrong."

As the wind whipped her wet hair across her face, something burst through her eyes. "Yes, I was wrong." Jaw jutted, she shoved herself away from him. "About you!"

Her words stabbed him. She'd taken his admonishment personally instead of assimilating it to improve her technique. Letdown shadowed the pride he'd felt earlier. "If you can't separate your feelings from the action, you won't go on any more missions."

"Would you two can it?" Miller glowered from the back. "You're waking the dead!"

Reece lowered his gaze to the pack between his legs. As the boat sped them back to the waiting trucks, he used the time to steady himself from the energy and mental rush. The thought of her dead at the bottom of Mumbai Harbor . . .

He'd lost control with her. He roughed a hand over his face, disappointed with himself. But she brought out things in him that nobody else had been able to—fury, passion, anger. He would need to talk to her. Get them back on track.

Back at camp, he grabbed his gear and caught up with her on the trail. "Shi—"

"Get off!" Shiloh drew back like a cat ready to strike. Fire poured out of her moonlit eyes.

"Listen to me."

"I heard you just fine the first time." She stomped in the direction of her hut.

Reece started after her, stunned that their relationship had taken a nosedive from the nearly euphoric moment on the beach to the volatile argument on the dark waters. He'd thought better of her, believed Shiloh top-agent material, even secretly toyed with recruiting her despite the indications from Langley that she was off-limits.

Was he wrong? Had he pushed too hard? Involved her in scenarios beyond the scope of her abilities?

Images of a blonde woman swam through his mind. An argument. Angry, hateful words. An explosion. Her death.

He swallowed—hard. He'd crossed that line he swore to respect this time. How could life repeat itself in such a painful way? Maybe the transference theory was right. Would Shiloh ever speak to him again? Would they go their separate ways? His fingers curled into a fist at the thought. He scowled as he stared at the hut sitting beneath the canopy of banyan trees. He didn't want to lose Shiloh, either to circumstance or to the grave.

"Don't let it happen," Miller said, his words barely audible as he sidled up beside him.

Reece glanced at his partner.

Cole Miller stood facing Shiloh's hut, the small fire in the nearby pit lighting his face. He squinted. "Don't let this thing come between you two."

"She doesn't understand my reasons, this life I live, or what it takes."

"Then make her understand."

With a soft snort, Reece shook his head. "You of all people know it's impossible to make anyone do something they don't want to."

"True." He still hadn't moved. "But love can level mountains."

A snappy comeback lit through Reece's mind, a retort that denied anything existed between himself and Shiloh. Was it better to release what happened on the beach, accept that Shiloh wasn't meant for him, and just move on? It would be safer. For her. For him. If he did, could he head off another disaster? Maybe that would salvage what was left of his belief that true love could exist and remain a burning flame instead of snuffing out before it had a chance to burn brightly.

"Chloe wasn't your fault."

Reece ground his teeth, his gaze skirting the camp and then falling on Shiloh's hut. He flexed and unflexed his hands. "People keep saying that." Even though this situation wasn't the same as Mumbai, the similarities taunted him. "I won't be the cause of someone's death again."

Miller chuckled. "Sure you will."

"You know what I mean."

With a hand on Reece's shoulder, Miller turned. "She's not Chloe, and she's not your prodigy."

Alone with his thoughts, Reece replayed his friend's words. With so many years of executing covert ops, he'd wondered if he even had a heart anymore. After Chloe's death, he'd walled himself within the confines of espionage, enjoying the anonymity yet finding himself lost and alone. Following his heart was a lot easier said than done. It meant breaking not only Langley's rules but his own.

But what if his *heart* broke the rules? He didn't ask to fall for the enigmatic woman. Yet she called to everything that was Reece Jaxon. Sultry softness lured him into wanting more, a lot more than a Christian man should. But his attraction was to more than her body—she amazed him, made him curious to find out what made her tick, what made her laugh. And since she was Jude Blake's daughter, Shiloh had been exposed to the Christian faith. With her tenacity it was only a matter of time before she examined her anger toward God.

At her hut, he peered through the screen. She bent over her cot and dug through her backpack. He rapped against the wood frame.

"Go away!"

Reece opened the door and stepped in.

Shiloh spun and beaned him with something.

The object had nailed his head. Touching the spot, he stared at her. Shocked. "Ow!"

She rolled her eyes. "You were supposed to catch it."

"I did." He rubbed his temple. "With my head."

She stomped across the slat-board floor and retrieved whatever had hit him. "Here." Holding it, she wouldn't meet his gaze. "The coin Baseer gave me. It's our next step."

He gripped her hand, his gaze unmoving from her face. So this was how she wanted to play it—shove aside her feelings and get right back to the game? So much the better. At least this way they wouldn't have to worry about romantic entanglements.

Tugging free, Shiloh took a step away. "When he gave it to me, he mentioned a name—Gerard Moore, remember?"

"Moreaux," a voice called from behind. "Gerard Moreaux."

Both Shiloh and Reece turned toward the door. Miller stood on the wooden steps, his hands stuffed in the back pockets of his tactical pants. "Sorry, I was coming to ask you to keep it down. Couldn't help overhearing." He stepped into the hut.

"Who's Moreaux?" Reece asked.

A wicked grin plowed into Miller's face. "French deputy minister of foreign relations. A powerful man in the way of peace negotiations. Heard about a snatch-and-grab based on information he provided to an asset in Paris."

"So, he's friendly." Reece smoothed his thumb over the copper piece.

"Quite." Miller lifted the coin and studied it. Humor fled his face, his blue eyes nailing Shiloh. "But the people who gave this to Khan aren't so friendly. As a matter of fact, if they learn Moreaux is connected to your man, he's dead."

"Then we need to get there fast." Shiloh shifted and crossed her arms over her chest.

"You're not going," Reece said.

Her nostrils flared against pinked cheeks.

Miller stared at them both for a minute, then met Reece's stare. "Partner, you won't get in to see Moreaux."

"Why not?"

"Because you're an operative." With a shrug, Miller leaned against the center support post. "He has tabs on just about everyone flying under the radar. Doesn't trust a soul, except those in his inner circle."

"Then I'll find the inner circle."

Miller shook his head, then glanced at Shiloh. "Did Baseer or Khalid ever mention anything to you about this group?"

"No."

Eyeing the piece, Miller nodded. "This is not just a coin. It has an embedded receiver that registers its first contact once activated." He flipped it toward Reece. "If Baseer activated it . . ."

Shiloh intercepted it from the air. "Then what? It has my biosignature?"

"Exactly." Miller looked pleased about something. "They don't talk to just anyone. The fact that Khan gave you this coin is what grants you access to Moreaux."

"Hold up." Reece waved his hand, then pinched the bridge of his nose. This conversation had taken a turn for the worse. "Let's back up."

Although neither Miller nor Shiloh said anything, Reece heard their annoyance in the silence that chilled the air. Arms folded over his chest, he drew in a deep breath. "What we're facing here is a lot bigger than a simple killing."

"Simp—"

"Let me finish." Reece rubbed the back of his neck. "Come with me." He punched the screen door and launched off the steps. Shiloh and Miller muttered as they trailed him to his hut. Inside he retrieved his rucksack.

"Okay," he said laying down a photo. "We have satellite images from Kashmir with obvious radioactive signatures that prove a warhead is being moved." He set out stapled pages. "A transcript from Abdul and an unknown male, and photos of a meeting between Baseer Khan and Abdul, and an indecipherable message."

He turned to Shiloh. "Where's the device?"

She held out the coin.

He tossed it in with the other clues. "That's what we have. Too many connections and broken links."

"All this about nuke codes?" Miller's brow furrowed.

"Exactly, there's something else lurking there, but not tangible." Reece peeked at Shiloh. "I have pictures of Sajjadi with his men. One of them is your guy, Kodiyeri."

Shiloh's eyes widened. "He works with Sajjadi?"

"*For*. He works for Sajjadi."

"These connections are hair-thin, Jaxon," Miller mumbled as he picked up the Abdul/Khan photo.

"But they're there. And each second I'm in the middle of it, the threads firm up." He faced the woman who'd captured his heart and the attention of a radical organization. "Don't think I'm just trying to be chauvinistic and get the beautiful damsel out of distress. These guys, this organization we're up against, have a deadline. That information tells me it's less than a week away. And let me emphasize the dead part. They don't care who they bury. They will do anything and everything to see this through. Right now I have to make sure the codes to those nukes don't get accessed or go live. If that happens, it's going to get all kinds of ugly."

Shiloh stuck out her chin and aimed her electric eyes at Reece. "Khalid's father gave the coin to me. He had a purpose for that. I'm going."

"Not happening." Risking her life any more wasn't an option.

Determination carved her lips into a hard line. "I'm going to meet Moreaux, and I'm going find out what this coin means."

Reece bit back the burst of panic—panic? When had he ever felt panic? No, this was anger. Rage at the control slipping through his fingers. No matter how hard he worked to steer Shiloh to safety, each development dug her in deeper. His innate desire to protect the woman he was falling in love with demanded he keep her safe.

The determination he'd seen in her face leapt into his own. He met Miller's gaze.

"You'll hit every brick wall, physically and metaphorically, between here and Paris. Like I said, you won't get in to see Moreaux." Miller grinned again. Then glanced at Shiloh. "But she can."

20

AT THIRTY-THREE THOUSAND FEET MORE THAN THICK OXYGEN SMOTHered Shiloh. Silence from Reece Jaxon did. Since she'd forced her way into this mission a day ago, he had spoken only when absolutely necessary. He'd berated her for intervening when the Maharashtra authorities had almost discovered him. Then he'd insisted she head back to the States. Was he that anxious to get rid of her? Had their moment on the beach meant nothing? She'd wrestled for hours that night over how much she'd enjoyed his kiss, how much she'd relished the security and pleasure of his embrace.

Her heart hung heavy over the awkwardness. Was this her fault? Had she created this void between herself and the one man she'd developed strong feelings for? This rang similar to her relationship with her father. Close for a time, then miles apart after her mother's death. But she wasn't the one to blame for that.

For the first time in years, that horrible night flashed into her mind like a virtual plasma screen. A broken arm shooting piercing pain into her shoulder. Crying. Her mother groaning as she struggled to pull herself from the upside-down car. They'd linked fingers when—*Bang!* Her mother went limp just as sirens blasted through the frigid night. Her father's career had killed her mother and jeopardized Shiloh's life.

And never once had he apologized or wished for things to be different.

And you're doing the same thing to Reece.

But she saved his life!

Shiloh sighed and stopped arguing with herself. What was the old saying? If you're pointing a finger at someone, you have three pointing back at you? Why couldn't he just be grateful she'd helped? All he had to say was thank you, or good job. Instead, he'd pierced her heart with his scathing assessment of what she'd done wrong.

Once the plane landed, Reece laced an arm around her waist as they strode down the concourse. "Just relax."

They stepped up to the customs booth together. She handed over her fake passport. The idea that someone could forge false identities so wholly and without error churned her stomach.

"You do not seem happy, Madame," the uniformed man noted as he studied her passport.

Tension bunched at the back of her neck. She hoped the technology that cost five grand would get them past this wiry little man with too many opinions.

Shiloh hitched an eyebrow. "Long flight."

He chuckled. "Ah, but this is Paris. The city of love." With a smirk at Reece, he stamped their passports. "Sir, it seems you have your work cut out during your stay."

"Indeed."

Flushed with indignation, Shiloh stormed through the concourse and out into the brisk Parisian air. "I can't believe you agreed with him."

His eyes came to hers, brilliantly blue under the morning sun, but he said nothing. After renting a car, she had to bite her lip to stop from laughing as he folded his six-foot-two frame into the tiny compact. Crammed almost shoulder-to-shoulder between Reece and the fiberglass body of the car, she suddenly longed for the cramped style of the airplane.

With each thrust of the stick, he inadvertently jarred Shiloh's shoulder as well. Yet the skill with which he'd handled the car and maneuvered through town proved he not only had a working knowledge of the city, but he was used to whipping through Paris. The revelation piqued her curiosity.

"How many times have you been here?"

He stared through the windshield. "A few."

So, he didn't want to talk about it. Or was it that he didn't want to talk about it with her? Shiloh swallowed the sour thought and pushed her gaze to the skyline. Buildings loomed like giants on either side. As Reece braked at a red light, a shadow fell across her shoulder. She looked up and drowned under the shadow of the Eiffel Tower.

Reece aimed the car down the road, granting a better view of the magnificent structure. She craned her head against the window and peered around the bustling city. The car slowed and pulled to the curb, where a dozen wrought-iron tables littered the sidewalk.

To her right, a river rushed past. "What are we doing?"

"Going to foot."

Shiloh jerked toward Reece, startled to see him stuffing a weapon into a holster at his ankle. Although her heart skipped a beat, she knew not to ask where he'd hidden that—or how! Instead, she climbed out and silenced the questions hammering her skull.

Across the street, café canopies swayed in the cool, gentle breeze. Couples sat talking and eating, while passersby seemed oblivious to the magnificence of the city. How could they not be awestruck by it? Yet with the monumental task looming before them, even she couldn't find a deep appreciation for the wonders that were innately Paris.

She turned back to the river, her attention snagged by a woman who sauntered past, eating what looked like a chocolate waffle. Shiloh's stomach rumbled.

"This way," Reece said, his hand on her back guiding her toward a bridge spanning the Seine. "We're a happy couple, remember?"

"Blissfully happy." The sarcasm felt as tumultuous as the river gurgling beneath them.

As they stepped onto the street that led to the Palais de Justice, Reece held her hand. She had to quicken her step to keep up with his long strides. If she weren't so stressed about what they were doing in the heart of Paris instead of meeting with Moreaux, she might entertain the jellies swarming her stomach as she walked with Reece . . . in Paris, holding hands. She shoved the romantic notions from her mind as they approached a Gothic cathedral.

Sainte-Chapelle. Her breath caught as they stepped through the arched doors. Glistening golds and warm amber hues beckoned to her. Peace pervaded the building despite the throngs of tourists combing its stone floors.

Reece slowed, pointing as if any other tourist, but he whispered in her ear, "Buy the postcard with the spire from the gift shop. Meet me back here."

Heat darted across her shoulders. *We're separating?*

He met her gaze. Smiled. Then kissed her cheek. "I'll be right back, babe."

Babe? Oh. Right. Happy couple. She spun toward the small in-house shop and forced herself to move away from him, pushing aside the jolt of pleasure at hearing Reece call her by that endearment.

She pressed through a group of nuns to the rack by the sales counter. A nun stepped into her path, colliding with Shiloh. "I'm sorry," she apologized to the woman in the black habit before moving to the spinning rack.

A brightly lit mirrored shelf behind the counter gave her a perfect view of the cathedral. Through the craziness of the visitors, she spotted Reece sitting on a lone bench, his head bowed. What was he doing?

Turning the rack, she let her gaze hopscotch between the cards and Reece. Another man sat at the far end of the bench. Her pulse galloped. Was he a contact? Is that what the visit to this cathedral was about?

Hand on the card, she lifted it, and shifted to the cashier. As she held it out, her gaze hit on the postcard. *Wrong one!* "Wait, please." Shiloh reached across the counter and grabbed the spire card. "Here." She gave a weak smile and paid for the card.

As she pushed back into the openness of the beautiful Sainte-Chapelle, shivers danced down her spine. Where was Reece? He wasn't on the bench. The other man seemed to have disappeared too. The crowds strangled her. Or maybe it was the haunting structure. Gothic. She'd never liked the style. Even in a church with stunning glasswork and warm lighting, she couldn't shake the ominous feeling soaking into her conscience.

"You okay?" Reece's words skated along her neck.

She pulled straight and sucked in a breath as his arm slid around her waist. Where had he come from? Why was she so off-balance?

He moved in front of her, brows knit. "What's wrong?"

"I . . ." Her gaze traced the arched ceilings, then the crowds. "I guess I just don't like this style. It gives me the creeps."

Once again, he took her hand and led her from the church. Back out in the brilliance of the afternoon sun, the chill faded. The steady rhythm of their feet on the sidewalk helped to distance her from the sense of doom that had nearly suffocated her. She let out a heavy breath.

"Always trust that instinct, Shi." Reece kept walking, his large stride a welcome pace now. "Something was wrong in there. I felt it too."

"What do you mean?" Even the strength of his fingers entwined with hers gave her courage as they strolled at a quick but casual pace so as not to draw attention.

Reece stopped at a vendor and bought something, his French fluent and . . . nice. She shook her head, chiding herself for slipping into the wrong state of mind. Back on the sidewalk, he handed her a chocolate waffle and a bottle of water. She smiled, surprised. Had he seen her drooling over the treat before they went into Sainte-Chapelle? Munching, she noticed they were walking much slower.

"Where to now?"

"The Louvre." He guzzled his water almost in one gulp, then capped the bottle, and tossed it in a bin.

"Seriously?" She eyed him, finishing off her waffle. "What's with all the tourist traps?"

Hands shoved in his pockets, Reece grinned. "What? I can't take my best girl to see the sights?"

Believing he meant that would put her heart in danger. She'd already tried that, and it didn't work out too well. Something was going on. She wasn't sure what, but she'd learned not to question Reece. He wouldn't answer anyway.

As they finally approached the bizarre glass enclosure, Shiloh discarded her empty water bottle and waffle napkin.

He paid their admission and handed her a brochure. Over the next hour, they circled a fraction of the massive museum in near silence, her mind buzzing. She had to admit that it stole her breath to see the artwork, to stand before a da Vinci, knowing the master himself had once stood before the canvas. To see Michelangelo's inspired works and wonder what stirred his soul most when he painted.

But her mind wouldn't quiet. All these paintings, the trek along the Seine, the visit to Sainte-Chapelle, the Palais de Justice, Paris . . . And Reece. It had all the earmarks of a perfect, romantic trip.

So why did she feel so empty?

As they lingered before a sculpture of Alexander the Great, Shiloh stole a peek at Reece. His eyes seemed to probe the piece. Her mind spun with recollections of kissing him, being in his arms. And then her thoughts seemed to spin backwards at the incongruity of the man. Tenderness oozed from his touch that night on the beach, yet those same hands had killed to protect her.

His fingers wrapped around hers again. He pointed at the brochure. "The Egyptian theme trail looks intriguing."

Huh? She glanced at the glossy tri-fold. One image was circled—a proud, standing Anubis, freakish and mythic. Her mind reeled. He didn't have the chance to mark it. Where had this come from then? Had he already made a contact? Again, her mind flashed—through the places they'd been, the people who'd bumped her—the man at the cathedral! The nun! So trapped in the frustration of being here without *being here*, she'd not paid attention.

She swallowed, mad that Reece had been testing her. "I've always liked Egyptian history."

His eyebrow hitched as they backtracked to the first stop on the Egyptian trail.

Anticipation built with each exhibit they admired, knowing that at the Anubis statue, something should happen. What?

Forty-three excruciating minutes later, the jackal-headed guardian loomed over them.

"This guardian walked the shadows of death," Shiloh mumbled, reading the sign next to his foot. "He determined which of the deceased would rise from the earth to become stars."

How appropriate. Sickeningly appropriate. If the contact came here, they would decide whether they saw Moreaux. Shiloh finally understood—she'd just had a major learning curve in the tactics of covert operatives. Her stomach clenched.

And soared! She'd figured it out.

"It is said," a man spoke, his voice a soft timbre that forced them to listen closely, "that he also weighed the heart of the dead and only allowed the pure to enter."

Shiloh's pulse sped. Reece's grip on her hand tightened.

The man smiled, his intense brown eyes grazing Shiloh and Reece. "I think he would look favorably upon you, mademoiselle." With that, he was gone.

Reece continued walking the Egyptian exhibit, seemingly enamored with the relics of history. At the gift shop, he purchased a small Anubis keychain and handed it to Shiloh. A memento, he called it. A sign that they would stand in the shadows of death, yet live.

Her mind whirled in a million directions. Had they failed? Was the Anubis man the contact? Or had they missed the real contact? Why hadn't Reece said anything or given some indication that they'd accomplished something? She fingered the small but heavy ornament on the chain. Was this her sign that she'd done well?

Or maybe it wasn't a test at all. Was he really just taking her out to show her the sights?

And was it her imagination or was Reece more relaxed than usual? He almost seemed lighthearted. At the car, he opened the door for her and ushered her into the safety of the compact vehicle. As they raced through the city, he still didn't speak.

"You're driving me nuts," she finally snipped.

A grin tweaked his lips apart.

"As much as I'd like to think you were trying to give me a romantic day in Paris, that was all business, wasn't it?"

"You'd like to think that, eh?" He winked at her, then returned his attention to the road. "We accomplished what we set out to accomplish."

"Very diplomatic, Mr. Jaxon."

He smiled.

"So. Where to now? Arc de Triomphe?"

He cast a rueful eyebrow toward her. "Didn't you hear? Moreaux approves of you."

She spun toward him, the seatbelt tugging against her. "That was it! I was right. Anubis man was the contact."

A chuckle rumbled through his chest. "One of them. Why do you think I bought the trinket? Your first mission, so to speak, and you sailed through it."

"One?" Shiloh paused, her exhilaration tempered. "How many contacts were there?"

"Does it matter?"

"Absolutely!"

"Three."

Mumbai, India

"They are in Paris." Ali Abdul mopped his brow.

"Then that is where you should be."

He pounded a fist on his desk. "No! I must be here. There is a large meeting with the UN tomorrow. I already have men in place to take care of these two."

"Good. Or your wife and children will pay for your mistakes."

"There is no need for that."

"You gave them the female agent before we got what we needed."

"She did not have any information."

"But you let them march in there and steal her right out from under your nose! You have let me down for the last time, Ali."

"Be patient." His breath hissed out. "The committee has already begun investigating the president, once he is . . . distracted, I can gain full access to the codes."

"That should've happened last week!"

"I will not fail!"

"Then kill these two or you will be next!"

Paris, France

She glanced at the five-story building, grey and darkened by age and the elements, and wondered how things would go inside, where she would take the lead. Captain Miller had explained the way things worked—that only she could ask the questions if they wanted answers. She supposed that's why Reece let her talk to the primary contact in the Louvre.

She studied the French Ministry complex, the dark alley on the right, the police car parked on the opposite corner and then the building again. Why did it look like something straight out of a late-night horror flick? She licked her lips. "What do I say?"

"We went over it on the plane. You'll do fine."

Throat cleared, she braced herself. "Right." Considering the half-dozen security cameras poised over the street like vultures, they were most likely being watched. She wiped her hands down her jeans.

"Shiloh?"

She glanced at him. Warmth and strength flowed from his beautiful eyes into her soul.

"You can do this."

She nodded. Her attention drifted back to the foreboding building. Why was she so nervous?

Because this was her first gig. The first time her effectiveness decided her fate. She had learned enough about Moreaux to know that if she didn't ask the right questions, they'd get nothing but fluff. As Reece said, they wanted the goose, not the down.

"Ready?"

Before she could answer, he climbed out of the car and shut the door. She groped for the handle. Panic beat an unsteady rhythm in her chest. If she couldn't even get her door open, how could she pull this off? Unwittingly talking to a stranger in the Louvre was one thing. Entering an official's territory to extract information . . . What on earth was she thinking?

Her door swung open. Reece's hand flashed into view. She drew up courage she didn't think she possessed, took his hand, and climbed out.

Reece reached around her and shut the door as he whispered, "I believe in you."

His soft words skidded along her cheek and into her heart. She wanted to throw herself into his arms and siphon off as much strength as he'd allow.

They crossed the threshold into the office building. Marble floors rushed into bullet-proof glass and a large reception desk. To the right, an enclosed waiting area, secured with the same heavy glass and secure-locks, greeted them. A sign read *welcome* in French and English.

Reece gently nudged her forward. She strode toward the window. Half-tempted to smile, she opted not to change her expression lest the security personnel deem it artificial and prevent her entrance. Closer, she spotted a man in a uniform with a machine gun tucked into the crook of his arm.

"May I help you?" the woman at the desk asked in French and then English.

"Yes, I'm Joselyn Hayes," she repeated what Reece told her to say. "I have an appointment with Deputy Minister Gerard

Moreaux." She inched aside so the woman could see Reece. "My assistant, Mr. James."

"One moment, please." She pressed a few buttons, spoke into the phone. Then she motioned Shiloh to the waiting area. "If you will have a seat, Minister Moreaux will be with you in a moment."

The lock on the door to the waiting area disengaged.

Seven minutes and a mound of tension later, a woman in a business suit escorted Shiloh and Reece from the secure sitting room. They followed her through a series of doors and security checkpoints until they were finally ushered into an octagonal office with rich, dark paneling.

"The minister will be with you soon." She left and closed the door.

"I—"

"Nice office, isn't it?" Reece shifted away and studied the bookcases. Intently.

Shiloh straightened. This wasn't the place to say anything they didn't want someone to overhear. They should look casual, comfortable, at ease. "I'd like to see the tower before we leave."

Surprise glinted in Reece's ocean-blue eyes. "It's overrated."

The door opened. A tall, dark-haired man entered. The air swirled, carrying with it a thick, heady cologne. Behind him the door seemed to move on its own and shut tightly. "Ms. Hayes, I'm Gerard Moreaux." He clasped her hand and planted a kiss on her cheek.

"Thank you for agreeing to see us." Shiloh again turned to Reece. "My assistant Simon James."

The silent handshake between the two men said more to Shiloh than words. He didn't like or trust Reece. Was it because of what Captain Miller said—Reece was a spy?

"Ms. Hayes, please, have a seat and tell me how I can help you." The man had a grace and style about him that seemed to shout his Parisian heritage.

Somehow, Shiloh knew not to mince words. "A friend gave me a gift." From her purse, she withdrew the coin Baseer had given her. "He said to see you about it."

"It's a nice piece." He clapped the box shut looking completely unaffected or impressed. "I'm not sure what this has to do with me. I'm sorry."

Shiloh's heart sped. "But, he gave me your name."

He handed it back, his expression almost stricken. "My apologies, mademoiselle, but I cannot help." Pearly teeth shone through a conciliatory smile. "My duty is to help the citizens of France and monitor foreign relations. Unless you have a problem there, I am afraid I cannot be of assistance."

Remembering Reece's tutelage not to let the man easily refuse her, she nudged the box back to him. "My friend gave me your name." She and Reece walked a fine line, not wanting to test the minister's patience lest they end up arrested. "I believe this coin may be the link between life and death."

The minister's face sat like stone.

Reece folded his arms, a hint to keep going.

"There is an old story I've heard about pieces like this." Shiloh took the coin and ran her finger around the gouged edge. "Of silly skirmishes over gold pieces where a man's family is threatened and his own breath cut from his throat. Sometimes, a man's son is blamed as well, and his life taken too."

Something changed in the minister's eyes. Had they widened? Or maybe dilated? He lifted the box and bounced it in his hand.

She held his gaze until she was sure she'd made her point that Khalid and Baseer were dead. Then she let out a laugh. "Silly folktales. It's a good thing our countries are more . . . civilized. Heaven knows the U.S. would not tolerate such actions."

He lifted a black pen from a cup, twisted it, then set it into an acrylic base. Without a word, he strode to his floor-to-ceiling bookcase and picked up a decorative pen set. On a wooden base, the two gold pens stuck out at forty-five degree angles. Moreaux removed the pens and pushed a nameplate on the front. Two trays popped out from the base. Striding toward her, he set the coin in one tray, then glanced at her. "Your hand, mademoiselle."

Though tempted to check with Reece, Shiloh lifted her arm, which felt like an anchor.

Warm and firm, his hand guided hers to the contraption. He pressed her index finger against the velvet pad. A blue light strobed beneath her flesh. When it glowed green, he released her, replaced the scanner in the canister and returned to his desk. The leather chair whooshed against his weight. "The room is secure. You have two minutes, Mademoiselle Blake."

Hearing her real name voiced in this foreign office sent fiery darts down her spine.

Reece leaned forward and rested his elbows on his knees. Another sign. Get on with it.

Shiloh turned to the minister. "Baseer Khan was gunned down right in front of me. So was his son—my fiancé—Khalid. When Baseer gave me the coin, he told me to come to you."

"Allah's Sword of Justice." Moreaux tapped the edge of his desk as he quirked an eyebrow at Reece. "Your *friend* is no doubt familiar with it."

Reece nodded.

"As a youth, Baseer joined them thinking it was a pledge of loyalty to his country. When he realized the truth of their ways and tried to get out, they threatened his family. Over the years, they dragged him deeper and deeper because of his knowledge and skill."

"We have reason to believe Ali Abdul is working with this group." Shiloh tucked her chin, hoping he would confirm or deny that.

"Ali is an ant," he spat. "No, the man you want is Osman Sajjadi." Moreaux eased forward, the chair squeaking as he did. "And I suggest you leave Paris immediately. If he learns you are here, we will all die."

21

SOMETHING WAS OFF. REECE PUSHED HIMSELF UPRIGHT. WHY WAS Minister Moreaux anxious to get rid of them? "What's the rush?" His question broke protocol, but he didn't like the power the man wielded.

Minister Moreaux uncapped a crystal decanter and poured a crimson drink into a bourbon glass. "Ever been to the Louvre, Mr. James?"

He wanted them to know he'd had them followed. That they'd been flagged from the moment they landed at the airport.

"Or perhaps Sainte-Chapelle?" He replaced the decanter and turned to Shiloh. "Have you ever had a chocolate waffle, Mademoiselle Blake? Delicious, especially with a walk down the Seine."

Stiffening, Reece mentally plotted a path out of here. Why had he thought this would go well? He listened to the hall for footsteps. Was there a hidden camera? Trouble was coming. He could feel it.

"What's your point?" Shiloh rose to her feet, bringing Reece up with her.

Moreaux considered them both for a moment. He then lifted a black remote and aimed it at the far wall. An oak panel slid back and revealed a large plasma television. The screen sprang to life.

A newscast blurred before them. The airport. A reporter ... Images of Shiloh and Khalid splashed over the TV, confirming the minister's warning. Shiloh moved toward the screen. Reece could almost hear her frantic heartbeat. It felt like a grenade detonated.

She pointed. "Th-that photograph was taken at the governor's ball last year—in San Diego!" She spun around, eyes wide. "How did they get that?"

Moreaux clicked off the television. "The coverage started about an hour ago. No doubt when you walked through the front door of the Louvre your picture was captured, and now Interpol knows you are here." He frowned and shook his head. "They're probably already on their way."

"Who's on their way?" Shiloh's voice pitched.

Moreaux went on. "Baseer was more than my friend. He was my cousin by marriage." From his briefcase, he ripped open the lining and removed a wafer-thin object. "By midnight, I will be dead. This is what you will need to bring down Sajjadi."

Reece stared at the piece, momentarily wondering if it was a tracking device too. "Why now? You know we've been after him for a decade."

A sad smile bled into his somber countenance. "I had assets to protect, but now they are dead. Our organization lived in the shadows of death. Like Anubis." His dark eyes moved to Shiloh with meaning. "Don't hold it against Khalid. He only meant to help his father."

Not good. Reece snatched the piece. "We'll be on our way."

"Wh-what do you mean? I don't understand." Shiloh's words tumbled out. "Hold what against him?"

"Thank you, Minister," Reece said, hooking hands with her. "We'll show ourselves out."

She jerked away, her brow knit tightly. "What do you mean, Khalid only meant to help his father? Help him what? It was Baseer. Khalid wasn't involved."

Pity stole the place of sadness in the minister's expression. "My cousin never wanted you to know. He hoped to disconnect himself and start a family with you. For Khalid's sake, I'm telling you now before you find things in your search or see it on the news."

"No . . ." Shiloh took a step back, shaking her head.

Moving in to break her line of sight on the minister, Reece locked eyes with her. "We'll sort it out later. Let's go." Though she met his gaze, she wasn't looking at him. He could tell her mind wrestled with the devastating blow about Khan.

Reece cupped her face. "Shi?"

She blinked.

"With me?"

A disconcerted shake and nod shouted her bewilderment. She touched his arm before giving a stronger nod.

"A bit intimate with the operative, aren't you, Mademoiselle Blake?" Moreaux cast suspicious glances between the two of them. "Is this how you honor—"

"Thank you for your time, Minister." Reece grabbed her hand again. He'd drag Shiloh out rather than let this Frenchman fill her head with doubts.

"Khalid was my best friend. Nothing will change that, Mr. Moreaux." Conviction infused Shiloh's words as she stole one more glance at the screen. "I won't stop until his name is cleared. I don't care what you say, he *never* would've done the things his father did!"

Moreaux hesitated, then inclined his head toward them. "Thank you."

Only then did Reece realize the man only wanted reassurance that the sacrifices his family made weren't in vain. Shiloh, a woman who had captured the heart of his nephew, gave him hope. Of course he wouldn't trust a covert operative.

Shouts echoed through the hall. Heavy thuds pounded the floor.

"You should go." Moreaux used the remote once more and opened a hidden door. "Down the stairs. They'll take you to the alley."

Behind Shiloh, Reece stepped into the tight quarters of the stairwell. He glanced back.

Tears glossed Moreaux's hazel eyes. He looked at Shiloh, then Reece. "Take care of her."

Thud! Thud! Thud!

"Go!" Moreaux slid the door shut.

Crack! "Where are they?"

Reece frantically motioned Shiloh down the stairs. She sped over the concrete steps. The stairs dumped into a short corridor. At the end of the hall, beams of light slipped in under a door.

They raced toward it.

Voices devoured the cement coffin.

"Out, right, left, left," Reece shouted as they burst into the alley. He kept pace with her. This pursuit rang eerily similar to the foot-chase in Mumbai. Just as there, being captured here meant absolute death.

Shiloh broke right down another alley where a group of dogs snarled and barked at them.

Behind them, a barrage of yelling shattered the noisy normalcy of the city.

No more than two feet ahead, Shiloh banked left. She slipped and yelped. Reece grabbed her arm and dragged her back into motion.

The slight change in her speed worried him.

One more left. If they could make it to the apartment, they could hide out. It was the only safe place. The safe-house had too many connections. They'd be found there. The very reason he'd refused to go back to their car. The reason he'd switched their baggage so the police would only find a duffel full of clothing and ambiguous items.

Concrete burst out. He ducked. "Almost there," he shouted to Shiloh, sensing she was losing her resolve.

As he rounded the corner, several pieces of data pelted his mind. The tail end of a car sticking out past the corner. The shadow of a man stretching into the darkened alley. The quiet.

Reece grabbed Shiloh and yanked her into a corner. "Shh."

She nodded, pain smearing across her sweaty brow.

He motioned to the side and led her into a storefront. They worked their way through the quiet shop and out the back door. Up a flight of groaning iron stairs.

"Where are they?"

Frozen, Reece held a hand up, staring down between the black diamond grate underfoot. Shiloh pressed back. Cement dribbled down.

A half-dozen figures drifted through the alley like ghouls haunting the living. Angry words shot back and forth. They were almost in the clear. *Thank God nobody—*

"There! On the fire escape!"

Reece dove into Shiloh, knocking her through the broken window. They landed with a thud—she yelped and arched her back. Without time to assess her injury, he pulled her to her feet. "We've got about fifty yards. Can you make it?"

"Yes," she ground out, her face pale even in the darkened room.

He nodded, wishing he could erase her pain. Later. They hurried through the building. Voices and slamming noises played hide and seek with them.

Finally, they slipped through a door into a furnished flat. Reece gently turned the lock. They jogged to a back room. To the matching bookcases flanking a tall window. He lifted the window seat, revealing a very cramped space. "Get in."

Shiloh sucked in a breath. "You're kidding."

"Do it."

She complied, her petite frame consuming a large portion of the space. He crawled in after her, their bodies tangling in the darkness.

"There's not enough room."

"Shh." He eased the lid closed, waited for it to catch.

Click.

Hands over his head, Reece applied a subtle pressure to the wood running perpendicular to the floor—a crawl space he'd rigged under the bookcase wall.

He nudged the panel out of the way. "Slide up."

Shiloh hesitated, then scooted into the opening. Seconds later, Reece dragged himself in and toed the panel shut. The space gave them just enough room to stretch their legs as they lay on the dusty cement. He settled his back against the wall, waiting.

"Anything?" A voice rang out.

Shiloh took in a sharp, quiet breath and stiffened. Reece touched her arm to reassure her.

"Nothing."

"Check all the rooms, cabinets, sinks, floorboards."

Seconds later, Reece heard the window seat open. He gritted his teeth.

"There's a window open in the upstairs room."

"Let's go! That's where they went." The floor rattled. Dust rained on Reece's head. He jerked his head, right into something solid—Shiloh's head. Pain shot across his brow.

Shiloh grunted.

He'd apologize when it was safe to talk. He gave up trying to be comfortable. Although he'd used this spot once before, he'd never had to share it with anyone. Next time he built a hiding place, he'd have to make the space slightly larger. Not much bigger, or it'd be too easy for the enemy to find.

He closed his eyes, his mind logging every creak and shift in the boards. It took more than twenty minutes for those who'd come after them to give up. Reece waited another twenty before whispering, "You okay?"

"I have glass in my back."

"Turn toward me," he said.

She scooted, her hand catching his jaw. "Sorry." Braced on her side, she let out a soft sigh.

Reece ran his hand gently along her back. Something sharp pricked his palm. "Found it." He determined the glass wasn't big enough to have dug too deep into her skin. He gripped it and tugged it out.

Shiloh groaned. She must've leaned into him, because her hair brushed against his chin. The fruity scent of her shampoo teasing his nose.

"I think that's it." He let his hand retrace its path along her back, convincing himself it was to check for more glass.

"Is this your apartment?"

"One of them." He propped his head on his fist. "Sorry, it's not the Ritz."

"We're alive."

Silence again draped their hiding place. He shouldn't admit how much this time alone with her satisfied a long-ignored ache. It felt good and right to be with her. His mind rushed to some moment in the future when their lives weren't in danger and they could slow down, get to know each other.

Shiloh hissed as she repositioned her legs.

"How's your ankle?"

"Fine." She sighed, her warm breath fanning his neck.

He liked this, having her close, being in each other's arms . . . sort of. His heart skipped a beat, realizing how much he enjoyed this.

And that was dangerous. Very dangerous.

He needed to steer his thoughts to higher ground. "You did great today."

"You're a good teacher."

He hadn't meant to teach her anything. Just get what they needed and get out. If she put her mind to it, Shiloh Blake could be one of the best covert operatives walking the globe.

Which meant she'd be in danger for the rest of her life.

His heart pulsed.

No. He couldn't do that. Not to *her*. He wanted her safe. In his arms.

"Let's move to the roof. We can scope the streets, see if they're still here. If it's clear, we'll go to a safe house." With that, Reece guided them out of the hiding place.

As they crept along the narrow hall, Shiloh guarded her steps and ignored the dull ache throbbing against her ankle. His hand curled around hers as they slipped over creaking boards and past peeling paint. Reassured by the firmness of his grasp and the confidence with which he stole through the darkened hall, Shiloh followed him to the dank stairwell. Nerves zipping, she tried to listen past her hammering heart. What if they walked out and were gunned down?

She tugged back.

Reece shifted, and she noticed the weapon he held. His eyes questioned her. When she didn't respond, he continued until they hunkered before the door to the roof.

"Wait here," he whispered. Carefully, he pushed back the door. It creaked. Groaned.

Shiloh hauled in a breath and held it.

With stealth and speed, he ran hunched over and then flattened himself against the roof. Only then did she let out the captive breath. He peeked over a two-foot ledge. Just as quickly, he jerked back. A sharp nod and tightened lips told of his frustration.

At his prodding, Shiloh scurried to his side. She lay next to him, propped on her forearms. "What's wrong?"

"They're watching the building. We'll have to wait till dark."

Checking the sky, Shiloh knew the wait would be at least an hour, maybe two. How could they just sit for two hours? When Reece rolled onto his back, a cool breeze carried his unique, crisp and clean scent to her.

Shiloh pushed her thoughts to the mission. Away from Reece. In the cramped space, his body heat had kept her warm. Up here as dusk blanketed the city in pinks and greys, a chill trickled down her back. She'd never admit how much she missed the closeness of those deadly minutes.

Danger leapt all around them, chasing and threatening. Yet she felt as safe and peaceful as if napping by a quiet stream. Unfortunately, that quiet stream led to the turbulent waters they'd encountered at Moreaux's. Khalid wasn't who he said he was. He'd lied, deceived her. His betrayal gouged a hole in her heart.

When Moreaux had mentioned Khalid's involvement, Reece hadn't batted an eye. "Did you know?" she whispered.

"No."

She peeked at him in disbelief. "You didn't know about Khalid?"

"I suspected, but didn't have proof."

Why was she the only one surprised by Khalid's involvement? "I can't believe he lied to me." Sorrow clawed her soul to pieces. "I thought I knew him." Tears burned the back of her eyes. She blinked them back but felt her composure crumbling.

Reece nudged her shoulder. "Hey."

The softness of his word drew out a tear. "The one man I thought I could trust—and I couldn't. It turns out I didn't even know him. This is just like my—" A sob choked her. She squeezed her eyes shut.

Arms encircled her. Reece rubbed her shoulder. "Shh."

Burrowed into the warmth of his hold, she let her agony free. All these years she'd run from the brutality of her father's career and the pain it had unleashed on their family, only to become fiancée to the exact same type of man. And now she lay in hiding, in the strong arms of yet another betrayer.

"You're different," she blurted, startled by her own yearning for Reece to be different.

He kissed her ear.

She turned her head to his, feeling his breath dashing against her jawline. "I hated you, thinking you were just like my father."

He didn't respond.

"I don't know that I can ever forgive him. When my mother died, I promised myself I wouldn't let that happen to me again. But it did—I walked right into the middle of it, and Khalid died. I didn't even see it coming." A breath shuddered out. "In a lot of ways you're like my father, too, yet different." Why was she rambling? Did she want to convince Reece she didn't hate him? Or convince herself?

"Jude Blake is one of my heroes." Reece's deep voice rattled her ear. "As a trainee, I studied his methods, watched tapes of him at work. Everyone admired him." His thumb traced maddening circles along her arm. "But nobody saw what it did to his family . . . until it was too late."

"When my mother was killed, it shattered me," she said, startled at the raw burning at the back of her throat. Normally, the pain came out with vehemence and fury. "I was terrified when my father went back to work. Wondered if I would be the next victim of his career. Oh, sure—he said the agency guaranteed my safety, but they said that about my mother too. All his talk about God and trying to make amends . . ."

"But if he gave up, if he surrendered, the enemy would've won."

"And when does the family win?"

On his side, Reece gently rubbed her back. "So, you vowed to remove yourself from his life, and if I know how stubborn you are, you probably also promised to remain in an innocuous career that would never put loved ones in danger."

She bit back a retort, silencing the defensiveness coursing through her veins.

"How did that work out for you? I mean, you're out there diving and through one tragic event, you lose teammates and, ultimately, your fiancé."

Her heart felt like it churned sand instead of blood. "What's your point?"

"Hey," he said in a low, soothing voice. He cupped her face. "Don't get mad. I'm just saying we can't control when bad things happen. That's not up to us. God can take the imploding mess of our lives and turn it around."

God? Since when did God turn anything around? Again, she silenced her urge to snap her thoughts. Somehow . . . somehow she felt she had something to learn from Reece.

"I'm proof. My parents were diplomats. Spent a lot of time in DC." Reece lay back, rocks grinding between his back and the roof. "My father was always away on business. Mom stayed home with my sister and me. She entertained regularly—weekends, nights, days."

Why is he telling me this?

"I was a senior when the scandal broke."

"What scandal?"

"Remember hearing about the Maryland Madame? The one who ran an elite call-girl ring, entertaining dignitaries, politicians, ambassadors, and executives alike?"

Surely he didn't mean . . .

"My father divorced her and abandoned her—and us. Two years later, he died of alcohol poisoning. I was bitter. Didn't care. Glad he was gone, even gloated that his death had been painful, that maybe he'd felt some of what he inflicted on me and my sister."

"What about your mother?"

"Federal pen for the last fifteen years."

"I-I'm sorry."

"Yeah, me too. Funny thing is, I hated my father more. Couldn't look in the mirror for a long time. I look just like him."

Shiloh searched his face and wished she could search his mind to see how he'd managed to become the incredible man he was with such a sordid family tale.

"How did you . . . ?" She swallowed. Could she ask that question? Dusk loomed, descending with the dark blanket of evening.

"How did I go on?" He had read her mind, and in his words, she heard the hint of a laugh. "Through no fault of my own. At first, I wanted to hurt anyone and everyone in my path. Even my older sister. She's like you. Doesn't take much flak. Told me to get straightened out before I ended up in jail. So I joined the Navy."

"Ah, that explains the haircut."

He laughed. "Six months in, a chaplain saw my pain and rode my case." Again he chuckled. "Said I was running from God. Man, was I ever, as fast and hard as I could. He helped me get turned around."

"You're a Christian?"

"How do you think I handle what I do? I give it to God every night before I sleep."

Curse the darkness! She wanted to see his eyes. See if he was serious. "My father claimed to convert to Christianity."

"He did."

Shiloh stilled, half expecting Reece to try to shove his religion down her throat. But when he didn't, she took the chance to ask him about it. "Don't you think religion's just a crutch? A label people use to cover their inability to provide answers for their problems? I mean, God hasn't exactly helped me."

"When have you let Him? He's not like Hostage Rescue—He's not going to come in with flash-bangs and door rams. If you've shut Him out, how can you expect Him to help when your brick and mortar world is bombed?" Quiet lingered as the darkness deepened around them. Finally, Reece tilted his head. Moonlight sparkled in his eyes. "You said I'm like your dad . . . going to hold that against me?"

"Maybe." The tease escaped before she could stop it. Shiloh shrugged as she looked to the moon. "We haven't spoken in years. I don't want him in my life."

"Just remember, you're the one who said I was different."

Now it was her turn to laugh. "You are." Since openness and honesty seemed to be the fare for the evening, she braved a question that had niggled her for a while. "Tell me about Chloe." Shiloh eased onto her back, stiffening against the prickles of pain from the glass cuts.

"Whoa." Hollowness poked his laugh. "You're not pulling any punches." He exhaled loudly. "All right. Even though this goes against my better judgment . . . Her sister worked for the agency and recommended her to me. After thoroughly investigating Chloe, I agreed she had what it took. So I recruited and trained her. She sailed through her first mission, following every nuance of my instructions. I'd never been so proud. But I made the mistake of letting my feelings for her cross professional lines."

"You had a relationship with her?"

"We dated. I got serious. She didn't—about me or the job."

"Did you love her?" The question swirled through her stomach, weaving a tight fabric of jealousy.

"I thought I did. I see things differently now. We never really clicked. Not like—" He cleared his throat.

Us? Not like us? Was that what he meant? So he felt things were natural and right between them too? Pleasure kneaded the longing in her heart.

"We had an argument. Chloe felt I was holding her back."

"Were you?"

"I knew things she didn't. Any trainee should know to trust their handler. She insisted I release her to go solo. I refused and told her she wasn't ready. Then we got the call that the Taj was under siege. By going against my wishes and without authorization, she was rogue. My hands were tied. If anything went wrong, she would be disavowed." He scratched the stubble on his jaw. "They found her body in a ditch a week later."

"I'm sorry."

"Me too."

Shiloh lay there, realizing how much he'd been through with his parents and Chloe. Why hadn't anger eaten him? He had said he gave everything to God. What did that mean? God didn't want her problems—He had a world full of them already.

And this woman who'd tied Reece's mind in knots. The one he thought he loved, what was she like? How had she captured his attention?

"What was she like as a person?"

"Smart. Feisty. Bad attitude." His thumb stroked her jaw. "But she had nothing on you. What is it—India? Does it bring out the worst in you women?"

"I love India. Well, not the clogged cities, but the people, the beaches and open areas. Just incredible." Shiloh smiled at the stars that peeked through the cover of night. "The caves are indescribable."

"You mean on Elephanta Island?"

"No, the ones underwater. Khalid and I found them weeks ago. We would spend our weekends exploring them."

Quiet plunked between them.

Next to her, Reece lifted up and peered over the side. He pushed up more. Soon, he slunk along the wall, peering over the rim.

"What?"

He hurried to the corner, glanced over—and jerked back. He returned. "Come on. I have an idea." Moving as if night had no effect on his ability to see, Reece jogged to the other end.

Shiloh followed close behind.

"Over there."

She followed to where he pointed—and her heart thumped. "What?"

"We're going to jump." Reece grinned. "Come on. It's only a dozen feet."

Only?

With a skip, he sprinted the distance and soared over the alley. Landing in a roll, he hit almost without a sound. On his feet, he turned and waved.

Great. She had no choice but to do the same. Palms sweating, she darted toward the ledge. *I am insane.* She threw her arms upward. Nothing but cool Parisian air below. The roof of the other building rose to meet her.

Shiloh hit. Hard. Against the side. She groped for a hold. Slid down.

A hand clamped over hers. Drew her up. Cement scraped her side. Finally, Reece hauled her up and held her close. "You okay?"

"Yeah." Her hands trembled. She hissed as the pain in her side registered.

"What's wrong?"

"Nothing." Shiloh clamped a hand over the scrape. "I'm fine. Let's just go."

Down the fire escape, they then stuck to the darker, stinky parts of the city. Reece's agile and swift moves challenged Shiloh to stay alert.

Thirty minutes delivered them to the stoop of a home in the Latin Quarter. "Where are we?" Shiloh inched nearer to Reece, feeling exposed in the light streaming from the front window.

The door opened. A woman eyed Shiloh, then Reece. She frowned as she stepped back and allowed them in. "Your faces are all over the news."

Reece nodded. "We need to get back to the States."

The woman shook her head. She lifted a device from a nearby table and handed it to him.

He looked at it and cursed.

"What?" Shiloh glanced between the two. "What is that? A pager?"

Something flickered in Reece's eyes for only a second before it vanished. He touched her shoulder. "Why don't you go shower? We'll head out as soon as I can get things worked out."

His words might as well have been a pat on the head. She wasn't a child. And she'd had enough. "I've just escaped a ministry building where I should have been safe. I've been shot at, gotten glass stuck in my back, lay for two hours on a roof, jumped off said roof, and hoofed it for the last half hour to get here." She raked a hand through her hair. "Now. Tell me what's going on?"

Reece's expression hardened. "*Everything's* going on."

The edge in his words pushed her back. He'd never talked or looked at her like that. What . . . what had changed? What was on that thing the woman had shown him? Or was this about something different? Maybe her and Khalid? Was this woman someone special to him, someone who reminded him that Shiloh was just a guppy? Did he think he loved her, only to realize he didn't? She eyed him and swallowed the swell of dread.

"Kit, take her upstairs." He started toward the back of the house.

Confused at the way he took charge, the way he ordered the woman who owned this house around, Shiloh stared after him.

"He's right, love." A strong Irish brogue sailed through the woman's words. "You should shower and change. Never know what will happen next." Kit guided her up the stairs to a room with a bed and private bath. "You don't look much bigger than me, so you'll have a change of clothes. I'll mend your back after you've showered."

Despair clung to Shiloh. She nodded, barely remembering the pain and stickiness in her back. Kit lifted a robe from a hook outside the bathroom, spun the knobs in the shower, set towels on the bathtub ledge, and then turned back to her. Brown eyes took her in, filled with uncertainty and . . . something else. "I'm sorry about your fiancé."

Surprised the woman knew so much, Shiloh tried not to react.

A smile slipped into Kit's beautiful face. "He's the best. He'll take good care of you."

"He hates me, I think." Even to Shiloh, it sounded so unreasonable, but something had changed with Reece. But still, she had no business talking about it with this woman. She accepted the robe. "Thanks." With that, she strode into the bathroom and shut the door.

Relief flooded her at being alone. Alone with her thoughts. Alone with her pain.

She slipped off her jeans. Then whimpered and cringed as she peeled off the shirt, the dried blood pricking her back with pain. Beneath the warm water, she pressed her hands against the white tile. What had she done? It surprised her how much she wanted to make this right, to see the smile that sparkled in his eyes even when he wasn't actually smiling. Desperately, she ached to have the strength of his support and feel like he had her back.

What did he have that she didn't? How could she be as strong and confident? Whatever it was, she wanted it.

God.

Anything but that.

22

WHAT'RE YOU DOING?"

Reece set the phone back on the cradle and turned calmly toward Kit.

"Don't give me that innocent goat look!" She stomped across the tiled floors, hands on her hips. "You're a better agent than letting some girl get silly over you!"

"It's . . ." He looked back to the paper where he'd written his notes, feeling helpless. No, desperate. "Don't worry. I'm taking care of it."

She cursed. "It's true—you've fallen for her." Kit slammed the metal tea kettle onto a gas burner. "How can you be so daft?"

He spun to her. "I said I'm taking care of it!" Then her slip of the tongue registered. "Wait. Who's talking?"

Her brows knitted together. Kit covered her mouth, her eyes glossing as she shook her head. Finally, she slumped and braced herself against the counter. "Did you learn nothing from Chloe?"

He stalked to her. "Tell me who's talking?"

"You've compromised her safety and yours." Sorrow plowed into her sweet face. "They'll pull you, Reece."

"No, they won't. We're in too deep." He returned to the table. Knuckles against the wood, he stared at his notes. The plan was there. Everything in place. Only a few more calls. "I just have to protect the codes, make sure they aren't tampered with. I'm too close."

"Yes, precisely."

He snapped up his head. "Not to *her*, to the truth."

"There's no difference. She's directly connected to the truth. Getting involved with a mark is a primary tactical error."

Reece flung the pen across the room. "Get off my back, Kit. I know what I'm doing." But did he? Why did everything feel like it was spinning out of control, right through his fingers?

"Do you love her?"

"No." The answer flew out and gave him away. The blunt force of a baseball bat against his chest wouldn't have knocked the wind out of him the way her question had. How could Kit, in less than an hour, know what he felt for Shiloh? He stared at his hastily scrawled notes. The flight numbers. Aliases. Times. If he went through with this . . . He started for the stairs. "I need to clean up."

"She thinks you hate her."

He stopped at the threshold between the kitchen and living room but didn't turn around. "It won't matter."

Kit's words haunted him as he trudged up the stairs. His plan had worked. Shiloh thought he hated her. But knowing that she believed it cut deeper than he could've imagined. As he walked past her room, he heard the steady cadence of water and music . . .

No. Not music. Crying.

His eyes closed. *God, this is too much.* Finally able to fall in love, have that love returned—he wasn't quite one hundred percent on that—and he has to surrender her. Walk away from the first ounce of joy he'd felt in years.

"What're you going to do?"

He straightened at the sound of Kit's voice behind him. Then his shoulders sagged. "Don't worry about it."

"Reece . . ."

"Don't." He took a step.

"My sister's death should've taught you more."

Anger stabbed through him. "It's a lesson I'll *never* repeat."

In his room, he showered and changed. This wasn't the first time he'd had to enact such an extreme plan, but it was the first time he felt as if he'd cut out his heart.

It had to be done. Once Shiloh was safe, he'd ghost himself. Then hack out a living in the Alps or maybe the northern Rockies. Anywhere he didn't have to think or feel.

On the edge of the bed, he made one final call.

"Go ahead."

"Where are you?" Reece reached into the dresser, slid a panel aside, and withdrew a set of bona fides.

"It's November. Where do you think I am?" Good. He counted on the man's predictability.

"I need a favor."

"I'm your man."

Reece delivered the flight information. "Make sure this happens."

"Got it."

He ended the call and tossed himself against the bed. Eyes shut, he let himself relive the kiss he'd shared with Shiloh on the beach. What he wouldn't give for a thousand more nights like that. He groaned. She'd awakened too much in him.

Female voices pulled him from his despair. He stuffed his arms into a navy fisherman's sweater and adjusted the white T-shirt beneath it. Best to just get on with this.

Not think or dwell on it. Smoothing back his short crop, he headed downstairs.

From the foyer he could see through the darkened living room into the kitchen. Shiloh sat at the table, a white mug in her hands. Kit leaned against the counter stirring a steaming pot.

Laughter shot through the room.

"You've got to be joking," Kit said.

Shiloh giggled and shook her head. Her reddish-brown tresses were dry and hung in loose waves. So beautiful . . . like autumn leaves of amber and gold. Tilting the mug against her lips, she took a drink.

"What else did he do?"

They were talking about him! He strode into the kitchen and took a mug from the cabinet. At the stove, he eyed Kit and gave her a warning look as he poured a cup of hot tea.

"He's a big lug, stiff and tough." Kit chuckled. "But he's also brilliant."

Reece sipped the tea. He singed the tip of his tongue and hissed.

"Or maybe not."

He glared at her and joined Shiloh at the table. "We head out in a couple of hours."

"Wow, already?" She toyed with her napkin, not meeting his gaze. "Is it safe?"

"Everything's set. Kit will take you to the airstrip, where you'll catch your flight."

"What about you?" Shiloh set down her mug.

"Separate flights."

Was he doing the right thing? It made sense. Sacrificing what he felt for her would ensure her safety. Her words about how her father's career had endangered her life gnawed at the core of his being. He would do anything to make sure Shiloh had another day to see the sunrise over the ocean. To make sure she wasn't hurt. It would be the death of their relationship. She'd never speak to him after tonight.

"Why are we splitting up?"

"You're easier to spot together." Kit set bowls of a yellowish substance before them. "Eat your custard before it's cold."

Shiloh nodded as she lifted a steaming spoonful to her mouth and held it in midair. "Then we'll hook back up, right?" Her blue-grey eyes seemed to search his very soul.

His heart tripped over the next few beats. "When it's safe."

"Then we can go in and stop this. Put the men who killed Khalid and his father behind bars." Shiloh's voice edged with a fierceness he hadn't heard before.

Part of him wished he could hammer the stuffing out of Khalid Khan. He'd knowingly put her in danger with his connections to Allah's Sword. And because of that, Reece had to take extreme measures to protect her.

Same thing with Chloe. She had felt abandoned. Her brokenness turned to rage and a dangerous determination that got her killed. He had to stop Shiloh from taking that same path. There was only one way to protect her. That conviction cemented his plans as they finished off their desserts.

Shiloh would hate him to the end of her days.

Sacrifice always has a cost.

"Why don't you two go in the living room and relax?" Kit stood and retrieved their bowls of custard. "I'm going to clean up in here."

Suspicion crept into Reece's mind. Kit seemed too anxious to move them out of the room. What was she up to?

Shiloh rose. "The custard was wonderful. Thank you for the food, the clothes." She smoothed a hand over the pale pink sweater. The tiny fibers seemed to tickle her face. Stunning. Beautiful.

A tiny sliver of doubt cracked his resolve. *God forgive me if I'm wrong.*

"I haven't had guests in a while. It's nice to do something for friends." Kit waved them out. "Now go on you two. I'll be there in a minute."

Reece hung back, scowling at the woman he'd trusted with their lives. Why was she so anxious to see them out of the kitchen? If she was double crossing them . . .

"Don't give me that look when I know full well what you're planning."

He drew himself straight, his hands itching to rout out what she was up to. "I'd kill anyone who tried to hurt her."

Kit's eyes twinkled, tears forming in the corners. "I know." She sniffled and rolled her eyes to blink away the tears. "And I'm so glad, Reece. So glad you've found someone to love and who loves you back." A tear dashed down her cheek. "I just hope you aren't royally screwing this up."

Love me back? "Just stick to the plan. Let me worry about the rest." He stomped out of the kitchen, his conscience agitating her words. Shiloh might hate his guts for the rest of her life, but at least she would be alive to do it. He couldn't say that for Chloe.

"Every man I've trusted has betrayed me." Shiloh saw the startled look on Reece's face and smiled as they sat in the living room. "Except you."

He moved to the window, nudged aside the curtain, and peeked out at the street below.

Shiloh tensed, anxious to smooth the ripple that had entered their relationship. "Reece, I don't know what I did, but want to apologize—"

He held up a hand. "Don't." A hazy blue light outlined his face, an echo of the streetlight. His jaw muscle bounced. "It's not necessary." He said one thing, but the cool distance between them said another.

"I see." A strange feeling surged through her chest. Jealousy?

He let go of the curtain and met her gaze. "What does that mean?"

The back of her neck heated. "Nothing. It's just been a long day." She brushed the hair from her face, determined not to be catty. "I'll go upstairs so you and Kit can be alone."

As she crossed the room, Reece hooked her arm.

Shiloh closed her eyes, knowing she'd crumble in a flash if she had to face him.

"Look at me." Emotion kneaded his husky words.

She braved the stormy blue eyes that had always left her weak in the knees.

Desperation tore into his rugged face. "I wish I could make you understand . . ." Something ominous haunted his words.

A strange, sinking feeling pushed against her waning courage. "What's wrong?" The way he stared scared her. It wasn't the confident, powerful man she admired.

"They're here!" Kit hurried toward the door, swinging a coat over her shoulders. "Come, Shiloh. We're short on time."

Reece cupped her face. "I *don't* hate you."

Her chin trembled as she melted at his reassurance.

His brow knotted. He hesitated, then pressed his lips to hers. Just as quick, he drew back. "I love you, Shiloh. Don't forget that. No matter what happens."

Stunned, she stared after him as he jogged to the back of the house. Out the rear door.

I love you. Had he really said that?

"Shiloh, please," Kit prompted, her eyes glassy, her voice cracked.

Something niggled at the back of her mind as she rushed into the back seat of the sedan out front. Shrouded in ebony, they spirited through the night toward the airstrip. The whishing of the tires against wet pavement lulled her senses. Had Reece really said he loved her?

She glanced over her shoulder, hoping to see a car pull in behind them. "Where did he go?"

A wistful expression took root in Kit's face. "Always it's the mission with him."

Mission. Right. Get on a plane. "I don't know what to do when I get there." Her imagination leapt to life. "I mean, the media has my picture all over the news because of what happened at the train station. How will I get back into Mumbai without tipping my hand?"

Kit covered her hand. "Trust him."

I love you, Shiloh. The words bobbed on the stormy sea of her life like a beacon. She knew he meant those precious words. In a different way and on a different level than Khalid. Or maybe it was that she returned Reece's love.

The thought stalled her mind and body. Did she? Did she really . . . ? She closed her eyes. *Oh, yes. I do love him!* And she didn't tell him before he left. Is that why he tore out of the house like an arctic wind? Because she hadn't confirmed her feelings for him? An ache wove around her chest, tightening.

"We're here." Kit turned to her and handed her a passport. "The plane is waiting to taxi." She indicated toward a small jet looming off to the side, wing lights blinking back at her. "Climb aboard, present your ticket and passport. They'll clear it. Speak to no one until you land."

Shiloh nodded.

"And don't worry. You'll be fine."

The wake and roar of the plane's engines stirred the cool Parisian air. Shiloh tucked her chin against the wind as she shut the door.

"Shiloh?"

She pivoted.

Kit stared at her over the hood of the car. The woman hesitated, looked at the plane, then down at the car.

"Yes?" Shiloh asked, suddenly feeling very off-center.

"Just remember, sometimes he does stupid things believing they're for the best."

"What?"

A howl kicked up in the wind. Shiloh glanced toward the jet, surprised to find a flight attendant approaching. "Ma'am, we need to get under way."

Shiloh met her, handing off the ticket and passport, remembering the instructions not to say anything. The flight attendant stomped back to the plane, ripping the ticket and checking the passport. She then escorted Shiloh to a seat near the door.

No doubt the setup on the plane was intended to bypass security cameras and normal security checkpoints. Still, she wondered in a day and age like this how Kit and the others had managed to get her on a plane so easily.

Once the plane leveled off high above France ten minutes later, Shiloh settled into the cozy leather seat. Cozy? No, cozy had been on the rooftop as she lay in Reece's arms.

She missed him already. But at least she had his words to keep her company. I love you. Words she never thought would carry the weight his had. Weight that anchored them in her heart and soul. They were on separate paths right now, if only for a moment.

The cabin steward delivered her a glass of water with a snack. Still full from Kit's custard, Shiloh didn't eat the snack. The water, however, she guzzled, surprised at how thirsty she felt.

As she recapped the bottle her head swam. She blinked, overcome by sleepiness. It was nighttime. Being sleepy would be normal. But why did she feel as if she hadn't slept in days? Why was her vision swimming? She blinked again. The water bottle caught her eye. Oh no.

Her head bobbed.

Darkness.

Arms and legs weighted, Shiloh struggled to break the fog of sleep. She moaned and rolled her head, willing her eyes to open. Bright light smacked into her vision. She clenched her eyes and groaned.

"Miss?" Someone nudged her shoulder. "We're landing. You'll need to set your chair upright."

Shiloh shook her head and tried to lift it. Finally able to move, she pulled herself up and propped her elbows on her knees and cradled her head in her hands.

"You okay?"

She jerked toward the masculine voice. Pain shot through her temples.

A grey-haired man smiled at her. "Probably shouldn't take more than the prescribed dosage of Dramamine."

"I didn't." Again, she shook her head, this time feeling more focused.

"I am a doctor, and I know when someone is coming out of a drug fog."

Shiloh stared at him, understanding lighting across her brain. Drugged? Why would she be drugged? Her gaze snapped to the window. Lush green acreage spread out below the belly of the plane. Green. Too green.

Panic shot through her. "Where are we?"

The doctor chuckled. "Landing at Heathrow in another minute or two." He patted her hand. "Don't worry. Most crashes happen on takeoff."

"Heathrow?" Shiloh squeaked. "I'm on the wrong plane."

He taunted her with his laugh. "A little late to figure that out, love."

She looked out the window again. He had to be wrong. "No," she whimpered. She'd be spotted right out of the gate. They'd arrest her and slam her in prison. How would she get back to India? She'd be of no help to . . . Reece.

Her heart rate climbed. "No." He couldn't have . . . wouldn't have . . .

Sometimes he does stupid things believing they're for the best.

Reece did this. He put her on the wrong plane. The revelation jolted her as hard as the wheels scorching on the blackened runway. She jerked with the violent impact.

Anger replaced panic. Anger at him. Anger at herself. *You idiot!* This is why he'd said he loved her. To set her off kilter, to get her mind scrambled so she wouldn't notice . . . She gritted her teeth. Dug her fingernails into the flesh of her palms.

The devastation worked through her system like a fast-acting poison.

"Miss?"

Why would he do this? Why hadn't she expected this? *Because I trusted him!*

"Miss!"

Shiloh whipped her head toward the flight attendant and scowled.

The woman handed her an envelope. "I was asked to give this to you when we touched down."

Shiloh trembled as she accepted it. She let it drop into her lap, then buried her face in her hands, fighting the tears. *Why?* Why would he abandon her? Betray her? She pounded a fist against the arm rest.

The plane slowed drastically, then veered toward the terminal. The authorities were probably waiting. She'd be extradited . . . imprisoned.

A phone rang somewhere.

Defeated, she hung her gaze out the window. Trapped in a plane. Trapped in a nightmare Reece had set up. How could he do this? Tears slipped down her face. *I loved him and this is what I get?* A cold pang smothered her.

The phone's cheery melody stamped out continuously.

Why wouldn't the person answer the stupid phone?

"I think your envelope is ringing," the doctor said, pointing to her lap.

Shiloh glanced down, numb. Her senses realigned, and she realized he was right. She snatched up the brown paper and ripped open the flap. Eyeing the contents, she spotted a black phone. Ringing blared against her hurting ears. Reece had given her a phone in Mumbai. What if it was him?

She pressed TALK. "Hello."

"Take the blue attendant jacket on the rack inside the galley," a strange voice ordered. "Disembark. Exit and use the first door on your right. Down the stairs. I will be waiting."

The call ended as the plane taxied up to the terminal. As the other passengers disembarked, Shiloh sat staring at the phone. Who had called her? How had he known she'd be on the plane? The only way was through Reece or

Kit. If one of them had told this person, then he was most likely an operative-friend.

Shiloh rose and donned the blue blazer. Heart in throat she strode onto the umbilical. With one glance over her shoulder to make sure nobody saw her, she pushed through the door and hustled down the spiral stairs.

23

India

COLD AND MERCILESS, THE RAIN PELTED HIS BACK AND NECK. THE PAIN FELT appropriate. The cold matched his heart. Reece downshifted and eased his bike through a turn. Six hours ago he'd knowingly put Shiloh on a plane to London. And he hadn't stopped since.

It was the right thing. The only way to protect her.

A bug splatted against his helmet, obscuring his sight.

Just as you let your fear obscure My plans for you.

The gentle reprimand pounded him. He aimed to the side of the road and rolled to a stop. Drenched and shivering, he cleaned the visor. His vision swam as he looked down. He wiped the rain from his face, and squinted down the grey stretch of road reaching into the mountains. He stuffed the helmet back on and got under way. He'd head up into the mountains where he shared ownership of a house with his sister. Lay low for a while, let the India conflict—now under the effective influence of Kit Fowler—get resolved, then he'd head to the Rockies.

It was the right thing. Best thing to do.

Reason said he'd done the right thing, but his heart cried foul. *God, forgive me.*

London, England

Wind whipped her hair into her face. The pungent odor of jet fuel burned her nostrils and eyes. As her toes hit the tarmac, a black Suburban slid into her path. Tires squawked as it lurched to a stop. A flurry of movement revealed two heavily armed guards in tactical gear. They hustled and flanked Shiloh, their backs to her. Soon followed a suited man. His dark hair rustled under the commanding wash of the jet's engines.

"Shiloh Blake?"

Instinct spun her around. She'd taken only a few steps when a weight plowed into her back. She flew forward, the cement rushing up at her. Fire lit down the side of her face as she kissed the pavement. Another weight dropped onto her neck, pinning her. Grunts and curses flew out as the men secured her limbs.

Options eliminated, she gulped back the nearly tangible fear. "What're you doing?"

A man with a slick suit and smile to match sauntered toward her and squatted. "You followed my orders right down to the jacket." With a swipe of his hand over the lapel, he dusted off the blazer.

"Who are you? How did you find me?"

"Agent Brody Aiken, British Intelligence." He cocked his head to the side and peered down at her. "Surely you did not think us so daft that we would let you get away with it."

"Get away with what?" she asked through gritted teeth as the men hauled her to her feet by the plastic cuffs.

He planted his hands on his hips. "Board a plane, escape a very deadly plot that you unleashed, and think we would welcome you with open arms?"

"I don't know what you're talking about."

His eyebrow rose and he grunted. "Oh, you are quite convincing, Miss Blake," he said in his taunting British voice. He started back to a black vehicle, waving behind himself. "Bring her."

The guards dragged Shiloh across the tarmac and hoisted her into the back seat of an SUV and buckled her in.

Shiloh stemmed the panic that made her palms sweat. "Where are you taking me?"

Doors slammed shut, and the vehicle lunged across the long runway. Trying to keep her bearings and sense of direction, Shiloh mentally noted several landmarks as they whizzed through traffic.

Aiken looked back from the front. "To think, he actually thought we would need to protect *you*." He chuckled.

"Protect me? Who—" She gulped. Reece!

His raking gaze seemed to assess her every reaction and move. "If I'm right, that's anger in your eyes." Another smile. "Brilliant. Tell me, did you not see this coming? Is that why you are so indignantly angry?"

Angry didn't cover what she felt toward Reece Jaxon right now. Reece sent her for protection? Not likely. He wanted her out of the way. *He betrayed me!*

"Huh. Fascinating."

"You're easily amused, Mr. Aiken." The gaping hole in her heart pulsed, growing with each beat.

"How did you do it? Deceive him so thoroughly?"

Ignoring his attempt to draw her into a confession, Shiloh pinned her gaze to a city that blurred beyond the heavily tinted windows. She needed to get out of here. When they got to wherever they were going, she'd bolt. Get back to India. Stop the insanity. Hurt Reece. Real bad.

"You see, this is all quite fascinating to me. I mean, I can't recall the last time he contacted me personally. Deep cover, American, working special ops in India. To boot, the very girl he sends for protection turns out to be someone we need protection from."

She narrowed her eyes. "What are you talking about?"

"Murder, Miss Blake." His smile disappeared. "You murdered two of our operatives."

24

Like a lamb to the slaughter.

Shiloh stepped into the steel trap and turned as the three men joined her. Agent Aiken punched in a code as two armed guards flanked her. Silence hung thick and heavy for several seconds as the elevator climbed then came to a stop. The steel barricade slid back, revealing another door five feet ahead.

Shiloh moved out, her muscles knotting. It wasn't a hall. Just a small box-like foyer that offered only one choice—a door. She glanced back. A grey wall glared at her. Where had the elevator gone? Unnerved, she traced what should be the outline of the box—and saw the faint impression of the door. The two guards stood on either side with their weapons ready.

"Miss Blake?"

She pivoted and found Aiken standing on a threshold.

"Your home. For now."

"I have no home."

Surprise leapt through her as she entered the room. A lavish apartment consumed her view. Wood floors gleamed under the tease of sunlight that came through four high-placed windows. Pale blue paint brightened the mood of the living area that slowly morphed into a kitchen with an island that served as the only divider between the two areas.

"Through there is a bedroom. You will find a change of clothing and a shower." He stood at the bar and lifted a phone. "I'm on the other end."

Which meant, nobody else was. But that wasn't what bugged her. It was the lavish apartment. "Am I missing something?"

Aiken glanced back at her. "How is that?"

"This is extravagant for someone accused of murdering your operatives. Where's the cement and iron bars?"

Aiken strode toward the door without a word.

Shiloh trailed him, her heart pumping hard. "I demand to speak with someone from the American embassy right now."

"Meals are served at seven, noon, and five." He chuckled. "Sorry, no afternoon tea. You are, after all, a murder suspect."

"I didn't kill anyone! I know my rights! I'm an American citizen and you must—"

"Good afternoon, Miss Blake." He reached for the door handle and eased it to. "I am certain you will be comfortable here."

"No." She gritted her teeth. Captivity, and he expected her to be comfortable? "I won't." Arms folded, she stood beside the window, staring out. A ledge blocked her view of the street below, but off a few miles to the right, Uncle Ben towered. With the clock-face not visible, she guessed herself to be south of the tower. Or was it north?

She heard the men leave. *Good.* Alone, she could figure a way out of here. She batted back the sheer curtains and bent, reaching for locks on the window . . . only, there weren't any. She turned to the door—and like the elevator, it had bled into the wall. The imprint of its outline barely noticeable.

She dashed through the living quarters looking for a window that opened, a door, anything that would let her escape. Nothing. The bedroom boasted a lush bed and thick comforter.

A tiled shower and sink huddled in one corner. Back in the main area, she turned a slow circle. Imaginary bars gradually took shape, closing in.

How? How could they possibly think she had killed anyone, let alone two operatives? She didn't even have time. Kit put her on the plane and . . .

Kit.

Shiloh's thoughts skidded into the face of the pretty woman. Was Kit dead? Is that who Aiken and the British accused her of killing? They said there'd been two operatives killed. Who else died?

She moved to the ornamental fireplace and traced a white statue on the mantle. An idea gripped her mind. She snatched the statue and smashed it against the window as hard as she could. The piece shattered into a million pieces . . . like her hope. Not even a scratch on the window.

She was trapped, blamed for murder, and locked up in a room with no doorknobs or window locks. And she had one person to strangle for this—Reece. Why would Reece do this to her? Hadn't they agreed to work together? Or had it just been his cover story until she gave him enough information and sources that he could finish the task on his own? She closed her eyes and hung her head. Her chin quivered as she thought about his last kiss and profession of love. He knew—*knew* what was coming.

For what felt like hours, she remained alone with only her reflection as company. The solitude gave her time to come to three important resolutions. One, she'd find Khalid's killers if it was the last thing she did. Two, she would never *ever* trust another man. Three, she would make sure Reece Jaxon paid for this—in a very painful way.

But first she had to get out of here.

She moved to the stove, where a ceramic cooktop sparkled back at her. After retrieving a towel from the bathroom, she rushed back into the kitchen. She flipped on the front, large burner and waited for the thing to glow a brilliant red. Then she dropped the towel on it.

After a few seconds, a slow spiral of smoke curled up, higher and higher. A spark twinkled back at her.

Unnerved at the desperate measures she suddenly felt ready to take to get out of here, she took several steps back, her eyes on the white towel turning grey with smoke.

Then . . . it fizzled. Stopped. The flames ate through, but did little else.

Overhead sprinklers kicked on, spraying cold water over the kitchen and Shiloh. Sizzling ensued as water drenched the towel and doused the fire. Only then did she notice the stove wasn't on anymore. She double-checked the knob. How—? She fidgeted with the dial. Tried another. Nothing. The stove wasn't working.

She wrinkled her brow and brushed back the soggy hair from her face. Why had the stove lost power? Moving out of the kitchen, she tested the lights. They worked. The living room lights. Yep. Finally, the sprinklers stopped. She lifted the phone. Immediately, it rang.

"Brody Aiken."

Shiloh blanched. Everything but the stove worked.

Which meant one thing.

"Why are you spying on me?"

"You killed two operatives. A deep-cover operative sent you here. Quite obviously you have secrets to tell."

"I. Did. Not. Kill. Anyone!" Shiloh dug her fingers into her hair. "I want to talk to an American lawyer!"

The door whooshed back. A Middle Eastern man entered.

"Change your clothes. Then tell Mahmud what you remember."

Shiloh hung up, her mind on escape. Shivering, she stared at her new jailer. Did he follow the Muslim faith as rigidly as many of his race? "*I'nsh Allah,*" she mumbled, hoping to gauge his loyalty.

He quirked an eyebrow, then smiled as he inclined his head. "As Allah wills."

Hope surged. She'd found an ally!

Groaning emanated through the wall. She glanced at the clock. Almost five. They were right on time. And so was she.

Bulb in hand, she monitored the plastic fork in the other. She'd have just one shot at this. If she was fast enough, she could escape, force their hand against the reader, and get to the garage. From there, she'd just have to trust her instincts.

The door opened.

A man in a uniform carried the food tray into the kitchen and set it down.

"Oh, is that coffee?" Shiloh lifted the cup to her lips. Lukewarm. Okay, so it wouldn't scald the guy, but it'd at least throw him off for a few seconds, which was all she needed. She worked her way in front of him, her mind on the guard who waited three feet away. With a quick flick, she tossed the drink at the uniformed guy.

"Argh!" Hands over his face, he doubled.

She smashed the bulb against the counter. Then she shifted her weight to the left, leaned and drove her heel into the guard's chest. He grunted. But instead of falling back, he flipped her leg up and planted her on the ground.

Her breath whooshed out. Stars sprinkled through her vision.

He lunged toward her, but she rolled. Using the bulb as a knife, she thrust it toward him. He grabbed a hand towel on the counter, snapped it at her, catching her arm. He wrangled it into a semi-knot and spun her around—straight into his fist.

Whack! Pain spiked down her cheek and neck, momentarily blinding her. She wobbled, and he punched her again. Everything went black.

"Miss Blake?"

Shiloh blinked. A blurry shadow bobbed over her.

"On your feet." The man who'd knocked her unconscious sat on the leather sofa, his hand wrapped in a bulky towel. An ice pack? Was her head that hard?

She lifted her shoulders, noting the plastic cuffs strapped to her wrist. She peeled herself off the floor—and tensed as pain speared her head. She hissed.

"Careful. I might have given you a concussion."

Shiloh moaned through the roar of aches as she struggled to stand. "Are those hands registered as a lethal weapon?"

"Actually, yes." He hooked her arm and led her to the door. "Former SAS commander."

Considering him, Shiloh chided herself for trying to fight the best of Britain. "Figures."

His stone-like face faltered just enough to reveal a very small smile.

He accessed the security panel and in seconds, the elevator opened and he guided her in.

"Where do I have the pleasure of going this time?"

"The director."

"Why?"

"Not for me to know or ask." They rode up for several seconds, and the doors opened—behind her. She turned, stunned to find a long hall stretching to the right. Doors lined the corridor. Her mind whirled—where was she? MI-6? The thought decimated her courage. Escaping one of the most highly secured buildings in Britain?

Mahmud emerged from the far end of the hallway. His lanky build, so much like Khalid's, quickly carried him to her. He offered a Styrofoam cup. "We'll go in here," he said as he accessed a ten-by-twelve room and allowed her and the SAS commander entrance.

Shiloh accepted the cup of cocoa—*cold* cocoa. She grimaced.

"Sorry." Mahmud's dark eyes sparkled. "Aiken didn't want you try to take anyone else out."

The laughter hiding behind his words did little to ease the tension in her shoulders or soothe her throbbing skull as the commander directed her to a chair at the head of a table.

Seated, Shiloh choked down a gulp of the cocoa. "Can I get some ibuprofen?"

Mahmud smiled and provided two green gel-tabs.

"You're my new best friend." After she downed the pills, she glanced around. "So am I still a murder suspect? I mean, I would've expected to be strapped to a board or something if I killed your spies."

"I can arrange that," the SAS commander said as he tossed the towel in a nearby bin.

A door slapped back. Two men in dark suits stalked toward them. "Miss Blake, I say! You took quite a beating trying to escape, now didn't you?" Brody Aiken greeted her as he sat two places down from her. His smile dropped. "Thank you, Commander Hadden. That will be all." He shifted to Shiloh. "Now, I believe it is time you provided us with answers."

She watched the SAS commander leave as she answered, "I already gave you the only answer I have: I did not kill your operatives."

Aiken rubbed the back of his head. "Ah, see, now that is where we have a problem."

"Why?"

"Because we have your fingerprints at the scene of the crime."

Shiloh's heart thudded against her confidence.

The second man leaned in and threaded his fingers. "What were you saying about not killing the operatives?"

"You're not British," Shiloh mumbled at not hearing an accent.

"Are you sure?" This time his accent hung as thick as his attitude. He scooted forward, his shoulders broad and threatening. "Don't try to play games, Miss Blake. We train operatives. We know the techniques of evasion and coercion." He lifted a remote and a screen came to life behind him. A fingerprint—several. "Evidence places you at the crime scene. Who do you work for?"

No way out. They had her prints and two bodies. She wasn't going to walk out of here alive or without some very intricate plan. "I'm an American graduate student on an underwater archeological dig."

"That's your cover. How did you kill them?"

"I didn't kill anyone. W-who did I supposedly kill?"

He waved the remote and two candids plastered the wall. "Kathleen Fowler and Jason Ganzz."

The photo of Kit was blurry, but her build and long, dark hair couldn't be denied. The other man . . . he drove the car to the airport. Shiloh remembered his eyes as he watched her in the rearview mirror.

"You recognize their faces," Brody said. "Your own eyes betray you, Miss Blake."

Shiloh licked her lips. "Yes, I recognize them, but not because I killed them."

"Then why do you recognize them?"

"I-I'm not sure I can tell you that."

"They're dead. You can't hurt them any more than you already have."

The accusation hit her with brutal precision. Reece . . . would talking endanger him? She drew up her chin. So what if it did? He'd sent her off on this little adventure. "Kit put me on a plane on the orders of Reece Jaxon."

The second man visibly flinched.

"What?" Her mind snagged on the only possible reason for that reaction. "Is he dead?"

"He might as well be dead for all the good he's doing us."

"I don't understand."

"Jaxon resigned his commission." Lips stretched taut, he hesitated. "Claimed he compromised his moral compass. Would you happen to know what he meant by that?"

Guilt chugged through her veins. He quit? Because of her?

A man darted into the room and handed a paper to Aiken. "We found Red One."

Aiken snatched the Intel. He scanned it, and then lunged to his feet. "Send in Scarlet." He nodded to Mahmud. "Take her back to her room. We'll talk soon, Miss Blake."

Shiloh hesitated and then pushed away from the table. She walked toward Mahmud as he opened the door.

"What was that about?"

Mahmud ignored her question.

This would be her only shot to talk to him alone, to convince him to help her. "I spent four months in India before Reece Jaxon interfered." She brushed her hair from her face, feigning as much indignation as she could. "What I wouldn't give to get out of here and teach that man a few lessons."

"Nobody escapes."

They made the trip to her cell in silence. She had to find a way to convince him to help her. Say something brilliant and capture whatever drove him to compassion.

As they neared her room, she eyed him. "I think nobody has escaped because they didn't have help."

Mahmud held her gaze unflinchingly. "Could be." He entered his access code and fingerprint.

The door slid back silently.

"Pakistan is a very beautiful country too. All things happen as Allah wills, yes?"

His eyebrow quirked.

She backstepped into her room watching him.

Just before the door slid shut, a smile teased the edges of his lips.

25

Northern India

FORTY-EIGHT HOURS OF TORTURE AND REGRET. REECE ROLLED OVER AND punched his pillow, once again unable to sleep. Face buried in the fluffy down, he let out a gruff sigh and shifted to look out the darkened window. Trees acted as sentries, guarding the small cabin. Of course, the real sentries sat in a metal box with a half-dozen tendrils that snaked into various cameras and motion detectors throughout the house.

Haunted that he'd abandoned a mission of critical importance to the protection of the world and walked away from Shiloh, Reece flipped onto his back. "I did the right thing." He pounded the mattress as his gaze traced the crisscross pattern of the beams.

He hadn't had a moment's peace since he kissed her and literally ran away.

He'd tried praying. Tried reading his Bible. Solace eluded him. A great time for God to go silent. "Was I wrong, God?"

Bleep-bleep! Bleep!

At the sound of alarm, he snagged his weapon and launched himself into the darkened corner. His gaze darted to the security panel. Back door. He scooted along the wall, inching his way to the door. Plush carpet gave way to teak floors. Cold. Unforgiving.

Like Shiloh.

He shook his head and blinked. Keep moving. He craned his neck and peered into the kitchen.

"Reece?"

His heart skipped a beat before evening out. "Julia?" He stalked down the hall to the alarm box and entered the disable code. In the kitchen, he hit the lights. "What're you doing here?"

She set a pack on the chair and unwound a scarf from her neck. Her gaze settled on the gun. She raised her right brow. "I should ask you the same thing."

"I own half this dump." He grabbed the coffeepot, filled it with water, and then stuffed it on the burner.

"So do I."

He flipped on the power. "I sent the code letting you know I was coming."

"I know."

Which meant she'd come intentionally. He made the mistake of looking at her.

Fire coursed through her golden eyes. When she spun away, he tugged two mugs out of the cabinet and returned to the island, where he peeled an apple.

Julia tossed papers across the counter.

Apple in his mouth, he scrambled to catch one that nearly flitted to the ground. And froze. He tried to swallow but had to remove the fruit. "Where did you get these?" Cold poured through him like an ice shower.

"Toby called me. He was worried." She crossed her arms. "So am I."

Shiloh. Pinned beneath the knees of tactical officers. Another—Shiloh hauled away like a slab of beef. Another—

her being led into an underground bunker. He lost his appetite and chucked the apple in the trash bin.

"Want to tell me how she ended up in British custody?"

He'd made a decision and would have to live with the consequences. "I put her there." He swept the photos back to her and stomped down the hall. In his room, he grabbed a sweatshirt and jammed his hands through the sleeves.

"And how did that happen?"

"Easy. I put her on a plane." The gurgling coffeepot drew him back to the kitchen.

"Don't get smart with me, Reece."

"Toby needs to learn to keep his mouth shut. This is none of your business." He groaned. "Never mind. I don't care. It doesn't matter." He rinsed a mug under the faucet, then shifted and retrieved the pot. While the smell awakened his senses, he dreaded the pungent taste.

"They're holding her for murder. She's been beaten and interrogated, Reece." Her rich, soulful eyes seemed to mourn her own words.

He snapped his head toward her. "Murder?" Coffee singed his hand. He shoved the pot back into the maker. "What do you mean?" When she passed him another photo, every semblance of control rushed out of him.

Bruised and bloodied, Shiloh's image gaped back at him. Her vibrancy had disappeared with whatever they'd done. "Why would they do this?" he mumbled, staring at the picture.

"She tried to escape. An SAS officer stopped her. MI-6 found her prints at a house in Paris."

Beautiful, sweet Shiloh—at the mercy of a soldier trained to kill. Shiloh, a woman who couldn't be re-strained. "What house?"

"The same one on the outskirts of Paris where a woman and man were found hanged, a dozen bullet and stab wounds."

Julia folded her arms. "I don't think you need the CIA dossier to know who they are and get the meaning of the execution."

"Kit." Grief wrapped a vise around his heart. "Who . . . why?" He yanked out his cell and hit the autodial for Ryan Nielsen. The line went to voice mail. He tried Aiken. Same. They were avoiding him.

Reece flung the coffeepot across the room. It crashed into the wall and poured brown down the taupe paint.

Palms planted on the counter, he panted through the rush of fury as he stared at Shiloh's battered face. "I put Shiloh on that plane—sent her to Brody. Now Kit is dead because of me." How could he have been so stupid to think Brody would grow a brain and handle this with intelligence? "Aiken should've mapped the timelines. Shiloh didn't have time to kill Kit and get on that plane. He didn't do his homework—and yet he does *this* to her!"

He pounded the counter. "I'll kill him. I'll kill that sorry—"

"Where's the little brother I've always been proud of?" She eased herself and her jangling bracelets onto a stool next to him. "Why did you leave her?"

"India was out of control—look at Kit; that's proof. Brody was supposed to keep Shiloh safe until the nuclear mess blew over."

"Why did you abandon the mission and quit?"

"I didn't abandon it. I transferred the files and information to another . . ." He let the words trail off as he realized the operative he'd handed over that authority to was now dead.

"What about Shiloh?"

"Things got too dangerous. I didn't want her involved. And now . . . now she's alive, and in that, I've accomplished what I set out to do." Fists balled, Reece tried to think past the acid pouring into his heart. "It's . . . unfortunate . . ."

He couldn't even finish the sentence. "At least she's safe. At least, she'll—"

"She'll hate you!"

"And she's alive to do it!"

His temples throbbed. Clenching his hands, he moved to the massive picture window overlooking the bluff. Dawn peeked over the mountain, draping the forest in its early amber hues.

How did it get all messed up? *God, where are you?*

Julia joined him. "Iran, Syria, North Korea, and South Korea, along with China, are all poised to sign this withdrawal pact. If that happens, then we will enter an era of nuclear terror that nightmares will pale in comparison to."

"You sure know a lot about that."

"I pay attention. My point is you bailed on a crucial mission."

Could his plan dissolve any more than it already had? He looked to where the edges of light crept along the horizon.

"Nobody, Reece—*nobody* can do the job that God called you to do." She joined him at the window, her hand on his arm. "You walked away from it. You walked away from *her*."

Glaring, he ground his teeth. "I sacrificed *everything* for her. So she would be safe."

Sympathy softened her expression. "Well, maybe now you've proven your love—for God and for Shiloh. But you were made for this. You have to go back."

Reece looked away. *God, please don't ask this of me.* His breathing turned shallow. "I can't." If she died . . .

"I think, dear brother, that it's time for you to carry out your duties." Julia placed her hand on his back. "I know you're afraid of repeating the same mistakes with Shiloh that happened with Chloe, but she isn't Chloe."

"Trust me," he said. "I know that. I've never felt this way about anyone. But I can't. I can't endanger her life any more.

She's been betrayed and hurt by everyone in her life. I won't do that to her."

"You already have."

Reece stared at her. Each beat of his thundering heart swished in his ears. "I put her in protective custody to save her life."

"You sent her away from the one man she grew to trust, and maybe even love."

The revelation pierced him. "I just wanted her safe. And no matter how much it kills me, she *is* safe. Behind a steel wall in London. That's where she needs to stay for now."

"It's not that simple anymore, Reece." Julia blinked. "She needs you to . . ." Swallowing, she shook her head and forced a smile. The tear streaking down her face alarmed him. Julia never cried. "I think you should—"

He rushed to her and held her shoulders. "What? What aren't you telling me?"

Her face contorted. More tears slipped down her tawny cheeks.

Reece shook her. "What's happened?"

"She escaped," Julia said. "It's not good. She escaped with someone she believed was an ally. A man British intelligence thought they had a leash on. He'd sworn his allegiance to helping them stop Allah's Sword, but they fear he might've been a double."

"Who?"

"Mahmud Sajjadi."

Shock ripped the breath from his lungs. "Sajjadi's son."

26

IT HAD BEEN TOO EASY. DESPITE HER INEXPERIENCE, EVEN SHILOH KNEW that their without-a-hitch escape from MI-6 signaled her stupidity. Hadn't she just vowed not to trust another man, and who did she pick to break that promise with? A man whose allegiance she'd managed to sway with two simple words. *I'nsh Allah.*

He's a means to an end. A means to an end. Even chanting those words to herself as they flew through British airspace hadn't persuaded her. As a matter of fact, the trip had dislodged them, leaving her courage hollow. The numbness in her legs and spine had little do to with the train vibrations. She'd do whatever it took to get back to India. If she could, then she'd make her way to the Green Beret camp, find Reece, and tear out his heart. After that, she'd hunt down those responsible for Khalid's death.

God, help me do this. Help me find Reece. Amazingly, the prayer didn't feel like it had hit a brick wall and bounced back in her face this time. Maybe God was listening.

Feeling the gravitational pull of the train as it sped around a bend, Shiloh stiffened to stop herself from sliding across the seat and directly into her traveling companion's lap. The train straightened out, its drag easing. Her thoughts flitted back to Reece. *I love you, Shiloh. Remember that. No matter what happens.* She savored the memory of his kiss, and then she remembered his betrayal. Voices whispered around them, warning of danger.

"I have the girl."

Heat spiraled into Shiloh's chest as the words snatched her from the dreams. She stilled her impulse to look over her shoulder at Mahmud. Who was he talking to? She didn't hear another voice, so he must've made a call on his cell phone.

"I know what I'm doing!" he said in Arabic.

Shiloh wished she'd studied the language more. He continued speaking, this time something about a father and Allah. He ended the call as the train slowed.

A nudge against her shoulder. "Miss Blake." Another nudge. "Miss Blake, this is our stop."

Feigning sleepiness, she stretched and yawned. "Are we here already?"

Mahmud nodded, his features taut.

Grabbing her pack, Shiloh tucked aside her fear. Her idiocy had gotten her into this mess. Now she had to let it play out until she could seize the reins of control.

They plodded down the narrow corridor to the door. A uniformed man stood on the platform and extended his hand toward Shiloh. Questions about what an American woman was doing with a Muslim man clearly lingered in his dark eyes as he glanced between her and Mahmud. Her lanky companion glared back, caught her shoulder, and tugged her away.

"Speak to no one," Mahmud grumbled as they entered the depot.

"I know In—" Shiloh bit her tongue when she saw the signs hanging over the door. They weren't in Marathi. Or Hindi. The signs were in Arabic. Which meant this wasn't India.

At the security checkpoint Mahmud handed over his passport. The guard glanced at the information in the official pages before he snapped a salute.

Unfazed, Mahmud nodded.

The guard considered Shiloh for several long seconds before Mahmud pressed something into the man's hand. Only when the guard looked at the object and sucked in a breath did Shiloh see a coin similar to the one Baseer had given her. The one with the symbol for Allah's Sword of Justice.

"My apologies for the delay, sir."

"I will overlook it this time, Captain."

Without another word, the guard again saluted Mahmud and stepped away. Shiloh took the cue and glided forward as the passport was handed back to her escort. It fell at her feet, and she stooped to retrieve it. When she saw the lettering next to the photo, her heart caught. She lifted the passport, staring at the name: Osman Mahmud Sajjadi.

His hand clamped around her wrist. Shiloh wrenched away, but Mahmud jerked her straight into his chest.

"You're Sajjadi's son."

"And you'd do well to come quietly and without resistance."

Her spine stiffened with resolve. "I'm not going to do any—"

The presence of four tactical officers behind Mahmud snapped her mouth shut.

Mahmud glanced at the men, then brought his gaze back to hers. And smiled.

The checkpoint guard shouted to the others, waving the officers away and mumbling Sajjadi over and over. Shiloh's heart slowed as the heavy firepower dissipated.

"We've drawn enough attention." Mahmud caught her arm and strode toward the front doors. As they passed through the glass, he released her but kept walking.

Suddenly, a hand slapped tape over her mouth. Suffocating darkness swallowed her as a hood slid over her head. A noose tightened around her neck. As her hands were yanked behind her back, she tried to scream past the tape. Hands lifted her from the ground. She wriggled and writhed, panic seizing her.

A sudden, sharp pain rammed into her head. She blacked out.

Hollow and distant noises seeped into her awareness. She moaned. Where was she? Why was it so dark?

Brilliance tore through her vision—a hood removed from her head, and with it went the disorientation. She'd been kidnapped. Taken . . . somewhere. Heat plumes writhed like dozens of snakes slithering through the desert. Shiloh cringed and squinted against the blaring white sand. She swept the area with her strained gaze. Several set of feet. Military tactical pants. Black shoes. Jeans.

"Are you hurt?"

The sound of that voice forced her to pause. Close her eyes. When she opened them, it took only a few blinks to clear her vision and see the man before her. She clenched her hands into fists. "What are you doing here?"

"It's not important why I'm here." He had more salt than pepper in his hair now. His sweat-drenched navy shirt accented his striking blue-grey eyes. Eyes just like hers. "What's important is why you are here."

Shiloh struggled for a breath not strangled by rage. "You never were good with openness and honesty, even with your own daughter."

Stepping from the brutal sun, her father entered the tent. He bent over a small table, palms against the wood. She blanched at his posture—so hauntingly similar to an event fifteen years ago. Him, hands on her mother's coffin, silent, unemotional, uncaring.

Why? Why did he have to resurface now?

He pointed to a map on the table. "Take a look."

She held her place. Did he really think she'd just obey? "All these years, and this is how you greet your only child?"

"Shiloh, this isn't how I wanted things—"

"I'm sure seeing me is the last thing either of us wanted. I left because I didn't want anything to do with you. That hasn't changed." She hated the searing retort, but the ka-thumping in her chest made it impossible to move or take back the words.

"You're angry—"

"Really? What gave it away?"

He hung his head. "Look, I'd do anything for this to be different, for you not to be involved, but this is where we are." He jabbed the table. "There's a lethal mission you're entangled in." He stared at her. "Are you with me?"

"No." But curiosity had always gotten her into trouble. "What mission?"

He cast a glance behind her. Shiloh looked over her shoulder and stiffened at the sight of Mahmud.

"He's Sajjadi's son! Don't trust him."

"His identity is the very reason he's here. You might want to pay attention and figure out whose side you're on." He glanced back to the articles on the table. "Mahmud will take you to his father's camp. It's possible you'll be interrogated, but Mahmud reassures me you won't be tortured."

"Why doesn't that reassure *me*?" She gulped at the thought of going anywhere else with Mahmud. Was her father crazy, sending her away with the son of a known terrorist?

"Don't worry. You'll be safe."

"Nobody can guarantee that. I might not be a spy, but I'm not stupid. No American is safe in Sajjadi's hands."

"Your father is right," Mahmud said as his lanky frame filled the hot tent. "The general intends to use you to accomplish his mission."

His words seemed to comfort him as if they were an obvious answer to this dark problem. But the meaning was lost on her. She looked to her father, who might've done a lot wrong where she was concerned, but he wouldn't intentionally put her in jeopardy.

Blue-grey eyes softened. "It means Sajjadi wants you *alive*. Shortly after you left India, Ali Abdul was arrested. With him imprisoned it's impossible for the Summit of the Agreed to go forward with their plan—"

"Which is?"

"To detonate a nuclear weapon in Kashmir in four days to frame India."

"And he thinks I'll finish that for him?" Shiloh scoffed.

"I would not laugh so easily," Mahmud countered. "My father has a way of making the unwilling become very willing."

"He's right." Her father whipped out another page. "I've seen that man powerfully affect leaders in ways you couldn't dream."

"Sir," a woman stepped into the tent, a baseball cap tugged over her brow. "The report just came in."

Shiloh gaped at the familiar white-blonde hair and bruised green eyes. "Edie?"

A simple nod. "Shiloh."

Her father turned to Mahmud. "Go with Edie. Give her any guidance you can." He moved around the tables and came closer to Shiloh.

Mahmud hesitated, dark eyes bouncing between father and daughter.

A smile, one Shiloh had recognized since childhood as fake and concealing, filled her father's face. "I'd like a moment with my daughter." He touched her shoulder. "Please."

Instincts warned her to keep her mouth shut and body still.

"Sir." Mahmud nodded and then left, leaving a clear impression he wasn't happy.

Her father hurried back to his desk. "Okay, we don't have much time." He drew out a black case, ran his fingers over the silver combination number, smoothed a hand along the side, and then depressed more keys on the lock. *Click!* The lid opened.

His clear eyes pinned her. "Shi, come here."

Although she wasn't going to play his spy games, having intel never hurt. She moved around the desk.

A green digital readout blinked at them. "It is my estimation that Sajjadi will have you retrieve the second half of the launch codes." He pointed to the readout where a series of letters and numbers glared at them in an angry red. "Got them?"

Just like that? He wanted her to play spy?

"Shiloh?"

"You're serious. You want me to—"

"Do you have the code?"

She flashed her eyes at him. "Yes."

"Good." He slapped the case closed. "You'll need to enter it—"

"No." The word felt foreign, yet good. Maybe not strong enough. "No," she said again, this time with more ferocity. "I'm not doing this."

"You don't have a choice."

"That's where you're wrong. I'm not one of your recruits."

His lips narrowed. "You're my daughter, tangled in one of the deadliest confrontations this region—*my* territory—has seen in decades." His eyes drilled into her. "Whether we like it or not, you're on the grid."

"Do *you* like it? I mean, all those years as a kid, is this what you were training me for?" Hard to breathe. "To guide me into this covert world of yours?"

"No." His words bore the surprise and hurt she clearly read on his face. "What I taught you was to make sure you never got snatched again." He shook his head. "I don't like this any more than you, but it's done, decided. You're playing."

Heat infused her cheeks, fueling her anger. "No. I'm not."

"For once in your life, look beyond your own interests." Though the words were quiet, they packed a punch. His chest rose and fell quickly as he brought himself back under control. "Set aside that hatred you have pinned on me, and for once—just once—trust me. There's more to this world than you and me. Millions of lives are at stake."

How could he do this? Stand there and act like they'd never missed a beat in their relationship. It had been fifteen years! Shiloh pressed the heel of her hand against her forehead and turned away. Didn't he care? Did he miss her? No, he didn't give a rat's nest about how she felt or what she'd gone through. He wanted to put their past behind them so she'd bend to his will and become what she despised.

"You're unbelievable. All these years you haven't spoken to me, and now you're standing there ordering me . . ." Her breathing deepened. "Ordering me to trust you?" The words cracked. Dust kicked up as she paced in front of his desk. "I'm not doing this. I'm not following your orders. I don't care—"

"I'm not ordering you, Shi." His soulful eyes stared. "I can't believe how much you look like your mom."

The words served as a line drive to her heart. "Don't. Don't bring her into this. I am not going to become like you. I *hate* you!" Tears threatened. She gulped back the swell of outrage. "All my life, you moved me around, ripping me from friends and schools. Then when you're off playing hero, I'm in an overturned car watching Mom bleed to death."

"Shiloh—"

"No!" Her pulse pounded through her skull. "I won't do that to those I love. I won't become a creature without a heart or conscience."

He drew up, pain etched into the lines of his weathered face. "I did everything I could—"

"All you did was screw up my life!" Tears flowed harder, defying her every attempt to stop them. "You ruined me. You're the reason I have seizures. I—" She covered her mouth as a sob wracked her body.

Quiet steps crunched on the sandy floor as he drew closer. "I owe you a thousand apologies. I'll never forgive myself for the months you spent captive, the experiments that left you with seizures. Killing the man who did that to you didn't erase the damage—or my fury."

He balled his fists and bowed his head. "It's your choice, your right, to cling to that hatred. I beg your forgiveness for all the ways I've failed you." He sighed. "But in the end, it doesn't alter the fact that we're in this together."

A piece of her glacier-like hatred broke off and drifted away, unnerving her. He was tricking her, using this time just to get what he wanted—her cooperation.

Shiloh shook her head. "No." She couldn't. Wouldn't. Too easy. She wanted Jude Blake to hurt, to feel the stabbing pain of betrayal. "I won't forgive you. I'll never forgive you."

With slumped shoulders, he returned to the table. He skimmed the pages in front of him. In that fleeting moment she saw something in her father she'd never seen before. Brokenness. Emptiness. A man who'd lost the woman he loved. Lost his daughter.

The thoughts surprised her. "Do you miss mom?" she whispered.

His blue-greys came to hers, streaked with heartache. "With every breath." He laughed, his chin puckering as if he fought off tears. "You look so much like her. That fire in your eyes . . . that's Jirina."

Jirina. It'd been so long since she'd heard her mother's name. She'd been a spy too. Maybe, just this once, Shiloh could honor her mother by doing something brave and heroic, the way her mom had done for many years. After all, her father said millions of lives were at stake, right? She couldn't exactly walk away from that if she had the power to make a difference. But this time only. Never again. Bolstered by the thoughts, she composed herself.

"I won't do this for you," she mumbled. "But for mom." Lip trembling, she sucked in a breath and batted the hair from her face. "What do I need to do?"

He didn't miss a beat. "Intel shows Sajjadi has half the codes already. We've got a plan, and I'll be in place—"

"So, you'll back me up."

"Every step of the way."

Shiloh nodded, amazed that his words comforted her, especially since she'd never trusted him before. "Go on."

He looked at her. "Nobody can know about this."

"You don't trust Mahmud."

"Not for a minute." His gaze was steady and focused. "But I mean *nobody*, Shiloh. Not even Reece."

Her chest spasmed. How did he know about Reece? "We aren't on speaking terms."

"You'll see him again." A smile marked with pain and sympathy pinched the corners of his eyes. "It's hard to be angry with someone you love when you'll never see them again."

Green Beret Camp
Northern India

Amid the dark shroud of night a shadowy figure emerged from the trees. "Knew you couldn't walk away."

Reece clapped his friend on the back as he entered the camp. "What's the latest?"

"Bad news."

"Give it to me."

"About two hours ago word came that Jude Blake was taken captive."

Reece froze as the revelation bungeed through his mind, snapping back with a thousand-pound kick. How did that happen? Where did that leave Shiloh? "What's the plan?"

"Hit fast and hard." Cole hiked up the hill toward the hub of the camp where the men knelt around the fire pit, packing gear, checking weapons, and whispering last-minute prayers. He tugged out a crinkled map and shone a flashlight on it. "Latest intel shows Sajjadi holed up in this warehouse north of the Gateway of India. Chopper will drop us at the pier. We'll get him and get out."

"Him? What about Shiloh?"

"There's no reason to believe she's there."

"She was with Sajjadi's son. It's plausible—"

"Jude's our mission."

"If Sajjadi has Jude, then he has Shiloh." Reece ground his teeth. "I could kill Aiken. One simple task, and he couldn't do it."

Miller glanced toward the camp. Then turned away. "Don't worry, we'll find her. She may not be my girl, but I liked her."

Reece quirked an eyebrow.

Hands raised, Miller laughed. "Hey, Aras liked her and that monkey don't like nobody."

"No . . ." Glancing around the camp, Reece tried to determine what his buddy wanted to hide. "What's up?"

Chatter rose up from the south end of the camp. To Reece's surprise, he identified Brody Aiken stepping from a hut, laughing. Every muscle in Reece went rigid. He dropped his sack.

"Reece, don't—"

His friend's curse was lost amid the wind rustling in his ears as he stomped toward Aiken.

The Brit turned, and his eyes widened.

Reece slammed a solid right cross straight into the man's face.

Crack!

With a hard uppercut, Reece brought the guy to his knees. Blood spurted from Aiken's nose.

He whimpered and coughed. "What's wrong with you?"

"One simple task, Aiken. Keep her safe." Reece drew back, fisted his hand—

A hard weight barreled into Reece from the side, knocking him down. His head slammed into the dirt with a resounding thud. He wrestled the opponent.

Two more heavy thumps landed on him. He recognized the odds: three to one. Outgunned. Someone grabbed his arms and pinned him to the ground. His breathing heaved. He glared past his flaring nostrils, past the knee at the base of his throat to the man looming over him.

Miller glared down at him, a knee in Reece's throat. "You in control?"

Humiliation swirled through Reece. He closed his eyes. Gave a curt nod.

"Let him up."

The two-ton boulders lifted. Reece sat up, slowly clenching and unclenching his fist. He spit to the side, air coming in short, staccato breaths. The release of pent-up anger had felt good. Too good. Arms propped on his bent knees, he sat watching the shadows from the fire dance over his pants.

Shiny loafers appeared in front of him.

Reece grunted when he met the familiar expression of Director Ryan Nielsen. "Aiken did everything he could—"

"Don't." Picking himself off the ground, Reece cringed and held his side. "What are you doing up here anyway?" He eased onto a felled log next to Miller.

"I was there during Shiloh's questioning. Intel came in almost simultaneously with her escape that the hit against our people was professional."

Reece snorted. "You people are—"

"Sajjadi's yacht is entering Mumbai Harbor," Nielsen said.

Reece and Miller exchanged glances. Why would Sajjadi go inland? He couldn't run if something went wrong.

"Chopper's coming," Miller mumbled and removed himself from the tension.

"Jaxon," Nielsen said. "I understand your anger—"

Reece jerked to his feet. When he saw Nielsen cringe, he patted the director's lapel. "You're a good director, but you aren't me. Just be glad I'm not going to repay you for your part in Shiloh's interrogation."

"I didn't lay a hand on her."

"I know." Reece let the sneer into his voice.

Ryan Nielsen didn't have the guts to get his hands dirty, especially when it meant going against Jude Blake, America's top operative and regional director. The guy no doubt feared retaliation and losing said operative. And for that, Reece would be grateful—just this once—that Nielsen didn't have a spine.

Shouldering his way past the grunt, Reece surveyed the men. In their countenance, he saw the raw determination that mirrored his own.

"Where are you going?"

Swiping the dirt from his face, he said, "I have a mission."

"If you can't free Jude, you know what you have to do."

The objective was the highest possible. Such a well-connected agent simply had too much secret information:

location of assets, identities of those who kept the balance of power in check, the missions no one knew about. His capture meant every man in this camp could be wiped out. Every operative this side of the world could die.

If they couldn't drag Jude Blake to safety, they had to neutralize him.

"The kill order applies to his daughter too. If she's there and you can't free her, Shiloh must be killed."

27

Mumbai, India

BEATEN, BURNED, WATERBOARDED, BUT NOT BROKEN.

Shiloh jutted her jaw. "This the best you've got?"

Her father had said Sajjadi would find a way to make her cooperate, which she accepted would happen, but he'd also said the sicko wouldn't torture her. Another reason not to trust her father again. Of course, she might die, but Sajjadi would be unable to finish this insanity.

Tingles from the electrocution still lingered on the tips of her fingers. *Please, God.* Was He even listening? She'd cast Him off like an empty dive tank when she left home. *Let me do this. For my mom.*

A cell phone rang. The goon with the magic wand answered the call. Seconds later, he grinned. Then headed across the cavernous space toward a door. Creaking and groaning echoed off the rafters of the warehouse as he pushed open the door and stepped into darkness.

Was it really night already? The hours had blurred. She had arrived, under the not-so-gentle manhandling of Mahmud—where was that creep?

A cool breeze wafted through the open door. A familiar scent snagged her mind. Water! A sea of ebony sparkled back at her. The docks. Had they brought her back to Mumbai? If she could get to the water—

Lifting hands weighted by shackles and chains anchored to the cement walls, she pulled forward and yanked backward. Pain darted through her shoulders. She sagged. She'd have to free herself, but these weren't your standard movie-style cuffs. Quarter-inch thick and clamped with two bolts, the steel dug into her wrists. Permanent reminders carved into her soft flesh. She considered breaking her thumbs. Could she swim with broken hands?

Outside, a noise clapped into her awareness. Shoes. Someone was coming, and it wasn't the goon who'd gotten perverted pleasure out of her screams. He'd walked heavily and sluggishly. This had a crisp, confident air.

Seconds later a tall, powerful form blocked her view of the water. The man hesitated, then strode forward, his steps now lazy and taunting. "I am told you have not been cooperative, Miss Blake." He stopped in front of her, the lone overhead bulb casting eerie shadows over his face.

Who was he? Sajjadi? Surely she hadn't drawn the viper from his den. "Sorry, but his high-voltage personality grates on me."

Surprise danced in his dark eyes. "Humor." He stepped closer, eyeing her as though she was a prize catch on market day. "Perhaps they have been too easy on you."

"I'm a slow learner."

A somber expression replaced his amusement from seconds earlier. "I will give you one chance to cooperate, Miss Blake." Easing himself onto a metal folding chair, he crossed his legs and smiled up at her. "I need you to retrieve codes from an associate."

If she jumped at the chance, he'd be on to her. But her resistance had elicited more anger than she'd anticipated and she didn't have much left. "O-okay. Okay, I give."

"I thought you might say that. But . . . you see, I need some insurance that you aren't going to walk out of here and change your mind."

Panic beat a frenzied cadence through her chest. "W-what insurance? I said I'd do it."

Without taking his gaze off her, he lifted his hand, flicked his fingers, motioning someone into the warehouse. He cocked his head, watching her intently.

A commotion ensued, bringing with it grunting and a scraping noise. Shiloh finally saw two men dragging an unconscious man into the warehouse. Blood stained his brown T-shirt and camouflage pants. Unease squirmed through Shiloh. Who else had they captured?

"I will help you remember, when you begin to doubt your choice." The man stood and stepped back, his attention wholly on her face. "I have found in my business that on their own, agents are forgetful, and often fastidious in the belief that their misguided ideals are heroic." He shrugged. "But what do they gain by death?"

The two men stretched their quarry between metal piping riveted to a wooden platform. They clamped vises on the man's hands and wrists. Knowing full well what it was like to endure waterboarding, she prayed the poor soul on the boards would survive. Watching it without experiencing it was one thing. Having that first-hand knowledge of the reflexive gagging as water rushes into the ears, nose, and throat and fills the lungs was another. And vomiting then swallowing the acidic bile . . . She'd blacked out and awoke as they strung her up on the wall.

"General," one man mumbled. "He's secured."

Sajjadi gave a curt nod. "Oddly enough, too many are willing to die. It is commendable, this willingness to die for a cause one believes in." He chuckled, then released the button on his coat. "However, there are few who will sacrifice those they love."

Those they love? Reece! Shiloh's gaze darted to the man on the board. Head turned away in the dark shadows, she could not make out his face. Was it Reece? No . . . no, he was bigger, stronger than this man.

Sajjadi moved to the captive, grabbed a fistful of hair and jerked the man's head up and toward Shiloh. "This is your father, is it not, Miss Blake?"

At the sight of her father's badly swollen eyes and bloodied lips, she froze. Anger shot through her. She tugged against her restraints. "Leave him alone!"

She cringed at her own foolishness. Sure, show the madman he's right, that she loved the man on the boards.

But she didn't. She hated her father. He'd ruined her life.

He tried to save me.

No, he messed her up. Made her a freak with seizures and a hyperactive imagination.

The imagination that kept you safe after everyone was attacked on the bay.

Sajjadi stood over her father. "Time to wake up, Jude Blake. The world is awaiting your death." He slapped him.

A slap—no big deal. Her father could handle that.

Sajjadi straightened, stepped aside, and signaled his men.

One reached for the water spigot. Within seconds the splat of water hitting cement snapped Shiloh's senses alive. *Don't react.*

The man stomped forward with a bucket. He dumped the contents over her father's face.

Thrashing, he jolted awake. Coughing, sputtering.

"Ah, so good of you to join us, Jude." Sajjadi chuckled. "A grand reunion, is it not?" He nodded toward Shiloh.

Her father met her gaze. No recognition. No change in his expression.

"What?" Sajjadi laughed. "You want me to believe you don't know her?"

"She's my daughter." The flat-line tone struck her harder than the blows from the torturer. "We haven't spoken in fifteen years. She hates me."

"Mm." Sajjadi seemed too amused. "I happen to know that is not entirely true." Attention momentarily distracted as he conferred with one of his men, he regained his focus.

Shiloh grew wary of the fierce determination now in Sajjadi's gaze.

"This girl is cut from the same cloth as you and your dead wife, yes? But your beautiful daughter has not been hardened. She hasn't murdered or watched her victims die as you have." He sauntered toward Shiloh and swept his grimy mitt down her cheek. "I think she will be a very loyal, *loving* daughter before we are done." A sick laugh ebbed as he nodded again to his man.

Her father darted his gaze to Shiloh, fierce. "Remember your mother."

Mom? What did he—

The promise she'd made. *For Mom.*

As the thug knelt and slipped the burlap sack over her father's head, Shiloh tightened her resolve. Jude Blake was a notoriously effective operative. Survived for years, organized and carried out innumerable missions, she reminded herself. Noble, so very noble. Something she'd always secretly admired in him—and Reece. High standards. High callings. Staying true to his convictions kept him alive. He'd most likely been tortured before, so he could endure it. She could do this—not let this man force her blind obedience.

"Begin," Sajjadi said.

One man hauled the hose toward her father while the other cranked a wheel on the far wall. A deluge of water blasted out, splattering her father's hooded face. Even from six feet away, she heard him gurgling.

Memory still fresh of being on that board, Shiloh clamped her eyes shut.

"Open your eyes, or I will make it worse."

She blinked her eyes open when she realized he'd stopped the torture. Braving the assaulting scene, she looked at her father's chest, heaving. Alive.

He coughed. "Is that all you've got, Sajjadi? See, she doesn't care."

I do care! The vehement thought jarred Shiloh, but she schooled her expression. Why was her father antagonizing him?

Anger roared through Sajjadi's normally controlled features. "More!"

Again water flooded her father. His arms, legs, and chest bounced and thrashed.

Stop. Please stop.

More water came. So much water.

How could he endure it for so long? Hadn't she blacked out at this point? Tears stung the back of her eyes, but she blinked them away. If her father didn't bend, she wouldn't.

Stop, she moved her lips in a silent, fervent plea.

Gagging. Gurgling. His head whiplashed side to side. More gagging.

"Sto—" She bit back the word.

Sajjadi arched an eyebrow at her, smirking.

Mom. Doing this for mom.

Mom died. Drowned in a pool of her own blood, unable to move beneath the steel car that pinned her and Shiloh.

A demonic-like sound emanated from her father. He vomited—choked. Gagged. He went still. Then thrashed again.

Drowning. He's drowning.

"Stop!" Hot tears streaming down her cheeks, Shiloh hung her head. "Stop! Stop! Stop!"

Images of lying in the overturned car. Gunfire cracking the night. The warmth of her mother's blood dripping on her cheek. "Please, stop."

She'd watched her mother die. She couldn't . . . *wouldn't* watch her father die.

"You now realize I will kill your father if you break your agreement?"

A lone tear streaked down her face, stinging the cuts and scrapes. "Yes."

28

Rope burned his gloved hand as Reece rappelled from the chopper. Cement rushed up at him. *Thud!* He hustled toward the building and pressed his spine against the aluminum. He slid down the face mask as the team regrouped in a line behind him.

Directly in front of him Cole squatted at point, weapon aimed at the door, prepared. According to intel, a small foyer led to the main area where Jude, and possibly Shiloh, were being held. That is, if the team had arrived in time.

A pat came to Reece's shoulder. The team was in place and ready. He passed the silent message to Cole, who shifted around and rested a hand on the door knob as he waited for the insertion command. Reece nodded his readiness knowing anything could happen once that door opened. The team could get blown into the Arabian Sea. He could get killed. Jude or Shiloh could get killed.

But that wasn't in his hands. It was in God's.

Okay, let's do it. He glanced to the team leader—

An engine roared to life somewhere in the thick night. The throaty rumble of a diesel vehicle carried heavily through the air. It was close. Reece jerked a gloved hand toward the last two guys in line. Stick and Bronco obeyed, sprinting to the corner. They cleared it and moved stealthily out of sight.

Refocused, Reece nodded at Cole.

The door swung open. Split-second recon revealed only dark mustiness in the foyer. He darted to the right, his spine against the wall as he swept his weapon and the team snaked in, stacking one in front of the other. In the empty facility, each noise carried like a detonation blast. Reece moved carefully, monitoring every squeak of his boots and each rustle of tactical gear. He eased up to the corner. Scanned. Bright green against his night-vision goggles, the hall posed no visible threat.

According to the map they'd studied, the opening to the main room lay in blue four. He led the team down the hall, zigzagging from door to door, clearing offices and the bathrooms.

Voices skated through the halls. Hurrying forward, they targeted the set of double doors that should lead to the main section. Reece nudged the door and peered into the area. Light jabbed its brilliant finger into one corner, but he couldn't see—wait!

Two tangos running toward an open door. He snatched the flash-bang, plucked the pin, and tossed it into the room. He held back, hand on the door, and waited.

Boom!

White light exploded.

Reece burst into the room.

One man grabbed at another, trying to pull him through the far door. Blood streamed down his face and ears.

Reece fired. He hit him, but the man spun and raced out of sight. Sidestepping, Reece spotted Tomcat slinking along the far wall, watching his back.

Crack!

Something slammed into Reece, center-mass. Oof. He stumbled. The momentum tripped him, but he shuffled and caught himself. Landed on a knee. Balancing with a palm against the cold cement, he looked up just in time to see Cole neutralize the man on the ground. A Sig Sauer dangled from the guy's hand.

"Tango down," Cole called. He jogged across the warehouse.

Thank you, God. If he hadn't been wearing a vest, that bullet would've paralyzed him. "I'm fine." Despite the thunderous ache emanating through his chest, he staggered to his feet, then pushed himself toward the door.

More shots echoed through the building—but this time, from outside. Seconds later, Bronco ambled in and nudged the body. "Lookee here. Got us a *dead* bad guy to match the one outside. Bingo!"

Stick came in behind him. "They're gone. Gave them a flat tire and shot out the windows but couldn't stop them."

No, not this close only to fail. "Check the building," Reece ground out. God, please! Amazing timing. Showing up just as Sajjadi leaves?

"What do you think?" Cole asked, as he straightened from checking their victim.

"He's playing with us. Leading us here, then—"

"Captain!"

They both pivoted toward the voice. Cole cursed.

There, across the cavernous space where a lone streak of light splintered the darkness, Reece saw the wall—but not just the wall. A dark spot . . . What was . . . ? *No.*

"Shiloh!" Sprinting across the empty facility, Reece struggled against the sixty-pound gear that slowed him like a nightmare.

His heart vaulted into his throat at the gruesome image his three-second dash pounded into his memory—Shiloh, strung up like a slab of beef.

"Get her down! Get her down." He rushed her, wrapping his arms around her waist. He lifted, easing her weight off the restraints. Blood from her temple dripped onto his cheek. Her matted hair hung over an angry red swollen eye.

"Stick, get the torch!"

"On it," the scrawny guy said as he aimed the small torch toward the steel shackle.

With her slumped against him, Reece ignored the acrid odor of her burnt flesh—she'd been electrocuted. "Shiloh." Was she still alive? He tried to angle her to see her face. She hadn't grunted, groaned—nothing! *Please, God. She can't be dead.*

Her head lobbed forward—smacked his forehead then slid down his face and came to rest on his shoulder.

"Shiloh." He bounced his shoulder, the sounds of the men working to free her from the chains a distant clamor. "Shiloh, can you hear me?"

Her right arm flopped down.

"Got a pulse," Map shouted.

The news should've made Reece relax but didn't. Couldn't. "Shiloh?" Another bounce. "Shiloh, come on, baby. Talk to me."

Limp and unresponsive, she almost tumbled out of his hold. They freed her left arm. He shifted her into a better position, her upper body resting against him now.

"Come on, come on, come on!" Reece yelled at the team. He scraped the hair from her face, looking for eye movement beneath her lids.

Her full weight dropped against him. Reece took a step back, guarding her carefully as he lowered her to the ground. Cole's skilled hands moved over her body with expert precision, assessing her wounds. "Nothing visibly broken. No obvious internal injuries."

Map knelt by her head. "Pulse is erratic."

"Chopper!" Bronco's deep voice boomed through the warehouse.

Tomcat and Leaf hustled through a side door. "Place is empty."

Reece glanced at the boards riveted into the floor. Waterboarding. His gaze drifted to Shiloh, to her tangled, damp hair. Every semblance of control boiled into his own personal Molotov cocktail that he'd love to lob into the faces of whoever had done this.

Tiny movement on the boards lured his attention. A droplet of water raced down a small indentation. Reece shifted, eyeing the strange markings. A slow smile came to his lips. Then a grin. Ragged and probably carved by fingernails, two letters glistened against the sodden wood.

JB.

Jude Blake. His mentor was alive.

Reece gathered Shiloh into his arms. "Let's move." As he hurried out of the building, salty spray from the sea, stirred up by the helo, stung them.

A moan. Tensed, Shiloh lifted her head. "Reece?" The whoosh of her breath tickled his neck. She tensed more. "Where—"

"S'okay. You're safe. I got you."

She slumped into him. Her arm snaked around his neck. Her muscles constricted as she held him in a vise-grip. Aboard the chopper, she refused to release him as they lifted into the air and returned to base camp.

Sobs wracked her body as she remained cradled against him. He slumped against the hard seat, his head resting on the bulkhead. Eyes closed, he tried to ignore the trickle of her tears sliding down his chest and neck. Focused on getting Jude back. Killing Sajjadi.

But amid the thunderous *thwump* of the helo and the wind that roared through the bird, he realized . . . Shiloh had been left there for a reason.

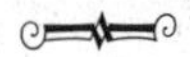

Green Beret Camp
Northern India

Never negotiate out of fear.

Shiloh knew the rule backward and forward. Inside out. Upside down. Lying on the medic's bed in the Green Beret camp, she stared up at the cobwebs twinkling in the low lamplight. Amazing how rapidly the rule had vanished from her weak brain even though her father spent years hammering it into her head.

Fear drives us to do things we'd never contemplate in a right state of mind, Shiloh.

Got that right. She'd vowed over and over she would never become a spy, betray those who trusted her. Yet she'd just signed her name on the dotted line—with the blood of her father. Sure, she'd gone along with her father's plan, but secretly, she'd hoped to find a way to turn the tide on this nightmare. Naive and Foolish were her new names.

Images spun and skated through her mind, pinching her eyes shut. Seeing him writhing for his life. The demonic-like sound of him hurling. Coughing. Gagging. Drowning.

And that dripping. That blasted dripping that fried her synapses. Each droplet sizzling with haunting reminders of her mother's death.

It had cracked her pride. Her arrogance. Her hard heart.

She'd do anything to keep her father alive. That angered her because of the power Sajjadi now held over her, and because two weeks ago, she wouldn't have cared whether her father lived or died.

Then she surrendered. Agreed to cooperate.

What scared her now was Reece. Somehow he always knew what she was thinking. Knew the *why* behind her actions. Would he figure this one out? Figure out what she had to do?

Outside voices drifted through the screen of the medic's hut. Amid them came Reece's. His tone now so different from last night . . . different from the words gentle with adamant reassurance that she'd be okay. Words as comforting as the warm flutter of his breath against her jaw and neck, as comforting as the concern etched into his rugged face. The heroic fury to settle the score with whoever had hurt her—yeah, she'd seen that clear as daylight in his beautiful blue irises.

Dull and heated, an ache kindled in her chest. Once he realized she'd aligned with Sajjadi, undone all his hard work, there'd be no forgiveness.

He abandoned you to the Brits. Didn't think you could cut it. No doubt he was thinking of Chloe. Compared her to someone who'd let pride get in the way.

Funny that. Her own pride and arrogance had blazed a path to where she was strung up on a wall and electrocuted. Tracing the raw flesh on her wrists from the shackles, she felt the tenuous strands of anger and knew that without them, she'd collapse in Reece's presence.

The screen door opened and closed.

This was it. She could sense his presence. Shiloh glanced up.

Reece edged closer, his expression guarded. "Hey."

Prying herself upright, Shiloh worried a thread from the thin grey blanket.

Metal clanged as he dragged a doctor's stool toward her and straddled it. "Doc says you're going to be okay."

Shiloh fought the way the relief in his voice crumbled the perimeter of her resolve. Having him here, staring at her with the intensity she'd always loved, the intensity that said he didn't do anything halfway . . . that he loved her . . .

If she didn't push him away, she'd fail this mission before she ever started.

But . . . she didn't want to lose Reece. She might even love him.

Warily, she watched him. Waited. Listened to the steady rhythm of his breathing. Admired the way his eyes looked like crystals sparkling beneath the tease of the warm sun. Remembered the kiss—

Shiloh jolted to her feet.

Strong, gentle hands caught her as she wobbled. "Hey. What's wrong?"

She pushed against his toned abs. "Nothing. Get away." Fire lit through her side and busted lip. "Just leave me alone."

"Are you mad that I sent you away for safekeeping?"

"Is that what you call it?"

"So you're still mad."

"No." Wait—there was her opportunity. "Yes." She shoved him back. "You wanted me out of your life, then I'm gone. Done. No worries."

He moved toward her. "Listen to me. Please." Never had his voice elicited such power as it did right then, stilling her, drawing her gaze to his as he cupped her face. "I'm sorry. I was wrong. I ran. Out of fear, I negotiated."

Shiloh's heart thumped at hearing her father's words on Reece's lips.

"I negotiated with myself, convinced it wouldn't bother me if I lost you because at least you'd be alive."

Move. Think. Do something! But she couldn't think. Couldn't move.

"I regret that my actions hurt you."

"But you don't regret *what* you did?"

"No. It kept you alive. That's what I wanted."

"Yeah, and is *this* what you wanted?" She pointed to her injuries. "Me tortured?"

"No." Vehemence speared his words and handsome face. "If you—" He clamped his mouth shut, and Shiloh knew what he wanted to say. If she'd stayed where he put her, this wouldn't have happened. And he was right. Which was why she had to fake this anger. She hated herself for fighting the painful attempt he'd made to protect her. Her rebellion cost her so much—maybe even her father.

"What about what I wanted, Reece? I wanted to get the men who killed Khalid." She swallowed against the metallic taste in her mouth. "I thought we were going to work together. You said you believed in me."

"I do. That's why I sent you away. I knew you'd stop at nothing to go after Sajjadi. But it's not as easy as you think to take him down. I've been trying for years."

"Point and shoot. Not real hard."

"And which of Sajjadi's seven guards do you hit first?"

"They have my father and you expect me to just sit here?"

"Jude Blake doesn't go anywhere he's not prepared to go."

Shiloh blinked. "What do you mean? He let himself get captured?"

"Think how he's stayed out of enemy hands for the last twenty-plus years. But suddenly, he's captured by the very man who has you?" He lowered his face. "We'll get him back. He's too important, owns too many secrets." He edged forward. "Do you really think I'm going to let my number one enemy kill anyone, let alone the father of the woman I love?"

"You still love me?" The words, unbidden, leapt from her mouth before she could catch them. She nudged him back. "No, stop—you're just trying to confuse me. I—"

Reece pulled her into his arms.

She wrestled against him, but he locked his arms. Held her firm and tight. She gripped his shirt, and although her mind screamed to shove him away, she couldn't. She wanted his strength. Needed it. She nestled in, the security a soothing balm to her wounded soul.

"We're heading back to Mumbai."

Shiloh eased out of his hold. "Mumbai?" She struggled to align the news of their return with her original mission objective. It was perfect. She had to get the codes from Abdul in a Mumbai prison. "Why? Why Mumbai?" It really couldn't be this easy . . . could it? "Is that where they took my father?"

"I have contacts there."

He didn't answer her question about her father, and that wasn't good. It meant they didn't know where her father was.

Regardless they were returning to Mumbai. Exactly what she needed. She slumped against the small bed, slowly feeling the wedge of her choice sliding between them.

"Julia and Toby are packing up now."

"Julia? Who's Julia?"

"My sister. She's . . ." He raked a hand through his short crop. "It's complicated."

Wow. He would all but deliver her into her mission. This couldn't get any more perfect—or worse! No doubt if they went back together, he'd want to keep an eye on her. There had to be an opportunity to get away from him in Mumbai. "What do I do? I mean, I don't want to get in the way."

A slow smile came to Reece's handsome face. "I want you in my way for the rest of my life, Shiloh."

She blinked. "You don't mean that."

"With everything that I am."

Only then did she feel those tenuous strands of anger slipping from her fingers. Strands she desperately had had to hold onto. But . . . was he saying he wanted to marry her?

His smile broadened. "That's exactly what I'm saying."

Shark's fins! If he knew these simple thoughts, did he know what she planned to do? "H-how do you always know what I'm thinking?"

Tracing the line of her jaw, he smiled. "I know where you've come from, what you've done. Knowing your heart, the woman

I've fallen in love with and the way she thinks," he said, tapping her temple, "I can figure out the rest."

He leaned closer, the smile lingering in his expression. "I've never been this clear on anyone, Shiloh. I know what you're thinking. I know what you're planning to do." The intensity in his gaze ratcheted.

A silent understanding passed between them as she nodded. "Dead reckoning."

"Yeah." He craned his neck forward. Then, warm and gentle, he kissed her. Once. Twice. Deepened the kiss as he pulled her into his arms.

When he figured out her plan—and she knew now that he would figure it out eventually—there was no telling where he'd send her. Since this was their last kiss, Shiloh wanted it to last.

Clap! "Whoa. Okay. Never mind." The screen door shut again as the doctor left. Despite the intrusion, neither of them broke the kiss.

Then Reece eased back. His smile vanished. Something slipped through his features—a challenge. Clear as day. Louder than the clap of the screen door that ushered in the good doctor.

Trembling from the kiss, she shuddered. "What?"

"I'm calling your game, Shiloh."

29

YEAH, WHAT GAME IS THAT?" CHIN JUTTED, SHE BROUGHT HERSELF UP straight.

One degree. Scientists said that if the Earth had been one degree off its orbit around the sun, the Earth would have ceased to exist. A cosmic collision. Earth and sun.

In the same way, Reece's world had shifted—in particular, Shiloh had changed. Subtly, but definitely noticeable. It awoke in him an awareness of imminent danger. If he didn't end this—and now—she'd end up just like Chloe.

Reece narrowed his eyes. He couldn't believe she was really going to ditch him and head out on a covert mission untrained and ill-prepared. "You've done and said a lot, but you've never lied to me before." He tightened his grip on his anger and panic. "Don't start now."

"What?" Her defiance flared. "What is it you think I'm lying about?"

Disappointment peeked around the edges of his anger. "Tell me why Sajjadi left you in the warehouse alive."

She drew back—not much, but enough to signal her admission. "How am I supposed to know what that loon was thinking?"

"Calling him names doesn't dumb him down," Reece said, trying to tap down his frustration. "What's your mission objective?"

"I don't know what you're talking about." She tried to step around him.

No, he wasn't letting her off that easy. He blocked her. "Come on. You aren't trained, you only have a cursory knowledge of the language, yet you seriously think you can pull off some harebrained stunt?"

Shiloh pushed him. "Leave me alone."

"Why?" He bounced back at her. "Does that make it easier to be a traitor?"

Crimson patches spread over her face and neck. "How dare you . . ." Tears turned her blue-grey eyes into pools of liquid silver.

"How dare I?" He moved in on her. "Quite easily when an amateur thinks she can go up against one of the deadliest terrorists." Staving off the panic proved harder than he thought. He had to stop her. "You do this, and you'll end up dead."

"Just like Chloe?"

Her words hit like an anvil. "This isn't about Chloe." So why was his pulse racing like a rocket out of a silo? "This is about you. About you thinking you can pull this off."

"What?" She tossed her hands up. "What exactly am I supposed to pull off?"

"Cooperation with Sajjadi."

Flames flickered through her stormy eyes. "You're out of your mind."

Those weak words of hers told him he was right. "The only reason you were left alive in that warehouse is because you're working with him now." Hearing his words broke the levee that held back the agony. "Shiloh, it isn't going to save your father."

Her complexion paled but he could see her clinging to the vain hope of rescuing Jude.

"It won't." He drew in a steadying breath. "I don't care what Sajjadi told you. He'll get what he wants and kill you both."

Her lower lip trembled. "My father's alive right now."

"You don't know that."

"I do!"

"You don't," he snapped. "Even if Jude is still alive, it's only because Sajjadi isn't done."

"I will do whatever—"

"Whatever isn't good enough. Whatever gets you killed!"

She barreled into him, knocking him off balance. Reece tumbled backward over the medical stool. By the time he regained his footing, Shiloh was gone. He lunged for the door.

In the arid night, Julia met him on the steps. Dark stormy eyes brooded. "Let her be, Reece."

He went around her.

"Reece, I mean it." Julia caught up. "Don't do this. If you push too hard—"

He rounded on her and gripped her shoulders tight. "I will do whatever it takes to stop her." His own words rang in his ears—*whatever gets you killed!*

"Isn't this exactly what you did with Chloe?"

"Why—" He cocked his head and looked away. "Why does everyone keep bringing her up? She's dead. Buried. Gone. This is about saving Shiloh." His sister's sympathetic smile grated on his last nerve. "What?"

"Does Shiloh need saving? Or is this you trying to control things again?"

"Controlling the situation is my job."

"But you're trying to force her to do what *you* think she should do."

"What I think keeps her alive!"

"Does it?" Julia arched an eyebrow, a corkscrew curl dancing in the light of the doc's hut.

"I'm not doing this with you, Jules." He started toward Shiloh's hut, only to see Gita stepping through the door. In that split second he realized his sister was probably right. If he pushed, Shiloh would be more determined than ever. But how could he just sit around and let her walk into that snare?

She'd never live to see another day.

Sacrificing love for lives made sense every day of the year.

Except today. Even as Shiloh braced herself in the ultra-compact car as Gita wove down the mountainous trail, she knew she was as good as dead where Reece was concerned. *Dead reckoning.* Yet he hadn't seen this coming, hadn't stopped her.

She didn't want to betray Reece. Didn't want to lose what they had. But her father—and a million others—would die if she didn't.

Okay, she wasn't a complete dolt. Sajjadi didn't bargain. She got that. But something in Shiloh tugged at her, urging her to at least try. While she and her father hadn't spoken in years, while she'd spouted off about how much she hated him, they were family. And she'd seen a different side to him and realized maybe things weren't quite so cut-and-dry.

Palm branches swatted the car. A truck-sized pothole pitched them forward and rocked them as they jounced back onto the path.

"Sorry." Gita's mumbled apology was lost amid the groaning and creaking of the car. She slowed the vehicle, glanced around and searched the dark, wet foliage. Was she lost?

Maybe this wasn't such a good idea.

Too late. She'd left the camp. Left the protection of the Green Berets and Reece. She was committed.

The car lurched forward and barreled between two boulders. "Almost there," Gita said as she braked, swung a hard right and squeezed around massive banyan trees, and then gunned the twangy little engine.

Within minutes they hit pavement. Shiloh relaxed and eased back against the seat, shooting her new guide a hesitant smile.

"He be mad." Gita's olive knuckles went white against the steering wheel. "They no let me back."

Awareness spun through Shiloh. For the first time, she realized what price Gita's assistance would cost. "But what about Stick?"

With a shrug, Gita faked a smile.

What had she done? When the woman suggested they take her car, Shiloh had seen it as a sign from God that she was doing the right thing trying to save her father. But would God bless her only to hurt someone else?

Confusion tumbled through her mind.

"He love you. Want you safe."

"Safe doesn't save my father." Shiloh leaned against the window and closed her eyes, feigning sleep in the hopes that Gita would end the conversation. But as they drew closer to the city, Shiloh choked back the fear that challenged her confidence. *What confidence?* Hadn't that died at the warehouse?

Sleep wrapped its greedy tendrils around her. Churning waters tossed her from Mumbai to Paris with the Louvre and the towering Anubis and then back to the mountains. To Reece's embrace suffused with warmth and love. To her father thrashing on the waterboards. To Sajjadi standing over her father with a weapon as water dripped down the burlap. He pulled the trigger.

Crack!

Shiloh bolted upright, grappling for her bearings.

A touch—Shiloh slapped it away. The soft gasp snapped her attention to the woman next to her. Gita. Not Sajjadi, but Gita. In the car. She blinked and glanced out the car window, steadying her breath as the ominous blue dawn pushed back the void of night. "Wh-where are we?" Lights twinkled nearby, indiscernible.

"There," Gita whispered. "The train depot you ask for."

Swallowing, Shiloh nodded slightly. "Okay." She reached for the door handle.

Gita caught her wrist. "You sure?" Sorrowful brown eyes implored her. "I take you back. Chief make all better? Fix this."

"No." Shiloh tried not to think about it, but the memories from far too recently skidded into her thoughts. Mikhail. Baseer dying. Khalid. So many lives squandered. And Reece would become a distant memory too. "No, I'm on my own now."

Shiloh gathered her backpack and smiled as she climbed out. "Thank you." On the sidewalk, she shouldered her pack and waited as red taillights faded into the darkness.

She braved one last glance at the depot and felt every ounce of the loneliness she'd trapped herself in. The tragedy at that station had switched the proverbial tracks of her life. Now she'd make someone pay for what they did.

Shiloh turned and hiked toward the government offices. The long trek bought her time to make peace with her decision. Or at least, battle with her decision. Peace wouldn't be hers. Not this time.

After a quick check of her watch, she quickened her steps. Sajjadi said her window of opportunity would be small. No room for mistakes. She jogged around to the back of the building. Just as promised, a small bag tucked behind a trashcan held a uniform and identification tag. Shiloh changed into the clothes, smeared the dark, heavy base they'd provided over her face, and stowed her pack.

About to step into the early morning, Shiloh spotted her own reflection in a dirty window—and halted. Did she really look that haggard?

As if on cue, a half-dozen women strode toward the entrance, their talk casual and dull. Bringing up the rear, Shiloh entered the facility with the entourage. At the first checkpoint, she swiped the provided card and walked through.

Though she ached to sprint down the long corridor, she hauled in the desire and walked as quickly as possible, remembering her instructions. Once in the kitchen, she tied an apron over the uniform and accepted the ready-made cart from a woman who gave her a long, hard look before motioning Shiloh off.

Squeaky wheels seemed to shriek as Shiloh headed toward Deputy Minister Abdul's special detainment room. Holding her breath, she aimed toward the two guards. Poised at attention, they flanked the door. Either they would let her in . . . *Or they'll kill me*. Yeah. Great.

One guard stepped into her path.

Shiloh pasted a smile on her face and presented her ID. He verified her card. Why did seconds like this tick by with the weight of anchors?

The guard glared at her, sized her up, then grunted and flung open the door.

Holding her practiced smile, Shiloh entered the cell, which was in reality a lavish suite. Persian, hand-woven rugs spilled over the marble floors and rushed toward the mahogany secretary desk and coffee table.

Abdul lounged in a chair at a richly draped round table, sipping a glass of water and staring at the large, flat-screen panel where garish images of some attack in a foreign country splattered over the screen. He glanced back at her before he waved at her in dismissal.

Shiloh nudged the cart toward him. "Fools exult in life while the pious prepare for the journey ahead." Had she gotten the proverb right? When he gave no indication that he was familiar with it, she lifted a plate and set it on the table before repeating the phrase.

Dark eyes remained fastened on the screen. "And what journey am I preparing for, what journey does *he* send an American spy to help me complete?"

"You have something he wants." Wasn't Ali afraid someone would hear him?

He sneered, the dark circles under his eyes evidence of sleepless nights. "He promised me wealth and power." Ali motioned around the room. "A prison? This is what I get?"

Shiloh moved around the table and faced him. Palms against the cold surface, she leaned forward and tucked her chin. "He wants the codes." And she wanted to get out of here before she was discovered.

In defiance he sipped his drink. "I want my freedom."

This wasn't going anywhere. She had to force his hand. "Give me the codes, and I'll give you the antidote." Letting her gaze rest on the glass of water before him, Shiloh hoped he got her meaning.

He swallowed. Hard. "He would not—"

"No doubt he has predicted your reluctance." This had to work so she could get out of here before something went wrong. Like the rumblings of a typhoon before it hits, she felt the trouble looming over her now. She gave a small nod. "Very well. May you find your virgins—"

His mocha-colored hand clamped over hers. Dark eyes rose to hers. "Your loved one will not live."

Her heart skipped a beat. Two.

Ali rattled off the code. "The plan is not what you think. And remember . . ." His eyes darkened and then drifted to the small barred window as he shoved her aside. "Nobody who works with him lives."

30

Mumbai, India

WHY?"

The Anubis keychain glinted back at him, mocking. Reece rubbed his thumb over the memento, his heart heavy with grief. She'd left him. Snuck out in the middle of the night. Everything in him railed at her naiveté. She had no idea what she'd walked into. She might think she did, but only those who had traveled that road knew.

The hurt surprised him most. Knowing she didn't trust him, that she wasn't willing to let him handle this with the skill and experience he had. Forget the experience. She intentionally walked away from *him*.

Keychain clutched in his hand, he leaned against the table and hung his head. Ignored the map. Ignored the schematics. *God . . . why?* Why would He bring Shiloh into his life only to have her storm out—straight into her own death?

A door flapped open, banging the interior wall of the U.S. Embassy conference room. He straightened and slid the key-chain into his pocket.

Brody Aiken stood with Nielsen, Toby, and a half-dozen other men. "Shiloh was arrested at the Mumbai ministry building."

Hope stabbed him. If she was being held, he could extract her. "Where?"

"Unknown. But the guys snapped a few photos of her being escorted for transfer. Once in the building, they couldn't trace her." Brody tossed three photos on the table and then tapped one. "Look familiar?"

Knuckling the table, Reece studied the pictures. "Kodiyeri." He eyed the men flanking Brody and noted the tactical stance, the rigid posture, the military haircuts. Special Ops. But not Green Berets if the glares and Cole's taut lips were any indication.

Someone had a plan they hadn't shared with him. His gaze rose to Cole.

"The girl never made it anywhere." The dark-haired leader said as he shuffled one of the images to the middle and scooted it closer to Reece. "This is the interior of the building. She goes in. Never comes out. Kodiyeri and his team load up in SUVs and that's the end of it."

"He has her." Reece stared at the last image of Shiloh.

"Maybe. But we can't search for her. Not now." Nielsen huffed.

This was the way of it. Without legitimate cause to tie up resources, Shiloh would remain MIA. She'd walked out and tied his hands. Just like Chloe. And a rogue agent must be disavowed. He mentally touched the Anubis keychain, remembering the cold, hollow feeling that coursed through him when he spotted the piece on his pillow back at camp.

"This looks personal."

Staring through his brow, Reece met the steely gaze of the new Spec Ops leader and detected the man's question and challenge.

Brody cleared his throat as he placed another photo on the table. "About twenty minutes ago, a UAV snapped Kodiyeri's ugly mug on *The Jannat*."

The very yacht anchored off the coast of Mumbai and from which the Summit of the Agreed would launch their vicious campaign to restructure the political map in the Middle East. Something wasn't right.

But the proverbial clock ticked out the countdown. The nuclear disaster was his primary objective right now—Sajjadi. Not Shiloh and whatever it was that niggled at him.

"Okay, gentlemen," he said, eyeing the schematics of the yacht. "Sajjadi has both sets of codes for the missing device, as well as two of our people."

"That can't be assumed," Brody said.

"Until she's back in our custody, that's exactly what I will assume." Killing two birds with one stone, as it were, kept Reece's hope alive that he would find her before Sajjadi decided she'd served her purpose.

"Just get the nuke back or neutralize it. Do that," Nielsen said from a nearby chair, "and you have a green light."

Surrounded by his Green Berets, Cole Miller grinned. "We're all yours. Tell us when and where."

"We're yours too."

Reece pulled his spine into line and stared the man down. "And who am I working with?"

"Navy SEALs."

Why didn't he know these guys? Had he been out of the field that long?

"Don't need no squids," Bronco mumbled.

"Hey, Friction," a blonde SEAL said, looking from Bronco to the team leader. "I think they're nervous we'll blow 'em outta the water."

Still locked in a visual challenge with the leader, Reece didn't respond. Something about the guy rankled him.

"They're on a yacht." Friction smirked. "In case someone missed the obvious—yachts are usually in water. Like Ditch said, maybe you're afraid we'll blow you out of the water. I mean, who better to call than the aces of the sea?"

Arrogant too. Although Reece didn't trust this stranger, something—maybe the complete lack of control he felt—told him to let it be. "He's right. We need every available shooter." Studying the map, Reece marked an *X*. "It's a 300-foot yacht."

"Top bearing 16 knots, comfortably." Friction nodded, his grey eyes darting over the drawings. "Aft skiff will be heavily guarded."

"Agreed," Reece said. "If we hit the aft, we'll lose someone."

"Or make something go *boom*."

"This a game to you, frogman?"

That stupid grin. "No, I play for keeps."

"Trust me." Ditch laughed. "How'd you think he got the call-sign?"

Friction's attention never left the yacht photo. He tapped the left and right of the image. "We'll have to hit the sides."

"They've been in the water too long," Cole said. "Don't worry, chief. We've got you covered. The plan's solid. We'll get her back."

The relief at Cole's words swirled through Reece, easing the rising agitation over the new team members.

"So, it *is* personal." Friction smiled again. "Good to know."

Reece grabbed the photos and started toward the door without another word. Because if he did say something, it'd be with his fists and the squid would be laid out flat. Minus one asset in taking down Sajjadi. Not good.

"Jaxon, where are you going?" Nielsen called from behind.

"Meeting someone." He raised a hand as he pushed open the door. "Get them in place. I'll be there." The guy was right—it was personal. And this was his last chance to check his sources and make one last-ditch attempt to locate Shiloh. Help him figure out what he was missing in the intel. Something just wasn't right. The whole nuke code thing made sense, but something else simmered just out of reach in this whole nightmare.

And still, his mind couldn't shake the trauma of Shiloh's betrayal. Why had God allowed him to fall in love with a woman who could so easily turn her back on what she believed in?

With each step, the pain pounded into his chest. He had hoped his love would help her abandon this path.

He rounded the corner to the campus. Time to get focused. Reach end game. He stretched his neck and strode past the fountain to the building. Perry always had the missing clues. A good friend, sometime mentor, and all-around good guy. Reece silently thanked God for the man.

He aimed toward the building—and a door flung back. Grey blurred toward the street.

"Perry!" Where was he going? And in such a hurry?

The man carried himself fast, not quite running, but not walking either. At his car, he tossed his briefcase into the backseat.

"Perry!" Reece darted toward the car.

Behind the wheel, Perry met Reece's gaze. A smile washed the tension from the professor's face. He rolled down the window. "Reece, thank God! We had it all wrong, but there's still time, *mera dost*."

The engine turned over.

An explosion ripped through the car.

Reece flew backward, struck by an invisible force that felt like a cement wall. Light flashed over the pavement. His feet tipped over his head; his body spiraled through the chilly air. Heat seared his back. Pavement rushed up at him. He tried to brace against the impact. His shoulder slammed into the ground. *Pop!*

Pain rocketed through his neck and spine. He flipped onto his back, writhing to look at Perry's car—now a hulk of metal engulfed in flames.

Agony worked into his muscles. Reece shifted onto his side, using his uninjured arm to push up. Each move sent shards of pain stabbing through his body. He'd have to jam the shoulder joint back into alignment. But first, he had to get clear of here. Whoever had taken out Perry wouldn't hesitate to finish off Reece too.

On his feet, he hooked a thumb through his belt loop, hoping to keep his arm immobile. Sweat dribbled down the sides of his face, from both the pain and the intense heat of the flames.

He lumbered back to the city, down the busy streets. What had Perry meant? What did they have all wrong? Still time for what?

Mumbai Harbor

If she had to die, at least it would be on the water.

Sort of poetic. Or maybe that was God granting Shiloh her last wish.

"Move!" The oaf shoved her forward, down the second flight of steps into the belly of the yacht. The beauty and luxury of the vessel belied its purpose. Despite shiny surfaces and leather sofas in the lounge, she knew what would go down here. The giant plasma screen up on deck and the computer rigged to it—no doubt, to enter the control codes she'd extracted from Abdul.

If she could pull this off, honor her father in this one last stand, she'd die in peace.

No. That wasn't true. She wanted to make peace with Reece first. Let him know she did love him—that she hadn't turned her back on him the way Chloe had.

As she stepped over a raised threshold, she saw a suit escorting her father across marble floors, past a cream leather sofa to shiny gold-trimmed stairs. Her heart caught in her throat. He didn't look good at all.

"Dad!"

When their eyes met, he blanched.

Okay, that wasn't good.

The oaf wrestled her out of the companionway. "Keep moving."

Prodded forward, she stole one last glance at her father. Concern burrowed into her, yet relief—he was alive. And would be as long as she cooperated. But she had another mission that begged her cooperation.

Who was she kidding? With the firepower on this boat and the brutality of those wielding the weapons, she and her father didn't have a prayer.

Prayer. Yeah, tried that. Didn't work.

Tossed in a room, she spun around to find the bad guy pulling the door closed. Shrouded in darkness, she hurried forward, searching for a handle. Smoothing a hand over the slick surface, she realized there was no knob.

She patted her hands over the wall until she found the light switch. *Click.* Nothing. *Click-click.* Still nothing. Suffocating darkness swooped in on her like a hungry vulture. Shiloh closed her eyes, pretending to be on a deep-sea dive. Cool waters teasing her muscles and rela—

How could she relax in a pitch-black room and at the mercy of terrorists? Her pulse sped.

She had to calm down. The kingdom, phylum, class . . . What was it? What came first? A jumbled list of Latin words and images flitted through her brain. Shiloh drove her back against the wall and groaned. She couldn't even think!

Sun star. It leapt to her mind and just as quickly, the order: *Animalia. Echinodermata. Asteroidea. Spinulosida. Solasteridae. Solaster dawsoni.*

Miss America.

Shiloh tensed, remembering Khalid's voice. Remembering how he'd died in the train depot. Sliding down the wall, she felt her hope fading. She hugged her knees. Tears, unbidden, sprung free. *Whatever gets you killed!* Reece was right. He was always right. During their plan-making, her father had mentioned Reece was one of the best operatives he'd ever encountered. And she ached for his strong arms to hold and reassure her. He would tell her to trust those instincts and do what they told her.

Smearing the tears away, Shiloh climbed to her feet. This was no different than diving at night. She couldn't see . . . but that didn't mean she couldn't *see* with her hands in the darkness.

I am the light of the world. Whoever follows me will not walk in darkness . . .

Whoa. Where did that come from? Shiloh paused, stunned as images assaulted her of the pastor standing over her mother's casket as he heralded the salvation of God to the world—those gathered under the mourning tent. It had angered and frightened her that he used her mother's death to scare others to God. Sort of like Khalid. He'd always told her to "get right" with God before it was too late.

Maybe now was too late. She was on a ship about to launch a nuclear weapon. Anyone with a brain knew the world powers wouldn't allow that, meaning they'd blow this tub to kingdom come.

But this time the verse felt different. Soothing. Like a lifeline. Tentatively, she grasped the thread of hope dangling before her. *God, help me. Please.* A surge of excitement raced through her.

She took a step to the right. And stubbed her toe. She growled and nudged whatever it was out of the way. *Clank!*

Shiloh stilled. That sounded familiar. She bent and groped over the wood floor. Her hand hit a cylindrical object and ran up to the top of the small sphere-shape. An oxygen tank! She dropped to her knees, feeling for the regulator. Blind, she attached it, released the valve and felt the cool, distinct flow of nitrox. She smiled and quickly cut it off. Stood and trailed her way around the room, hoping against hope that there was a window. If she could get it open—even if she had to smash it—she'd have a tank and could swim to shore.

Since she couldn't feel the vibration of the engines beneath her feet, she guessed they were far enough from the coast that Sajjadi felt safe. And minus the sounds of choppers ferrying guests to the upper decks, all the players must be in place. Which meant she didn't have much time.

Finally, her fingers snagged a window sill. She jerked back the curtain—and precious relief flooded her at the dim blanket of stars that met her. Gold glinted under the tease of moonlight. She traced the ledge searching for the hatch-locks. She found one and released it. The window swung open. Shiloh quickly rigged the counter buoyancy device on the tank and threaded an oxygen cable through it like a rope to lower the tank to the water and anchor it in between the window.

The lure of freedom cinched her by the throat. *Just climb out the window.*

She stopped. Her father. She couldn't leave him.

He never cared about you.

Not quite the truth but one Shiloh had always touted when she wanted to shove him away. Yet now, standing here at the portal to freedom—the great sea of black glistening at her—she understood for the first time the sacrifices he'd made.

Realized the danger he had intentionally placed himself in to make the world a better place. For her. For everyone.

Glancing back into the room, she knew that she knew that she knew she couldn't leave him. Was there another tank? Ah, there! Carefully, she eased the window shut, the tether to the tank sandwiched between the window and sill. Stumbling past a couch and end table, she reached for the other tank.

The door clobbered the wall as it flapped back. Light burst through the room. Her nemesis, Kodiyeri, loomed in the doorway. "Let's go!" Roughly, he dragged her out of the room, back up the companionway, and tossed her toward the stairs.

Choking back the fear that she'd lost her one opportunity, Shiloh trudged up the narrow steps, her mind locked on the tank.

As her foot hit the floor of the upper deck, she froze.

Dozens of men, dressed in slick foreign suits and wearing gold Rolex watches and sneers that told Shiloh exactly what they thought of her, laughed and socialized on the upper deck as if this were some grand celebration or coronation. They mingled amid white table-clothed tables sporting silver and luxurious floral arrangements. The air, suffused with merry music and salty sea humidity, wrapped itself around her.

This was it.

"Gentlemen, friends," Sajjadi's voice rang through a loudspeaker just as the guard hooked Shiloh's elbow and hauled her toward the aft, where a balcony jutted over the lower level pool and hot tub. "Tonight will be remembered forever!"

Only as the guard wrestled her around the deck did Shiloh see her father.

"This man, this *American* has spied on our countries for decades. Until recently, his location and identity were unknown.

But," Sajjadi said as he smiled broadly. "My son has delivered the spawn of the Great Satan to our hands."

In that moment, Mahmud Sajjadi emerged from the crowds and joined his father. As cheers drowned the spectacle, Shiloh went rigid at the sight of the man who'd brought her here, claimed to be an ally of the US and Britain. And they called her father the spawn of Satan?

"Together, they cannot stop us. Yes?"

She'd love to toss them into the deep sea with no nitrox and see how unstoppable they really were.

Sajjadi ordered his right-hand man—none other than Kodiyeri—to press her father to his knees.

"No!" Shiloh started forward, only to be restrained.

"And our night is even further blessed by Allah. We have the daughter of this pig, and she has agreed to help us, with a little encouragement."

Laughter filtered through the crowds.

Shiloh speared Mahmud with a deadly glare. If only she had as much power in her glare as the nuke had in its belly.

"And now, after years of meticulous planning, it is on this night we set ourselves apart. Allah's Sword of Justice will be known throughout the world as a deadly force, one willing to obey the Prophet Mohammed, peace be upon him."

"Peace be upon him," those gathered repeated the blessing.

Sajjadi banged a fist against the table. "We will start with those who have embraced the Great Satan, who have compromised their faith for money," he snarled.

The guard pushed Shiloh toward a large electrical panel.

Sajjadi slid a key into one access portal. His son slid a second into the other. "Let it be said," he nodded to Shiloh.

Resisting the urge to look at her father, Shiloh shifted toward the instrumentation. Stemming the trembling in her limbs she reached for the keyboard. *Please, God, if you've ever been there . . . be there now. Let Reece find out what I've done.*

Mahmud stood beside her and slid in another key, then prodded her. Swallowing, she entered the codes. And spotted a small hand-held device next to the panel. Numbers flicked down. *A timer.* Shiloh pressed the final key on the panel.

Whiiiirrrrrr-p.

Did he have another bomb? As the panel died and the screen went blank, Sajjadi's dark eyes widened. "Wh-what is wrong?"

Shiloh checked the hand-held. Still ticking. *Oh dear God . . .*

Mimicking his father's response, Mahmud stepped back. "I don't understand."

She looked at her father. How could she let him know? She gulped. Glanced at the small device. Ten seconds had passed. One-hundred twenty remained. She darted a panicked look to her father.

"What have you done?" Sajjadi shouted at her.

Backlit by the sea, her father smiled. Good job, his expression said, echoed by the twinkling stars and the sparkling waters behind him. He nodded.

Crack! Gunfire rent the air.

Her father's face went slack. He blinked and leaned forward, his mouth open. A dark circle spread over his chest. The suited guard leapt away from the unfolding nightmare.

Shock froze her—Sajjadi shot her father! As if in slow motion, Sajjadi turned toward her father once more.

Shiloh drove her elbow into the goon's stomach and sent him spiraling.

Sajjadi took aim.

Summoning everything she had left, Shiloh launched herself over the thin table and slammed into her father. He caught and held onto her. They dove over the rail.

Water gathered them into its dark, icy depths.

31

PHEWT-PHEWT!

Reece caught the crewman as he slumped forward, drugged from the dart, and laid the body on the deck. Crouched, Reece placed two fingers against the man's neck as he watched Friction and Cole slip over the stainless steel rails along the port side. Beside him waited Ditch.

The distinct sound of something very large hitting the water drew him up.

Screams splintered the night. Shouts engulfed the chaos chased by cracking gunfire.

"Go, go, go!" Reece hustled down the starboard gangway with Ditch covering him. Cole and Friction worked port-side. The captain of *The Jannat* and his team would be held or neutralized, depending on their resistance, by Stick and Bronco.

Hunched beneath the wall of windows that lead into the main lounge and saloon, Reece eyed the back of the stairs. Guards could be waiting there. Most likely were.

A fluid signal sent Ditch darting up under the stairs. Reece whipped around to the front. *Thud!*

"Tango down," Ditch called.

Reece joined the man. M4 raised to the opening onto the upper deck, he took the first step up. Adrenaline spiraled through his veins with each squeak of his Deep Sea Amphib boots against the lit steps.

"Primary one in sight," came Friction's smooth, steady warning. "Doesn't have a clue we're here."

"Find and kill them!" Hours spent listening to recorded conversations embedded the coward's voice in Reece's brain—Sajjadi.

But why was he ordering his men to find them?

"We're blown," Ditch mumbled.

"Negative," Friction said through the coms. "Guy's going ape trying to find someone. Stick to the plan. We're—"

Phewt-phewt!

A grunt. "Now we're blown," Friction said.

Eyeing the layout, Reece saw the best point of cover—the bar, six paces past the stairwell. With a deep breath, he burst onto the upper deck. A spray of bullets whizzed over him. Ditch cursed as he slid into Reece behind the shield.

He raked a gaze over the man and spotted a slice just below Ditch's shoulder. "Already looking for a medal?"

Surprise danced through Ditch's brown eyes. Then he grinned. "Any I can."

"Chief, he's comin' your way."

Reece drew himself into a crouch again, his ears trained on the crunch of glass that grew louder. One.

Crunch-click.

Two.

Crunch-click-click.

He punched to his feet bringing up his M4 as he did.

Sajjadi stepped back.

Two armed men rushed from the side. Fired.

So did Reece.

Fire tore through his shoulder, shoving him backward—Sajjadi seized the moment and darted around a half wall and vanished down into the lower deck.

Reece groped for stability. He blinked through the pain.

Someone steadied him. "Easy, Chief."

"Stop him." Reece caught the grab rail and dragged himself upright. In pain and losing blood, he went for the stairs. Stumbled down them. Tripped. But kept moving, following the shadows of Sajjadi's trail. "Lower deck. Primary One."

"Roger, lower deck," Cole called. "On our way."

Propped against the entry that opened into a companionway, Reece shrugged off the tingling in his arm. This wasn't over until he found Jude. And Shiloh. "Crew's quarters." With a huffed breath, he dropped down the stairs.

Clambering behind him told him of the team's presence.

"You're hit."

"He's down here," Reece said, swiping at the dribble of sweat near his ear.

Friction eased forward and took point. It felt good but weird to work with another SEAL again. To operate with grace and automatic protocol without having to explain or direct. Respect sifted past Reece's suspicions of the squid as they cleared one cabin after another.

"Like a rat in a cage," Friction mumbled as they worked their way toward the bow.

"Never did like rats." Reece gritted his teeth, cringing over the blood that slid down inside his gear. The vest stopped him from getting killed but didn't make him invincible.

Friction flung open a door.

The galley yawned before them, sterile and white. Pristine. Undisturbed. A half-dozen wide-eyed workers, panic streaked across their faces, stood to one side.

He's here.

"Rat stew." Friction scissored in, his weapon sweeping the semi-cavernous room.

"Nobody move," Cole ordered as the team spread out, taking a wide arc and slowly closing in around the two long stainless steel prep tables where the workers remained immobilized.

"Need him alive." Reece backstepped toward an area where a mound of vegetables, bright and colorful against the sterility of the galley, sat before a young girl who held a large knife. Would she try to use that on the team?

"Easy," he whispered as he gently lifted it from her grip.

She gasped.

Phewt! Phewt-phewt!

Reece pivoted at the sound of the muffled fire just in time to see Sajjadi flop onto the floor three feet away. Something clanged to the ground and spun. Stepping on it with his Amphib boot, he paled. A meat cleaver. A very large one.

He rushed to the terrorist and flipped him onto his back. A ragged breath wheezed through the man's chest. "Get the doc!" Reece pressed a hand against the wound to stem the flow of blood. "Where is she?"

Sajjadi's gaze flicked to Reece's. A crooked grin came as a stream of blood slipped over his lip and down his jaw.

"Where is she?" Reece growled, pushing hard against the wound.

Sajjadi gasped, gurgled. Laughed.

Rage coursed through Reece. If Sajjadi didn't tell them, if he died with that knowledge, then Shiloh could die too. He hadn't come this far to lose her!

Doc dropped to his knees and checked the injuries. "Doesn't look good."

Reece grabbed Sajjadi's uniform and jerked the man up. "Where is she?"

"Chief!"

"What did you do with her? Where's Shiloh?" He shook Sajjadi. Hard.

"Chief!" Doc clamped his hands over Reece's. "Let go. Him dying doesn't help us."

A hissing noise issued from Sajjadi. "You think"—cough—"you stop me." He wheezed. "One last jihad! You won't find it . . ." Cough. "Or her." His eyes rolled into his head.

Finally, Reece released him.

"He's not dead. Just very, very close." Doc unfurled his pack and went to work on Sajjadi. "You won't be getting anything out of him for awhile."

Defeat wriggled into Reece, painful and desperate. He stared at the general, disbelieving their one source—

"Wait." Reece struggled to his feet. "Where's his son?"

"Upper deck." Friction adjusted his black gloves. He pointed to Reece's shoulder. "Want to get that looked at?"

"I'm fine." Chin tucked, Reece stumbled down the companionway, past the crew, over bodies. "Stick, Bronco," he spoke into the coms. "Give me a sitrep."

"What did he mean about one last jihad?" Friction asked from behind.

"The same thing the niggling in my gut means." Reece pushed himself to the upper deck, listening to the chatter of the team calling off their sitrep.

"So you think there's something else?"

"Definitely. This was too easy."

The twumping of choppers reverberated through the hull and cut their conversation. Right now, the only thing he cared about was finding Shiloh and Jude. Knowing she was missing, knowing every second could be her last drove him crazy. As he dragged himself up the last flight, he ignored the grinding pain.

The dignitaries sat at the tables as if eating and enjoying a fine meal on the open sea. But their faces belied the calmness of the yacht. A giant, steel bird descended toward the helo-pad at the bow of the ship.

"Chief, over here."

Pulled in the direction of Stick's shout, Reece spotted two boats out on the water.

Stick knelt beside Mahmud, bandaging his chest and side. Avoiding the dark stains on the deck, Reece drew closer.

Just then, he heard the familiar twang of a Zodiac boat on the black waters. Two splinters of light fractured the void. Long and shrieking, a whistle rent the night. A red tail snaked through the twinkling sky. *Boom!* A flare turned night into day.

"What're they looking for?"

Stick straightened. "Jude and Shiloh."

Bullets had nothing on the revelation. Reece stilled, his gaze back on the dark sea. "How long?" How long had she been out there?

"Ten, fifteen minutes, maybe more."

She would be fine. Excellent swimmer. Pro diver. Shiloh would be just fine.

"It gets worse." Stick rustled his hair.

Darting a glare to the scrawny kid, Reece's heart churned like the Arabian Sea.

"Jude was shot point-blank in the chest. According to this guy here, Shiloh lunged at her father and they both went overboard." The thin face looked taut. "Chief, he doesn't have long. Not in this water."

Shiloh. What was she thinking? He studied the waters, trying to replay the event in his mind. His attention plummeted to the blood on the deck. Jude's. *God, help me! Help Shiloh.*

Friction leaned on the grab rails, watching the boats circling and probing the deep waters. "No way any normal person could survive that. Especially mortally wounded."

No, Reece wouldn't accept that. Shiloh had surprised him more than once. If she went into the water she saw that as her only hope. Rankled, he descended to the lower deck and strode toward the dive skiff.

But it didn't make any sense. This far out and supporting her injured father she couldn't swim to shore—a shore that was a solid five miles out. And what about sharks?

"Let's suit up."

"Chief," Friction said, catching his shoulder.

Reece nearly dropped from the blinding pain. He rounded on the guy.

Hands raised, Friction took a step back. "No offense, Chief, but you aren't in any condition to dive."

"I'm *not* leaving her out there."

"They're probably already dead."

"No," Reece snapped. He had no energy to fight with a man he didn't know. A man who didn't care about saving Shiloh. Jude . . . Jude might—probably was dead. But Shiloh had a chance.

"I can have you grounded."

He jerked toward the SEAL, his mind and soul warring. Who was this man, who'd charged into the middle of this and tried to take over the mission? Didn't matter. Reece wasn't going to sit around while Shiloh drowned trying to save her father.

"Do what you have to." He sat on the edge of the skiff. "I wouldn't expect you to understand."

"That's my brother out there. Shiloh's my niece."

Burning squeezed her lungs hard. Shiloh tapped the blue-lit dial. *Oh God, oh God, please . . .* Her arms felt rubbery. She fingered the hole in the nitrox tube. Minutes vanished like seconds with the wounded tank. A bullet must have pierced a hose as they tried to dive out of range.

Her father treaded water next to her, using the regulator. His eyes told her he understood the predicament but also that he fully expected to die. And they couldn't go back up to the surface without getting killed.

Only one choice. The caves! Scissoring her legs, she pushed downward, praying she'd made the right decision and had her bearings right.

The depth squished her ears and chest.

She kept swimming.

Reece would find her. He had to. *Please God—help him remember. Save us.*

As she swam deeper, guiding her father, she came upon the oil piping that lead from Butcher Island to Wadia. She used the steel tube to drag herself closer to the cave system. Only . . . something wasn't right. What was that? She angled the light from the nitrox dial toward the bulky object sitting on the pipe. And her heart stalled.

Her father stiffened visibly. She pulled him away—away from the piping and toward the caves, but he resisted. No doubt he knew what she knew. That wasn't coral or driftwood.

It was a bomb!

Nothing. They'd spent thirty minutes searching the choppy waters for Shiloh and Jude.

Reece dragged himself back onto the grate of the yacht. As he swiped the water from his face, he met Cole. "What's up?"

"We're pulling out." Cole stood on the aft skiff with Brody and Nielsen.

"You can't be serious." Reece panted from the swim but drew himself up. "She's down there with her father!"

Frowning, Brody looked away. "Reece, listen. I don't know how to say this any other way. They couldn't have survived. They're probably dead."

"No!" He fisted a hand. "She's alive. And I'm not giving up on her."

"She did what Jude asked her to do—she entered counter codes, which neutralized the nuke. There's nothing left to do here, and we can't waste manpower."

"I'm not leaving. If you take the men, you guarantee her death—and that of one of your top operatives."

Brow knitted and dark circles under his eyes, Toby looked forlorn. "I don't like this either, Reece, but we've found evidence connecting the Agreed to the violence in the Kashmiri Mountains. In light of the tense relations, it's vital we do this—*now*."

"Hate to say it, Chief, but he's right," Cole said. "They've been terrorizing the villages near the camp for years. We have one shot to take this down before they know what hit them."

"How many times have you said one life for thousands?" Nielsen sighed. "Well, we have to save thousands, possibly millions, of lives."

Reece couldn't argue. He glanced up as a suit escorted Mahmud to a flight of stairs. The man held something in his hand and strained down to see as he moved his thumb.

Reece's pulse spiked. He leapt up, caught the upper balcony, and hauled himself up over the rail. "Mahmud!" He dove into the man.

In those seconds, Reece saw a light spinning out of the man's hand across the deck.

He pinned Mahmud. Scuffled. The man threw a fist. Reece nailed him with a right hook and knocked him out cold. The guy wouldn't hurt anyone else.

Reece pushed off and scrabbled across the deck to the device. He picked it up—and moaned.

"What is it?" Friction raced toward him from the stairwell.

Propped against the wall, Reece held up the black device. "Twenty minutes." He pushed off the wall and headed to the bridge of the ship to access the computer maps.

Where would they have planted a bomb? Was that where Shiloh went? As he thought and trudged through his memory banks, he felt a presence behind him.

"Where do we start?" Friction moved to the opposite side. The blue-white glow of the backlit map cast ominous shadows over his face.

"If we had unlimited time, I'd say work the grid, piece by piece."

Dark brown eyes came to Reece's. "That's a million-five square miles of water surface."

"Exactly."

"You a praying man, Mr. Jaxon?"

"I am."

"Then start praying. Because only a miracle will find my brother and niece."

Reece couldn't help the grin. "I've been telling God that for a few days."

Friction paused. Smiled. Laughed as he raised his hands. "And look who He sent you."

"So, guardian angel, what do we do?"

"Find out what's of interest to jihadists."

"People. Banks. Trains."

In the distance a lengthy horn blew through the darkness.

Their gazes rammed into each other. "Oil."

32

RED IS DEAD. THE METER HAD DROPPED TO THE LAST MARK IN THE RED. With hand signals, she promised her father she'd find a way to come back, but they had to get to the air in the underwater caves first.

When her hand grazed a rare patch of coral, her heart alighted. She was in the right area. But now . . . now the trick of finding the right opening.

Coral scraped her fingers and dug into her flesh as she used the small shelf to pull herself toward the cave opening. Arm anchored around her father, Shiloh resisted the demand of her body to take a deep breath. *Come on, come on! Where are you?*

The shelf rose. Yes! Shiloh readjusted her hold, and in that instant, her father jolted. His arms flailed out. Legs kicked. Bubbles flourished under his rapid movements. He thrashed against her and spun away.

She lunged at him and curled her fingers into his shirt. Dragged him back down. Swam hard toward the opening. If she didn't hurry, it'd be too late. Beating her legs faster she could only pray. *God! God, help us!*

What if Reece didn't remember about the caves?

As she paddled downward, she lured her father around to the right, aiming for the spot where she'd found that pocket of air last month. From behind, she locked her arms around him and propelled them into the gap. Rocks scratched and clawed at them as she maneuvered through the small opening. A sliver of pain sliced down her thigh. She clenched her jaw but kept moving. She had to volley them up. Harder. More.

They broke the surface. Shiloh gasped. Greedily gulped the air. But no time to savor it. She adjusted her father, tilting his head back so he faced the roof. She yanked her hands into his abdomen and drew him against her chest. Both of their heads hit the cave ceiling. She repeated the thrust to evacuate his lungs. Nothing. Just the disturbance of the water.

"Dad!" She pulled upward into his lungs again. And again. Her whimper ricocheted off the limestone like the glow of the regulator dial in the pitch-black dome. "Dad, please."

Water finally burst from his mouth. He coughed. Gagged. His head lobbed backward, smacking her cheek. Pain darted down her jaw and neck, but she relished the feel of his chest bulging against her arms.

She released him. "Dad?"

"I . . ." He coughed. "I'm here." With a trembling hand, he reached for an outcropping and kept himself afloat. Forehead propped against his arm, he sucked in several long, painful-sounding breaths. "The bomb. Have . . . to . . . the bomb."

She'd never seen him so frail. So expended. "Dad, we can't. There's nothing we can do. It's too far away. We can't swim in time to disable it."

Shiloh swallowed hard. They were trapped, and the explosion would bury them at sea.

"Save the light," he rasped.

She twisted off the lamp on the tank and let darkness descend to save the battery, to save her from having to face the reality of his near-death experience.

"Is this the only cave?" he asked, clearing his throat.

"No, there's a system. A beautiful one fifty yards back that Khalid and I loved to explore."

"We need to get there."

"You can't. You nearly died."

"I've been through worse."

"Yeah, well, I haven't!"

His ragged breath echoed in the confined space. "Give me . . . few . . . need to try for . . . the bigger cave."

Of all the thick-headed— "Why do you have to push so hard?" Surprised at her burst of anger, she reeled it in. Told herself it was the adrenaline bottoming out.

"No." His eyes drooped. "Bigger cave . . . safer if bomb . . ."

It made sense but also scared her. Could they reach that cave without nitrox? She might be able to, but he certainly couldn't. Quiet descended as if pounding in the reality of their situation. Shiloh braced herself against the ledge. But with each passing second, the quiet grew louder. She strained to hear her father's breathing in the void that held them hostage.

Was he still alive? Water sloshed as she lifted a hand toward him. Fingers grazed flesh. Cold, wet flesh.

"Need . . . go."

A shiver snaked through her body as the cold water clung to her, chilling her skin. He just didn't quit, did he? "Dad—"

"No." He grunted. "Have to . . . the . . . bomb."

"I know. But we can't do anything yet. Just . . ." If they tried to swim this soon after the trauma, he might not make it. But staying here put them at risk from the bomb.

Either way, he was dead.

I am not going to let my father die. "Okay." She drifted closer. "Let's use the tank to tether us together."

"Good thinking."

Teased with his praise, she unthreaded one strap of the tank from her shoulder and guided his hand and arm through it. She winced as something pinched against her leg.

"Okay, let's go."

"Butcher Island."

"Oil refinery," Friction said as he hacked into the computer network on the yacht and quickly drew up maps of the piping. "Wow, that's a lot of plumbing."

"Too much to cover in twenty minutes."

"I'll send my team now. But . . ." Friction's gaze came to his. "Think they're still down there?"

"Yes." And that ate at him. He ground his teeth together. "She had a reason for going down, I just don't know what. Is she aware you're here?"

"Hopefully, neither of them have any knowledge of my presence in the area." Friction leaned against the table as he relayed orders to the team, then glanced at the map. "And actually, my identity as Jude's brother is a national secret kept by high command. I haven't talked with Shiloh since her tenth birthday."

"Seems rifts run in the family."

Friction laughed. "You know us well, then?"

Reece paused. "How'd you know they were in this situation?"

"My position within the agency grants me certain access."

"Ah, spying on your niece."

"Let's call it protective monitoring."

"Want to explain why you chose to surface now that they're in mortal danger?"

A smile crinkled Friction's dark eyes. "Sorry, I don't cave under interrogation."

"Interro—" Reece froze. Wait. *Cave.* Like a vacuum sucking him into its void, he stared at a series of circles on the map. "She took him to the caves!"

33

I DON'T WANT TO DIE! WHAT IDIOT WOULD ATTEMPT ANOTHER TREACHER-ous journey through dangerous depths to get from one cave to another? Apparently, Shiloh. What a way to die—leading her father through black waters to a cave where they could lie down and die. With no food, no oxygen, no—*nothing*!—die was all they could do.

As they crept over more rocks, Shiloh angled her shoulder so the light on the dial hit right. There. The opening to the Mammoth, as Khalid had called it. Coming down here had been a totally different adventure with him and the proper dive equipment. Now she was fighting for her life, petrified her father would be given up to the watery depths.

His grasp on her shoulder tightened.

At the silent signal, she swam faster. Through the opening. And jutted upward.

They broke water, gasping. She scrambled for the dry ground. The limestone sloughed off and scraped her knees. She didn't care. They'd made it!

He crawled to a large, flat rock and slumped onto it, holding his shoulder. "I knew . . . you could do it."

Swallowing, she wet the roof of her mouth. As she flopped onto her back, cool water lapped at her ears and chin. Her breathing slowly returned to normal. Her stomach rumbled.

"This doesn't make sense." She cupped a hand over her forehead. "We're farther into the caves. Farther away from help. We have no food. No supplies. And Reece probably has no idea where we are."

"I met Reece about five years ago."

Shiloh paused, not surprised he'd completely evaded her objections.

"He sat through several lectures I gave at Langley."

She didn't want to think about Reece, didn't want to think about never seeing him again. "Dad—do we really need to talk about this?"

Her father eased himself down and let out a relieved sigh. "Graduated top of his class. I think he actually made a couple of perfect scores and scared the Academy spitless."

"He does that to everyone."

Her father laughed, a wonderful sound, even though its weakness bounced off the cave walls. "A few years later . . . on a complicated mission . . . I tapped Reece." He lay quietly for a while, then continued. "He did it. Pulled it off. Like a pro. But . . . in debrief . . . he got mad, lips flat, eyebrows tight."

Shiloh couldn't help but smile. She'd seen that look more than once.

He drew in a ragged breath. "Asked him what . . . wrong." A gurgled chuckle echoed around them. "He quoted my lecture, verbatim. Told me I was either wrong before or I was lying right then." He panted as though out of breath.

Shiloh rolled her head to the side, concerned at the way her father panted from the effort of just talking. The glow of the lamp enabled her to see his smiling profile.

He coughed, his chest seizing. "Vowed to drop . . . if I didn't come clean. *'I can deal with half-truths, but not lies, not from the man I want to imitate,'* he said." Her father swept his wet hair from his face. "I'd never had a trainee . . . call me out like that."

She relaxed a little at the way he'd been able to finish that sentence. Maybe he was okay. "Is there a point to this walk down memory lane?" Although she taunted him, Shiloh was enjoying the story, glad her father thought so highly of Reece. Yet part of her flirted with jealousy that Reece had had more interaction with her father than she had in the last fifteen years.

He gave her a pointed stare. "Reece loves you, right?"

On her back again, Shiloh licked her lips and tasted the salty sea. "Wh—Are you going somewhere with this?"

"Aren't I always?"

She couldn't help the smile. "Okay, yes, Reece said he loved me."

"Then don't doubt him. If he could remember something from my lectures two years prior . . . he'll remember . . . conversation you've had in the last few months."

Kneading warmth spread through her chest at his words, infusing her with a solid dose of hope. Yeah. Her dad was right. "So you think he'll figure out about the caves?"

"Mm . . ."

Shiloh peeked at him, confused by his distant answer. "Dad?"

He didn't respond.

"Dad?" She stumbled to her feet and slogged toward him. "Dad, are you okay?"

Nothing.

"Dad!" Shiloh nudged his shoulder. She pressed her fingers against his neck—startled at the chill of his flesh. A faint pulse.

"Please, Dad . . . just hold on." He looked pale. Or was that from the blue lamp light?

Shiloh lifted his arm around her shoulder and burrowed against his side, hoping to keep both of them warm. She realized that in that dark moment God had given her something she'd longed for since she was a little girl—to be in her daddy's arms.

But what if he died—left her alone in this cave? Cuddled against him, she closed her mind against the stillness and fear. Amid the repetitive dripping of water, she was carried back to her childhood. A night when her mother placed her hands over Shiloh's steepled hands.

The Lord is my shepherd
I shall not want
He makes me lie down
Beside the still waters . . .

Voices scampered through her dreams, tugging at her. Shiloh sat up. The images floated in and out. Dark ones—the careening of her life as her mother died. Odd ones—her father as he sat alone in his bedroom with her mother's picture. New ones—when Reece laughed and chased her through the waters of the bay. A large splash. Water spraying a thousand tiny droplet images across her face.

A bright light stunned her. She winced and turned away.

"Shiloh!"

Hand shielding her face, she glanced over her shoulder. Blurry vision confused her.

"Shiloh. Thank God!"

Again, she blinked. This time, Reece's face loomed before her. She gasped. Was it really him? She reached for him. Touched his dive suit and cold face. "Reece?" She tried to shake the cobwebs from her mind. "Am I dreaming?"

A regulator dangled below his smile. "Do I look that good?"

With a guttural cry, she grabbed him and yanked herself into his embrace, arms tight around his neck. "You remembered. You came." Then she shoved him back. "We have to get out of here. There's a bomb."

"Wait," one of the other men said. "You saw it?"

Shiloh looked at him and blinked. "Uncle Shaun?"

"Shi, the bomb. Where did you see it?"

"Above the caves." She brushed her hair from her face. "On one of the pipes leading from Butcher."

After securing a mask and tank to her father's unconscious form, Shaun hoisted him toward the water and looked at Reece. "Can you take care of that?"

"On it." He off-loaded a secondary tank and helped her into the straps. "I want you to take me to it. Once I see it," he said as he slipped a dive mask and regulator over her head, "I want you to make for the surface."

And leave him?

"I mean it, Shiloh."

She stuffed the regulator in her mouth and dove into the water. Within seconds, they cleared the main entrance to the cave. A heavy wave stirred around her. Bright and steady, a beam of light sliced through the dark waters overhead. In the dispersed beam and murky water her uncle and father headed to safety.

Reece swam up next to her with a dive prop, the engine churning the waters. With two fingers, he tapped his watch. In other words, they were running out of time.

She grabbed the handle of the prop and pointed in the direction of the burdened pipe. With the motorized propellant, they made the site within minutes. Reece approached the device carefully, motioning her back.

Keeping her distance, Shiloh watched him. Amazement and admiration rippled through her with an unnatural dose of fear. She didn't want to die. Maybe there'd been a time not too long ago she wouldn't have cared, but now that she had Reece and she'd made her peace with her father, she wanted to live. Wanted Reece to live.

Yet there he treaded water, laboring over an explosive that could blow them both to heaven in the blink of an eye. *God, protect him!*

He swirled toward her. Shook his head. Behind the mask, she saw the worry in his eyes.

They were going to die?

No. They weren't. An idea lit into her. She tapped Reece, made a few hand signals. At first, he objected. But he reconsidered.

With great care, he freed the bomb straps from the 8-inch pipe. Together, they secured it to the dive prop, using delicate moves to fasten the straps and tighten them. If they couldn't get it to stop, then they could scuttle it into the deep ocean. No one would get killed, and the city would be safe.

Her heart thrummed like the engine as they revved it. She checked the gauge. Less than two minutes! Holding the sides, she waited as Reece rigged the prop to maintain full throttle.

He pushed her away, resolute.

Shiloh gulped but propelled herself away. Wasn't he coming? Surely he wouldn't try something stupid. *Reece, please . . .* She slowed her pace, the distance between them growing. Her heart staggered as another few seconds passed without him.

Like a rocket, the prop angrily bolted from Reece.

Relief swept through her as he launched toward her. Shiloh paddled her legs furiously.

The bomb sped through the distant, dark waters. Not visible, but deadly dangerous all the same.

Shiloh kicked harder. Up. Away.

She'd no sooner seen Reece's dark form glide next to her than a deep rumbling rent the serenity of the sea. He reached out and grabbed her. The concussion of the explosion tumbled them faster. Shiloh dug her fingers into him. With the near-centrifugal force rocketing them through the sea, there was no telling where they'd end up. At some point, the force ripped them apart.

Like a missile, she sailed up. Out of the water. And plopped right back in. Shiloh pushed herself back to the surface. Above water, she flipped off the mask, turning, searching. Where was Reece? Where did he go? "Reece?" Her head spun. Ears rang. She scoured the darkened water for him but only saw flames dancing over the tumultuous sea. "Reece!" A spurt of water hit her temple.

She jerked to her right. Where was he? "Reece?" Water hit her again. This time—she saw where it came from and grabbed at the spot, realizing she was getting gleeked, hit by a stream of water.

Laughter suffused the night. "Okay, okay. I'm here."

"I can't believe you're playing around."

"Why? We beat the bad guys. Defied death yet again. I daresay you might be getting Anubis a bit miffed."

She laughed. "You really enjoy this, don't you?"

"Beating the bad guy? Absolutely." He waded closer to her. "You did real good, babe."

"Babe, huh?" She wrapped trembling arms around his neck. "You knew I wasn't going to help Sajjadi, didn't you?"

"I don't fall in love with terrorists." He motioned behind her where a black boat pounded across the waves toward them. "So I knew whatever idea you got into that beautiful mind of yours, I had to trust you. No matter how much it killed me to let you go."

Shiloh smiled at the man before her, a hero and guardian, just like her father. "So, guardian, do I get to be a star?"

"Why would the sun want to dim her brilliance?"

She laughed. "Kiss up."

Reece grinned unabashedly as a strobe of light struck them. "If you insist." He leaned down and pressed his lips against hers. "So, I know this preacher . . ."

Epilogue

READY?" REECE GRINNED AT HER, REGULATOR POISED IN FRONT OF HIS mouth.

With a grin, she shoved backward off the boat, launching into the warm waters of Mumbai Harbor. An hour ago Reece had rushed into her flat and announced that a clearance for an archeological dig had just come through the consulate's office. The professional archeological team would arrive in two days. That gave Shiloh twenty-two hours to scour the site and see what they were coming after. The temptation was too much. She'd fled the apartment with him to the open water. Miller waited with Bronco and Stick. Because Toby had provided the information, he'd bartered his way onto the trip with Julia.

Three months after Sajjadi had been taken down and all she had to show for the nightmare were two small, pink scars. Reece called them her red badges of courage. She wagged her feet, propelling herself toward the ocean floor. Rumor of Greek pottery twenty meters below lured her deeper.

Reece swam into view, the blue glow of his shoulder lamp shattering the darkness around him. His presence spurred her on. He had promised to help her train for the Pacific Rim Challenge, but it just didn't have the allure it had once held. She was right where she wanted to be for the first time in her life.

Another ten meters provided the first signs of coral. She took her time, surveying the area and videotaping it, so the team on the surface could track their movements and mark the location. If they did find something, they could come back with better equipment.

Five yards to her right, she spotted a mound in the silt. She tapped Reece and paddled toward it. It didn't look ancient. As a matter of fact . . . She lifted the object, confused when a wide-mouthed jar in the shape of a monkey smiled back at her. What . . . ?

Reece removed the lid.

Inside, she spotted a black object. Too bizarre. She reached for it. Her fingers tracked over the black object.

His light flared into the jar and hit the box.

A *jewelry* box. She peered at him through her goggles, her heart stuttering.

He shrugged.

Shiloh lifted it and popped open the lid. A ring gleamed back at her with a princess-cut diamond. She widened her eyes. Looked at Reece.

He cocked his head and raised his eyebrows, as if saying, Well?

She catapulted toward him. He caught her and wrapped his arms around her tightly. They spiraled through the water in each other's embrace. After a moment, she touched down on the sea floor with Reece. He pointed to the surface.

Torpedoing upward, she gripped the ring tightly in her hand. Light fractured the blue-green waters, streaking out from the dive boat. Memories of months previous when her life had turned upside down darted through her mind, but she shoved them behind her. Her future felt promising for the first time. Reece had been patient, but firm and loving with her.

Once-a-week dinners with her father had built the bridge to restore their relationship.

A school of fish swarmed around her, as if they, too, celebrated her discovery of the ring. His proposal. Yes, absolutely, she would marry Reece Jaxon.

She broke the surface, bright sun flashing at her. Regulator out, Shiloh wiped her face and hooked her arm over the grate of the rig.

Reece glided up next to her, his regulator already dangling down his shoulder. "Like your treasure?"

"You did this. Plotted against me." She laughed as he swept her into his arms and kissed her.

"You ready?"

She frowned. "For what?"

He nodded toward the boat. "Now or never, chicken."

She glanced up at the deck of the rig—and gasped. A white tent stretched the length of the boat and billowed under the teasing fingers of a warm wind. Julia and Toby waited with Miller and two of his men . . . and a man she didn't recognize.

"That's Pastor Roy."

She darted Reece a glance. "Right now?"

"If I gave you time to back out, you would."

A slow smile stole into Shiloh's face. "I think you were afraid you'd get cold feet."

"Not on your life."

With one last look to the guests, she climbed up on the grate and removed the tank. "I don't know . . ." She held the open box, admiring the way the sun caught the brilliance of the square stone.

Reece hauled himself aboard and unloaded his gear. He took the ring and slid it on her finger. "That belongs on your left hand. I belong in your life. What's to know?"

"Hey!" Miller shouted over a gull's call. "Are you two getting married or what?"

Reece cocked his eyebrow and held out his hand. "What say you?"

"Are you sure you want to be married to a spy?"

His forehead wrinkled. Then he blinked, the shock registering. "You mean . . ."

"My clearance came through this morning. I am seizure-free, and my synapses have regenerated. I'm good to go."

Pulling her into his embrace, Reece kissed her soundly.

"Hey! You aren't married yet," Miller taunted. "You better hurry before this pastor gets cold feet."

Laughing, Shiloh let Reece lead her under the tent. Her love and excitement burned such that she barely noticed the loss of the sun's warmth beneath the white canopy.

Holding hands, they stood before the pastor.

Reece nodded. "Go ahead."

Discussion Questions

1. The title of this book, *Dead Reckoning*, is a navigational term that means the process of estimating one's current position based upon a previously determined position, or fix, and advancing that position based upon known or estimated speeds over elapsed time and course. How does this play a key role at the end of the story? Have you ever been so intimately aware of someone that you have been able to predict their reaction, or even prevent something bad from happening?
2. Shiloh is an underwater archeologist with one goal on her mind. What is that goal? Does she achieve her goal? What does Reece say is the real reason she's in the region?
3. Do you believe Shiloh understands what true love is or what it means? Why? She makes a decision in Chapter 10 that could alter her life. What do you think drives her decision?
4. The Doctrine of Competing Harms comes from English common law and refers to the judicious use of deadly force when one feels there is a legitimate threat of bodily harm or death, or in other words, the lesser of two evils (kill or be killed). At the train station (Chapter 14), Reece is forced to protect Shiloh with the use of deadly force. What is it? How do you think he resolves situations like this with his faith?
5. Shiloh harbors a lot of anger and bitterness toward her father because of his life as a covert operative. What does the Bible say about anger and bitterness? Do you have any unhealed hurts or anger? Is there one thing you can do that would open the door to reconciliation?
6. Espionage operatives defend and ensure our freedom throughout the world, using covert and often dangerous means. Yet these men and women must use deception

and sometimes deadly force to accomplish their objective. The Bible warns us against lying lips and deceitful tongues (Psalm 120:2), which would seem to suggest that the means employed by a covert operative is sinful, yet even King David used spies to gain the advantage. What do you think about espionage and the agents who protect their countries and put their lives on the line without ever being acknowledged or thanked?

7. Shiloh falls in love with India, a beautiful but pagan nation that predominantly practices Hinduism, a faith that worships thousands of gods. Although Shiloh does not embrace the beliefs of the country, she also does not embrace Christianity. Why? Can you relate to her hesitancy toward spiritual things?
8. Reece is a strong, heroic character who thrives on being the one to save the day. Where did this drive come from in his life? Also, what is it that enables him to cope with the gruesome realities of his occupation?
9. At one point in the story, Shiloh finds comfort in a memory long suppressed—her mother praying with her the Lord's Prayer. What verse in the Bible gives you comfort or has helped you through a particularly difficult time in your life?
10. How would you describe Shiloh's spiritual journey? What role does her father play in it? Why is she so determined not to be like her father?
11. At the opening of the story, Reece is still struggling with an event that happened two years earlier. What is it and why did it impact him so deeply? What similarities are there between that event and what's happening in his life now?

Want to learn more about author
Ronie Kendig and check out other great
fiction from Abingdon Press?

Sign up for our fiction newsletter at
www.AbingdonPress.com
to read interviews with your favorite authors, find tips
for starting a reading group, and stay posted on what
new titles are on the horizon. It's a place to connect
with other fiction readers or post a
comment about this book.

Be sure to visit Ronie online!
www.RonieKendig.com